Praise for *Hindred Spirits*.

Wrought by the hand of a skillful, insightful, and empathic writer, *Hindred Spirits* is a treat of a literary horror story. This is *The Lovely Bones* as told by Shirley Jackson, with a little *Firestarter* thrown in for grit, supported by the confident scaffolding of a top-tier thriller.

In *Hindred*, Perratore eloquently explores themes surrounding the oft avoided and very real horrors of childhood abuse and neglect. Some might wish to avoid such a subject but that would be a mistake, as they would be denied this author's deft handling of his subject, as well as his engaging plot and layered characters.
— Samantha E Talbot, author of *A Thunderbolt Into Nettle*

A typical ghost story this book is not. It's a tale about spirits, both corporeal and incorporeal, both belonging to the soul or essence of what it means to be human and of what it means to be inhumane.
— K. L. Davidson, author of *Ten Thousand Fields* and *Nectar Haven*

Lock the doors if you read *Hindred Spirits* alone late at night. Tragic events enable an unsuspecting couple to buy the house of their dreams, one that becomes the house of their nightmares when it's haunted by a previous occupant, a mean little girl with a big grudge and an unusual ability: She can fly from her body and go "ghosting." When important work is sabotaged, their baby is threatened, and the house itself turns against them, the family must decide whether to fight back or leave. They flee, leaving the house to a haunting spirit now drunk with power, one who continues to torture new residents—a mom, dad, and two kids who don't always get along. Can they unite in time to drive this spirit far from home? Perratore's plot twists will keep you reading to find out.
— Leslie Ware, author of *Dear Miss Bryant: The Life and Murder of a Remarkable Eccentric*

I love a good ghost story, and the author has definitely delivered one. There were areas in the novel that hit home and I could relate in a deep manner that I was one of those children. Well done!
—LaVoné Holeva, author of *Wife: A Supernatural Horror Short Story*

Hindred Spirits

ED PERRATORE

Other works by Ed Perratore

Fiction

The Coven Tree

The Knock from Nobody

Nonfiction

One Man's Journey: A Walk on the Croton
Aqueduct Trail

Published by Boat Tail Press, Fort Myers, Florida, 33966

BOAT TAIL

PRESS

ISBN: 978-1-7376069-2-5

https://edperratore.com

DEDICATION

To Elena, my bride and editor, for your loving heart
and unerring eye.

To Jack Cotter, my pal in Heaven, for the many, many hours
we spent reading, watching and talking all things horror.

ACKNOWLEDGMENTS

Cover design by Ruth Anna Evans
www.ruthannaevans.com

Cover photograph, "Sunday Morning in November," by Henri
Senders

Author photograph by John F.X. Walsh

"You got me floatin' across and through
You make me float right on up to you
There's only one thing I need to really get me there,
Is to hear you laugh without a care."
—Jimi Hendrix

"Unbeing dead isn't being alive."
—E. E. Cummings

"Dying! To be afraid of thee
One must to thine Artillery
Have left exposed a Friend..."
—Emily Dickinson

PART 1

1

"Did I say I was going?"

Kim Leffingwell speared the roast that was about to slide off the cutting board as if on its own power. Its pinkish juices dripped over the side and collected in a widening swirl at the raised edge of the Corian counter. The air conditioner, she happened to notice, had cut out again; this raised temperatures as well as her husband's temper. And the breeze entering the kitchen window, this early in September, was scant.

"N-no, George, I didn't hear you say. I just...thought it would be nice if you took, w-well, a bit more interest in Natalie's studies. A child needs the support at home that she gets in..." Her voice trailing off, the woman reached up with her forearm to push back the lock of wavy blonde hair that had dangled over her forehead. Hands wouldn't do, not while they tremblingly held the steaming roast in place.

Kim blocked the eye round beef from any further motion and turned to stir the gravy on the stove. The mashed potatoes, which she'd prepped awhile before, were covered. So were the beans.

She softly sighed and took a deep breath. So far, so good. With any luck, her husband of ten years would cool down before their daughter came to the table. And sometime, perhaps in a public place,

1

they could have a good conversation about their marriage, what their goals had been, what happened to them, and what the two of them needed to agree on, going forward. They were still young, she knew, and things didn't...have to be this way.

George was tall and thin, nearly five foot ten. His blue eyes showed little of the frustrations of the past three years, and his smile, seldom in view these days, she remembered as cheery. His nose, somewhat crooked, could suggest either confidence or guile—depending, of course, on his attitude.

Kim wasn't happy about much these days, but the occasional look in a mirror helped. She was five inches shorter than her husband and was pleasingly thin, with a broad smile that, she'd been told, lit up her face. The small, turned-up nose and her light brown eyes contributed to the effect.

Tonight, she was more concerned about their daughter.

Kim winced from a recalled pain as she lowered the jet beneath the gravy and turned back to the roast. She cut off the end and cut a few more slices for starter portions. At this point she paused—George was too quiet—and then slowly withdrew the knife and laid it beside the meat. She turned around, absorbed the scowl she knew had formed on her husband's lean face. "Okay," she sighed. "W-well, I mean I-I can go. I'll go, and tell you—I'll tell you if they talk about anything important. All right?"

"Listen." George Leffingwell's Adam's apple bobbed as he further loosened his necktie. His face, still tanned from a summer of road trips, wore a dark stubble that remained evident even after a morning shave. He now slammed the flat of his hand upon the polished pine tabletop. "I don't pay all these goddamn school taxes to go to little monthly meetings and tell the teachers how to do their jobs. *We* pay *their* salaries—they tell *us* to go to meetings?"

"Ge-George, these meetings are just a chance for us to know what kind of...approach to education the school is taking." Kim placed a few slices, with gravy, onto her husband's plate and returned to the kitchen for the potatoes and beans. "Natalie! Dinnertime!" She stepped back into the narrow dining room to the first seat, the head of the table, and laid down his plate. "Natalie's already in the fourth grade. It's time we took more of a r-role in what kind of person she will bec—"

George pounded the table again, catching the plate, which spun up and sent the meat flying. Gravy and all, the plate struck the ledge of the table, flipped over and shattered on the floor. "And I never said *you* were going to any goddamn meeting either, now, did I? *DID I?*"

"N-n-no, Ge-George, you d-didn't say—" Kim bent over to retrieve the pieces but straightened up again, wringing her hands on the flowered canvas apron. She knew the situation would get worse if she didn't clean up the mess at once. Yet...recent experience also told her he wanted a fresh dish.

Wanted it now, in fact.

"Natalie!" the man growled. "Didn't you hear your mother? Get down here *now!*"

Seconds later, the little girl crossed the living room and entered the dining room. Natalie stood four-and-a-half-feet tall, thin, with straight, shoulder-length blonde hair and a smallish nose. She wore a tie-dyed T-shirt with a V-neck. Below, she wore tight, elastic-waist blue jeans with a mid-calf cut, and slippers. The girl took in everything as she passed through the living room: the colorful Tiffany lamp with a ceramic cat and two Hummel figurines beside it, a Niagara Falls ashtray, a bowling trophy on the mantel beside a bowl with dried flowers, and, on the wall, a framed photo of a city skyline and a painting of an empty boat on a lakeshore.

She sat down in silence and tried to look at everything that was not her father. A set of wooden chimes, which barely moved in the faint breeze of the hot dining room. The mug tree on the counter. The "round tuit" potholder and cookie-shaped magnets on the refrigerator door; she could see them from the table. And her favorite, the perpetually drinking bird decoration. It swung back and forth on a shelf above the sink.

Her eyes, blue like her father's, scanned the dinner table, on the mashed potatoes—her favorite—and string beans they were having tonight. As her mother suspected, Natalie had again been watching, and listening, from partway down the stairs. She'd probably also seen the plate in the air. Kim knew well that their daughter would neither show that she had seen it nor, indeed, act as though anything whatsoever was amiss. Other than her stony silence, anyway.

Not a skill a mother expected her child to need.

Kim picked up what fragments of the broken plate she could and, with a glance over her shoulder, swept up the remaining fragments she saw with a paper towel. It would take too long to wipe up every bit of the gravy, she knew. And she needed the precious few seconds her daughter's arrival might distract her father to get him another plate. Once George began eating, he usually settled down for a while.

Then she could serve a few small slices to Natalie, who would immediately go for the potatoes. Another few shards, including the dry, blackened end, Kim had cut and put off to the side when the roast first came out; they had cooled long before. She liked roast beef better that way, she told herself.

* * *

If not for Kim's anxiety, she later told herself, the terrible scene following that evening's dinnertime—far worse than any airborne plate—might not have occurred. If only she'd cleared the table by herself without asking her daughter to pitch in. If only she'd had time to wipe *all* the spilt gravy from the floor. Kim told herself these and more once she'd quietly helped Natalie clean and stow the last of the dishes and carried her daughter, exhausted and throbbing with pain, up to bed.

Emily Sanders, the school nurse, had been at the late-August PTA meeting, a kickoff get-together held just prior to the semester's start. She'd been present even though, Kim was sure, the woman had no children, was not even married—and had contributed nothing to the meeting. She'd introduced herself at the end and, Kim realized later, had likely noticed a mark on her arm that she'd concealed with a windbreaker she'd worn...but forgot about, during the meeting, when she felt hot. Moreover, the nurse had asked politely whether everything was all right at home. That question alone told Kim she'd been watching Natalie.

The woman didn't need much to interpret that the girl was not the same child who'd scampered down the steps so cheerily last June.

Tonight, in anticipation of the meeting, Kim had fully expected Emily to approach again and inquire how she was. A purely casual question, of course. But Kim had no doubt as to what the woman was really asking. She in fact had decided, really decided, that it was time to confide in someone about the regular...turmoil.

Especially since, more and more, their only daughter was also a target of her husband's wrath. She shook her head, fighting more tears and trying desperately to keep the most recent episode, of only a short while before, from running through her head yet again. Thank God, she thought, the poor thing was already asleep.

Kim raised the weights hanging down from the cuckoo clock after its eight-thirty chime. The PTA meeting would probably be over by now, and she busied herself by engaging in a dusting spree that she'd hoped her husband would see as what most needed doing. She was beyond guessing what would set him off. Irregular banging sounds echoed up the steps leading to the basement—George was in the basement, at the workbench. Given that, she predicted, the remainder of the night would be better.

She was in the dining room, putting away the masking tape, which Natalie had left behind from an afternoon school project, when Kim noticed that one drawer of the china closet, the usually locked one, was ajar. Gingerly, she opened it, glanced inside, closed it, and locked it with the key they hid on top. Recent burglaries or not, she would somehow have to talk to George about removing what she once declared would never have a place in any home of hers—"declared," that is, back when what she said didn't earn her a face smack or a swollen lip. It was nothing to have around a house even without a curious child living there, and she'd have to find some way to deal with the matter.

But that was for another time. Perhaps things would turn up for George soon, and then...

The tears were coming again.

...and then things would be all right again.

Kim decided to dust in the small office adjoining the living room, and she reached above the locked roll-top desk for the certificate her husband had earned, from his prior employer, for a solid year of above-quota sales. Holding it in her hand, feeling the sharp edges of the brass-plated chrome of the frame, she thought about the man he had been. His eyes were younger then but no less piercing, and he had a way of cocking his head as he smiled, of knowing what was on her mind. That was the mark of a true salesman, wasn't it?

* * *

They'd met on the ferry connecting the city with nearby Littles Island—he on his way to a sales conference, she off for the weekend with a coworker friend from her accounting position at a local university. Drivers were told to pull their vehicles close to those ahead to meet the vessel's maximum capacity, and as she'd inched up her Corolla, she'd tapped the rear of his Mercedes convertible.

He'd rushed out of the car, his lips tightly shut with apprehension until he saw no damage had been done. Feeling certain herself that it was nothing, Kim came out anyway to show her concern. Some people, after all, would take you to court for ten dollars if they thought you were acting superior—say, by remaining in your car after a fender tap. But instead of showing annoyance, the man who soon introduced himself as George Leffingwell now seemed only friendly. "Looks totaled to me," he said, then grinned. His suit jacket was on a hanger in the rear, and he seemed ordinarily very well dressed, and naturally so. Rubber bumpers forgive, she remembered his saying, and the conversation had gone on from there, as lightly as the sea air wafted about, until Kim's friend rolled down her window to say the ferry had docked.

The following weekend, she was having the first of many dinners with George. Over wine, she listened to stories of his new job, this stockbroker who'd already won a handful of lucrative corporate accounts through his assertive, breezy style. It was almost love at first sight. He was an irresistible man with a promising future; she, a career woman who had nevertheless been ready to marry if ever the right man came along.

She supposed she should have heeded the warning flag that unfurled about a year later, the day Kim met Randolph, George's father and the patriarch of what George jokingly referred to as the Leffingwell clan. Getting out of her then-fiancé's car, Kim wanted to pinch herself: They'd passed between marble pillars with busts that flanked the opening to a winding driveway a quarter-mile long. Lavish lawns with rolling hills and manicured trees and shrubs abounded, and now she saw an immense mansion with a horseshoe driveway and a front door that, fully open, would fit a horse and carriage. From a stone fountain at the center of the front lawn, a Romanesque cherub brandished a horn from which water erupted and poured down to the bowl, around which was an array of resplendent flowers.

In amazement at the estate she'd never dreamed her companion might possibly inherit, she didn't immediately realize what was going on. A butler, one George hadn't met, had greeted them at the door. The servant then led them, past myriad paintings and carvings, to a second man, a tall, silver-haired one with steel-blue eyes, heavily bagged, and a graying goatee, who stood silently before them without saying a word. Kim had waited for an introduction that was not forthcoming. She'd looked at the man with a polite smile, then to her fiancé, and wondered whether it was or wasn't polite to elbow him to get him, *one* of them, to speak.

"Hello, Father," George eventually said, almost in a whisper.

"George," the older man returned. Then, to her, he said, "You must be...Kimberly."

"I'm very happy to meet you, Mister Leffingwell."

In response, the man called over his shoulder. "Pearl," he said as if he were summoning a servant.

At once, a woman entered the passageway from a room out of sight, and Kim knew at once this was George's mother.

"At last, Kim!" the woman exclaimed and rushed up to embrace her. "We've heard so much about you!"

The same servant who'd brought them in now asked what they'd like to drink, and he nodded to a younger man, who scurried off and returned, soon after, with a tray once they'd sat down in a vast living room that could fit a dance floor. But from her impressions of George's stone-faced father and the servants—even Pearl, who had largely shrunken into the background after the introductions—there was no music in this house.

"George...tells me you're an accountant," his mother finally said after a longish sip at her drink.

"Yes, I am," Kim replied, wondering how much was too little to say at a first meeting, and what was too much. At any rate, she decided, *somebody* had to talk. "I've been on the staff of Miller U. for about two years now, and I'm up for a possible promotion at the end of the year. People don't tend to leave the place, so that means waiting for retirements. But the people are mostly nice, and the benefits—you know, the health plan, 401K and another pension— are better than I've had in earlier jobs. And..."

She stopped when she realized George's father was staring at her, his face betraying what she could only call a glower. She took a sip of her Chablis, barely noticing its fine quality, and wondered what she'd done wrong.

"We're looking at houses in Hollister," said George. "We think we've settled on one, a smallish starter home. It'll do for now."

More silence ensued until his mother chanced a reply. "That's an easy drive from here," she said.

Before they'd even sat down to dinner, Kim felt she could understand why Sarah, George's older sister, had left home right after college for a job in the city, never to return. Or to marry. She believed she also knew why George himself had initially seemed troubled about the idea of marriage. He had described his father to her as eccentric; had the man even said his name to her? But what she was seeing was something far deeper.

Over a leg of lamb that was, without question, the finest she had ever tasted, an argument began—or, perhaps, a longer one resumed—over George's apparent place of work, which his father derisively referred to as "that little brokerage."

"Father," she remembered George's stating in a slow, controlled voice, "I have my own life now, and your wish for me to take up in your company, instead of going it alone, has nothing to do with me. I wish you'd get over it."

Kim could still remember the way she had shivered at the old man's cackle, which told her the discussion was not over. At one point, after she and George's mother went off for "the grand tour," Kim excused herself to use a bathroom. On her way there, she could not help but hear the rest through the thick double doors of the library.

"Marry the little snip if you want," Randolph said as if they'd been arguing over the proper tennis racket to buy. "I don't know what was so bad about Meredith Filbert. A fine family, and more opportunity than you'll ever get in that..."

Kim felt guilty about her slowed step—and disappointed that she could not hear her intended's reply.

What she could not miss was her future father-in-law's next words: "Perhaps I'll also get over any foolish notions about my will." She'd turned around, then, to notice one of the servants standing behind her—and, from what Kim could tell, choosing not to interrupt her apparent eavesdropping.

"I'm sorry," the servant now said. "Do you need something?"

These days, Kim still could not forget how coldly silent the old man had remained the rest of her visit, not to mention their later wedding. But she wasn't so sure what transpired that day of ten years earlier. Repeatedly dusting the same frame, Kim dried a tear and pondered the old man's words. Randolph Leffingwell had died three years before, two years after his wife's death. As he'd promised, he'd cut out both his children from the will; he'd donated the entire estate to a historical conservancy. It was now a park. But had her husband truly inherited nothing?

George had surely been a confident man, and at the workplace much of his father's business sense had apparently rubbed off. From how he spoke at the dinner table, with Natalie then a toddler in a booster seat, he was clearly on the VP track. Lunchtimes were typically for client meetings, and the president often invited him to lunch at his club—didn't that mean something? And her husband continued to bring in big clients for the next few years.

Then, things began to change. George was working longer hours some nights; other nights, he was trying to be the father his own dad never was, to spend time with his daughter in her early school years. He tried to attend every PTA meeting and never missed a parent-teacher conference. Feeling ever more thinly spread, George became increasingly irritable, his anger occasionally surfacing, and his voice rose as he told his wife she didn't, couldn't, understand how clients cared only about what you were doing for them this week.

Soon, George's biggest victories were all in the past. By then he was taking shortcuts, rushing headlong into deals without spending the time he needed to look out for his clients. One night he pledged to attend a recorder concert Natalie's first-grade class was putting on at Hollister Elementary, and stayed to the very end, when he could hug his daughter close. "I'm sooo proud of you, Natalie!" he'd said to her.

Mid-concert, however, the news had broken about a huge class-action suit against a company whose stock he'd been recommending, in a big way, to a Fortune 500 client. He'd been warned when he still could have alerted clients, but he'd put his phone on mute—and didn't check it till they got home.

Only a few months later, George was selling not blue-chip stock but plumbing supplies. His confidence all but gone, he made his rounds with a disgust for the job that was all too apparent.

George had not made it back from that peak, though Kim alone believed that his newer position had great potential of its own. Nevertheless, it didn't take long before the blaming, the rages, the accusations that, somehow, this was her doing.

Then came the beatings.

They started with an occasional tap or shove, followed by an apology that, over time, began to ring all too hollow. A specific altercation would not have happened, he began to say, had *she* not said something to set him off. First, it was when she, or poor Natalie, needed to ask him something while he was scanning job ads on his laptop...*never* a good time. If she mentioned an old friend she'd heard from, he'd grill her on what her husband did for a living—and suggest she was cheating on him if she knew too much about the man. If she knew nothing, she was evading the issue—an obvious giveaway.

George was never much of a drinker, a fact that had once comforted Kim. But in a way, that made their time together all the worse. It meant that her husband had become a walking powder keg all of his own doing. No telltale whiskey bottle warned of possible trouble later, and no level of alcohol in his blood would impair his ability to hit—and to hurt—exactly where and how hard he wanted. For a wiry man, he was unstoppable when he was angry.

It took very little these days to get him angry.

Kim first fought back, with words and even efforts to grab his arms, to wrap them around her, to remind him she was a person, one who *loved* him, and that they needed to work on these problems together. But the fact that he cried as he shoved her away, and hit all the harder, gradually broke her will. Her only consolation, that he never laid a hand on their daughter, was only temporary. This very night, after dinner, was only the latest example.

Three months before, Kim had been fired from her latest position, to which she had risen to run a department of four bookkeepers and an office manager. Too many sick days, she was told, and she could provide no clear explanation for why she couldn't get her act together. Kim took this blow the way she took the others, with a blank stare and a stiffening of her entire body that only eased when her husband went to work and she'd dropped Natalie off at school.

Then the tears would come, and Kim had even taken to driving home by a less traveled, roundabout route that took her past several parking lots of businesses she knew did not open till ten. She did it for one reason: Each day, in all likelihood, she needed to pull over the car for a good cry...the only release she felt, more and more, that she deserved.

* * *

The ringing phone snapped Kim's reverie, but in her surprise the framed certificate slipped from her hands. Its glass shattered, the small shards fanning out toward the living room—and the open basement door. "Damn it!" she heard from below. The phone rang a third time as she stared at a rip across the middle of the document. Her husband's hurried footsteps told her this night's turmoil was not over.

2

Two weeks earlier, while on her bed, Natalie had thought she was dreaming. The little girl watched, entranced, as a transparent finger—her finger—gently rose from her right hand. The reflected glow from the corner streetlight, a steadfast friend, gave the finger a bright, fuzzy glow. The rest of her hand followed, then the arm.

The girl soon realized she was leaning forward, yet she felt she had done nothing but push back against the pillow at the revelation of what was happening before her. On impulse she turned her head...and realized she was staring into her own face. The blank expression she wore made her gasp. Had she...died?

But no—she wasn't dead at all; Natalie's spirit watched as her chest, the chest of her body, rose and fell with every breath. Yet, somehow, here she was above it.

Looking down.

The child froze in fear. At nine years old, she was old enough to know this wasn't...*supposed* to happen. A year before, her mother had explained how her Grandma Rosie's spirit had left her body and gone up. To Heaven. But Grandma Rosie was old; she'd had something called a "stroke." Natalie's slim body on the bed, by contrast, was physically in fine health but for the bruises. And the only thing "up" in her room, besides the overhead light, was a scallop-shell mobile. It clattered occasionally in the warm nighttime

13

breeze that wafted into the room.

Her body lay perfectly still, the flowered sheets tucked around the hem of her lavender nightgown. Her long, silky hair was draped across the side of the pillow near the wall. Some of it hung down over the blue eyes that stared blankly at an invisible point high on the opposite wall. One side of her thin, smooth face seemed to shine in the reflected glow of the streetlight.

She was awake, now...wasn't she? It was true, then, what she'd overheard from the Miller boy the other day.

Overheard, yes. The boy—her parents called him "disturbed" though she knew only that he stuttered and was ridiculed every day about it—had been talking to his collie, Jasper, on the other side of his family's tall, wooden privacy fence. "In spirit," he would meet his dog at night after his family had long turned in for the night. His older brother, Mark, would be asleep in the next bed, and he would not see even if he woke up. But Jasper knew.

Natalie grew afraid, even as she lifted the other arm from her physical self. In her own childlike way, she recognized that even here there had to be rules. Floating inches above her motionless body, she suddenly wondered whether she would be allowed to return. She thought to spin about, face the ceiling as her body did, and lower herself slowly. Her spirit responded as if she were moving muscles. Her hips joined first. Then she settled completely back into herself. She moved her hand—all of it—and sat up. She was back inside! It was easy, she realized. And the night was young.

Moments later, she again concentrated to the point at which she could again rise out of her own body. She felt freer to explore her room, this time, in a way she had not done before. Misjudging her direction, she floated into the shell mobile and flinched by habit as if her father had come into her room, angry to have been awakened by the shells' gentle clatter. But her mouth hung open when she realized that she had *passed through* the mobile. For several moments, she flitted about in a delirious dance.

She passed her hand through her music box and its little ballerina, her half-finished watercolor of the evening street scene (the streetlight prominently featured), and even the mirror that hung above her dresser. *"I'm Wendy in Peter Pan!"* she said aloud but covered her mouth immediately after. She listened for the banging that her parents' oak headboard, on the other side of the wall, made when someone was getting in or out of bed.

14

Her parents were light sleepers.

Especially Daddy.

For those few anxious seconds, she blew air at her curtain. The fabric didn't move any more than the night breeze was already rustling it.

Still, she heard nothing. Natalie floated to her bedroom door. Passing through that as well, she peeked into—literally passing only her face through the wall of—her parents' room. Her mother lay on her side, facing the corner of the room by the window, where all her plants were. Plenty of sun came in that window in the morning, though by night it was dark as a forest. Next to her lay her father, asleep in jeans and T-shirt and an old pair of sweat socks. The little girl entered the room completely and giggled as she stuck her finger through a hole in his left sock. Oh, what freedom! Again she looked up: No one had heard her.

Walking to the middle of the room, Natalie put her hands up to her mouth and yelled, *"Fiiiiiirrrrre!"*

No response. The little girl laughed: They really couldn't hear!

She checked once more in her own room, where her body remained in place. Then? She explored the rest of the house. She crept facedown along the ceiling in the kitchen, the bathroom, the living room, even her father's private, off-limits workbench in the cellar. Delighting in her new perspective, Natalie passed through walls, ran between the layers of the very structure of the house with all its insulation, floated up and down the chimney, and, of course, peeked inside the closed refrigerator. In time, she stopped at the bay window of the living room. A whip-poor-will was singing on a branch of the cherry tree.

Until that moment in their quieted household, Natalie hadn't considered that she might be able to hear sounds without anyone being able to hear her own. Now she not only could see and hear the night flier as it sang its name...she also could greet it!

She floated out through the closed windows toward the tree. The bird, however, abruptly cut off its song and flew off in the other direction. With a frown, Natalie came up with an explanation. It was like they said in a ghost story some boys were telling in the schoolyard: that animals always know when there's a ghost. That's what she was when she was floating around, wasn't she? The Miller boy's dog, Jasper, knew, though he somehow didn't care. The whip-poor-will knew.

Natalie lowered her head, ashamed as she sat on one of the high branches of the tree. God didn't allow such a thing, did he? She didn't know how she had done this...this act of leaving her body, but she was sure it was wrong. It was just too much *fun* to be allowed. Aside from what the Miller boy had seemed to say—Gerald, that was his name—she'd never heard anyone talk about it. Grownups, she supposed, didn't want kids to know some things. That was it. Her father would surely find out if she spent another minute away from her body. He would come out and find her in the tree, and then she'd get it good. She had to go back.

That was when she noticed the other children. In the gleam of the streetlight, Giselle Harper was sitting in the front seat of her father's shiny new pickup truck, her hands trying in vain to turn the steering wheel. She was an orphan who'd only recently been adopted; by day, she cried a lot in class. Two children she didn't know were playing peekaboo in and out of the sewer gratings that dipped down at the corner of Mason Street and Oak Drive. And from down the block, a dog was running. Natalie recognized it as Jasper, Gerald's collie. And high above, flying way above the power lines was Gerald, the stutterer, smiling and laughing while his dog, below, panted to keep up with his master. The boy saw Natalie, waved and kept on going.

The young girl smiled. She would find no grownups here.

Later that night, she'd passed from above through the ceiling, and was about to head toward her bedroom when a sound from behind her made her spin around. Her mother was in the hallway, her eyes open though she was apparently asleep, her arms open and extended. Toward Natalie.

The little girl gasped and withdrew till half her body was in her bedroom. Still she watched, however, and her mother no longer seemed to be staring at her. She kept her arms outstretched and weaved slowly back and forth. Searching. "My baby...my baby...where's my baby? My baby is..." Looking faint, she fell to her knees.

Natalie had dashed back into herself and opened the door of her room. "Mommy!" she gasped in her loudest whisper—her father wasn't to be awoken except in emergencies, whatever those were—and wrapped her arms around her mother.

Kim had awoken, then, and the two hugged as they crouched outside the spare bedroom, her playroom. "Oh, Natalie, my baby,

Natalie, you're here..."

"Mommy, were you having a bad dream?"

Her mother nodded. "Yes, Sweetheart. But everything's all right now. I love you, my dear sweet Natalie. I'll always protect you, always...protect you..."

Natalie buried her head in her mother's bosom the way she had as an infant. "I love you, too, Mommy. I...know you will."

* * *

That first night had frightened Natalie as much as it had thrilled her. Despite her youth, she'd sensed that what she had learned was a secret she must jealously guard, even from her closest friends—not that she had many friends, close or not. They never came over these days.

She *had,* at least, spoken to Gerald Miller, secure that he would not reveal anything about it. Passing by his backyard one afternoon, soon after that first night, she'd heard his voice and the collie's barking, and had called his name out twice before the boy climbed up to peer over the six-foot security fence. "N-Natalie, r-right?"

She nodded.

"I-I...don't s-s-see you m-much d-d-during the d-day."

The little girl tightened her grip around her books. She flashed her eyes left and right. "I have to ask you something," she said.

"Ab-ab-about what?"

"You know."

The boy paused as if considering the situation, then dropped from view. Moments later he unbarred the gate to let her in. The fence provided some welcome shade.

"Y-y-you d-don't have any brothers or s-s-s-sisters," he said as if it were an accusation.

She shook her head.

"S-so...wh-who told you?"

Natalie blushed, suddenly convinced that the boy could read minds as well as do...whatever it was they and a few other children were doing. "I'm sorry! I-I was just—"

But Gerald was laughing. "It's o-o-okay, it's okay, y-you d-d-don't have to t-tell m-me." He leaned close. "M-my older br-brother t-t-taught me."

Forgetting her embarrassment at Jasper's approach, the little girl suddenly was confused. She had seen Gerald's brother, and he was at least fifteen. In all her incorporeal escapades, the oldest child she'd seen was Desmond Wilson, whose older brother, Tyrone, delivered one of the local papers. Desmond was eleven, she knew.

This time Gerald must really have read her mind, or at least her expression, as he watched her pet his dog's head. He also began to stutter less as they talked, something he never did in class. "B-but he can't do it anymore. It's, l-like, cool—he told me a c-couple years ago in the s-summer. He was having a lot of em-emotional p-problems then. And we went out together a f-few times. It was...you kn-know...what you thought the f-first time."

Gerald stopped, wiped his brow with his hand and, for a moment, looked as though he might cry. "B-but school started. He g-got busy"—the boy shot Natalie a sideways glance—"with *g-girls* and st-started acting d-different, and one day I asked M-Mark if he w-wanted to go out tonight, me and Jasper were g-going 'ghosting.' Anyway, th-that's what he c-called it."

Ghosting. Natalie felt the word on her tongue and decided she didn't like it. She turned back to Gerald, whose face had grown very red. Jasper left her for his master, and the boy wrapped his arms around the dog's neck.

"He l-looked r-right at me and...s-said, 'G-g-ghosting? Wh-what the hell are you t-t-talking about, Gerry?' I...I tried to re-remind him, even s-said what it was and th-that he sh-showed me how to d-do it.

"He started—he st-st-started l-laughing! He said wh-what are you high on, ki-kid. I s-saw in his eyes. He *f-forgot!* I went away cr-crying l-like...like...I am...now, I g-guess, and...figured out that it, it's only for k-k-kids, for s-some k-kids. When you g-grow up, m-maybe just a t-teenager, it's gone like you never knew how to d-do it. And I..." He trailed off, embarrassed.

"That...wasn't nice" was all Natalie could say. In the night, the two would meet often and play together. They'd talk, too, with Gerald's voice virtually free of emotional impediments. But here, in the boy's yard on a sunny afternoon, they were just two nine-year-olds, one boy and one girl, who could never be seen together by schoolmates.

"Um...I have to go," she said and reached for the gate's latch.

Gerald nodded. "B-before you g-go, y-you remember one th-thing. A-abou-abou-about—"

"About what, Gerald?"

18

If he stung from the interruption, he didn't show it. "A-about w-watching your b-body in c-case of danger. Even fr-from f-far away, N-Natalie. Right? Never, ever f-forget."

Somehow, she already knew this, she assured her friend before leaving. On her evenings out, she floated as with the breeze to wherever in the neighborhood she chose to explore. Once, however, she had known from blocks away that her father had just opened her bedroom door and, in an instant, reunited with her body—just in time to get a smack for leaving the cap off the toothpaste.

At only nine, Natalie managed to understand how many families apparently had problems, and their kids suffered for them. Suffered greatly. Otherwise, she'd have been alone in her nighttime excursions. It wasn't fair, she thought, it wasn't....

The girl snatched up a tiny stone and, without a thought, flung it at a chipmunk as the tiny animal ran to hide behind an elm tree. She watched as the stone struck the rodent. It cried out, squirmed in place for a few moments and then struggled to its feet long enough to slip beneath Gerald's fence. Natalie watched the blood-sprinkled tail as it disappeared from sight.

She continued toward home, disturbed by her actions but hardly understanding why. It was not guilt that ate at her conscience, although Natalie could easily remember when she'd once saved part of her sandwich roll to feed the sparrows on her way home.

Rather, it was her eventual realization that she felt no remorse.

* * *

What Natalie could appreciate was fear, and it was fear that kept her apprehensive about leaving her body. But the bruises that so stung her small shoulders, back and legs were in fact the reason she continued her practice nightly. Apart from her body, after all, she felt no pain. Her body could recover while her spirit soared, and were it not for the approaching sunrise and her parents' alarm clock, she might stay away for much longer.

The night of the PTA meeting, for instance, Natalie had just finished dinner and was helping her mother clear the table when she slipped on a bit of gravy, from the earlier incident. She'd kept her grip on the plate, but her elbow had swung out and struck the front panel of the aging dishwasher.

"Nice little dent you put in this machine, kid," her father was quick to react. "What's next on the bill? Gonna—"

"George, it wasn't her fault. I—"

He lashed out and slapped her squarely on the side of her face; she spun to her knees and stayed there, her tears rolling onto the brick design of the laminate floor.

"It wasn't *her* fault, it wasn't *my* fault. Then who the hell's fault *is* it? Maybe if you cleaned the goddamn floor once in a while, we wouldn't have such a neat skating rink in our kitchen, now *would* we?" He turned back to Natalie, who had opened the dishwasher and was putting in the dish she had rescued.

"Oh, no, you don't—give me that goddamn dish." He charged at her, took away the dish, and dropped it into the sink. He grabbed her by the waistband of her jeans and shoved her up against the dishwasher door. The old appliance's knobs bruised her ribs where she struck the console.

"D-Daddy, noo—"

"Daddy, no? Daddy, no? Do you have any idea what it cost for this goddamn dishwasher? Tell me! Do you?" He let her drop to the floor, where she knelt, heaving up her dinner.

"Answer me!"

The girl violently shook her head, the vomit spilling out the edges of her mouth as she did so. Her mother took a step toward her but stopped in her tracks with one look from the man she married.

"I didn't think so. Well, kid, tonight you'll learn. After you clean up this mess you're making on the floor—I trust you won't be slipping on *that*—you're going to learn just how valuable the dishwasher *is* in this house." He opened the machine and made a racket as he withdrew every dish, glass, and utensil, stacked the items high on the counter and slammed the dishwasher door.

"I want every one of these dishes washed spotless, rinsed and dried—*by hand*—before you go to bed. Understand?"

Natalie was heaving up nothing by this point. The nine-year-old looked up, her eyes red, her chin tan with what had been gravy. "O-okay, Daddy," she managed to whisper between sobs, and her father turned to head down to his workbench in the basement.

"Good girl," he said before descending.

* * *

By the time she'd gone to bed, Natalie was nearly doubled over in pain. With great difficulty and much help from her mother, she had washed, dried and stowed the dishes, pots and other items. Upstairs, Kim tried to help her daughter change into her nightgown. To skip the nightclothes would invite further punishment should her father discover the infraction, but her intense pain gave her no choice. Her mother quietly acquiesced, this time, to Natalie's wearing her street clothes to bed, and to change during the night—at least before she went down for breakfast—if she awoke and felt up to it. She would do her best to keep her father away.

Natalie's tearful eyes widened as she lifted her top and caught a glance at her battered frame in the mirror; the welt, from the dishwasher knobs, seemed to further redden as she stared. She felt the urge to lean to one side, both from the stinging burn at her ribs and from her shoulder, from when he had yanked her arm. And even though her mother had slipped her a banana and a biscuit once they'd finished in the kitchen, the girl's stomach still felt hollow from having brought up her entire dinner. It would take time, but Natalie seemed to know she'd be all right...eventually.

For now, though, she had to escape. She knew her mother sneaked down a few white pain pills when he hit *her* too hard. But she felt more sure that no pill, even if it were okay for kids, would do a thing for what she felt tonight. She needed something else.

Natalie tried to lie down. It hurt too much to recline in the usual way—and while she was away, it didn't really matter whether she was in a supine sleeping position. With difficulty, she maneuvered into a relatively comfortable position, her knees up and her hands clasped in front, her back against the headboard. She leaned her head back and felt the frilled cushion of the headboard's top edge against her neck. That would do, she thought, particularly since she believed her father was probably through with her that evening.

The girl closed her eyes. It had grown much easier to "ghost" since she'd first done it, two weeks before. Still, she needed to concentrate. For the few moments it took for her to separate spirit from body, Natalie had to focus on a total release from her pain.

She began with her still-trembling arms and legs, felt her skin tingle with anticipation. She thought hard about her bruised ribs and aching stomach, worked on pushing them away, however much the pain was a part of her, and within seconds she felt far removed from the intense throbbing. In the short time it took for her mind to disengage from all that could be called physical, she looked down at her arms and suddenly saw another pair stretching out from her bruised body. The difference between stinging pain and none whatsoever was remarkable, and were it not for her desperation to relieve her suffering, she would have gone back into herself, again and again, to marvel anew at this remarkable power.

For several minutes she danced around her bed, up and down the walls, upside down from the ceiling. She balled her fists and beat her chest like a gorilla. She even leaned through her wall to flap her arms and give the raspberry at her father, but he wasn't in her parents' bedroom.

Then she was off, this time a little farther. The day had been overcast, and Natalie had been thinking she'd like to touch a cloud. It didn't matter either, she'd found, how far away you were from your body. When someone came near, she knew it immediately— and could flash back in an instant. It would be as if she'd never been gone.

Natalie met up with Gerald along the way and invited him along. He thought it a fine idea and instructed Jasper to wait down below, as if the dog could otherwise follow his young master to such a destination.

"Hey, W-Walt! Larry!" Two faces looked up from beneath the roof of the soda shop on the corner of Mason and Walnut, two blocks from Natalie's home. Gerald turned toward Natalie. "The more, the merrier. Right?"

"I—I guess..." This was not her idea of escape, but she quickly decided that, yes, this was just what she needed: company. "Yeah, sure. The more, the merrier!"

By the point the group had risen skyward and thrashed about with glee within some low-lying fog, it had grown to seven children. Natalie forgot the horrors of her evening, didn't feel the pain or the ravenous hunger that was enveloping her body, in the romping and frolicking that made her feel, for the first time in years, like a normal kid.

Among the group, Natalie recognized a few classmates from earlier grades, knew their names but had never spoken to them before. Outside their bodies, she realized, a different code governed them from the treacherous rule of schoolyard politics. Where below the quiet, the different and the troubled were shunned and even victimized, apart from the physical world all were one. She laughed with her newfound friends. She was warmed by the knowledge that through the power they shared—this power God seemed to reserve for the troubled children alone—the friendships formed in the night would extend even to the classroom, to the everyday.

Her home life had been making her an outcast, but all that would change now. She could go home after the night was over, and everything would be all right. She could face anything.

So long as she had friends like these.

3

Kim's hands trembled as she picked up the handset. "H-hello?" She glanced over her shoulder. George leapt up the stairs and headed straight to where she'd dropped the frame.

Now he was storming toward the kitchen, where she'd answered the landline.

Right toward her.

"Hello, Mrs. Leffingwell, this is Emily Sanders. I'm the school nurse at Hollister Elementary. We met at the last PTA meeting, and I was hoping..." But Kim barely heard the voice. Her every sense had braced for one simple reality: *He's going to kill me.*

"You little—"

Kim screamed into the phone. "Help me, please, *help me!* Hurry! He's—"

George slammed his hand on the hook switch to break the connection, and the handset crashed to the floor. "Who was that? Who was on the phone!"

"Nobody, I didn't hear her, it—"

"What do you mean, *her?*" He had grabbed her arm and now twisted it till she fell to her knees. He was leaning over her now, and

Kim was barely hearing even him now. Her body was stiffening as if preparing for death, even as she knew this wasn't only about her. She needed to make it, if only for her little girl.

"Do you hear me? I said, how the fuck do you know it was a *her* and don't know who it was? Tell me, damn it!" He swung down and struck the side of her head. Her vision blurred, her knees buckling anew as she'd struggled to rise, Kim raised a hand to avert the second blow. This one, though, came from the front—his knee hit her face. She felt herself crumbling to the floor, blood draining from her broken nose.

"Over here!" He was dragging her, by one limp arm, out of the kitchen. Staring down, the woman stared at her reddening blouse and the thin, red trail she was leaving behind first on the laminate floor, then on the parquet hardwood.

George released her where she had dropped the award and pulled her by the shoulders to a sitting position. The air conditioner struggled, then clicked on; the cool air from a nearby register made the blood dripping from her nose seem all the wetter. She shook her head and spat out blood. A tooth was loose, she noticed. "George," she said, her voice sounding foreign to her own ears, "I didn't mean to do it. I was dusting it, and—oh, George, I love you—"

"You didn't mean to do it. You didn't mean to do it! The only thing I earned in my whole fucking life that I haven't lost, and you didn't *mean* to do it! I won that goddamn thing, Kim. I was the best goddamn broker in the business, and they shit on me! You saw it all, and I know how you thought, well, it couldn't happen to a nicer guy—"

"N-no, George!" Kim couldn't control her sobbing. "I *love* you, George. I *cried* when you lost your job! We can't go on like this, George, we—"

"You *love* me!" He spoke the word like a swear as he stepped into the dining room and reached up for the key to the china closet's locked drawer. George unlocked and opened the drawer. Reached in. He returned to where she lay, struggling to stand, and gripped her wrist with one hand; with the other, he brandished the revolver. He held it up before her face, its barrel an inch from her forehead. "And I suppose *love* is pulling out the gun as you're dusting"—he was sneering—"and playing with it. What would it be like, you wondered, to just point this pistol at my sweet George, who I *love,* right between his eyes...and pull this little trigger?"

Something in the lowered tone of his voice terrified her all the more.

"Is that what you call LOVE? You think I don't know exactly where in this drawer I keep the goddamn gun? Think I wouldn't notice if you took it out, just for fun, and—"

"George, it wasn't m—" She broke off in horror. Of course it had been Natalie. It must have been. Kids get curious. It was what she'd been wanting to tell him all along, that a child naturally would want to examine such a thing and could find the key just by standing on a chair.

But in doing so, she perhaps had sealed her daughter's doom as well.

"So let's go ask Natalie then, shall we?" he tightened his grip on her arm.

"No! Leave her alone! You've beaten her already tonight! Just..."

He smacked her again across her face, and the loose tooth dropped to the floor. *"I* decide when the child's had enough of a whipping." He pulled her to the stairs and began dragging her up, each step a shock to her hips. "Get up here, bitch."

"George, noooo..."

"Move."

They reached the top of the stairs, and George dropped her on the landing. He looked down the hall. To Natalie's door, a few steps before theirs.

* * *

Still propped against the headboard, Natalie's body breathed gently, in and out, doing what it could, at its own slowed speed, to repair the damage of the evening.

Far away, the little girl and her friends had just floated out of the cloud, having noticed that it had strayed far from Mason Street during the past hour or so. Even Gerald's dog, Jasper, was nowhere to be seen.

"There's my father's office building!" chimed in Sandra Berkow, who sat two seats up from Natalie in class. "He took me to work a couple of times!"

This brought a chorus of cheers from the wispy crowd, who all knew very well exactly where they were. Like cats taken far from

27

home, no child among their group could not find his or her body in the blink of an eye.

The game, however, was in figuring out how to get there by the local landmarks rather than their own homing senses.

Natalie had been having the time of her life, but she could not forget the pain she'd felt that evening before her "ghosting"—for want of a better word—especially because her body, back home, could hear them arguing yet again. The next day was a school day; her parents forbade her to stay home, unless she felt very sick. And her teacher, Mrs. Genovese, had been looking very funny at her lately, almost staring.

She thought next of her body and could picture it sitting exactly where she had left it, leaning up against the headboard. Natalie somehow knew that her wounds would heal, but...what if she died? Would she know death was coming, like those pictures of a hooded skeleton with the big sharp blade on a pole? Would it appear to her, here among her friends, say, "Come, dearie...it's time to go," and lead her by the hand back to her body for a last visit? Would it—

The little girl shook her head and started listening to a conversation that Gerald, Sandra and Wendy were having. It was creepy enough, she thought, thinking about what had happened only a week or so before.

That night she had been exploring the house again, hovering for a time above her father's workbench, entranced by all the power tools, the hammers and wrenches hanging on a big, white pegboard, everything neat and clean. On her way up she'd noticed in the dining room the drawer that had the gun in it. She'd known about the gun since one of the first nights she had roamed the house unencumbered by her body.

Darkness was no hindrance to her, and she'd peered into each dark drawer of the china closet, stopping when she found it—and the key hidden above. By day she might return to the scene, just to touch it for a minute. But for now, all she could do was look.

* * *

Kim had barely enough strength this night to lift herself up, let alone lunge at her husband before he reached their daughter's door. Somehow, she found the energy, and George fell down on his face, tripped at the ankles. She climbed on top of his flailing body but he quickly shook her off and rose to his feet. Next, he swung the butt of the revolver; it crashed against her knuckles an instant after she covered her face with her hand.

The room, she thought. If she could get into their bedroom, she might get George to follow her in and forget about Natalie. She lurched in the direction of the doorway and tripped over the threshold. "I'm c-calling the police," she announced and lifted the handset of the extension phone with her uninjured left hand, "and you can't stop me."

Before she could raise the handset to her ear, though, her head began to spin anew, and she barely noticed when her husband grabbed her shoulders and hoisted her to her feet. *It worked, she vaguely realized.* She began to fall—but regained her posture at the sight of the gun barrel inches away from her eyes. "It's time," her husband said.

"Nooo, George, don't, George, you'll go to ja—"

"Shut up."

She shut her eyes for a moment and reopened them when she felt cold metal touch the palm of her hand. "Whaa...?" She was holding the gun. Her husband was smiling.

"Kim, m-my father was a great man. He ran his family the way he needed to, and he did it because he knew, deep in his heart, that his wife and children didn't have the *guts* to kill him if they had the chance. I'm...finished, Kim. I lost another job today. So here's your chance. Raise the gun. I-I won't move an inch. It's loaded, and the safety is off. You can pump as many bullets into me as you want, Kim.

"Aim carefully. Pull the trigger. It's that simple."

Police sirens were growing louder, coming very close. Of course! The phone call. The woman—who was it? She'd called 9-1-1.

Maybe she could just keep him here, hold him till the police came up. But no, then he'd be free in a few hours. He'd come home, madder than ever, and finish what he'd started, confident she didn't "have the guts." And anyway, she couldn't be sure she'd remain conscious long enough to hold him.

"I'm still here, Kim, if you have the *guts* to do it. Come on, never mind the sirens, you can dooo it..."

If I...do it, she thought as she tried to remain standing, I might go to jail. If I don't do it, he'll win. It won't stop until both Natalie and I are...that was it. She had to do it. For Natalie. Having no father was better than this monster who beat her—

Her finger tightened on the trigger, but her knuckles screamed from the cracking they'd gotten out in the hall. Her knees were buckling. Come on! You can do it...just...

The siren had stopped, and someone was banging on the door.

"Damn it, Kim, do it, do it, do it, do it do it..."

"Oh, George..." Her eyes opened wide at the realization. In his eyes she saw desperation, pleading. Somewhere in there...he knew what he had become. He was her husband, and—

"KIIIM!"

"George, I love you!" She pulled the trigger. Shots rang out again and again. Her knees weakened. The first bullets went wild— through the wall above the headboard. The lampshade. A seascape painting he'd bought her. Then George fell, one bullet lodged between his eyes, another through his left lung. Another went past him, into the ceiling, as his wife's knees fully gave out.

The banging from below was louder; someone downstairs was breaking in. Her husband lay across their bed, his eyes open, his face locked in a mad grin. Natalie! She had to...had to somehow....get to her. To tell her it was okay. To tell her everything would be all right, that the police would believe them, that everything would turn out fine. They'd move away, Natalie would start in a new school, and everything would be okay.

She stood up now, and, her weight against the wall, made her way out of the master bedroom.

Moments later, however, she began to scream. Pain ripped throughout her body. The blood running from her nose and ears was choking her. The hallway was spinning. The chandelier above swirled in a wide ring, and Kim knew she had to be lurching closer to the railing, to the stairs, to her death, but was too weak, too ravaged to do anything more but watch the light swirl, swirl around as she crashed against the wall and rebounded away, away from the wall, against the corner. She watched herself tipping away...toward the stairs.

Her rescuers had broken through the door, but they were too late. The first policeman on the stairs watched, helpless, as Kim tumbled over the first step and rolled, headfirst, to fall limply at his feet.

4

Two weeks passed, and a key turned in the lock of the Leffingwell home. In came a policeman, another man wearing a navy blue suit, and a woman whose slightly graying hair was bound tightly into a bun to keep it off the padded shoulders of her gray suit and ermine coat. She shivered after the door closed and further tightened her thin lips. "I didn't realize the heat would be off," she remarked.

"Sarah," the dressed-up man was saying, "you can see that the house has remained in virtually the same condition as it was the night the...incident took place. We haven't even been allowed to clean the place up, to which Officer Burke can attest."

He glanced in the direction of the policeman, who nodded blankly as he stared more closely at the dried blood he'd spotted from the doorway. "Yes—oh, yes," Burke said, realizing he was being addressed. "Yes, Ms. Leffingwell, we're still conducting our investigation, so we were hoping to keep the place sealed until...until our boys could wipe down the floors, clean up a bit. Public service, you know."

The woman herself had barely been listening. She had taken a few steps ahead of the other two, into the dining room, and now gaped at the scene of the incident. At the laminate floor in particular.

"Was it necessary to leave *this?*" She directed her question to the man in the suit.

"Sarah, you know the police haven't finished checking over the place. I'd have preferred you and, um, your brother's other relatives

31

stayed away from the house, at least until I straighten out the estate. It's all in probate, as you also know, but..." He shrugged his shoulders. "You wanted to see what's left behind, to know nobody's walked away with anything. The police chief owes me a favor, so..."

"So we may as well see the place then, shall we?"

The lawyer and policemen exchanged glances as Sarah led the way around the first floor. The woman looked carefully at everything, with an eye totaling its potential value. She surveyed the furniture, the jewelry, the china—a set still worth a few dollars despite three missing plates. She occasionally touched things, despite Officer Burke's repeated instructions that she only look. And she took notes with a gold pen on a yellow legal pad.

Her face, though she was no older than forty, seemed twisted in a knowing smirk. Her family had the legal muscle to wrest this house away from those *other* people, after all. She just thought she'd get an idea, firsthand, of the worth of her late, stupid brother's paltry property. The woman shook her head and shielded a grin. Thought he was leaving Papa behind, did he?

Having summarized the basement and first floor in a single sheet of the yellow pad, Sarah advanced to the stairway. But she soon realized that something...something was wrong. She stopped on the fourth step, looked back at the pair—what remaining legalities she hadn't already trampled required they accompany her everywhere on the premises—and suddenly felt an unsettling chill. The room was already bitingly cold without the boiler running, but this was...different. It was an intense cold that brought with it a wave of despair, pain...anger. It seemed not to be a breeze but...a wall of ice through which she, with one step, had passed.

"Sarah?" The attorney, directly behind her, was looking up at her questioningly.

The woman shook her head. She had learned from youth to hide any hurt she felt, yet she was uncertain she had done anything of the sort. She was doing what she had to do, she was convinced. The Spencer family hadn't built this household—no, not Kim (what a name!) with her paltry bookkeeper's salary. Not her. Whatever terror her idiot brother had instilled upon his family, *he* had paid for their possessions.

All she wanted was to keep things in the family, at least her splintered segment of it. For whatever it was worth.

The feeling grew more intense, as if something on the stairs directly above her had descended a step to meet her.

"There—there's something...a window. Someone left a window open. Officer Burke! Have children been throwing rocks at the windows?"

"No, Ms. Leffingwell. If you want, I'll go up first and check whether..." He reached the step beneath hers, then dropped back. "Say, that is a chill. A...brrrrr! From one step to the next. Like..."

"No, that will most certainly *not* be required." She continued climbing. "I can certainly manage a few steps—"

At that moment, something passed literally into the same space Sarah Leffingwell occupied. The woman shuddered and threw herself against the wall. "Uh-uhhh—huuu-uhhh...uhhhhhhaaah..." She began to rock violently and kick out at the balusters, snapping one of them. "Ahhhhh! Leave me alone! Leave me—uhhhu—uhhhuhuhu—uhuh—uuhhh, uhhhh...leave—"

"Ms. Leffingwell!"

Officer Burke grabbed hold of the woman in the hopes of guiding her down the stairs and tried to ignore the dank chill that was permeating his own body as well. He wanted to release her and run, to get out of that house as fast as he could, to forget about the house, forget about being a cop, get as far away as possible. What he felt was his own soul gripped deep within him. Someone, something, had reached in and was holding tight...hands around his very being.

And his soul was being shaken. Throttled by something angry. Very angry.

But strangely not angry at him, he realized with a flash. He swung to look at Sarah Leffingwell. Angry at *her.* The policeman stepped back, and the feeling left him. It had but one target. Burke sighed. He had to forget his own troubles, get this woman out. Could he ignore what his every instinct was shouting?

The woman's eyeballs were now rolling in their sockets as she continued her involuntary, jiggling dance against the wall. "Uhhuhuhuh...not me...I didn't mean...uhuhhu—no," she muttered with less energy by the syllable. Blood dripped from a corner of her mouth, then from her ear. "It wasn't..." she said. And then her eyes went blank.

Sarah Leffingwell slumped down from the wall—barely conscious and devoid of expression—to fall into both men. The policeman caught his footing and, with the white-faced attorney, raised her up at the foot of the stairs. Each man wrapped an arm behind her, but her feet barely lifted to walk to the front door. They eventually dragged her, one Fendi shoe left behind, as they made their way to the attorney's car. Relieved to be back outdoors in the early autumn air, Officer Burke agreed to clear traffic along the way to Hollister Medical Center's emergency room.

The policeman made a mental note to return later and retrieve the legal pad she had left behind. You never knew, after all, whether anything she'd jotted down could help explain what had just transpired.

He returned the next bright, sunny morning and could not find the pad anywhere. Somehow, though, he was not surprised.

5

The chilly breezes typical of a late September morning made the idea of an open-air garage sale less than a great idea, but the woman the bank hired to run the event preferred the driveway of the Leffingwell house to anyplace within the already storied home.

Whatever sold at this point, she already felt some satisfaction in having persuaded a local furniture dealer to lend a hand, for a healthy discount, by hauling off some of the home's larger pieces. As for the rest, the woman shrugged and held her lined windbreaker tightly against her, watching the first leaves fall and wishing she'd donned her Under Armour before leaving the house; the early-morning rain hadn't helped. Inevitably, some sales she ran involved long, boring hours with an occasional customer stopping by. This one? There were plenty of browsers—just no takers. She felt she were hosting a museum exhibition.

What took her some time to realize was the extent to which the house's reputation as a site of brutal crime had permeated the community. Few people knew that three cleaning teams over the past year had independently seen and heard things that had sent them racing out of the house, pay be damned. But for a chance to see the *Leffingwells'* things, the turnout was great.

"There's the dishes," she heard one middle-aged woman whisper excitedly to the man who accompanied her. She stopped to count. "Looks like there're a few pieces missing."

The man shrugged, staring into his phone. "Maybe someone else had the same set and only needed a couple of pieces."

"Uh-huuuh," the woman returned with more than a hint of sarcasm. The two moved on.

Two young boys had been moving from table to table, uninterestedly staring at the collection of household items. Their eyes scanned the storage containers, the utensils, the power tools, and the office supplies. One of the boys then stole quietly away from the other, walked around to the left side of the house, past the street lamp toward the back, and stood looking up at one of the windows.

A few moments later he collapsed.

"Gerald!" shouted the boy's friend as he ran over.

Several people rushed from the driveway to the boy's side, but Gerald was just coming to. He looked up at his friend, darted his eyes toward the house and shot to his feet. "G-g-g-got t-t-t-to..." He took off down the street and stopped only when he was home, safely behind the six-foot privacy fence with Jasper.

* * *

"Oh, Phil...it's even more beautiful in the fall!"

The man with black hair cut into a high-fade, longish on top, and a scruff beard of two days' growth nodded as he pressed to unlock the car's back door. "Almost winter, feels like. I still wish we'd been able—"

"There you go again." Jennifer, his wife, pushed her long, straight red hair out of her vision and mimicked him, saying, "Can't move in sooner, the bank won't clean the place up, it's too cold outside, my toenails are getting long..." until he began to chuckle with her. "And besides, we did get a good price on it, didn't we?"

A baby's cry interrupted their hug, and Philip sighed. "So do you hear something, Jen? A siren, maybe?"

Jennifer slapped her husband playfully on the back. "Let's get her out of there. It's been a long trip for her. But let me," she said, as she pulled down her sweatshirt and extended her arms to accept the infant, "carry her over the threshold."

"Hey, waitaminnit, I wanted to carry *you* over."

The woman strode toward the house and looked back once she climbed the few brick steps to reach the door; of course, she'd set him up for this. "So who says you can't? I'm *almost* back to my old weight, after all. It's taken long enough."

36

Philip Carter grinned and joined his wife and daughter at the door. He propped the storm door open, turned the key in the lock and gave the main door a push. He grunted as he lifted both of them up and over the threshold. "So *there,*" he said proudly and set her down with a deep exhalation.

Jennifer shook her head as she surveyed the living room.

"Problem?" inquired Philip.

"Vera said they put everything they didn't sell into the garage. But look. There's art on the walls, this Tiffany lamp, ceramic cat, all this stuff in one part of the room. We didn't want to have to clean up..." She shrugged and turned to her husband. "I guess it won't take long, but...people do as little as they can get away with, don't they?"

Her husband nodded. "Or as much," he replied, noticing a musty smell a moment before his wife did. Philip took off his black, horned-rim glasses, wiped his brow and put them back on. He suddenly looked into his wife's bright hazel eyes and touched her hair. She met his stare and lowered her eyes, smiling.

The baby in her arms had barely opened her eyes since they came indoors, but now she was fully awake. Jennifer held up the baby so she could face her father. "This is your daddy, Carolyn. He's the greatest man in the whole world."

A broom that had been leaning against the wall outside the kitchen fell over, slapping loudly against the parquet floor. Philip and Jennifer started.

"Can't get good cleaning help anymore, can you?"

His wife giggled, and Philip went over to pick up the broom. While she waited for him to return—he'd apparently made a turn and headed into the kitchen—she picked a spot on the carpet, leaned against the wall and began to nurse the baby.

Jennifer felt blessed today. She had been anxious over the past few months, what with the approaching delivery of her firstborn as well as the dealings with the bank over the house, a corner property with three bedrooms in a quiet, safe neighborhood. Her dream house, she'd called it, although she'd dared not call it that in the presence of Vera, their realtor.

She recalled the day she and her husband had visited the house for the first time. Their seventy-ish realtor wore too much makeup and smelled as though she applied her perfume with a pneumatic sprayer. She at least had been marginally helpful, though, which was more than they could say about most others. And she'd been sure to make the obligatory fuss over Jennifer, rosy-cheeked in her eighth month.

Philip had been wearing a red-plaid flannel work shirt despite that day's temperatures in the seventies, and she remembered the first thing he said when he'd walked in the door: "You know, I'm surprised the owners had the gall to show the place without at least paying someone to clean it up some. Haven't you been here before?"

The woman shook her head with a plastic smile that said she thought a sharp eye could see through the dust and realize the place was a bargain despite its recent neglect. "No, I'm sorry," she said. "It *is* a foreclosure, after all, and the listing did say 'as is.'"

The man glanced at his wife, who shrugged. "So Vera," he said, "we've been looking in this area for several months now, and we've had house after house grabbed out from under us. Okay, so not many people move here from out of state. But the houses *are* going, and quickly. Why not this one?"

Jennifer's father then knocked on the door, and stepped in. "Oh, hi, Daddy," she'd said to him. "I'm glad you could make it over—and sorry you needed to take the train. Wherever we move'll be your place, too, and you've got more experience in the process. You ought to be looking at these with us." She approached and hugged him.

Grant O'Keefe scanned the room. Wearing a cotton driver's cap, light blue polo, windbreaker and khaki golf pants, the old man looked thinner and a bit frailer than even a week before. His hazel eyes, deeply bagged, still took in everything, a mark of his career as a builder. In better days, he'd been five-foot-ten and broader-shouldered, with a tanned complexion from plenty of outdoor projects. These days, he walked with a slight stoop, took stairs with caution—like those he spotted, which apparently led up to the bedrooms—and tried, generally, to count his blessings. Like his daughters and his still-new granddaughter.

Philip nodded to her father with a rather dismissive air, she thought, and returned his attention to the realtor.

"As I was saying, Mr. O'Keefe, just as you knocked," she was saying, "the house is a bit underpriced because the bank foreclosed on it. A house gets a bit neglected as affairs are set in order—by the day it's back on the market, it looks more like a handyman special, and people start to be anxious about it, so their imaginations go to work. The house has even gotten," she chuckled at this last point, "a *reputation* as of late. Can you *believe* it? But...I'm sure it will brighten up *considerably* once there's a little life around the place again."

There was something about her father that seemed to brighten things up at once, Jennifer had been thinking. He took off his cap, revealing the bald spot on his head. There wasn't a pretentious bone in his body, she knew. And there was something about the way he'd seemed to see through the dust and clutter—"Saaay, what a place," he said—to feel it was a nice house to live in.

Despite appearances.

* * *

Now in the baby's new room, next door to the master bedroom, Jennifer thought about their day. She had marveled, earlier, over the layout of the house: the bay windows, the trim kitchen with the little shuttered window she could see from where she'd stood in the dining room. A dining room! Their cramped apartment in the city had merely had an open area, at the end of the living room, into which they'd crammed their dining-room table—sans leaves. There hadn't been space for the full length of their table.

Of course, most of the old furniture had since been removed from the house; that was one point on which they'd insisted. This "quiet" family, from Vera's description, who'd apparently died in an accident abroad, had had decent taste in furniture, but there simply wasn't room for all the Carters' pieces along with the Leffingwells'. But though both Jennifer and her husband had wanted to start in their new home with only their own things, she had nevertheless taken note of how the former owners had arranged everything before the last estate sale had taken place.

Take the Leffingwells' china closet, for instance; Jennifer had wanted one for years, and the one left in the house could stay right where it was. Right by where the broom that fell had been leaning against the wall. Speaking of which, where was Philip?

Carolyn, at her breast, was fussing. After three months, Jennifer had surely felt she had the hang of the routine; still, some feedings were easier than others. She gently guided the baby's face toward her nipple, but the hungry infant began to cry in frustration anyway. It's right here, she thought to say. She imagined, with a wry grin, the baby replying, "Never mind this pink thing, where's the breast?"

It would take time for both of them—no, now the *three* of them—to get used to the baby, she thought. She couldn't forget her father, who would be in the guest bedroom for...however long he had left. Philip had objected initially to the idea when she'd first proposed it. Colon cancer or no, her husband worried about the long-term effects of a live-in parent on their relationship. Couldn't they find nearby, to use his euphemism, a nice "long-term care center"?

Jennifer had persisted in the end, mostly because her father's illness seemingly took a turn for the worse during their discussions. You couldn't tell from looking at the man—his energy and optimism were boundless—but he would live his final days in that house. Long-term effects were no longer a concern. Her only concern was the stairway.

This argument had convinced her husband. What may also have helped was Philip's enthusiasm over his new job marketing a new line of smart devices—several of which he planned to install at home—that, he felt, could well get some attention should buyers agree to pay more to a company that pledged strict protection of their personal data. Maybe, too, he had fallen in love with the house after all and didn't mind a little extra company for a while. Philip, Jennifer felt glad to notice, seemed to speak more highly of her father than ever before. A change of heart, maybe? Might the two get to know one another well enough to get along?

Or was the whole thing a bad idea?

Jennifer didn't want to think of that. Her baby had fallen asleep at her breast, and her husband was...where was Phil, anyway? She laid her baby down in her porta crib and headed for the stairs.

A horn blew three long blasts outside. Philip hurtled out from the kitchen, not noticing her or the baby's crying as he rushed out the door to meet the moving van. His face was paler than she'd ever seen it.

* * *

Today, thought Grant O'Keefe, he felt he could face anything. He had ridden over with the van for the whole two-hundred-mile trip on a theory he knew was true: that even the most unmotivated movers worked much more carefully when they liked you. It was a common-sense business acumen that had served him well throughout his career as a builder, and it was universal enough to make a difference here, too.

The two Latino movers had resisted his presence at first; though the cab easily fit his thin frame, they were naturally used to their own company. They'd spoken little, and when they did it was usually in Spanish to one another.

Eventually, though, he'd engaged them in conversation—first one, then the other, then both together—and had begun to pull down the walls. One man, the driver, was a father of a pair of toddler twins; Grant used the occasion to ask what advice he could pass along to his daughter regarding their three-month-old infant.

He'd sensed the other man was perhaps in the country illegally from the man's reluctance to answer a casual question about where he lived. Suppressing his usual objections, Grant had eased the conversation into America's pick-and-choose method of recognizing other governments based upon what was politically expedient at the time. The losers were the refugees, who simply wanted better for their families than they could sometimes get in their native lands, and now wanted to be Americans. You couldn't generalize about people, he said—and came to believe it as he spoke it. He was sure there were plenty of people in the U.S. who didn't have papers but were nevertheless making worthwhile contributions to the economy.

Before much longer, it seemed he had won over the second man, too. And when they'd stopped for lunch, the three chatted like they'd known one another for years.

These two men would treat his daughter's household goods like they were cases of nitroglycerin, he knew. He had done what he'd set out to do, and it had kept his mind off the nagging pain in his lower abdomen.

He had fixed things, all right, but he hadn't expected the kind of greeting they received from his son-in-law.

The man came stomping out of the house, slamming the door behind him; from behind Philip, Grant could faintly hear the baby's shriek through the open door.

"Hi, Grant. So okay, guys, let's get hopping. You're already a half-hour late. What the hell kept you?"

"Phil," the old man began to explain, "we stopped for lunch. I said it was all ri—"

"Grant, *I* hired them. You can't just..." He trailed off and turned to head back into the house, hands in the air in exasperation. "I'm sorry. Never mind."

The storm door closed behind him, again with a resounding slam.

Grant made a mental note to tighten the screw on the door's piston; then he looked back toward the two movers. One was already in the back of the truck, tossing canvas covers out and rolling dollies to his partner. They kept their voices low and mumbled in Spanish, as they would do for the remainder of the day.

Jennifer called out to her husband as he came in and again passed her by. "Phil, what's wrong?"

Philip stopped momentarily and shook his head. "Nothing, nothing. I'm just getting madder by the minute that all this *shit* is still all over the house. The living room, the dining room—all that glass that nobody swept up—and the kitchen. I bet the upstairs hasn't been cleaned out, either."

He slammed a fist into the other hand. "So I'm calling Vera. I don't know what the problem is, but..." He tried her phone, hit the realtor's voice mail and hung up.

His face dropped, and he met his wife's gaze as he paced the room, unsure what made sense to do next. "Jen, could you direct the movers while I...go around and throw this crap out? I'll just get it all together before it becomes permanent."

"Mmmmm, okay. Wait, Phil." She caught him as he climbed the stairs. "How about tossing it into the garage till we can get rid of it? We'd better not leave a big pile in the driveway without knowing the garbage pickup day—and we might need to tell them it's here. The things could be there for days. Besides, some of them might come in useful."

"Like the year-old calendar in the kitchen?"

Jennifer grinned but got no smile in return. She held the baby more tightly as a sudden chill made her shiver. "Use your own judgment, Phil."

Her husband charged up the stairs. Was that a "humph" she had heard from him? That wasn't like Phil, she thought. Sure, the managing agents hadn't done their part in getting the house ready. But they were gone now, it was the Carter place now, and it just wasn't worth being mad over.

Darn if the air hadn't suddenly gotten very...stagnant. For a moment it seemed to downright stink. What could...

She decided the place just needed a good dusting. With all the opening and closing of the doors—

The storm door cracked open, slammed shut and then opened again. Jennifer jumped. What was getting *her* so uppity, now?

"Dad...it's so good to see you," she said when she further opened the main door. Her father wrapped his arms around her and stepped around to see Carolyn's face.

"She's back asleep, looks like," he whispered.

"Not for long." Jennifer's bedroom dresser was on its way up the walk, carried by two very muscular men who didn't look very happy to be working. "Dad, I need to tell them where to put everything. Would you mind just...holding Carolyn for a while so I can..."

"No problem." He tossed his cap and jacket into a corner. "Pass the little bundle on over."

"Thanks, Dad. And have you noticed the air is..." Jennifer stopped, staring at nothing, then turned toward the open doorway. The first man was backing in with the dresser. "Now it's...you know, it's fine in here now. But just a few seconds ago, the air seemed to have a...smell of some—" She turned to her father, who was grinning.

"Mover sweat," he said.

"No," she replied. "They hadn't yet..." Again she trailed off. "Okay, so I imagined it. Humor me, please?" she asked.

The old man smiled with love. "I've done it for thirty years now. Once more couldn't hurt, I guess."

6

Jennifer opened her eyes and, in the dark, realized her husband was sitting up against the headboard, wide awake.

He'd been plenty active that day. First, he scrambled furiously to take the Leffingwells' old things out to the garage. Later, he'd unpacked several boxes and hung enough clothes in the closets to make the three of them feel they had enough to wear over the first few days. After everything else, he'd installed and set up the wireless router—the prerequisite for connecting not only their laptops and phones, but also all the smart doodads he wanted to learn about to help his new position. It would add meat to his presentations, he'd once explained.

Philip was exhausted, she knew, more than she'd seen him in recent memory, even over the first days after she and Carolyn came home together for the first time. And she could bet his back hurt. Who could blame him?

Yet here he was, sitting up at three-thirty a.m. and staring at nothing in particular. Sure, it would take time to adjust to sleeping in the new place. But tonight, thought Jennifer, he shouldn't have needed any coaxing. She paused before touching him, taking in everything about their new bedroom, in their new home. She was realizing that a new home had new sounds, none of which was familiar. Still, she herself would need little persuasion to return to dreamland tonight.

"Phil...?" She laid a hand on his shoulder, and his head jerked in her direction. He was not only awake; he was *wide* awake. "What's wrong?"

Philip shook his head as if annoyed. "Nothing. It's...nothing, Jen." A pause. "Go back to sleep, huh?"

She stared at him for a few moments—he, unaware she still watched—before she closed her eyes and drifted back to sleep.

The two of them had been fortunate so far regarding Carolyn's sleeping habits. Although the baby had cried half the night for the first week or so after coming home from the hospital, the past few weeks, including tonight, had seen the infant falling asleep while being nursed, at about nine or so. And now that their young daughter was old enough to sleep in the crib in her own bedroom, they could check on her via the video monitor linked to the baby cam in her room. It was the first of many niceties Philip would set up from his company's new line.

Sleep, however, was not necessarily a given. Infants, they'd been told, changed a pattern as soon as they settled into one, so it was best for new parents to sleep whenever they could. You never knew when you'd be woken up, after all. Jennifer had quickly taken that advice to heart, especially since an awakened baby was usually a hungry baby. Philip had, too. Except for tonight.

He got out of bed carefully so as not to awaken Jennifer and worry her more. The baby hadn't made a sound in a while, and Philip stopped in his daughter's room to listen until he could hear Carolyn's quick breathing—normal for this age, the new parents had come to know. What little of her face you could see behind her hand was half-covered by a pacifier. The baby sucked occasionally in her sleep, comforted by the pacifier's reassuring presence.

Philip got back into bed and lay on his side, facing away from his wife. He hadn't told her what had happened earlier, partially because he had no intention of frightening her. Especially so soon after their child was born and they'd moved into their first house, far from their roots.

As he lay in the bed, still wide awake, he also realized there was nobody he could talk to about it. Jennifer, of course, was out of the question. Grant, his father-in-law, was also no one to tell; the man had enough troubles as it was. He deserved to have some peace for as long as...he was around.

He couldn't tell any of the new neighbors they'd met that day, either. Even if he knew one of them well enough to consult, Philip sensed there was more to the history of the house than Vera or the managing agents ever let on. That, in fact, was what he'd wanted to call her about, although he realized later that he'd be better off looking elsewhere for the truth.

The first tip that something was, well, not right came when he took a break from filling the garage and, responding to a wave, chatted with a new neighbor from down the block. This man—Howard Perkins was his name—had wished the four of them welcome and offered Philip a beer. He popped his own open, took a drink and began talking. "Y'picked the right town, all right. It's pretty nice around here. People helping people, all that." The man rubbed his unshaven chin and brushed a yellowjacket off his windbreaker.

"So that's good to hear," Philip replied. "I bet it'll be strange for you, seeing people in this house again after...what? A year?"

The man seemed to frown for an instant before he shrugged and smiled. It was the kind of smile that made Philip wonder if he'd committed some *faux pas.* "You bet. But I'll tell you," he said, turning slightly as if to leave, "it sure is nice to have a nice, quiet family living here."

Philip, bewildered, asked Perkins what he meant. The neighbor looked equally confused for a moment—he stared into Philip's eyes—then smiled again. "Well, uh, you know how people worry when new people show up. Loud parties, radios, motorcycles. Y'know, the stuff teenagers are into."

"Oh, I see what you mean," Philip had replied, trying not to read too much into the quickened tempo of the neighbor's talk. "So, well, you don't have to worry about that for a while. My daughter can't even turn over yet, let alone rev up a motorcycle."

Still smiling, the man excused himself with an open invitation for Philip to stop by anytime for a beer or if he ever needed a hand with anything—"preferably, haha, for a beer." Alone by the garage, Philip wondered whether, in some strange way, Howard had been referring to the Leffingwells. The key word both he and the realtor had used regarding this family was "quiet." Was there another side to the story of this poor family who'd met, as he'd heard, a tragic end abroad?

That discussion was the first tip. The second, much more troubling, had been a scare, one for which Philip could arrive at no good explanation. He had just picked up the fallen broom in the doorway of the dining room when he glanced into the kitchen.

Something dark was along the edge of the counter. Moving slowly away from the sink.

Philip stepped into the kitchen and then felt the chill. The windows—was one open? He walked closer to see that no breeze swayed the blinds; the windows on both sides of the corner, so far without curtains, were closed tight. The boiler was running, too, so heat was coming up. Crossing his arms, he leaned over to see what must have been a bug. This was a house, he told himself, not an apartment. You had to expect things to get in now and then, especially since the place had been empty for so long.

It was an insect, and it had turned the corner of the counter and was moving down a portion of Corian counter that was perpendicular to the wall. Philip was sure it was a large cricket, so far as he could tell from across the room.

But...something was wrong. Philip had known it from the minute he got closer and he saw the thing. It had traveled half the length of the counter, a total of at least two feet. Behind it, a wet trail of some liquid had followed it, then dried.

The cricket's legs did not seem to be moving.

Its two large, hind legs were dangling straight behind. Even he, born and raised in the city, knew they should have been arched, ready to spring at the slightest threat, ready as if set to a hair trigger. The insect's four other legs also hung behind, curled beneath and pointing in the direction from which they had traveled. Philip felt he could almost hear the legs slide wetly down the counter, a squeaking pitch like that of a fingertip rubbing a wet dish.

One of the insect's antennae was bent under the dark brown, crusty body. The other was missing; it was on the floor, near a spot in front of the sink, where more of the yellowish liquid lay. He stared for a moment at the wet stain on the brick-design laminate.

Someone

something

had killed the cricket. On that spot.

Philip stood frozen into position, the chill making him tremble but also rendering him powerless to act, to cry out—he mustn't—or to do anything but stare. A dead insect was moving across the counter, its legs limp behind it, its body flattened. How?

His own legs would not move. Philip watched. His jaw dropped as the cricket stopped its forward motion. And turned...

No!

...toward him. He took a step to the right, then back to the left. It rotated as well, both times, stopping as it was, in a position facing him. But there were no eyes. Its head was obliterated, yet it was...

looking?

He had...he had to get out. Get Jennifer, too. And the baby. To get out of the place. Something was wrong here. Some things...just didn't happen. He was seeing one of them. He had to—

The cricket flew at his face.

Philip cried out, raising his arm too late—fortunately at the moment the horn blared—and he needed no more prompting. He sprang from the room, looked at his watch and realized he had been in the kitchen for ten minutes. Where had the time gone? What the hell had taken the movers so long?

What kept him awake now was the incomprehensible way today's incident fit in with all the good things he and Jennifer had to think about right now: young baby, new job, new town, new house. He had to make things work out.

Even if it meant coming up with some incredible explanation for what he had seen.

Other bugs. That was it, he thought. When an insect died, other bugs—ants, maybe—carried away its remains to their nest for a fiesta. The cricket was reasonably large, certainly big enough to have hidden any small thing beneath that strained under its share of the weight. Ants were carrying it away. That would do, he thought.

Then why did he see no ants?

What crushed it?

What brought it up to the counter after killing it?

And...

what...threw it?

* * *

Again, Philip got out of bed. Jennifer had had the foresight to pack away a number of critical, day-to-day things they'd need right away. He went for the small traveling bag and felt around till he found the penlight.

Even with the small light, the hallway was unfamiliar. So were the stairs. Shadows leapt up in a mad, unchoreographed dance, and a shutter by one of the windows above the stairway creaked as the autumn winds blew it gently one way, then another. It didn't swing widely enough to slam in either direction. It merely creaked unrhythmically—a breeze here, a stillness, a slight shove...

Someone was downstairs. A floorboard creaked—Philip didn't know which room.

He slowly descended the stairs, being sure to keep his footfalls soft.

In the scant beam of the penlight, Philip felt assured by the bare walls, on which they'd soon hang their paintings, their framed photos. The house would feel more like *they* owned it, just a little bit more, with each passing day. And now whoever was here was going to be sorry he ever—

A dark form sat in the recliner.

The chair was tipped back. Philip sighed, shook his head and chuckled. "Grant. You scared the crap out of me."

From his half sleep, the old man looked up and grinned. "Phil...sorry about that. I guess you're not used to my being around."

"No. Not yet, I'm not." He sat down on the couch and felt, at last, that he could fall asleep right there. Near the...*safety* of his father-in-law?

Philip blinked, and his eyebrows curled downward as he dwelled on that notion. Sure, why not? Perhaps it was merely that he was *someone,* that without needing to explain anything he had an ally against...whatever. But there was more; it wasn't just that. Something he couldn't quite put his finger on.

He stood up. "So I-I have to check on something I think I left in the kitchen."

"Some cold cuts and a kaiser roll, maybe?"

Philip held his chuckle within as if it might warm him, but he didn't need to; the kitchen was not cold in the slightest. The boiler was working fine, he realized, *most* of the time. He switched on the range hood's nightlight, and nothing at all seemed out of the ordinary. His wife or father-in-law had even tidied up earlier, removing the insect and giving the counter and floor a good wipe.

Still he struggled to explain even some of what he'd seen that day. Something, Philip thought, must have coincidentally fallen down and flattened the cricket. A spice jar from the rack, maybe? No, the spice rack had been on the other side, beside the refrigerator. He could see the outline on the wallpaper where it had been mounted. And anyway, anything that could have rolled off the counter and killed the insect would still have been there earlier.

The movers—they must have dropped something onto the bug, and then some little bugs were carrying it away. But no...the movers hadn't yet arrived.

Some mugs on hooks attached to the cabinet above, maybe? Wood gave way sometimes, and if one of those weakened at the right moment and fell...but no. There was nothing above, or anywhere nearby, that could have killed the insect.

Something had to make sense.

Philip shut the light and returned to the couch, shaking his head. "So..." he said at last. "Couldn't sleep?"

Grant shook his head. "Not tonight. Hurting all over till I took something for it. You don't want to hear about that, though—I feel a little better now."

"I don't mind hearing about it if you want to talk—really," Philip graciously lied. "How do you like your room so far?"

The old man laughed quietly to keep his voice from making it upstairs. "Fine, fine. And—oh, don't take this wrong at all—there's something full-circle about sleeping next door to a nursery. I'll be heading back up there shortly."

Philip nodded, appreciating the irony, then got up to head back to bed. "Well, have a good sleep, anyway. That's a nice chair—I've caught a few Zs in it myself—but a bed's always more comfortable."

"Right you are. Good night."

At the top of the stairs, Philip stopped and stared blankly down the hall while his mind returned again to the quest for a rational explanation. It could've been anything that killed the cricket. Grant, his wife, a stray box, lots of things. Lots of good explanations.

But solving what had *killed* the cricket left open the other question.

A much thornier one.

7

It was Halloween. Anxious for the final bell to ring, the children shuffled in their seats. Many of the students still enjoyed dressing up and going door to door for candy—though at ten years old, they might not admit it to everyone in the class. Others, of course, anticipated an evening of chasing those sissy trick-or-treaters down the street and pelting them with a well-aimed egg or two. The egg ran best down the hair of girls, they joked among themselves, and down the backs of, well, just about anyone else.

And then there were those select few for whom, in their own special way, nearly every day was Halloween.

A dark-eyed boy from the back of the room was snickering to a friend as a lone girl stood in front of the room, reciting her essay on Halloween. In her anxiety, she mispronounced the word "body," pronouncing it more like "booty," which drew a chorus of yo-ho-hos from the audience. When she said "fly" as "fry," the heckling changed to hissing sounds like those of the local hamburger joint's deep-fat fryer.

Still she continued her recitation, stuttering occasionally and pausing often to slow herself down. It was a basic technique of speech class, but the slow breaths she took in between efforts were audible enough to resemble gasps. "She got azma," someone whispered.

"...I learned...from this ex-per-ience...how we live in a small...world. In my night as a g-ghost—"

"B-b-boooo!" A student bellowed.

"—as a ghost I learned how t-temporary our world is. I learned that we must...be fair...and k-kind to one another because our lifes— our lives—are too short to hurt...one another. I sp-spent one night as a...ghost, and my l-life...is richer because...of it."

The classroom had grown quiet, and Mrs. Genovese rose to her feet from her chair on the side of the room and began to applaud. "That was just beautiful, Cynthia!" No one else was clapping but for a thin rail of a girl in the last row, the one who spent each day with her eyes affixed to the blackboard, never asked a question, and scored straight As. "Class?"

A few students mockingly touched their hands together in response. Many others stared at the girl clapping, mostly because she was the "class corpse," who spoke to almost no one, particularly when addressed. The rest of the class was looking toward Cynthia's desk as she spun in to sit down, her gaze meeting nobody's.

"Oowwwwwwwww!"

The classroom exploded into hysterical laughter when Cynthia sprang from her seat. Her hand reached behind, felt the thumb tack and pulled it loose. She held it up—its moist point was red—and hurled it down. It bounced under a desk.

"Hey, she's right! She does fly!" shouted the dark-eyed boy from the back.

"Cynthia, are you okay? Raymond, class, I demand to know who is responsible for this cruel joke. Cynthia? Cynthia!"

The classroom door creaked as it swung gently closed.

Hours later, it was growing dark. A dry breeze wafted more leaves onto the porch where Cynthia and her only friend sat. Their feet had already crunched down on all the leaves that had blown up against the steps, and Lana's munching of an apple sounded explosive in the dusky stillness.

"You didn't have to write about it," Lana said with a mouthful of Macintosh.

Cynthia shook her head, and some of her brownish hair fell out of her striped woolen cap. She hated her hair; it was brown, it was blonde, it was green, it seemed—it was no color in the world that she or anybody else could put a finger on. Come to think of it, she hated all of herself today, and waiting for the sun to set with Lana scolding her only worsened her mood.

"I wanted them to leave me alone. Is that so bad?"

"They're animals. They won't leave you alone. They won't leave me alone. We're just...different. And then you have to go and tell everyone about it." She swallowed the last bit of apple and shook her fist at her friend. "You're just *lucky* you didn't mention *me!*"

"Lana, it was a story. I told it like it was all a story, just a story like a fairy tale of Halloween. Nobody thinks it was *true,* you know!"

"You better hope not. Hey, it's getting dark—they'll be out soon."

Cynthia looked up. "Yeah, okay. Better run and take the shortcut."

"Yeah. See you here in...maybe ten minutes?"

"I'll be here." She paused and grinned. "Just...not in *material* form."

"Right." She started to run off.

"Hey, Lana?"

Her friend stopped and turned back around, hands on her hips. "Whaaaat?"

"Thanks for clapping."

Her friend shrugged and continued on, though even from behind Cynthia knew she was smiling.

* * *

"No, let's face her away from the TV."

"Right." Philip lifted a wide-eyed Carolyn out of her new playmat, handed her to Jennifer and oriented the mat in the opposite direction, not that it mattered much with their daughter on her back, facing up. Here, the baby would be closer to the baseboard but not too close, just as far from the windows—drafty things, Philip had commented—and, most important, away from the big screen. Before long, he'd come home from work talking about market share, and his wife would be talking about what nasty thing Oscar the Grouch said to Big Bird today. It was natural, he knew, and the educational shows wouldn't be so bad for the kid to be watching. But if they could put it off for just a while...

"There," he said. "So how's that?" He took Carolyn back.

Jennifer grinned and plopped herself in the middle of the sofa. "You know I'll agree to practically aaaanything tonight, Phil."

"Anything?" Philip glanced upward, toward Grant's room. The last of the few trick-or-treaters they'd seen had come and gone, her father had gone to bed early that night, and if Carolyn fell asleep on the mat the way she was supposed to, well, the two of them might have their first chance to be close since halfway through Jennifer's pregnancy.

Blushing, Jennifer cocked her head to the side. "Maybe...just maybe." She patted her thigh. "A girl fits back into the jeans she wore before getting pregnant, she feels good. But let's not get our hopes up too much. We have yet to witness the dazzling effects of this thing you insisted on bringing home."

Philip sighed. "So for this age, it seems like all the rage, from what I can see. Hey, let's turn off the TV."

The television had been a comfort for Jennifer since they'd moved into the new house. At a time that practically everything in her life was new, it was a relief to sit down and know she could ignore the same mindless sitcoms they showed in the old apartment far away.

She shut off the TV and lifted her head just in time to see Philip lay their daughter back into the so-called Deluxe Kick & Play Piano Gym Playmat, replete with bright colors everywhere, plastic rings dangling from a semicircular loop encircling baby, and a little foot-operated keyboard. Once he got the baby in place, she stared, her head tipping placidly from one side to the next. Carolyn's small, dark eyes seemed to take in everything as she decided just what she thought of this strange little world.

A few moments after Philip settled into the sofa, his arm draped around Jennifer's shoulder, the baby made her decision: "WAAAAAAAAAAHHHHHHHHH!"

"Okay, okay, okay," Jennifer whispered. It was a vain belief of new parents that their child will respond in the same tone of voice at which they are addressed. "So, we'll put you in front of the TV." She turned the set back on and lay Carolyn in her infant seat; the baby continued to scream. She switched the channel to a sitcom featuring a family of six children of various races and ages living with their adoptive parents from the planet Jupiter.

Carolyn stopped crying and stared up at the TV.

"So look at her—she's entranced," said Philip.

"Of course," she replied. "She's what they call the 'target demo.'"

He was shaking his head. "I dunno about this here Gym Playmat," he said. "She looked a bit too entertained to get sleepy."

"Oh, just come here, my man, and hold me," she said, taking her husband's hand. "We haven't done just that for a while."

She was right; it had been a long time. Philip forgot his worries about the house, about the job, as he held his wife close, enjoying the feel of her head against his shoulder. He hadn't thought enough lately how he felt about her, hadn't thought that all this newness in their lives was for them, for the family they were building together.

He looked across at the infant flailing her arms and legs, moving to and fro, and never taking her eyes off the TV screen. Yeah, he thought, and all this is for you, too, little one. You, little cherub, who I haven't gotten to spend very much time with since you showed up.

Philip knew he was impatient with this period of his daughter's life, however important he knew these times were, too. He wanted her to be walking, talking, going to ballgames with him, smiling at the sight of a double-scoop ice cream cone with sprinkles. Anything but crying and insisting on being held virtually every moment she was awake.

"Penny for your thoughts," his wife whispered beside him.

"So I was thinking," he lied to talk about something different, "about how sexy you looked across the room in that poetry class. You wore all olive green that day, and I saw that flowing red hair and those eyes—I thought maybe you noticed me, too."

"Mmmmm, I remember *you,* Mr. Across-the-Room. Two weeks after the semester started, after everyone got used to where they were sitting, *you* decide to move your seat from over by the window. To the one in front of mine." She reached around and stroked the stubble on his cheek.

"Well, why not? It worked, didn't it?" Philip clasped his hand over hers.

"That old excuse you gave the person who'd been sitting there didn't, though." She mimicked his voice from that day in college. "'I'm sorry, I have a new prescription on my contacts, and the light from outside is hurting my eyes.' Poor baby!"

"So, he did go away, didn't he?"

"Well, you stinker, you've never worn contacts a day of your life."

"The better to see you with, my dear."

She sat up and kissed him, glancing once to notice the baby looking in their direction to make sure they hadn't sneaked away.

A few moments later Jennifer was leaning against her husband again, her mind drifting back to other pleasant memories. "Phil, do...do you remember the first talk we had about getting a house?"

He chuckled. "You mean the time you said you didn't think we'd ever be able to afford one the way the prices kept going up?"

"Yeah," she replied with a nod. "You sure showed me, though."

"Mmmmm." Philip, though, didn't want to talk about the house. "So I liked your parents' house a lot," he said. "That country style, wood everywhere—"

"That's my father for you."

"Yeah. I'm a little too impatient with him, I think. He's really a good guy under all..."

Jennifer's smile told him she saw it coming. "Under all what?"

"Under all that kindhearted exterior."

She leaned back again. "You haven't always respected that in him," she commented.

"So yeah...yeah, it's taken me some time to realize...to realize that a kind person can still be a...very strong one. This point in his life, I guess, he's showing me a lot. Hey, Jen?"

"Mmmmm?"

"Thanks for talking me into having him live here awhile."

Then they kissed again. It had been long, thought Jennifer, too long, since they'd gotten to—

A commercial without music came on, and Carolyn started whimpering.

"Quick," snapped Jennifer. "Sing a jingle!"

"I—I don't know. Uh, uh..."

One came to mind just in time, and Philip began to sing to his daughter in a mock operatic voice: "I have an annuity, but I need-cash-now!"

"J. G. Wentworth, really?" Jennifer whispered. "Is that the best you can do?"

"Hmmm..." He raised his index finger. "One-eight-seven-seven, Kars for Kids—"

"Never mind..." she said and pointed to Carolyn.

The baby had stopped crying. They looked. The baby was looking up at her father, her deep brown eyes clearly a match with his. It was the first time, in fact, that Philip could remember the baby actually looking at him; it didn't come easy at that age.

Again, the show came on. The moment passed, and once more Carolyn watched the same bad actors parroting the same old jokes—though all were brand-new to her.

"So you know," Philip continued, "I remember your telling me

58

once that your father was really big on helping people in need. He isn't a rich guy or anything, but he did what he could for people stuck on the road, friends and co-workers low on cash, neighbors who needed things fixed…"

"He still is. With a little less steam, though. Hey, Phil, why all this talk about my father? You're in *my* arms, you know."

"Yeah, Hon. Sorry. Whatcha wanna talk about, then?"

She gave him a quick kiss on the neck. "The house."

"Mm. Nice place, huh?"

"You don't like it very much, do you?"

"So what makes you say that, Jen?"

"Oh…I don't know."

"I guess…" he said, not wanting to admit she was right, "I guess I don't quite feel like it's ours yet. Maybe I still feel funny about the idea of the people who'd lived here before having died."

"Mmmm. That would give me the willies if I thought about it too much."

"So maybe it was all that crap lying around that I threw in the garage—"

"Do you think we should throw it out?" Jennifer asked.

"Maybe we should. So there's the cheapskate in me, though. There might be something there we'll want to keep for ourselves."

Jennifer lifted her head and leaned back against the sofa. "I've already nabbed the spice rack. And, oh, the china closet stays—it's just like one I'd pick out—though it might need refinishing sometime."

"There. See? I guess I keep thinking this really isn't our place, that somebody is going to come in and say, 'Okay, you can go now, give it back.' So, I mean, I guess every new homeowner feels that for a while. I mean, is all this really ours?"

Nodding, his wife agreed. "I feel that sometimes, too, yeah."

"Maybe once I've installed more of my company's things besides this smart baby cam"—Philip gestured toward the camera's LCD monitor-speaker, currently situated on the coffee table—"I'll feel more like it's ours. Bring it into the twenty-first century or something like that." The monitor's image was static as the crib upstairs, in Carolyn's bedroom, lay empty.

An awkward silence followed, as if the two of them had agreed to sit back and absorb the atmosphere of their new house. Aside from the generic blue glow of the TV screen, only a dim lamp on a nearby end table lit the room. Shadows sprang from behind the table legs, the magazine rack, and a few family photos on an end table.

Eventually they noticed it had been raining, and the dull patting on their roof had been going on for quite some time. Jennifer walked over to the bay windows; Philip joined her. And the two of them gazed way out toward the right, toward the corner streetlight, invisible but for its beam making its way through the storm to reach into the room when she parted the curtain. A few moments later, Philip looked back to check on Carolyn, who had finally fallen asleep.

"Pssst," Philip whispered, pointing at their daughter. Gently he reached down and lifted the baby while Jennifer shut off the TV once again, along with the lamp. She gestured for Carolyn, but Philip shook his head and walked, ever so slowly, upstairs.

Jennifer watched him on the baby cam's four-inch screen, smiled as he set her gently down in the crib, checked the baby cam and left the room. Moments later, he walked downstairs, took his wife's hand and led her upstairs to their bedroom.

Five minutes later, Philip would return to retrieve the LCD monitor, which they were keeping overnight on Jennifer's nightstand since Carolyn began sleeping in her crib.

What he missed, in those brief minutes, was a glimpse of their sleeping baby being lifted into the air, suspended as if by invisible cords, and laid snugly against a shoulder not of this world.

* * *

The ten-year-old, slightly heavyset girl stood up just in time to see the shadows of four boys appear down the shadowed street. They weren't dressed in costumes, she knew. They were walking down the middle of the street, hardly the path for ringing doorbells.

Cynthia stepped into her house and switched on the porch light. Bad kids or no, somebody would be out trick-or-treating that evening. She wished she and Lana could help watch out for them.

"Trick or treat!" shouted a voice from the recliner in the corner.

"Hi, Mom," Cynthia mumbled as she headed for the stairs.

"Cynthia, c'mon back here, girl. Lissin."

The last thing the little girl wanted was to listen to her drunken mother when she needed to go upstairs, lock her door and...be free for a while. Her father sat in the opposite corner of the room, his face covered strategically by the broadsheet newspaper.

"Mom, I don't feel good. I want to go upstairs, please."

"Didn't you eat your dinner?" came her father's voice. He didn't put down the paper but rather spoke through it.

Cynthia thought of the frozen dinner that lay ignored in the microwave oven. Her mother had set the timer for her but forgot to hit the "start" button. It didn't matter, the little girl thought. She wasn't hungry, anyway.

"Here," the woman said. Cynthia drew closer while keeping her customary distance. "What'd you do in school today—oh. Hey!" She gestured toward the TV; the remote lay at her feet. "Turn it to Channel 7."

Cynthia retrieved the remote and obliged. Her mother yawned, lay down her beer on the arm of the recliner and drifted halfway off to sleep. One arm reached up to rub her eye, and it fell to knock the beer can onto the carpet. Her father continued to read the newspaper as the fluid soaked into the rug; it wouldn't be the first time. Tears in her eyes, Cynthia bounded up the stairs, closed her bedroom door from within and locked it.

It took only a few moments, even though she'd done this thing just a few times before. She wondered what it was called, and why only she, Lana, and an autistic boy from a few blocks away were able to do it.

Only the weirdos.

The thought hit her like a wall of incredible logic that somehow she had been staring at, but never recognizing, as it stood before her eyes. Of course! She'd been the subject of ridicule since the first grade. Lana was what they called noncommunicative, withdrawn—though she knew better. And that boy made three. He seemed weird even to them, but still they'd all played together once. "There are no outcasts een the night air," Cynthia remembered Lana saying in a Bela Lugosi-like Dracula voice, and she smiled. Well, here goes nothing.

She melted through the side of her house to find Lana waiting down below.

"Shhh!" her friend said, as if anyone could hear them in their incorporeal form. It was a new ritual they both enjoyed, and if one of them didn't say it, the other did.

The two floated together down the walk, and they moved aside to allow two trick-or-treaters to pass. One, a child of perhaps six, was dressed as a pumpkin; his older brother, who looked ten, wore a skull mask only and carried his own bag.

"I like the pumpkin," said Lana.

Cynthia knew what was coming next, and her friend's lips parted in a mischievous smile.

"He would make a de-*light*-ful pie!"

The two were laughing so loudly that neither noticed the others following the boys till they passed by. It was the foursome from before, Cynthia guessed, only now there were twice as many. They wore old, tattered jackets. All carried eggs—one boy, who looked about nine, carried two cartons—and all breathed heavily as they walked, as if they'd been running. "They're goin' to the haunted house!" one boy exclaimed.

Cynthia recognized this boy. It was Raymond from class, the one she'd decided had probably put the tack on her seat. How she wished she could solidify her foot just long enough to trip him and send those eggs flying.

"Readja mind!" said Lana.

"Oh, shut up! Let's follow them."

The pair of trick-or-treaters not only were heading for the haunted house, but they were going right up to the front door and *ringing the bell*. "Shit, man, they're crazy!" whispered one voice in the shadows of the corner streetlight.

"Batshit!"

While the door of the house was opened—Cynthia was surprised to see that the woman looked like she could be anybody's mother, only younger, and she held a baby—Raymond led the group across the street and off to the side of the house. They would wait here in the dark until their quarry passed by, and then...

The door closed, and the trick-or-treaters were dead ahead. "Charge!" Amid a chorus of cries, Raymond began to run toward the two, who saw them and took off in the direction they had come. He hurled two eggs, three, four—"Hah! Got the little one!"—and then realized he'd been alone in his charge.

He could see one member of the group, far behind him, jumping a fence to cut through in a neighboring yard. The others?

"Hey, where'd everybody go?"

He heard voices, muted voices, and panicked cries for a moment. Then he heard nothing. He had run a quarter of a block after the pair, and now, jogging back in the other direction, he returned to where he was, at the corner of Mason and Oak.

In the distance, one of his friends was just rounding the corner.

Behind him, Cynthia and Lana watched closely, their every instinct telling them to hurry back, to return to their bodies at once before...whatever it was could find them. It couldn't be someone like them. No. The boy that had been chased—no, pushed—into the rosebush and had staggered away bleeding had been proof enough of that.

It was coming again, and the dark-eyed boy stood transfixed as...something, covered in...a *sheet,* of all things, floated down from the roof of the haunted house. It was as if someone had dressed as a ghost, in a sheet with eye holes, and rigged some way to slide down from the house.

"Heh heh. Right. Nice trick!" He called up toward the second-floor windows.

It kept coming, close enough now that he would be able to see, clearly in the streetlight's glow, any ropes or pulleys attached to the Leffingwell house.

There weren't any.

"N-no!" shouted Raymond. He began to run. The two girls followed from a distance, holding back for their own safety yet too excited by what they were seeing to leave. The thing was almost upon him! It held...eggs in its blanketed hands, and the girls thought they heard a chuckle as the boy slipped on a broken egg and crashed, face-first, onto the pavement. He tried to get up for a moment, his face awash in a stream of blood gushing from his nose, but was pushed back down. His head faced up toward the night sky through no effort of his own. "No...no..." The thing was upon him and the girls heard a throaty cry before the boy dropped into the middle of the street. Whatever was in the sheet—it seemed to look toward the girls for a moment—disappeared behind some tall hedges and was gone.

The two girls approached the boy from the opposite angle, watching carefully to ensure the thing indeed was gone. It wasn't after them, they felt. Two porch lights had turned on nearby; they suddenly felt too self-conscious to stay. But first...one look.

Raymond lay on the asphalt, barely moving, his face turned in the direction of the streetlight. From the corner of his mouth, along the neon stream of blood and yolk, a few bits of crushed eggshell ran down his chin and formed a small pool in the street.

8

"...pray for us, oh Holy mother of God, that we may be made worthy of the promises of Christ.

"Glory be to the Father, and to the Son, and to the Holy Spirit..."

Grant O'Keefe finished his prayers and closed his eyes as another spasm of pain rippled up from his abdomen. This one wasn't as bad; the pain was receding, he believed. At least for now.

He looked at the clear brown canister that lay open on the nightstand beside his bed. The codeine-based medication had done him well for a time. Now, in his daughter's new town, he'd gotten a referral from his former doctor, the one who'd originally diagnosed him and done the best he could through two surgeries, to an oncologist who agreed with the treatment plan he'd begun two years before.

The new doctor, he'd heard, also believed that once the pain became too much to handle, it was time for morphine—if not something even stronger. As much, in fact, as he might need to ease his last days.

Oh, he was getting there, thought Grant as he rose from his side and finished off half a glass of water. Either he was getting too used to the codeine, or the cancer that had begun in his colon was now eating away at other organs, newer cells that would help form the new majority before much longer. Most likely, it was both.

How long did he have? Till New Year's, at best. Out with the old, in with...now, now, he told himself. No room for cynics in this world. It would be nice to see another year come in, though. That would surely be nice.

But he wasn't asking the Almighty for that kind of favor, he'd resolved. All he'd asked for, in the prayers he said twice daily in his room, was that he pose no hardship to his daughter and her family. And that he could welcome death, when it came, as he'd imagined Emily Dickinson had: "Because I could not stop for Death—/He kindly stopped for me..."

Funny thing, he was thinking, about the feeling he'd gotten several minutes ago on the bed. Through clenched teeth he'd been praying for relief—never mind dignity for the time being—and had suddenly felt that, somehow, he was not alone. The room grew cold; he felt he'd opened a refrigerator door on a hot summer day. But this was different; he thought it...unnatural.

Strangely, he didn't fear it. The enemy, he decided, was right there on the bed. It comprised the cells of his own body, which had staged a mutiny and declared war against his spirit. Whatever had just entered the room, whatever it wanted to be called, it could just take a seat and wait its turn.

In his pain, he felt he was growing delirious. A rattan armchair stood across the room, on the other side of his closet door, and he could swear its green corduroy cushion had moved slightly as he watched. He closed his eyes; it was getting bad. Oh, why hadn't he gotten a new prescription *before* he'd come here?

When he opened his eyes, he spied another movement—a wrinkle in the bend of the corduroy fabric seemed to have widened. Someone...it seemed someone was sitting there on the chair, though he could see no one. Watching him.

He shook his head and smiled. Lord, he thought, if...this is my time, I'm sorry and am...willing to go. But are you usually so dramatic?

He managed a grin as he thought about his wife in her last days. Also a cancer victim, Roberta had hung on long enough to vividly describe a departed sister who, his wife insisted, awaited among the living at her bedside, to accompany her to the Great Hereafter.

Whatever it was he imagined was present, in his present condition the notion of company for the journey ahead was a comfort. Was there, he wondered, a power shared among all the living in their final days on Earth?

"Hi," he whispered in the direction of the chair. "I...I'd offer you a chair, but..." He grinned despite the spasms coursing through his body. Perhaps it was letting up—the medication had to take effect sometime—but if the pain was leaving him, it was squeezing him all the way out.

"Must...be a slow day for you, you need to come up—or down—and...watch me die."

The wrinkles on the chair changed. It seemed that whatever had been sitting had gotten up. And was standing in the middle of the room. The cold was more intense now, and Grant watched his panting breath turn to frost as it passed his lips. It was closer, yet...his pain was easing up.

Death was closer, but it strangely had not come for him this time. How could it? The spasms were lessening, losing their strength, their frequency, with each passing moment. Yet the chill remained.

"You can...stick around if you want, an old man always likes company. But the...fun's over for now, I think..."

The chill was gone, as completely as if it had been encased in a large, airtight container and someone had suddenly carried it away. He was sweating again, as he'd been a minute ago, but now he felt almost good enough to get up. He'd finish his prayers before attempting anything.

And he'd thank the Lord for the kind introduction to his fate. He could bear it now, he felt. It had meant him no harm.

* * *

"Hi, little princess!"

Jennifer had brought Carolyn in, her eyes staring out at shades, patterns, and barely focusing on her grandfather's or anyone else's smiling face.

"Dad...you don't have to do that stuff. We can afford to have someone come in, you know. Really."

Grant waved her away and continued slowly patching up one of the holes someone had made in the wall between Jennifer and Philip's room and the smaller adjoining room, which presently lay empty but for the crib, a changing table, and several boxes of baby shower gifts. If he had any ideas on how the holes got there, he wasn't volunteering them. "I intend to earn my keep, daughter. Philip, by his own words, uses a hand tool like a surgeon wearing a catcher's mitt. Just like I couldn't market my way out of a paper bag.

Neither of you want a penny for room and board, so...how does that look?"

He must have put some kind of backing behind the hole, thought Jennifer. Once the room was painted over, you'd never know the hole was ever there, it was so neat a job.

Grant saw the look on his daughter's face, grinned and continued talking. And you, little girl"—he was addressing the baby—"you won't know your room when I'm done with *that*. Not that you know your room now, of course." He couldn't resist a snicker. "You've barely been *in* it."

Jennifer noticed the cord on her lamp, which the movers had all but torn off the base in one of many moments of carelessness the other day. Her father had replaced the cord, too. "Oh, Dad..."

"Dear, the day I stop fixing things is the day I'm gone from this world."

She shook her head. "Dad, let's not talk about that."

Her father smiled, appearing more comfortable with the subject than she'd ever seen him. "Then let me at those broken things, kiddo! I'll stick around at least till the job is done. Agreed?"

Jennifer looked away, smiling sadly. "Agreed. I don't know what I'm agreeing to, but thank you. Again, you don't have to do it."

"Course," he added, "the jobs're never quite done."

She followed him to the baby's room, where he'd earlier noticed the door squeaking when opened. He stood in the doorway, moving it back and forth and reproducing the sound he'd heard. "Hear that? Imagine making that unearthly sound in the middle of the night when you get up to check the baby."

"Top priority!"

"You bet." He bent over—painfully, she noticed though she dared not comment—and retrieved a small can of WD-40 lubricant from a leather bag. With a punch and small hammer, softly to keep from surprising the baby, he inched the hinge's pivot pin up and out, then caught it and sprayed a bit of lubricant before tapping it back in place. He repeated the process for the other hinge and swung the door back and forth, silently, to get the liquid around the moving parts.

"Let's see what's next," he said, passing the two of them and heading downstairs.

* * *

Philip forgot all about the library until he'd turned onto Oak Drive, having passed the building a half-mile back. He pulled over his Toyota, letting by a tractor-trailer, and swerved around to head in the opposite direction. It wasn't that he couldn't look up what he wanted on his own, using any available search engine on either his laptop or his phone. He wanted to hit the library to get some solid, uninterrupted research time—between his manic prepping for his first big presentation at the office and, at home, the unpredictable hours leading to the baby's bedtime.

He was too late. Accustomed to big-city libraries, which were often open late a few nights a week, he hadn't realized how once you got away from the city, things slowed down a bit. This branch was open past five only one night a week, and tonight wasn't it. In fact, Philip had a dinner meeting scheduled that evening with some clients from the West Coast.

Eventually he would get there, because Philip had gotten curious about the house's history. He wouldn't yet go so far as to say the realtor had lied—although Vera certainly had had reason to leave certain things unsaid. Still, he'd begun to wonder about the previous residents. He couldn't back it up, of course, but the incident of the other night, however ridiculous it seemed in retrospect, was what had gotten him thinking. If it hadn't been his first week on the job, with introductions and meetings with other department heads besides the rush preparations for the upcoming dog and pony show, he wondered how well he'd have been able to concentrate.

That other night, Philip had finally sunken into a deep sleep. All the moving and, later, his experience in the kitchen had caught up with him, and if he'd had nightmares since, he didn't remember them.

Sometimes, however, he didn't need to dream. The patent impossibility of what he had seen in the kitchen—or at least his inability to explain it—had initially left him edgy both at home and on the job. The day after they'd moved in, after the baby had woken them both up, he'd glanced half-asleep at a shaded portion of the bedsheet's floral pattern and had shot up, one leg hitting the floor, before he realized there was nothing amiss.

At his office the next day, he was waiting for his secretary to stop in when he noticed, from the corner of his eye, a dark shape beneath the shadow of his desk.

He was surprised to see that he...could not *look* at the thing, couldn't bear to find that it was the same insect, its body flattened and crisp, shuffling with unmoving, dragging legs toward his polished leather shoe.

This was ludicrous, he thought. The thing the other night had been no big deal. Just one of those freak things. And this...whatever it was out of the corner of my eye, it was nothing. Something I dropped. Some plain, ordinary thing found in any office, and I'm going to look right—

He couldn't turn his head.

It came closer, he felt sure without daring to direct his vision down. He wanted to move his foot, to get it away from this thing, to move it before it reached his shoe, left a thin trail of its yellowish fluid as it dug into his sock, brushed its dragging legs against the thin cotton barrier and made its way up, under the pant leg, to his bare...skin...

A hand reached down toward the floor, and Philip straightened in his chair as though he'd received an electric shock.

Nina! His secretary. She was standing there—dumbly, it seemed, looking at him. She was...he eventually noticed. She was handing him something.

"Your binder clip, Mr. Carter. You dropped it? It looked like you couldn't see it there."

He reached out and took it, turning his head to look down at the now-bare spot on the floor. "Th-thank you, Nina. So, y-you wanted something."

The woman pulled away the iPad she'd been holding under her arm and held it up. "You needed a few contacts?"

Philip shook his head. "Oh, boy. Yes, I did. Uh, so give me ten minutes. I just got a strange phone call."

"Yes, sir." The moment she walked out, Philip closed his eyes, took a few deep breaths and paced around his desk. Until he felt he could sit back down.

* * *

Though Carolyn had outgrown the bassinet, Jennifer still used it sometimes to keep her daughter nearby. She did so now while unpacking gifts from the shower a friend had thrown at her former workplace, where she was managing editor for a trade magazine.

Unexpectedly, thoughts of the previous owners came into her mind. They must have been a charming family, supposed Jennifer. From what little she'd heard, they'd seemed like pleasant enough people.

She stopped at one of the two windows and looked out. Embarrassedly she caught herself playing with a few strands of her hair. Some people never grow up, she thought with a grin.

Out the window was the corner of Mason and Oak. Leaves fell from a tall maple to blot out bits of sidewalk, and several of them blew up against the black painted base of a streetlight she could barely glimpse. There will be Carolyn's nightlight, Jennifer thought. She'd had no such problem growing up in the city, she reminisced. Aside from several street lamps within view, she had a blinking red glow from an all-night bakery, the passing flashes—with accompanying roars—of planes landing at the nearby airport, and the usual buses and cars.

Jennifer felt both grateful and wretched for her gratitude that the baby slept so much in this phase of her infancy. Philip had been fine, she thought, as new fathers go. He gave Jennifer a break now and then, carting Carolyn off to roll her around on their bed in an effort to extract a smile. But so much was left up to her: most of the diaper-changing, the getting up in the night if the baby awoke, the dressing for bed and, for that matter, every occasion whatsoever.

She felt wretched wishing for a break, for the opportunity to take a walk, even for fifteen minutes, once a day by herself. She'd caught herself feeling disappointed in her mother, who'd died ten years earlier, for leaving before she could teach her how to be a mother. Of course, Jennifer adored her new daughter—it was instinct, wasn't it? But what she'd needed to hear from her mom was that it takes a bit longer to understand that, for a time, whatever she happened to want was secondary. To accept lovingly that the newborn's universe consists solely of herself.

The baby had been asleep for more than an hour, Jennifer noticed with a glance at her phone. The time didn't yet matter very much, as Carolyn hadn't been around long enough to establish any kind of sleeping patterns they could bank on. But Jennifer hurried all the same, putting away what clothes were still too big and putting those she could use now in a handy place.

She walked over to the closet; she'd forgotten the room had one, it was so small. Some of the clothes that came with hangers she could put here. Oh, and there are two shelves, she realized.

Standing a few feet away from the open closet, Jennifer spotted the music box. It had been pushed almost against the back wall of the upper shelf, and Philip must have missed it when he'd scoured the place for the Leffingwells' things the other day.

Jennifer leapt up and, with a grunt, grasped it by a corner and pulled it to where she could lift it down. It wasn't very big—perhaps six inches across, five inches deep and high—but it looked new enough for a closer look.

Jennifer opened the box, and a lithe ballerina pirouetted as an unfamiliar but pretty tune played. It was a lovely gift.

Gift? Where had *that* word come from? She had found it, almost hadn't. It was no...

But as she listened further to the tune, she nodded in agreement with her initial impression. For the box, in some strange quirk of fate, *was* a gift for her newborn child. It was a gift from some previous resident: Had the Leffingwells a child she hadn't known about? Regardless, this would be the last baby shower gift. And, however sad it made her feel, it was perhaps the best.

"Thanks," Jennifer said with a smile.

9

Grant buried his face in the wrinkled copy of *Newsweek* he'd been thumbing through. Of course it was *that* kind of waiting room; no embarrassment was necessary among other cancer patients. But there were patients' family members here, too—people who hardly wanted the sight of an ailing old man to remind them that their own loved one perhaps faced a similar challenge.

He could feel his wrists shaking and knew that eyes were upon him. Here...it comes again, he thought. The magazine was growing moist at his sweaty touch despite the air conditioning. If he could only...

"Mr. O'Keefe?"

Grant raised a hand for an instant, and a nurse spotted him and rushed to his side. "I need help here," the nurse directed toward the reception window. Immediately an attendant came over; the doctor followed soon after.

"Can you stand, sir?"

The old man nodded, and he felt arms supporting his as he struggled to his feet. On his right was a more powerful grip; this was the doctor, he supposed. The last thing Grant remembered before he passed out was the gaping mouth of a short, silvery blonde-haired woman with glasses who had the corner of a magazine peeking out of her sequined jacket.

When he came to, he was staring into the eyes of the first nurse who'd seen him. "H-hi," he said. "This the hospital?" The woman wore too much makeup and had her straight, dark hair tied primly into a bun. She also reeked of perfume; maybe that's what woke him up, he thought. And, he became coherent enough to think, it's what might put him back out again, too.

She shook her head. "We keep a couple of beds here at the clinic for just this reason. Dr. Bennett gave you a quick shot of morphine. How do you feel?"

Grant smiled. "Like a hospital bill," he said.

"Pardon?"

"Like a million bucks, I mean."

The nurse huffed like a disappointed schoolteacher, but her smile betrayed some cheer from his manner. "You've been here for three hours. The doctor asked me to let him know when you came around. Be right back." She left the room.

Three hours? Why, Jennifer must be worried sick! Grant spotted a telephone nearby. He picked up the receiver and began to dial before he remembered he had a cellphone in his jacket pocket. He didn't recall, though, his new landline phone number. Almost two weeks in the place, and he'd never needed to dial it.

The receptionist had it; Grant had read it to her when he'd made the appointment. He'd better go see—

Before he could put his hand on the knob, the door swung open and caught him on the nose. He reeled backward for a moment, then caught his balance. Dr. Bennett grabbed his arm; the nurse was there, too. But he was all right, just startled.

Grant looked his new doctor straight in the eye. "Doc, I've decided you're a *jinx.*"

The doctor's grin vanished as he looked at his patient's nose. "Uh, huh. Well, Mr. O'Keefe, your nose looks fine, anyway." He glanced at his nurse, and she left the room.

"I'm pleased to see you're in good spirits, Mr. O'Keefe. Dr. Feller passed all your files along to me, along with some instructions to take extra good care of you."

Grant rubbed his nose. "So far, so good. Say, could you have someone call my daughter? She's at home with the baby, and—"

The doctor smiled, took his wrist and began to take his pulse. "We called your daughter but advised her to leave the baby with someone if possible."

"You're holding the wrist of the backup caregiver, Doc."

"Right. So I think your...son-in-law is out in the waiting room, instead." He stopped and jotted the results onto a clipboard. "How is the rest of you feeling?"

"I'm...happy to say I can't complain for the moment. The morphine?"

He nodded and helped Grant off with his shirt. "Mr. O'Keefe, I'm not one for rushing into advanced pain therapy." He began cupping the cold diaphragm of his stethoscope over Grant's chest, but looked up to see a troubled look on the man's face. "Not one for rushing. I prefer to be told, by my more rational patients, when it's time to prescribe morphine or even one of the truly heavy hitters."

"You call me rational? I got a visit from Death in my bedroom last week."

"Uh-huh. Dr. Feller warned me about your jokes." He grinned, but with a vague sadness. Or was it admiration?

The doctor continued. "Dick Feller warned you I'd want to take a few tests over again, Standard procedure for new patients. In the meantime, *you* tell *me*. Out in the waiting room, you looked like the codeine-based medications aren't doing so much for you anymore. Based on the test results I've already seen, Feller's forecast isn't going to change considerably. There's no reason for what happened outside to happen again."

"If it does," said Grant, "I'll scare your patients away."

"So...what do you think?"

"I think..." He sighed, shrugged and attempted a grin. "I think we're ready for the morphine."

* * *

Philip was silent as the two drove back from the clinic, and it took a while before Grant dared speak to his son-in-law.

"Phil, you didn't have to come, you know. It's a short trip—I could've taken an Uber taxi. That's how I got there in the first place."

Philip shook his head, his sunglasses hiding his gaze when he glanced quickly in the direction of his father-in-law. "Sure I did, Grant. We were worried about you."

"I sure appreciate it. But it's one in the afternoon! I know you're big stuff at your new company, but you still can't take time off without warning—"

"So family emergency, nobody bothers you."

Philip, it occurred to Grant, had too quickly snapped out his answer. He had gotten some guff from somebody, and he wasn't talking about it. Grant shook his head and looked at his knees, which looked frailer these days than he cared to consider. He wanted to look outside the car, to be outside the car. He'd gotten his son-in-law into trouble at his job, and he wanted somehow to undo the damage. He'd never worked for such a company, a big manufacturing concern where image was everything, but he was sure that, like any job, people could make things plenty uncomfortable for you if they thought you weren't pulling your weight.

Philip swerved to avoid a Corvette that had cut sharply into his lane, and he blew his horn for three long seconds. "Damn these kids!" he shouted.

Grant was silent.

"So Grant," said Philip, his eyes fixed straight ahead. "Um, I know you're thinking you're...putting a big load on me today or something. I don't like to talk about these things, but...I didn't catch shit for leaving to see you. Not at all."

The old man held his sigh of relief. "Then, what...?"

Philip shook his head and switched lanes to exit the highway. "So I had a presentation this morning. Big client, twelve reps in all plus the big kahuna—their CEO. I had my notes, I had the hardcopies for them, a thumb drive with the Powerpoint file, everything...*everything* in my briefcase. I packed it away, checked it, went up to the bathroom once more before I left, and when I got to work, it was all..."

"Gone?" Grant asked incredulously.

"Gone. The clincher was that my laptop is also missing. I'd've needed to scramble to print everything again, but I could've run the presentation from the laptop, too. It was in the car—in the trunk—from last night. No sign whatsoever that the car was broken into.

"So it was...bad enough I slipped on a fucking *roller skate* on my way down the porch steps. Where the hell does a roller skate come from, the only kid we have around is only three months old? The other kids in the neighborhood, I don't even—I don't even see them go by the house. A few of them on Halloween, that was all. They cross the street like we live in a house of plague or something. So...where does this fucking *skate* come from?"

"Damnest thing I ever heard," the old man said with all sincerity, wishing his son-in-law would slow down a bit.

"Sure, the bag went flying when I did—I didn't tell Jennifer this, so don't you, please—but nothing came out, so I was sure everything was okay. I mean, I would've seen it if it spilled out across the lawn, wouldn't you think?" The exit came up, and Philip glided into it too quickly and slammed on his brakes before the horseshoe curve.

"Take it easy, take it easy."

"Easy for you to...sorry. You're right." He sighed deeply, then continued. "So I...I blew that presentation, Grant. I was so *damn* flustered that I stumbled on what I could remember, tried to remember the figures, though *of course* a visual means *everything,* and...I caught a world of shit for it." He was shaking his head. "Lots of shit for something I can't explain for the life of me."

The two of them reached Mason Street, and Philip swung into the driveway so quickly that the car caught the edge of the mailbox post. The mailbox swung forward at the passenger window like some rabid beast, its post wrenched out of the ground, and Grant raised his arm to defend his face.

The glass of the window broke, but none of it came loose. "Fuck!" shouted Philip as he pounded the steering wheel. After a few moments that seemed far too long, he turned to his father-in-law. "I'm sorry—very sorry. Are you okay?"

The old man nodded, rubbing his nose for the second time that day. "We'd better get out on your side."

"What's the matter with your nose?"

Grant tried a grin, which turned sincere when he noticed his daughter, running down the walk clutching Carolyn in her arms. "Flirted once too much with the nurses," he quipped.

Shaking his head, Philip exited the car and helped Grant out. Jennifer didn't know whom to run to first, and she decided to head toward her father. Except that he was already leaning over the battered mailbox post, evaluating the damage.

"Doesn't look too bad," he was saying when the others came over. "Little digging, maybe, but the post looks all right."

"Dad, forget it. This is one you are *not* going to do." Jennifer shot a look at her husband; seeing he was okay, she was now going to lambaste him. "What are you, drunk?"

The old man was muttering as he got to his feet. The mailbox itself was lying on its side, its red flag extended outward at an angle, its door open halfway. Grant could see something sticking out. "Looks like you got some mail."

"Can't be, I picked it up an hour ago," said Jennifer.

Grant shrugged; in his day, it seemed mailmen came a couple of times a day—more if a letter looked important. "Let's see..."

Inside the box were several typed notes, a thick set of printouts and the missing thumb drive.

"My God..." Philip's mouth hung open for a few seconds. Then he ran into the house shouting, "I can't believe it! I can't *fucking* believe it. This isn't..."

Jennifer and her father exchanged looks an instant before the baby woke up from the slamming door.

"Let's—let's go inside, Jen."

* * *

He wasn't happy about it, but the word "triage" was repeatedly popping up in his mind as Philip dealt with his professional crisis in the best way possible.

If...*things* could possibly happen to a project he'd prepared in supposedly off-hours at home—his presentation, this time—then he had to treat the likelihood as he would any other potential hazard.

Had he another shot at the presentation he had so bungled before important clients, Philip already knew what he would do: duplicate the PowerPoint file. He'd email it to himself, at his personal email as well as his professional address. He would complete the client packages days before, print and bind them at the office, and leave absolutely nothing to chance at home. He'd also leave very early that day, with enough time to look around for anything that happened to be missing—such as his laptop, which had turned up, of all places, in Carolyn's room. This way, he'd never again be caught trying to rely on his memory.

Given that bit of hindsight, he realized also that he needed to better familiarize himself with the entire product line he managed. It wasn't enough to read and reread spec sheets, pricing, feature bullet lists and the like. He managed the hawking of a growing handful of smart products for the home, all controlled via his phone, laptop or both, and he needed to know them better than anyone but the engineers. And with each upgrade, he would know what was coming before it happened.

To better know these devices, he would get on with installing them throughout the home.

The front door lock came first—a locksmith had already installed it mechanically. But instead of everyone's having to use a key, he could open and close the lock remotely using his smartphone or laptop. This meant that if Jennifer, for instance, had locked herself out, he could open the door for her while he was at work.

Next was the smart doorbell, equipped with high-res video he could view from anywhere using his phone. Philip added both to the device list on his phone's app, followed by the video stream they were already getting from the baby cam in Carolyn's room.

By evening, he had added a garage door sensor, a smart thermostat connected to the heating system, a robotic vacuum and several smart AC outlets and lights—all of which he could manage with his phone. More would come, but these were a good start.

Philip grew in confidence two ways: He felt, first, that he could better explain to clients and reporters how this product line worked from a homeowner's point of view, which would surely restore any confidence his boss had lost in him that morning.

Second, he was assured, though he couldn't explain why, he held the reins of a house he couldn't quite believe was his, given these odd experiences troubling him. Whatever might be...lingering here, there was nothing like modern technology to chase it away.

10

Dinnertimes were hit-and-miss at the Carter household. Owing to Carolyn's whimsical howls of hunger and a knack for catnaps that ended just as meals were on the table, the three adults present had come to appreciate an uninterrupted meal as a blessing from God. It took divine intervention to keep the microwave idle for a change.

Philip had wanted to cook tonight—it took his mind off the work week and gave his wife some sort of break—and he placed the steaming casserole dish on a trivet in the center of the dining-room table.

Jennifer, rising to get a serving spoon, noticed she hadn't turned the baby monitor's LCD screen around to face them. Its row of blue lights flashed across the display, indicating a clear connection. The device then settled down and emitted a low hiss.

"That's the sound of the rising food smells, I think," Grant commented.

"Uh-huh," replied Jennifer from the kitchen. "I knew someone would figure out what wakes her up so often during dinner."

Philip grinned as he spooned out the chicken dish to his father-in-law. "So notice she isn't waking up," he said. "She already knows it's me cooking and has decided solid food is overrated."

The three sat down, Grant far more slowly these days, and Philip and Jennifer began to eat before the old man raised a hand to pause and say grace. "Please," he said.

"Oh, I just remembered," said Philip immediately after, still with food in his mouth. "Jen, so did you get to pick up my suit at the cleaners this afternoon?"

Jennifer grinned. "Sure did...thanks to Dad."

Seeing Philip's puzzled look, Grant slowly began to explain between bites. "You left that yellow slip on the bulletin board beside the phone—I remember seeing it."

"Uh-huh. So?"

"Yesterday morning the slip was gone," said Jennifer. She turned to her father. "Tell him where you found it."

Grant chuckled as he swallowed. "Please...pass the salad. I, uh, found it under...my hammer on the workbench, in the basement."

"The basement," Philip repeated.

"Yep. The basement."

Philip grew quiet, and both Jennifer and her father knew what he was thinking.

"Phil," said Grant softly. "It isn't my medication."

His son-in-law shrugged.

"He's right, Phil. Things like this have been happening since we *moved in.*"

Philip swallowed his bite with an audible gulp. She was right, he thought. The loss of his presentation materials had perhaps been the worst...mishap since the day they moved in, but the little things had been too frequent, and too arbitrary, to attribute to Grant. Items in the medicine cabinet or the spice rack were frequently rearranged. No clock in the house, from one day to the next, seemed to have the same time as another no matter how often he reset them all, and he swore he'd had to hunt for his car keys ten times in the past week or so. It was a weird house, he maintained, and the neighborhood was no Nirvana, either.

He turned to Grant. "I'm sorry. I know it's not your fault."

"Well, Halloween's past," said Grant, trying, in his usual way, to lighten up the mood. "Maybe the goblins will move on."

"Oh, God, I hope you're talking about something else when I come back down," Jennifer said, rising. "This stuff is scaring me, with that *attack* down the street..." She went upstairs to check on the baby.

You and me both, Philip thought. He had decided to talk privately to Grant about the house after all, but the doorbell rang before he could begin.

Before he rose from the seat, Philip checked his phone app to see who was there: It was the police. Two officers: one tall, white, older; the other, shorter, Hispanic. Neither looking anxious. He went to the door.

"You're here about the boy from the other night, I bet. We heard."

The first officer nodded. "I'm Officer Giangrande, sir, and this is Officer Morales."

"Phil Carter. Come on in." Grant was just getting up from the dinner table, and Jennifer was coming back down the stairs.

"This is my wife, Jennifer, and her father, Grant O'Keefe."

"Pleased," said Grant as he shook both their hands.

Jennifer offered them coffee.

The one named Giangrande shook his head. "We'd like to ask you all a few questions, then be on our way."

"I imagine you're going down the block hitting all the houses," she offered.

"Yes, ma'am," said the other policeman, "but your house in particular seems to be involved."

"Our house...?" said Philip.

"What do you mean, Officer?" Jennifer asked.

"There's no need to be alarmed, I'm sure," said Giangrande. "It's hard to piece together, but it seems there were several boys chasing two others—one a small boy, about six or so—with eggs, shortly before the incident."

"The pumpkin!" said Jennifer. "I remember those two. I told the older one he should have on more than a mask if he wanted some candy, and—"

"Yes, well, do you know which direction they went?"

Jennifer shook her head. "Well, no, but I think they were facing...up Oak Drive. No...um...I don't remember, really."

Giangrande continued: "They went the other way, down Mason, toward where they live. They said they'd been chased, but...the boy who was attacked—he's still in the hospital—was on your street. He came back in this direction, and was chased, it seems, half a block down."

The other officer spoke up. "One boy was cut up very badly in your rose bush. Did you know that?"

"No!" said Philip. "So I mean, we were all home that night."

"We certainly are not responsible for any of this," remarked Jennifer, growing angry.

"Mrs. Carter, I apologize for our questions," said Giangrande. "What happened is, the boys who were out egging claim they saw someone...a person in a sheet jump down—they actually said 'float down'—from your roof."

"Nobody saw the attack," said Morales, "but the boys insist someone who lives here was responsible for what happened to the boy. Mind...do you mind if we just look around?"

Philip looked at his wife and shook his head. "Hell, no. So go right ahead. Our daughter's asleep upstairs—step lightly, please."

"Daughter?"

Philip's eyes rolled. "Three months old, Officer."

"Yes. Well, thank you. We'll try to be quick."

"I'll...go with them," Jennifer said to her husband.

Philip stepped into the living room; he'd start the dishwasher once they were alone again. As he hoped, Grant followed. After the old man had settled into the recliner—Philip helped him tilt it back—the conversation began.

"Grant, so I've been wanting to talk to you about something, without Jennifer being around. I hope it won't disturb you, but—"

"About the house, you mean."

"Yeah. How did you know?"

The old man shuffled a bit in the recliner. He'd seemed less alert since his last visit to the doctor, and Philip hoped this wasn't the wrong topic to discuss with his father-in-law. "I...have been wondering about the place, too. Especially since the mailbox trick."

Philip nodded. He felt like having a beer but thought it best not to give the policemen any ideas about drunks playing scare games with the neighborhood kids. Their talk had to be quick, anyway. "The mailbox...that sure wasn't anything any of us could've—would've—done. The roller skate I slipped on that same day was one of a pair that I'd thrown into the garage, along with everything else, when we moved in. So it couldn't have come from a neighbor's kid."

He ran down the list of other strange things he had been noticing, out of concern deleting the cricket incident from his discussion. "Haven't *you* seen things, too? I mean, Jen thinks the place is a bit weird, or that I'm overworked, which is true, or both. But if she's scared of the place, she's not telling. And that's not like her, I'm sure you know."

"I...know exactly what you're talking about, Phil. A few times lately, I noticed..." Hearing footsteps, she didn't finish.

The policemen came downstairs now with Jennifer behind them, holding a swaddled Carolyn. They looked toward the dining room and back to the living room's adjoining office, and Jennifer looked their way and smiled.

"They seemed real interested in the upper rooms," she said. "The rosebush boy thought the guy in the sheet came down from there. I told them we'd have to have a pretty strong clothesline for that! This isn't a *Zorro* movie set, last I checked."

Philip and Grant looked at one another. Jennifer held up Carolyn for the baby to see the policemen; she stared wide-eyed at them, barely blinking, and then began to cry.

"Ohhh, Honey, it's all right. It's okay. Just a few policemen." She leaned close to her daughter. "I told them you're too little to go to jail. And besides, you didn't *do* anything."

The crying continued till Jennifer, sighing, excused herself and took the baby upstairs to nurse her. Philip, in the meantime, pretended to have more to do in the kitchen, where he could keep an eye on the policemen and also hear their comments, and when they were ready to see the basement, he walked down with them. They exited out the cellar doors, which opened out to the backyard, and apologized once more before they moved on.

"So if it means you're through worrying about us, we're glad to give you the tour," said Philip. "We did move in just a short while ago."

"Thank you for understanding, Mr. Carter."

"Have a good night," said the other officer.

And both of you just leave us the hell alone, thought Philip as he shut the door. He glanced over toward the workbench on his way upstairs, thinking again of the dry cleaner's slip.

Back upstairs, he found Grant exactly where he'd left him but wincing in pain. "Please...my pills are upstairs. Could you...?"

"Sure. Hang on." He charged up the stairs, opened Grant's pill bottle and poured him a glass of water.

"Phil? What's wrong?"

Philip poked his head into the master bedroom, where Jennifer was nursing the baby. "Your dad needs his pills."

"Oh. Is he..."

With a cursory nod, Philip hurried back downstairs and helped the old man tilt the glass back for a drink with his pill. This morphine was strong stuff, he was sure, even if other, newer meds packed more of a punch. They'd have to finish their talk some other time. In the meantime—

It was Friday, Philip realized. The library was open late, till nine that night. After a few minutes, Jennifer came down with the baby and sat in the living room with her father. Philip excused himself, saying he was heading out for diapers, and drove off in the car.

* * *

How could he have been so stupid?

The old man had kept the kitchen light off to keep the shaft of light from announcing his descent. Sure enough, there was that sound again.

Chink. Tap tap.

Gentle sounds coming from the workbench in the basement. Sounds that he'd heard before, or thought he'd heard, an instant before he would go down the stairs to his workbench.

His?

He'd been stupid, Grant thought. Or, giving himself the benefit of the doubt, perhaps it was the medication, old and new, that was clouding his judgment. A few weeks ago, Death had visited him in his bedroom, the house's former playroom. At least he'd thought it was Death.

How could he have been so stupid?

It was all very nice, now, to have conjured up such foolishly romantic notions of the hooded timekeeper standing by his side in his final throes of life. Since he'd gone on the morphine, however, its numbing effects had given him what he felt was a true understanding of what was approaching. Death was no gentleman, extending a gracious hand to the willing and speaking in respectful, hushed tones. Rather, it was a sea lamprey that latched onto its moving target, using its rasping tongue and rings of piercing teeth to suck the life out of its victim. Sometimes it was a quick process—an artery providing short work, within seconds. Else it took days, weeks, months. Years.

Grant now knew the image of the grim reaper for what it was: merely man's lame effort to shape the intangible into something that can be seen and heard. The image of the lamprey, though another perhaps feeble attempt, seemed more true to life.

Or death.

Death, in other words, was not something that could be seen or heard or, in truth, understood before its time.

Or felt?

Yes, and about the cold he'd felt: Of course, he often experienced chills during his most painful spasms. But this was different. And it was morphine, not the codeine he'd had that day in his bedroom, that was strong enough to cause hallucinations.

Something had been in the room with him that day; the weight on the chair's padded cushion had been no hallucination. And Grant was now sure it was the same...whatever...that had been toying with his son-in-law.

The old man had never been one to believe in ghosts. You died, then you went to Heaven, hell or, for a time, purgatory. That was the way he'd been raised, and it was what he had clung to throughout his life...even now, while memories of his wife stirred up a certain open-mindedness he could not begin to explain. So what was a ghost? Someone who'd died unprepared—or who was *too* prepared? Someone whose will...transcended the usual boundaries? That didn't make sense, either. You could say till the day you died where you were headed in the afterlife, but that would be so many wasted words. All we could do was pray for salvation.

Then what, or *who,* was it?

He tried to think clearly, although the effects of the morphine lingered in his system, along with some of the pain. In anticipation perhaps of this approaching moment, he'd taken only half the recommended dosage. Yes, he needed his wits about him for this one.

Let's see, he thought. Philip, since they'd moved in, had hardly seen a day go by without some bothersome occurrence. There was the thing about his presentation. And something had seemed to be bothering him from the first day they'd spent in the house.

If Grant had seen anything, however, it was the work of the most potentially gracious goblin on the face of the earth. Since that day in his bedroom, three times had he found items lying on his dresser that he thought he'd lost. When it came to socks, this was no trivial matter. Once he'd spilled his glass of water on the carpet after taking his medicine. He had fallen asleep for a while on the bed, and when he woke up, a full glass of water awaited on the nightstand. It could have been Jennifer or Phil, he'd first thought. But they had taken Carolyn out shopping and didn't return for an hour after he awoke.

Assuming the impossible, whomever this...ghost was, it didn't seem to like Philip very much. And Jennifer would've spoken up at once if she felt she—or, Heaven forbid, the baby—were in any way threatened.

Tap. Tap. Clink. Sssss—chink.

If he didn't know better, he'd swear it was a...*a kid* playing at the workbench. Touching things, moving them around into other positions, the way he often found them when he went downstairs. There once had been something of a playroom in the house: his room, now. But kids didn't want to play with their own toys for long. They wanted to play with the unsafe, the forbidden.

Tap. Chink. Tap tap tap.

He gripped the rail, leaning his weight against the wall for support as he slowly descended the stairs in his stocking feet.

I may not be able to get back up again, he considered.

He shook off the thought and took another step. He thought he could see a bit of light, a strange bluish glow that reached the landing below, and smelled the usual trace of mustiness. He also caught a faint chill but shrugged it off.

He had to know what it was.

* * *

The Broward County Sun. The Hollister Register. That must be the one, he thought. Philip was using one of the library's own computers to do his research, expecting the library to have some sort of pass to get him into online stories without hitting the paywall. No such luck, he realized.

Near where he sat, however, he noticed several binders labeled with newspaper titles, including the two he'd been perusing online. Philip took the newest for *The Hollister Register* and opened to the end—but realized the last bound issue was more than twenty years old. Maybe he did need to spring for the online account, which annoyed him since they had already begun getting the paper edition delivered.

On a lark, he decided to ask the librarian, who might be helpful— town records of some sort might be available—but the crowd of college students flocking about made any aid he could get highly unlikely. You never know till you try, Philip told himself, so he stood in the vicinity of the desk and stared in the librarian's direction.

Eventually the seventy-ish, bearded librarian turned his way, expecting to see yet another kid who hadn't seen the inside of a library in years. "Oh!" he said when he saw Philip. "Sorry to keep you waiting. How can I help you?"

"So I'm looking...for information on the residents of a...house that my family and I recently moved into. Um..."

"Has the house some historical significance that you're aware of?"

"Um...I don't know. It's a strange old place, and—what I'm actually trying to do is verify the background, whatever, of the people we were told lived there before. So I'm not sure we were...told the truth. Just a hunch."

The librarian smiled. "Breakthroughs are made on hunches, as you know." He sighed. "I think, though, that you might be better off at the town hall. They'd have whatever records are available—tax records, too, with names—of former residents. But they closed hours ago." He stared for a moment at Philip, as if he suspected the man was actually a private detective.

"Mmmm. Okay, thank you very much for your help." He turned toward the door.

"Oh, just a minute." The librarian had already started talking to another student, but he broke away with this further revelation. "You never told me which house we were discussing."

Philip walked back over. "So it's the former Leffingwell house on the other side of town. Corner of Mason Street and Oak Drive?"

"Oh...*that* house." The librarian gave an emphatic nod. "Forget the town hall. We've got a little file on the place right here." He started walking, then turned back for a moment. "I have to warn you...it's not pretty." He withdrew to a caged-off area behind his desk and emerged with a thin, red-plastic file. Having led Philip over to an enclosure away from where the students were congregating, he laid a hand on Philip's shoulder a moment before he returned to the line at his desk. "Here you go," he said. "Photocopier's over there. Have fun."

* * *

Grant reached the bottom stair and knew, by this point, that anyone or anything in the basement had by now detected his presence. The noises had stopped, but the feeling remained.

It was here, he knew. In the darkness.
It waited for him.

11

The handle of a screwdriver floated a few inches above the hardwood surface of the workbench. The flat of its tip came down

dududddd, dududdd

again and again on the bench. Whoever was holding it apparently liked the sound, for it continued

dududddd, duddd, dududdd

as Grant approached the back corner of the basement. The only light now was a muted glow making its way in from the streetlight, out the window to his left. A bit of it reflected off the shank of the screwdriver.

The drumming stopped.

The old man, awash in sweat, struggled to ignore what his senses were telling him. Standing some eight feet from the bench, leaning against one of the basement's Lally columns, he knew he felt too weak to run or even stagger back up the stairs. Perhaps he'd feel more up to it later. In the meantime, he had someone, something, to meet. Something that...*seemed* to mean him no harm.

So far.

Grant took a stab at the truth. "I...know you're here. I've been wanting to meet you since you visited me...in my room."

Silence.

A dull pain had returned to Grant's abdomen; he could almost feel his cancer clutching hold of new, clean cells. Making them its own. He wondered how he was going to get back up the stairs;

perhaps it would not be necessary. "You've been very kind to my daughter and me, and her baby, since we moved in. I think...you like us, and I think that...maybe I'd like to get to know you a little better."

dududddd, duddd, dududdd

"I see you like my tools."

The screwdriver fell to the floor. Grant watched it as an invisible hand gripped it, dropped it once, and then lifted it up to its previous position. *dududddd, dududdd...*

"There were a lot here when we moved in. Were—are—some of these your tools?"

DUDUDDDD, DUDDD, DUDUDDD, DUDUDUDD, DDDDDDDUDD...

"D-do they belong to someone you care, cared, for—"

The hand holding the screwdriver began to thrust at the wood of the workbench. It stabbed furiously, again and again, the tip sticking into the grain, being twisted and wrenched free, each time plunging yet again. And again. Grant wanted to draw back, to pull himself up the stairs with any strength he could muster. Somehow, he instead did what he had to.

He moved forward, the hardest steps of his life.

"Wh-who are you?"

The screwdriver dropped to the table.

"Will you tell me?"

The chill permeating the space seemed more familiar this time. A few nights lately he'd woken up, conscious that he'd felt cold, so very cold, as he slept. Had he had company again—someone who sat, for hours at a time, in the padded rattan chair?

Grant felt the space growing colder still, and he sensed that whatever stood before him was now no more than about five feet away. The aching within grew stronger; he tried to suppress it through his will. Oh, why had he skimped on his dosage?

"aaaaaaaahhhhtaahhhlll..."

The voice was high-pitched, the soft voice of...a child. He heard it from the chilly blackness ahead of him, yet it seemed to echo from all around him. It seemed to resonate throughout his withering body as well.

"'Atle'? I...don't understand you."

"aaaaahhhtaahhhhlllleeeee..."

"At—Atolie. Atol—Your name is Atole? Anatole?"

"NNNNATALIE!"

Grant dropped to his knees, the force of the name had been so great. As though a strong blast of wind had bowled him over with the very mention of the name.

"N-Natalie. Natalie. A...a very nice name for a g-girl. M-my name is G-Grant." He struggled to his feet.

"Miiiister Ooooo Keeeefff..."

They were speaking. He was conversing with a spirit. He tried not to dwell too much on that, if he could avoid it. He had his purposes, after all: to protect his family in whatever time he had. "S-so formal. But if you want to call me that, that's fine. Natalie...c-could I see you? Please?"

A few moments passed, and she was before him. About four-and-a-half-feet tall, with a serious face and long, straight hair that fell around big eyes that appeared blue from a glow that tinged her very presence. The old man's mouth dropped open. It...it *was* true, it was really true. Before him stood a...spirit from the great beyond, a being who somehow—but, he realized with surprise, he was less afraid now that he could see her. Stories he had read as a boy, comic books he had read...they seemed not far off, from what he remembered.

One thing they could not have captured, however, was the stillness. The apparent suspension of time and space that would prove but a delusion of the mortal in the face of the immortal. He was in the basement, he reminded himself. It was...after eight p.m. But before this young will-o'-the-wisp, in his physical state, Grant felt he himself would soon be a ghost.

He could see the glint of the bench vise behind her, through her, where it stood bolted to the edge of the workbench. Yes, this...this *girl* was the one who had stayed with him in this room, as though he were *her* grandfather, and she were at his deathbed—which could soon well be true. This was the little girl who had been spending a lot of playtime at the basement workbench he'd claimed by default when he'd moved in with his daughter and her family.

This...this girl was the one who had already displayed more than a casual dislike for his son-in-law.

Spirits, said the old books and movies, were of a forgotten time. Should ghosts indeed exist, he'd thought once in his youth, he expected they'd wear the garb of the eighteenth century. Ruffles, lace, all the trimmings that adorned the long dresses of the period.

This child, in contrast, wore street clothes that you might find in

93

any Walmart. He couldn't tell the color—everything visible was bathed in the same faint bluish glow—but its style, the tie-dyed T-shirt and jeans, seemed distinctively modern. This was no Victorian spirit.

And Grant had been right about her, he knew. She wasn't out to hurt. Not him, at least. He had to know her intentions, though...a little bit at a time.

He already knew something of her powers.

"Natalie...did you live here before we moved in?"

The spirit nodded.

He pointed upward in the direction of the garage. "D-did the things in there belong to your family?"

Again, she nodded. It seemed easier than speaking.

"Natalie, I'm sorry, but...I want to ask you a...hard question. Did...did you die in this house?"

The spirit crouched down to the floor, shaking her head and crying tears the old man could not see. She remained there for a time, then looked up at Grant and nodded. *"M-my faaaather haaad guuun aaand..."* She resumed sobbing.

"N-no! You-your father killed you?"

The little girl alternately nodded and shook her head.

"I...I don't understand. He did? Or he didn't? Please...tell me."

The girl's voice crackled as she spoke, and her voice occasionally faded in and out like the sound of a radio signal troubled by interference.

"He...huuuurt me...uuurt 'yyy...huuurt my mmmooother and sheee..."

Grant forgot his pain in the conversation. "Your father...did he...shoot you?"

The spirit shrugged and could not seem to further explain. *"...waaas ouuut 'oo plaaaaaay and 'aaas baaad 'oo staaaay awaaay."*

"You—you were out playing and upset your father. Natalie. Excuse m-me for saying so, but your father d-doesn't sound like a very nice man." Her gaze grew hard at this—Grant wondered whether he'd gone too far—but she merely nodded in agreement.

"mmmeeean mmmaaaaan..."

Natalie snapped her head to the left as though she had heard something. Grant knew his hearing wasn't quite as good as when he was younger—too much heavy equipment, too little ear protection—but he had heard nothing at all.

Then the spirit was walking with a strange fluid motion. It looked to the old man as though her feet glided above the floor on some steps, dipped below on others. He followed her away from the workbench, past the washer and dryer and a disheveled basket of laundry. Toward a high window that looked out onto the side of the house, with a view of Mason Street.

The little girl was staring out the window when the question occurred to him. "Natalie, two policemen were here earlier tonight."

She glanced quickly at him but returned her attention to whatever was outside. He was having trouble seeing her face in the light of the moon, though the lower half of her body remained in view.

"Did you have anything to do with that boy, the one who was...hurt the other night?"

Her mouth opened, but with none of the reaction he'd expected he might see. Natalie brought her hand to her mouth in recognition, and an instant before she vanished—rather, floated up and out the window—he saw the look on her face. It was a smile.

Not quite an evil smile but a smile of a child who, from the living...

What about the question?

...had a secret.

* * *

"Shhh!"

"Oh, shut up," Cynthia told her friend.

"What?"

"We're not supposed to be doing this. What do you mean, 'What'?"

Lana looked around her, past the tall hedge that lined the front of her yard, down a street blanketed with dried leaves that would not ordinarily allow quiet approach. The unease they felt when they'd first begun these nocturnal adventures, that even in spirit form they would be visible to someone nearby, no longer occurred to them. Still, Lana scanned up and down the street.

What frightened them might make no sound in the leaves, or anywhere for that matter. Something felt wrong.

"So, you still want to go over there, right?"

"Not *in,* you know."

"I know *not in!* Cynthia, I'm not daring you. I just wanna, well..."

Cynthia trembled in what could only be described as a shiver despite the fact that her body lay blocks away, in bed, her bedroom door closed though her mother would not venture near. Her mother, after all, was out cold from a six—at least—of Coors and wouldn't be upstairs for hours. If at all. "You want to look for the ghost."

Lana sighed. "We don't *know* if it *is* a ghost!"

Shaking her head, Cynthia started down Oak Drive. "But if it is, it won't be able to bother us, I know, I know..."

The house loomed a hundred feet ahead, looking as ordinary as any in the neighborhood. It was painted white, an aging coat that hadn't been freshened in several years. That added to its reputation, the two girls were certain. Its front porch was just wide enough to stand on before the few brick steps took it down to a concrete walk. Its wide first floor was topped by a half-roof that slanted up to just beneath the windows of the second floor, through which there seemed to be a hallway.

Which led to where the murders took place.

A one-car garage was off to the left, past where someone—even the car was haunted, Lana had joked—a few weeks ago had driven over the mailbox and torn its post from the ground. Along the wall leading to the garage, though, were a few flat windows at ground level; they led to the basement. Lana hadn't noticed these before, but was not surprised now that she was giving the place such a look.

"Lana..." Cynthia said, stopping and touching her friend's shoulder.

She looked up from the basement windows to see a young girl, their age or slightly younger, standing in the driveway. She, like them, was *immaterial,* as they'd jokingly called it between themselves.

The girl was shyly waving to them.

Cynthia and Lana exchanged glances and shrugged before approaching her. Neither of them could explain the girl's presence, especially since Hollister had only one school for children their age. They'd have seen any new girl, right?

"H-hi," Cynthia said to the stranger.

"Hi," the girl replied. "My name's...Nancy. What's yours?"

There was something unusual about this girl that neither Lana nor Cynthia could put a finger on. Or maybe, thought Cynthia, it was just that they didn't recognize her. Of course, how was one supposed to greet someone in this strange, incorporeal world? You couldn't just say, "Hello there. I see you also are hanging out without your body. My name is Cynthia. What's yours, and what's your problem?"

When she and Lana had first spoken, it was while both were *immaterial,* but at least they'd seen one another for a couple of years—however much they'd both kept to themselves. For them, there had been first recognition, then instant friendship. The school outsiders, ironically, often avoided other outsiders for the same reason these classmates were generally shunned. But for Lana and Cynthia, their nightly excursions had made them the best of friends.

"I-I'm Cynthia. This is Lana."

"Are you from around here?" asked Lana.

The girl sat down on the grass, which wasn't unusual since it wasn't easy to be caught trespassing. The girls, in fact, occasionally chatted in the middle of a neighbor's chimney—but only after the family had lit the fireplace. "No, I'm from..." she pointed down Mason, in the direction of the highway leading to the city. "Down there. I lived around here once, though. I miss it."

"What house did you live in?" Lana persisted.

The girl looked down at her knees for a minute and tugged down the hem of her top as if she were cold. "I don't know. I was little when we moved. It's around here somewhere, though."

"I live up the block," said Cynthia.

Fine, Cindy, Lana wanted to say. Why don't you just give her the key to the house while you're at it?

"Do you go ghosting a lot?" the girl asked.

Cynthia wrinkled her brow. "'Ghosting'?"

The girl named Nancy chuckled—a strange, hollow kind of laugh—but her smile was friendly. "I thought it was a funny name when I first heard it. It's not really a nice word, but..."

"But it's better than anything else you came up with, right?" replied Lana.

Nancy nodded, and all three laughed.

"Well, I like the word myself," declared Cynthia.

"Of cawse, my dear," snapped her friend in her best British accent. "The word *myself* has been used for yee-ahs!"

"Hey, let's go fly over the school!" cried Nancy.

Lana and Cynthia exchanged glances once more. "Okay! But only for a little while," said Lana with caution. "I don't want to leave so much homework for the weekend."

"Let's go, then!" said their new friend.

* * *

This was turning out to be a wonderful night, Natalie had been thinking. First she had spoken to Mr. O'Keefe—her friend, she'd known from the start—for the first time. Now, she had made the first friends her age in months. They'd be good friends before long, she felt.

So long as they believed her story.

The three of them talked and joked as they floated toward the school, a mile away, with Natalie hesitatingly asking questions about the neighborhood. As they conversed, now and then her mind went back to her conversation with the old man, to the questions he'd asked about her former life.

To the events that made that evening her last.

She had initially assumed her father had to have fired the gun. Yet he was the one who had died first, his blood running down onto her parents' bed and soaking into the sheets. She had seen her father before the paramedics had taken him away and had found it hard to believe he was gone, and worse—that the crumbled mass of flesh and clothing now at the bottom of the stairs was all that remained of her loving mother.

She thought of her return to her bedroom, on a night very much like this, after playing with Gerald, Wendy, and the others. She'd realized something had happened, felt a sudden emptiness within her that—from the way they suddenly looked at her, her companions had seemed to sense—and flashed back to her bedroom only to see her body lying face down on the bed, blood flowing from a hole in the back of her head. Her first instinct was to re-enter herself. But when she tried, she passed through as though her body were a wax figure. A bleeding wax figure.

She had been shot...by a bullet that came through the wall from her parents' bedroom. She spotted the hole in the wall, above her headboard, an instant before her mother swung open the door, muttering her daughter's name.

Natalie cried out "Mommy!" at the sight of her mother, who at the same time saw Natalie's body and began to scream.

"Noooooooo! Noooooo!" She leaned over her daughter and touched her face, as if her touch could make things right again. "M-m-my baby, my baby, it can't be, it can't be, Natalie, m-my baby, it caaaaan't be..."

Above her, Kim could not see or hear the screams of her daughter hovering above, her spirit uncertain what to do next. The little girl's senses could have detected a physical threat had someone entered the room, or even knocked on her door. But the bullet that destroyed her body had given no warning whatsoever. She was trapped! Natalie's body was as closed to her as if it had been someone else's, and she watched, helplessly, as her mother staggered out of the room, into the hallway, toward the stairs. This time she was not dreaming.

Policeman had broken through the door, but they were too late. The first man on the stairs dodged as Kim tumbled down the stairs and landed, head first, at the feet of her would-be rescuers.

* * *

"Nancy...?"

She looked back, then down, to see that she had passed by the school. Lana and Cynthia had already started to descend, their bodies floating down slower than parachutes to the slate-covered plaza before the main doors.

"Which school did _you_ want to see?" yelled Lana.

Natalie headed down to meet them, her mind snapping out of its reverie. Those times weren't important anymore, she told herself. What mattered now was that she had _friends,_ what she wanted most in all the world.

"When did you go here?" inquired Cynthia.

"Oh! Well, I...didn't go here. My—my big s-sister went here, but my family moved away before I started. I...just like the place. It's not like my school in the city—big, gray, ugly place with dirty windows."

Lana nodded; that sure did sound like how she'd imagined city schools. "Let's go in!"

The three passed through the roof to find themselves in the cafeteria. Natalie kept relatively silent as they toured the kitchen, the ovens, the offices behind, and then the boys' locker room adjoining the gym. At one time, with former friends, she might have had a great time joking about certain teachers, the principal, the rotten food in the cafeteria. Fortunately for the long run, however, Cynthia had questioned her before she could reveal how well she knew the place. Lana had lived in Hollister for only a few years—she was among the last Russian adoptees released to American parents—but

Cynthia had grown up here. She'd have remembered seeing any girl from her own class, though possibly not everyone in other classes of the same grade. Natalie was about the same age and could not remember having seen either girl.

She'd have to talk about the school, as well as most of the town, as if it were a distant memory of a child who'd moved away at about age five. Not as much fun, she conceded, but it would have to do.

"Hey," said Cynthia, "wouldn't it be fun to open up all the lockers and hang up all the boys' shorts in the principal's office?"

"Better still, let's put them in a few of the girls' lockers," replied Lana. "I know *just* which lockers!"

"Yeah, let's do..." Natalie stopped herself when she realized that her two friends had been fantasizing, not actually conspiring. She'd forgotten that the living, while "ghosting," did not have the ability to touch objects. Her powers to materialize, to hold objects, had developed immensely, even with objects too heavy for her in life. And it wasn't difficult to raise suspicions about the fact that she was

dead

different.

"Do what?"

"Only kidding," she replied, embarrassed but also growing angry at Lana's persistent doubts. Natalie decided she wanted to show them something, just a taste of what she could do, without making too big a deal about it.

The opportunity arose when they passed through a wall adjacent to the student records office. "Let's play a game," she said.

Cynthia grinned. "Okay, what?"

"Well," she began, enjoying herself yet choosing her words with care. "This is where they keep all the records, right? The *permanent* records?"

"Yeeeah?" said Lana, playing along with a hint of skepticism.

"You tell me who's the meanest boy in school. Then we go into his *permanent* record and..."

"Aw, c'mon, we can't really *do* anything!" Lana complained. "This isn't very much fun."

"Yeah," said Cynthia. "And besides, I better get back to study."

"Wait!" She was losing them, Natalie realized. They were friends, especially Cynthia, and she needed them far more than they needed her. She'd wanted to keep it all a game, but now...

Now she needed to get serious.

With the two girls' attention on her, Natalie reached behind the locked top drawer of the student record files and felt behind for the catch. Over time, she'd gotten good at learning how locks worked, and she could solidify her finger, or a portion of it, to exert pressure in just the right place to—

"What are you doing?" asked Lana in a tone both curious and exasperated regarding this Nancy.

The two schoolgirls gasped when they heard a click, and Natalie reached for the drawer's front handle, pushed over the button, and opened the drawer.

"Whaaaa?"

"You can't do that!" cried Lana. "How did you...?"

"Nan..."

Natalie shrugged. "It's just something I learned from ghosting. My...big sister taught it to me. When...when she still remembered how."

"How come we can't do that?" Lana asked.

"Yeah!" said Cynthia.

Here goes, thought Natalie. "I don't know," she said with a shrug. "I think that...the longer you know how to...leave your body, the better you get—the better you get at doing this. But only a little at a time. It...it hurts a little."

Lana understandably looked confused. "Hurts? Like pain? But your body—your body is in the city, right? So how can it—"

"I think it—takes away some of your energy...the body's energy. So you can't do it too much. I think, if you do, it...makes it harder to get back into your body. That's what my sister said."

"Woooow!" The two said almost in unison.

"So...who's it gonna be?"

Cynthia was shaking her head. "I would pick Raymond but...but..."

"But what?" inquired Natalie.

Lana had no such trouble with this one. "He's almost dead, mon." Her eyes lit up. "From 'alloween nahhhht!"

Oh, brother, thought Cynthia, I thought we watched the same movies.

"Oh." Natalie shrugged. "Who else?"

Lana and Cynthia exchanged quick glances, and Cynthia came up with another boy: "Jason Pleva!"

Thinking for a moment, Lana subsequently nodded. Jason was a friend of Raymond's, though the two hadn't been together that fateful night. Even though he was only in the third grade, he already was acting like one of the older class jocks, coming into class each day wearing a smug grin and combing his hair several times an hour.

He, the two friends agreed, hadn't an ounce of compassion toward them or anyone else, probably not even his well-to-do parents. "Jason Pleva," Lana stated again for the record.

Natalie had already gotten the bottom drawer open, being sure to pause momentarily, sighing, before reaching in to withdraw a file. "This file says, 'TO BE INPUT.'" She gingerly thumbed through the pages till she found the right one. "Pleva, Jason."

"Look!" said Cynthia after Natalie opened the file on the desk's top. "'Discipline problem!' it says."

"'Re-prim-anded for insub-ordination,'" Lana read. "Every year he gets into some trouble with the principal."

"One more problem, and..."

"He'll be out, I bet!"

Natalie pulled out the blue card, the one recording his borderline grades, and reached over for a black pen nearby. "Uhhh," she grunted as if in pain.

"Y-you okay?" asked Cynthia. Natalie knew she had them, at least for now. Her friend was worrying as much about the possibility that "Nancy" might not be able to continue as she was about her overdoing it.

"Yeah. I'll be all right. Yeah." She picked up the pen and carefully wrote over several of the grades recorded on the card, changing Ds to Bs, Cs to As, but being sure to do it sloppily—in a child's hand— and not to eradicate the old grades completely. "When they find it, they'll think Jason did it."

"Wooow!" said Lana. "I can't wait till—I mean, I wish I could be here when—hey! What if they don't find out?"

"Yeah! What do we...?"

Natalie gingerly returned the card to the file and closed it. She carried it over to the cabinet and slowly slid it into its place—almost all the way. She closed the top drawer completely; the bottom drawer, she left slightly ajar. "Okay?" She reveled at their gaping smiles.

Sometimes you had to do things the hard way, Natalie thought. To earn their trust, you had to give them something to...make them *like* you.

Natalie needed the girls to like her. She wanted to feel close to Cynthia and Lana as much as she needed to gain their trust. The house, after all, was a lonely place. The old man would die soon, and then there'd be nobody she could talk to. Nobody, that is, unless...

Unless she could bind someone as tightly to this strange, dark world as she was herself.

12

In the old days, his shop was a solace from the problems of the world. Not that he'd desired an escape from his wife and two children—no, Roberta and the girls were no hardship whatsoever. But Grant O'Keefe, like many people, needed what he called his "quiet" time among the tools to keep his perspective about the world. There was nothing in the world you couldn't fix, he'd once told his wife, when you had the right tools for the job.

But that was a long time ago, he thought. Roberta was gone now and awaited him, he was sure, in Heaven. Jennifer was close by, a pleasure for which he routinely thanked God, and he heard from his other daughter, married and halfway across the country, more often than many parents did from offspring who lived closer.

Could he solve the problems of the world today? He looked down at the belt sander on the worktable, its metal trim dully reflecting the LED bench light. Morphine and driving didn't mix; that much he'd figured out for himself. But morphine and power tools? He hadn't thought to predict that one.

After Natalie had left him so suddenly, the old man had decided to resume work on a birdhouse he'd been making. If she came back, he'd have plenty more questions for her—some very important ones, in fact. If she didn't, well, that was fine, too. He supposed he'd eventually see her again, now that they'd had a formal introduction.

A few minutes into the job, however, Grant stared at one side of the birdhouse and sighed. He'd carefully secured it to the side of the bench, doubling up a rag to cushion the soft wood from the jaws of the metal clamp. But his control of the tool had been off. He had applied way too much pressure on one side, and at one point, he leaned too far over and almost ran the sander off the wood and into the edge of the bench. At that point, he powered off the sander, set it down...and wept.

This was the way the disease hit home, he thought; it stole everything he'd taken for granted throughout his life. Of course, Feller had warned him about what to expect of his cancer—having metastasized, it would quickly do a great deal of damage. Grant had been taking it with some small degree of stoicism when he occasionally coughed up a bit of blood in the bathroom. He expected the medication to occasionally make him oversleep or, other times, keep him wide awake for hours. This resulted in his having breakfast or lunch alone, or skipping it altogether. It was hard to eat regularly with family, after all, when he couldn't count on getting up with the sun.

No matter what warnings he had received, however, for some reason Grant had imagined he'd somehow be able to work, slowly if necessary. He realized now that power tools were off limits to him; hand tools like screwdrivers and wrenches, he supposed he could use with care. For at least a few more days or weeks, at best.

He felt like sleeping, but at the same time he feared slowing down. He wanted to talk to someone, but he also knew that this wasn't something he wanted to dump on his daughter or her husband. He began to pace, from one side of the basement to another, and then trudged slowly up the stairs, pausing every few steps to take a breath. Once at the top, he decided to head toward the door leading to the garage; Philip and Jen had apparently gone upstairs for the night. He opened it and walked in.

Of course. This was where Philip had put—more like thrown— the personal articles the Leffingwells had left behind, awaiting a trash pickup he hadn't yet gotten around to scheduling. Most of the furniture that was left behind after...*whatever happened* had apparently been sold, but the room was crammed full of other items. Too many for Philip to have thrown out for the weekly trash pickup.

He switched on the light; no bulb. Some light, at least, came in from the streetlight. Grant scanned the room's contents: a mantel clock, several paintings including one of a mountain stream, a few shelves with grooves for displaying decorative plates, a flashlight, assorted curtains with rods, a few dishes and utensils, ashtrays—a virtual houseful of family effects, such as a ceramic cat, potholders and a cuckoo clock.

In the corner he spied a child's toy box. He tried the flashlight; its batteries were weak but usable

(like me)

and he opened the box.

The smell of pine hit him immediately. Next came the sight of a white sheet that had been wadded in a rush and dropped in the corner of the spacious box. He set the light down on the lid, which rested against the wall, and held up the sheet to see three holes crudely cut through the middle—like eyes and a mouth. "What the heck..."

The question he'd asked Natalie remained in his mind, and he remembered the accounts he'd read of the attack that had recently taken place just outside the house. While most of the boys who'd been out egging that night preferred to talk with no one, two of them told stories that made local TV reporters dash for their typewriters—or their iPads, whatever doodads they used these days.

"Like, it was a ghost. That's all. It floated down, and I was, like, gone," the first had said.

The other boy was more eloquent. "I heard some kind of flapping sound, and I turn around and there's this guy, or someone, inside a blanket with eyeholes coming down, floating, slow-like, from the roof of the haunted house. But he's, like, going too slow. And I didn't see no ropes, nothing. I dropped all my eggs in the yard and climbed over the hedge."

A blanket with eyeholes.

What kind of child was this?

More to the point: How could he protect his family? It was clearly up to him—he, after all, was the only one who knew...something about the spirit.

"Daddy? Everything okay there?" It was Jennifer.

He answered her from where he stood. "F-fine, Jenny. Just, uh, looking around."

"Want some company? Phil's still outside. Carolyn's great to talk to, but she isn't much for conversation."

"Um, I think I should be alone for a while. Sorry, Jen."

A pause. "Okay," she said resignedly. "See you later."

"Yep."

Grant folded the blanket, laid it in the box and closed the lid. He hated to be that way with his daughter, especially since he knew he lived there—and not in some institution—through her kindness alone. Still, he knew he would eventually have a meeting he couldn't miss, his second with a little spirit named Natalie.

* * *

He had stepped back down to the basement, shut out the lights and was dozing on the futon when she returned. Under the medication, which could also cause insomnia, sleep came quickly sometimes. Too quickly for his preferences.

When he opened his eyes, Grant realized it was the touch of a hand upon his shoulder that had done it. She had reached out and somehow materialized her hand to wake him up. Like how she'd gripped the screwdriver. It had been an odd touch, a feeling that frightened him, deep within, however much he told himself he had nothing to fear from this spirit. It was not a feeling of evil but of...wrongness. The chill of her presence bothered him little; the cellar's dank humidity cloaked anything coming from her. But the memory of her hand on his shoulder, he knew, would remain. Long after he returned upstairs to the company of his family.

"Mmmmiiiister Oooo'Keeeefffe..."

He sat up until his head stopped spinning, then stood up to face the little girl. She looked virtually the same as before, but something had changed from earlier. Of course, she was dressed in the same clothes. But her face—it was brighter. Natalie seemed almost happy, if that emotion were possible in her situation.

"Natalie...it's good to see you," he managed to say.

"Hiiiiii..."

"H-hi yourself. Where did you go?"

The spirit looked down for a moment and shrugged. *"Oouut 'oo pllaayy."*

"Out to play," he repeated. Grant again felt she was hiding something, but realized there was no point in pushing her. He needed her trust, after all, and of course he was no relation of hers. "I guess you must get lonely sometimes."

Natalie shrugged again, then nodded.

"Do you like my daughter's family, Natalie?"

She looked down. Was this the same child who had been

tormenting his son-in-law? Who'd worn the white sheet he'd found, in a demoniac Halloween rampage, and dashed the head of a young boy into the pavement outside? The ambulance had picked up the boy before Grant went outside that November 1—All Saints' Day, he'd noted—but a trace of eggs and blood, diluted by the later rain, still stained the single yellow line painted down the middle of Mason Street.

"Natalie." She looked up.

"I bet you like the baby, don't you?"

"uute baabeee...prrettyy baabeee...liiike the baabeee..."

Spoken like a true little girl, Grant thought with a smile. "Do you know her mother is my little girl?"

The spirit nodded.

"Do you like my daughter, Natalie?"

Through the haze, he could see her grin. *"...gaaave 'eer 'iii mmmuussic booox..."* Her voice was still breaking up as she spoke, making it difficult for Grant to understand her.

"Music box? Something about a music box?

"Iii gaave...hhheerr..."

"You gave her your music box. That...was very kind of you, Natalie. I'm sure she appreciated it."

The little girl seemed to know what was coming next.

"aake Phiiill go 'wwaay..."

"Phil? Natalie, why don't you like Phil?"

The door to the basement stairs opened, and light streamed down the stairs. "Dad? Who're you talking to?"

"Um...what talking, Jen?"

"Dad, I heard your voice and just thought I'd check—"

"Just a few prayers, Jenny. I'll...I'll be up soon, all right?"

From her bedroom, the baby began to howl loudly. Jennifer sighed and closed the basement door without another word.

In another moment Natalie had returned; this time she had a mischievous grin on her face.

"What? What is it?"

The spirit shook her head, the grin slowly fading from her face, and they resumed talking.

"About my son-in-law..."

"Haaate Phiill..." Her voice, now, seemed less broken up. Was it her own doing?

"Natalie, he's a good man. He—"

"Meeean mmaaaann..."

"No he isn't. Natalie, he just wants a nice, safe home for his family."

"Mmyyy hhhomme..."

The room grew colder, and Grant saw Natalie's stance become more resolute. "W-what did you say, Natalie?"

"Myyy hooome..."

So that was it, he thought. It was natural, he supposed, for the little girl to feel possessive about the house, and unwelcoming to the first family to live there since she died. Especially since the place had never really been cleaned out. As far as she was concerned, it was still her house. And he supposed the girl demanded more respect than the stashed clutter in the garage, the Leffingwells' possessions strewn about, had suggested. It was clearly something he had to work on—later, after he had discussed things with Jennifer and Philip. And after Natalie had cooled down.

The old man realized his next question would touch upon a topic that had often dominated his thoughts in recent months. He would find out much about the true nature of death before long—that expectation, perhaps, was what had attracted Natalie to him—but still there was much he could find out now from this child.

"Natalie...why do you stay here, in this house?"

She shook her head, the bluish cloud leaving fleeting trails as of mist behind her head. *"...caaan't leeeave..."*

"But, Natalie, you must be able to leave. There—I'm told there's a place where the dead go when it's time for them...to go..."

"NO! Nooplaace tooo gooo.... Caan't leeave...'aan't lleeave..."

"But..."

"'aan't leeeave..."

* * *

"Hi, Jen." Philip gave her a quick peck on the cheek as she leaned against their headboard, nursing a fussy Carolyn. "So where's your dad?"

She shook her head, still a bit annoyed at him for rushing off to the 7-11 with barely a word to her. The baby had been awake since a while ago, when she was talking to her father, and she hadn't had much luck in calming her. Who'd have thought such a small baby could throw her pacifier so far out of the crib while asleep? "In the basement, last I checked. I've been all around the place with Carolyn, so he could've slipped by and gone upstairs."

He shrugged. "I'll go see."

"Phil, can we talk about the house, what's bothering you? You've been awfully jumpy, and it's scaring me. Not to mention the baby. I know babies can pick up on these things—or at least it seems so. Why don't you—"

"Later, Jen. Please." He left the room.

"Philip!"

He wasn't in the living room, dining room or kitchen, Philip knew. The younger man's small office adjoining the dining room was a place his father-in-law would feel he were trespassing if he ever went in without asking. Which left the basement.

The basement lights were off. All of them.

He opened the door and reached in to turn on the light switch. No sounds, except...something.

A sobbing?

Shaking off his caution, Philip ran down the stairs and immediately saw the old man on the cold concrete floor near the workbench. He lay on his side, his back to Philip, and he was crouched into a near-fetal position.

My God! Philip thought. *This was it.*

"Grant," he said without thinking. "Can you speak?"

To his surprise the old man nodded, but slowly.

"So I'm going to call Dr. Bennett. Here...can you make it over to the futon here?"

Grant was shaking his head. "No, no..."

"Can't make it? Should I...what, Grant?"

"N-no doctor. I'll be okay. Help...help me upstairs, please, and br-bring me my medicine."

"Are you sure, Grant? Grant, listen, so I'm going to call the doctor anyway. Just to be safe."

"No!" The old man nearly shot up off the floor for an instant, then settled down again. "I mean, I'll be okay. Ju-just help me, would you?"

With a sigh, Philip took his father-in-law's left arm and draped it around his shoulder. It wouldn't be easy, but if he took his time and clung to the banister, he'd be able to carry Grant up the two flights of stairs to his bedroom.

As he led the old man upstairs, he had other things on his mind.

By the morning, for instance, he hoped to have decided what to tell his wife —if anything—of what he'd learned that night. Never mind telling his father-in-law. Philip wondered, in fact, whether their earlier conversation had contributed to Grant's having gone downstairs...in the dark, and collapsed there. It was entirely possible, he was sure.

As he carried the old man up the stairs, he could still see the headline that had leapt out at him as he opened the folder at the library—an entire folder on what he, only days ago, had regarded as their dream house. The headline:

DOUBLE KILLING, SUICIDE
VEX HOLLISTER POLICE

Nine-year-old's death
termed 'accident'
despite earlier beating

The words, he knew, would be hard enough to purge from his memory. The accounts from the three local papers detailed how Kim Leffingwell, nearly dead, had fired at her husband, killing him but also—by a stray bullet through the wall—her daughter. She then had jumped, perhaps fallen, down the stairs.

But then there were the photos, the shots of the house with three bodies in lean plastic bags being carried out the front door of what was now his house. One of the officers pictured was the one called Giangrande, who had visited earlier. No wonder Philip's family—as residents of *this* house—had been thought to be involved in the recent killing.

The three newspapers also quoted an anguished woman named Emily Sanders, the school nurse, who had suspected George Leffingwell of beating his wife and probably his daughter, but hadn't acted in time. "I knew he was a beast," she'd been quoted as saying. "I was just too late, too late."

What a guy, Philip thought.

Was there such a thing as a sick house?

13

"Dad?" Jennifer opened the door wider to see her father still lying in bed. It was Saturday afternoon, nearly three p.m., and he'd retired to his bedroom immediately after breakfast, during which he'd barely spoken a word.

Grant lay on his side, crouched similarly to the way Philip had found him the night before. His back was to his daughter, although he had shifted slightly at the sound of her voice. Jennifer knew he was awake.

She noticed his water glass was nearly empty, which wasn't necessarily a sign that he'd been taking his medication. Still, however, she worried about his use of the morphine—it unquestionably could alter moods—while feeling assured it was helping to ease much of his increasing pain.

In what little time Jennifer found on her hands, she had done some checking up on the drug. Often used to help heroin users beat their addictions and for other less controversial medical treatments, the drug had also won longtime support for just the reason her father had gotten his prescription: pain treatment when nothing else would do, when fentanyl and other stronger drugs could be overkill, and when survivability was unlikely enough for the threat of addiction to matter very much.

Other side effects, however, concerned her. There was loss of appetite; she was seeing this here, and it was important for her father to eat when his body allowed him. Nausea and constipation? He could deal with those problems as they came, she knew. So could he handle the euphoria. But confusion, disorientation? That one bothered her enough to consider calling Dr. Bennett.

Too many strange things had been happening lately. Her husband didn't have to tell her about the medicine cabinet or the spice rack. Even with Carolyn to tend for, she cooked enough to notice when the salt or pepper moved from one shelf to another overnight. The baby's room frightened her the most. Occasionally a toy seemed to have made its way from the dresser to the crib, or the changing table to the dresser. She had regarded these occurrences as no more than lapses in her memory.

But that morning, she had taken Carolyn, along with the music box she'd found in the closet, into her room. She remembered that earlier, about three in the morning, the baby had awoken her and Philip. Having closed the door and opened the music box—Philip was a heavy sleeper—she'd sat on a bean-bag cushion beside the crib to nurse the baby while the music box played its gentle, soothing melody. In that several-minute interlude of believing the baby might or might not have fallen back to sleep, Jennifer had stared at the dancer and lost herself in the growing distance between each note of the melody. Too, she'd contemplated how the dancer twirled ever more slowly until she came to a halt, seemingly meeting Jennifer's eyes in appreciation for the attention.

Jennifer had even thought of the dancer as she herself fell back asleep, the pleasant tune slowing down with the windings of her own weary consciousness.

Hours later, back in her daughter's room, she had opened the box—to find the little brass ballerina frantically rotating with the music. It performed its lively dance but for an instant, when Jennifer's mouth dropped open and she slammed the box shut. Carolyn started to cry. Gasping, Jennifer clutched the baby against her and hurried out of the room.

Who had wound it up again?

Her husband, she knew, wouldn't have gone into the room to wind it. And her father hadn't left his bedroom, except for breakfast, since Philip helped him up the night before.

Or had he?

"Dad, you really should come down and have something to eat."

Grant turned onto his back but stared straight ahead after meeting her eyes for an instant. "I-I'm not hungry, thanks."

The look in his eyes revealed what she had suspected earlier: that his defenses were down. Way down. Her father, in his mind, had at least temporarily stopped fighting his illness. It was natural in mortal illness—in fact, she'd wondered how he had been so successful in combating the inevitable depressions. Perhaps the fact that he'd been doing so well made his present feelings all the lower.

"Dad, please...talk to me."

He closed his eyes, and Jennifer saw a tear stream down his cheek. She rushed to his side and wrapped her arms around him. "Dad...Daddy...it's okay. We love you. We're all...rooting for you, Daddy."

The tears came more easily now, his eyes already red from earlier. "I'm...I'm afraid, Jenny. I...don't know what's there..."

She pulled away, confusion apparent on her face. "What's there? What's where?"

"What's...out there. What I've thought was the...*great beyond.*"

Downstairs, the baby began to cry. Rather, she had been crying for a while, but Jennifer somehow hadn't noticed. Some mother I am, she thought. She could hear Philip's voice as he attempted to soothe the baby, probably with a bottle of formula. They'd decided to accustom the baby to formula as well as breast milk, in case Jennifer eventually decided to return, at some point, to another job like the one she'd had. After Carolyn got a little older. And her father...

"Daddy, it's still *there*. Why, you've always believed in God and the saints, in Heaven, in being good. You even got me and Phil sometimes going to Mass again. Wh-why should you think...there's nothing there waiting for you?"

Her father didn't answer. He dried the last tear from his face and turned back onto his side, mumbling that he'd be down sometime soon.

When she went downstairs, Jennifer found her husband looking very much at peace with his daughter. The baby sucked away at a small bottle of formula, her eyes half-closed as she lay in Philip's arms. He looked up at Jennifer's approach. "Shhh," he softly whispered.

Approaching the recliner, she sat down and leaned all the way back for perhaps the first time. She smiled at her husband, but it was a faint smile, the kind one wears without fully believing it belongs. The long rays of autumn reached into the window, bathing the wall of the dining room in a weak, yellow glow. From the boiler downstairs, the heat came steadily up to warm the house as much as they needed before winter came. In the chair she felt relaxed, wanting to take a nap herself. Another priority, however, was more at hand. One that made the fall, usually her favorite season, only a frightening time of loneliness and uncertainty.

She sighed, leaned forward and took a seat on the couch beside her husband and daughter. "Phil," she whispered.

He looked down at the baby, now asleep, then to his wife. "Yeah."

"What's...wrong with this house?"

It was his turn to sigh. Reaching over to a pacifier on the coffee table, he took the bottle out of Carolyn's mouth. Before the baby began to stir, he inserted the rubber end of the pacifier between her parting lips. "So I don't know, Jen. I have the feeling there's something...wrong. With the house, I mean. I don't know—"

"What could it be? I mean, I know what you're saying—I think. But it sounds like you think that house is..."

Phil shrugged. "Haunted?" he said with a nervous titter. There. He had said it. He didn't believe these things happened these days, if they ever did. Or, at least, he didn't want to believe it. But what else—

Jennifer, he saw, was hardly laughing at him. "The things happening," she said. "I don't think you could blame them on any one of us. I've found myself suspecting Dad, too, just as you did. Oh...Phil?"

"What?"

"Have you or my father been in Carolyn's room today?"

He started to stand, perhaps forgetting that *he* had the baby, then sat down again. "So what's...what's wrong with her room?"

"N-nothing! I...I mean..." She relayed the story of the music box to him and watched his face pale. "But I thought maybe my father went in and wound it up just for a minute before coming down."

"Not likely, from the way he looked." He was thinking something else. "Jen, where did you get this music box?"

"I-I found it in the closet in Carolyn's room. I think it was left here by the people who lived here before—"

He was nodding. "Ohhh, boy. Yep." He stood up and carried Carolyn upstairs to her crib. When he returned with the LCD baby monitor, he also held the music box. He set down the monitor and headed left. Toward the door.

"Phil, what are you—"

But he was out. Jennifer listened as her husband walked across toward the garage, lifted the lid of the old metal garbage can, dropped the box in with a dull clank, and closed the can. "I'll buy her another one," he said once back in the house.

"Phil, I *like* that music box. Why did you throw it away? There's nothing wrong with the thing itself. I said, I just thought maybe—"

"So Jennifer," he hissed, trying to keep his voice low, "I *emptied* that closet. I took out *everything* from those upper rooms, the *whole* damned house, and I remember taking that music box down, too. It was on the upper shelf, way in back. I'd put it in a big cardboard box, in the garage, with a bunch of other crap on top. There's no way it could have..." He trailed off and, shaking his head, sat down in the recliner.

Jennifer began to giggle despite herself, the situation too much to bear otherwise. "S-so what do we do? Do we call a medium? A priest? *Ghostbusters?* Are we...in danger? Is the baby?"

The thought alone made her leap off the couch. "I think maybe she shouldn't even be upstairs *alone.*"

She started upstairs but slowly returned. "We can't...keep her down with us every second," she said. "It would be wrong to just live in...fear of whatever this is. And this is why we have the monitor, anyway. It hasn't *really* hurt anybody. Maybe...I think maybe it can't."

Philip went into the kitchen and came back with a beer. "So you know," he began, "I keep thinking about these movies where people find their house is haunted. They see things, hear things—which we're not doing, not really. Nothing has come around and said 'Boo,' for whatever *that's* worth.

"But there always seems to come a time, always much longer than the audience would, when they say, 'Fuck this place'—"

"In so many words," his wife replied.

"Yeah, right. And they clear out and never come back. Don't get their things, just leave and do...what? So is it really so easy to just *leave* a two-hundred-grand house? I mean, what the hell are we supposed to do about it?"

"That's...what I'm asking, Phil."

Philip shrugged and took a long drink of his beer. "I guess we could put the house on the market," he said. "But so soon after that weird attack, I dunno. People remember things a bit longer than that, and they already thought the place was cursed or something before we moved in. And, if you remember, the realtor—I'd like to hang the smug bitch right now—did say the place had a *reputation*. She said it with such a chuckle that I'd..." He slapped the back of the sofa from behind. "Ha ha, big fucking joke."

"I-I forgot all about that."

"So there's another thing we have to consider. I hate bringing this up, though I guess I should've talked to you about this a long time ago."

"Which is?" Jennifer didn't drink, but at this point she was considering getting a beer herself.

"Um...I guess I've hinted at this, but...my luster at the company hasn't been quite the same since I botched that presentation on account of those missing materials. So I've done what I can, you know. Spoken up well at meetings, watched my end of the operation closely, sent the right memos to the right people at the right time— but somehow, I don't think I'm taken quite as seriously as when I was hired. At my interviews, I was Jim Garrett's golden boy, the bright new star who relocated from the faraway big city. Now? I don't know. The company went out of its way to help us settle here. I don't know how well they'd view the attention I'd have to pay to selling the house and getting a new one."

"I guess your mind is on the house more than you've been letting on," said Jennifer. "I didn't think about this much till a few days ago. And I didn't know I'd been wondering about things till your dry-cleaning slip turned up on Dad's workbench."

"Dad's workbench, yeah." He took another drink to empty the can. "So that workbench seems to have something to do with all this, doesn't it? The basement, anyway. It's where the slip turned up."

"And it's where you found my father."

"Yeah...with the lights out," added Philip. He got up, went to the kitchen and came back with another beer. "So Jen," he said, "there's something else I need to talk to you about. It has to do with the reason I went to the library last night." He came over and sat beside her on the couch.

"The library?" She dwelled on this for a moment. "I'd wondered what was so important that you had to run out like that...we had plenty of diapers."

"Yeah. I didn't believe the realtor's story about the nice, quiet family. Maybe...maybe it would've been better if I had."

* * *

There was something missing. Plenty, in fact. He was getting stupid in his old age, Grant thought. He had continued thinking about what Natalie's spirit had told him the night before. Yes, she had died in this house and for some reason was trapped in this world. He was being ridiculous, and perhaps the effects of the morphine had contributed as well. She was unable to move on to another "plane of existence," as he'd heard it called.

But the years...years of faith had taught him to look for the proof he needed, every day. The proof of God's promise. He saw it in the smiles of strangers. He saw it in the way things really did work out sometimes—or, at least, you could begin to understand if you studied a situation long enough. He saw it in nature, in the intricacy of the designs and instincts of the most minute animals, and in the sky at night, how there was just enough atmosphere to support life—with emptiness beyond. Grant even smelled it when neighbors lit their chimneys on autumn evenings. Fine enough to permeate agnostic lungs, he remembered once commenting to someone.

With a sigh, he decided it was time to get up, to head first for the bathroom and then downstairs, to apologize to his daughter. He'd try to eat a little something to tide him over till dinner; that should help.

Then, if he felt up to it and Natalie came back, he'd try to have another talk with her.

On his way out of the bathroom, however, he heard Philip and Jennifer talking in the living room. He gripped the banister for support and noticed, for the first time, that a few of the balusters partway up the stairs were newer than those of the railing above. Funny thing, that. Even more interesting was what Philip was saying about what he'd uncovered at the library.

"...a whole folder on what happened here a few years before we moved in. I didn't want to tell you this, but...I think I'd better. You see, the last people who lived here, the real Leffingwell family...well, they died here. The husband was a really mean son of a bitch who beat his wife and their daughter. They got into a big drag-out fight, and there was a gun they had around, I guess for burglars. He maybe started firing—the facts aren't clear—and she seemed to get it away from him and shot him. The kid was in her room on the other side of the wall, leaning against the headboard. She'd been beaten up pretty bad that night and might even have been unconscious. One bullet...went through the wall and got her, too. The stories go that the wife...left the bedroom and fell—or threw herself—down the stairs."

"Oh, my God!" was all Jennifer could say.

They sat in silence, their arms wrapped around each other, and the mood broke only at the sound of Grant coming, not so easily, down the stairs.

"D-Daddy!" Jennifer ran up and helped her father down the rest of the way. "How do you feel?"

Her father shrugged and managed a weak smile. "Been better, I guess. But I think I could say the same about you two."

Philip pulled away from his wife. "What do you mean?"

"Sorry to eavesdrop. I might be able to help, though. You see, I think I've..." He went no further. In a flash, Grant realized that, owing to the morphine he'd taken, anything he might say about the night before would sound like so much gibberish. An old man spouting ghost stories, even to two people primed for just such talk? It wasn't the time.

He was better off talking to the spirit himself again—to help her, however he could, and his family in the process. "Oh, never mind. I was just seeing a connection between the things that happened here before and...I guess, the things that are happening now."

Philip gave a smirk and took another drink. "So that's what we've been talking about. We think the place is...well, haunted. It's stupid, I know. But we can't explain anything that's going on in any other way. Something is just plain weird about the place, we dunno."

"It's all just too strange, Dad. I'm worried about what to do, whether Carolyn is in any danger, whether—"

Upstairs the baby started crying, and Jennifer beat her husband to the stairs and ran up. When she appeared at the top of the stairs, Carolyn in her arms, Philip sighed and went back to the living room.

"Pretty good sprinting for a few months after delivery," Grant commented, referring to his daughter.

"Good old mama-bear adrenaline," Philip replied, downing the rest of his beer. "So I'm at a disadvantage. I had to find the stairs first."

"Think you...might be overdoing it a little?"

Philip leaned forward on the couch, anger in his eyes. "Yes, I am overdoing it. Yes, I *know* I am overdoing it. But damn it, tonight I think I have the right."

Grant merely shrugged, wondering how well his son-in-law would have fared the night before at carrying him up to his room if he'd been drinking then. With those creaky basement steps, it's possible the house would've had two more ghosts dwelling there.

On that matter, his eyebrows rose as a new thought hit him: If there were three deaths, why was there only one ghost?

He had so much to learn tonight.

14

Grant O'Keefe was not the only one who had been listening to the living room conversation. Natalie had been learning to conceal her omnipresent chill whenever necessary, weakening the once-inevitable effect it had upon anyone near. It was a handy power, one of many she'd found at her disposal over the year she'd spent alone in the Leffingwell house.

Her house.

The child was attentive to the Carters' references to her. But she was hardly sympathetic to their predicament. She didn't like how the father raised his voice and cursed; it was all too familiar. She remained furious over his treatment of her family's belongings, the way he'd run all about the day they moved in and treated them like so much garbage, piling almost everything up in the garage.

And now that he was drinking, she loathed him even more. Though her father hadn't been a drinker, Natalie remembered his temper like it was yesterday. In Philip, she was seeing anger, frustration, aggression—everything that, once before, had turned this house into a hell for her and her mother.

Time had begun to harden what had once been a nine-year-old girl. Her development, the natural maturation of young girl into blossoming preteen, had halted completely at the moment of her death. The desires of a nine-year-old girl reigned over her as they do any living child of a similar age. But the usual rules, imposed by grownups, restrained her no longer.

Rules meant beatings, and nobody would hurt her ever again. If they tried, well, she would hurt back. Natalie considered her treatment of Aunt Sarah, during a visit so soon after her family's tragedy, as little more than an accident; the girl had gotten caught up in the moment, reveling in her discovery of such power and enjoying the mean woman's dance. She'd felt some slight regret over the boy on Halloween, the egg-tosser, but had later shrugged it off. The two boys at the door a minute before had been nice; she'd have liked the older one as a playmate. And when she watched what followed, she simply...lost a little control, she supposed. Still, it was fun.

The previous Halloween, less than a year before her death, a similar gang of boys had hit her in the head with an egg. She had gone home sopping wet, having tried to wash the egg out of her hair, and off her jacket and pants, using a neighbor's garden hose. And with her cheek stinging from a smack in the face—"I'll teach you to come home soaked!"—her father had sent her to bed without supper, let alone a single bite of Halloween candy.

Nobody would do that to her again.

Perched on the railing of the second-floor landing—a hazardous spot for the typical child—Natalie recalled the immediate aftermath of her and her parents' deaths. Recalled the time before her grief turned to anger, a child's black and white judgment that accepted no excuses.

* * *

The house had lain empty, the police and medical personnel long ago having removed the bodies and made all the notes they were going to make on their clipboards. Two smoking policemen stood watch outside; one stared blankly at a flapping end of the fluorescent yellow ribbon they'd tied to slim pine stakes to cordon off the property.

The two men joked nervously, neither of them relishing their assignments but admitting it was better than making drug busts miles away in the city. The action was all over, after all. All that remained were the imagined echoes—and the memory of the woman who had hurtled down the stairs from the second-floor landing.

What neither man could hear were the sobs of the nine-year-old girl who still called for her mother, even her father, as she lay across her bed. The indentation of her body had remained on the blood-soaked bedsheet, and it was no coincidence that Natalie's spirit filled the exact depressions in the bed that her body, now at the morgue, had made.

She was alone, and through the foggy shroud of her grief came questions regarding her predicament. Her mother had explained that when you died, you went to Heaven if you were good and obeyed your mother and father. If you weren't good, well, there was a bad place where you went.

What kind of girl stayed in her room, by herself, and went to neither place?

She began to cry again and eventually thought to kneel down beside her bed—her hands, of course, would not rest on the edge of the bed but rather melted in—and say her prayers the way she'd been taught.

Her parents could not hear her. Could God?

And where were her parents? Surely they went somewhere when...they died. Yet she had not. Was it...because she had not made it back in time? Because she had broken the rules?

"It's not fair! *It's not fair!* It's not fair! It's not...faaaiiir..." Her voice made no echo in the still room.

Outside, the sun was rising. In the next room, the electronic alarm clock went off, its rhythmic beeping all that remained of life as Natalie knew it. The girl jumped, and a brief smile came to her face. Every moment she expected to hear her father's hand slam down upon its button. *Now* it would happen. Now—no, *now* he would do it!

Her game grew tiring as another wave of loneliness swept across her. She hadn't wanted to leave her room, still unwilling to view the wreckage of the previous evening. She hadn't wanted even to glimpse the blood she knew would be everywhere, considering the last fight her parents must have had. But she also couldn't stay in her room forever.

Forever...?

Again she cried, the alarm beep continuing, and this time didn't stop until more policemen showed up to look around some more.

"What the hell is *that?*" one of them asked himself aloud.

Both of them, however, knew exactly what it was. Neither spoke until they climbed the stairs, and one went into the room to shut off the alarm. He paused to wipe his brow, realizing what room he was in, and looked up at his partner. "Creepy shit," he said.

His partner shivered. "Cold breeze—damn cold. Went through me!"

"Breeze?" It's hot as hell in here. You...oh, yeah. Yeah. Hoooo, there it is! Damn! I'm freezing. One minute I'm sweating, next...shit, man, we only came in to check the place out—it checks out, okay? Let's book!"

"Fine with me, buddy."

"Don't go away!" Natalie was saying as the pair headed for the door. "Dooooon't go awaa-hay-hay..." She had only wanted to be near them. To listen to their voices, to look at their uniforms and just...be with them. Natalie had even, she hadn't noticed, *walked* down the hall from her room. Floating was the way you did ghosting, a game she no longer wanted to play. And where she could walk, she wanted to walk from now on.

Of those children who did have the power to leave their bodies temporarily, they rarely did so during daylight hours. The night, after all, offered more chance for uninterrupted play. The day was taking forever, a word Natalie didn't like to think about. She was thinking less about her parents and the loneliness, but was running into new things that made her want to cry at every turn.

She couldn't explain it, but she felt thirsty. Natalie sat on the kitchen table—its chairs were pushed in—and stared at the refrigerator. She was thinking about lemonade. About cold milk, and milkshakes, and plain old ice water. She hadn't thought enough about how nice it felt to have a cool drink running down your throat, and the reality of being denied such simple pleasures brought the tears, at least the impulse to cry, anew.

A moth had found its way in with the policemen's entry hours before, and Natalie soon grew bored and frustrated cupping her hands over its fluttering wings, only to have it pass through. She did notice, however, that the insect seemed to know she was there—it never landed, even near the light, and it moved as if chased by an enemy. That cheered Natalie; any acknowledgment was better than none.

On the windowsill she lay down her arm. On this kind of sunny day, if she'd kept her arm there long enough she would eventually feel a warmth that told her that her skin was tanning. She soon grew tired of waiting; truth was, she didn't want to wait long enough to be reminded the sun would never again be the same friend.

The metal pantry door had a particularly loud slam if you flung it closed from a half-closed position. Natalie acted out opening the door and giving it a swing; she shut her eyes and pretended it had slammed.

"Who did that!" she shouted, pretending to be her father. She rushed over to the doorway and hunched her shoulders, drooping her head gorilla-like and looking in the direction of the cabinet. "How many times do I have to tell you, brat, you don't slam that *cabinet!*" Natalie grinned. She ran over to where she'd been standing, cocked her head and looked up innocently.

"But Daddy, I didn't mean to..."

She ran back to the doorway and assumed the same apelike stance. "I didn't ask you what you *meant* to do, you little..." Her game trailed off. She was staring at the dishwasher, its dent barely perceptible in the sunlight that streamed in. The console knobs that so brutally dug into her side only the evening before glistened as she stared. They seemed to say, *Come closer, dear, you don't have to be afraid of me, just come a little closer,* the way an old man—the police had caught him last year—used to approach kids at the schoolyard.

She also could no longer ignore the trail of blood that started in a little dried pool near the hanging phone receiver and led toward the office room. She wanted to mop it up, but she couldn't do that, either.

The cuckoo crowed five o'clock as she felt the memory of another dry tear on her cheek. "I...I *hate* you, Daddy. You got...*so mean* to us. I'm glad you're dead, and you're not in Heaven with Mommy. I know it, I know it."

* * *

Once the sun had fully set, Natalie went up to her roof, atop its chimney, to watch for a friend to pass near. Not an evening had passed, of those nights she'd gone exploring, that she hadn't seen someone. Gerald and Jasper, in fact, seemed to be out every night.

An hour passed, then two. It had to be past nine o'clock, she thought, and still nobody came near. The only living things she saw, she knew to be adults and, therefore, no one who could hear her.

Another hour passed, and Natalie left her post to check the clock in her parents' bedroom: it was a quarter to ten. Where was everyone? Sitting on the roof had to be the best lookout, but...maybe it was time she did some searching for her friends. She felt most comfortable at home, empty as it was. It was the only constant that remained for her, the place she felt closest to her mother. But she'd have to leave it behind for a while, if only to see where everyone was.

Her first stop was at the Harpers', across the street; Natalie had seen Giselle, the adopted girl, playing in her father's pickup truck the first night she'd gone ghosting, and they'd played together twice at night since then.

Natalie stopped at the front door. She had walked across the street, as if she were going for a real life visit. She sighed, and now stood hesitatingly at the front door. Looking at the knocker.

No, stupid, she told herself. You don't *knock* at the door, you just go in. You don't even have to use the door. You just...go in.

She pushed her head through, just a peek, before entering. The memory of the chill the policemen had felt stayed in the back of her mind, and if she had been responsible for it, she would be better off keeping her distance from the far end of the room.

She saw the Harpers' family room and spied Giselle sitting on the floor with a comic book and a teddy bear. Her father sat in a worn easy chair, watching television; her mother sat at the kitchen table, within view, working on a laptop beside some papers. She was an accountant, the visitor recalled, whatever that was.

Nobody stirred when Natalie stepped fully into the room. The girl wanted to attract Giselle's attention, but knew she was powerless unless her friend left her parents and decided to leave her body behind for a few hours. Maybe she just doesn't want to go out tonight, Natalie reasoned. Giselle wasn't out *every* night that Natalie had been; maybe she had just decided to stay home.

Natalie stood there for ten minutes, merely watching while the Harpers spoke little to one another. When they did, it concerned the weather, the national news, baseball. Finally Giselle's mother raised her head from her work.

"But what about the bruises?"

Giselle's father's head snapped up. "Bev, I said this isn't the *time* to talk about this. We've already talked about this enough, we've scared Gissie enough already, and I think we should—Giselle." He looked at the hour on the grandfather clock. "You should have gone to bed a while ago."

Natalie recognized the look in her friend's eyes.

"Daddy, please let me stay up longer, please, please let me. Just for tonight." Her straight blonde hair fell across the tattered comic book, which she obviously had read several times before.

"But you have school tomorrow, Honey. You need your sleep."

"Daddy, please..."

"Bert, it's okay. Just for tonight, Gissie."

Natalie decided to leave before the hitting began, the beatings she knew just had to follow. In her rush to move along, she missed Bert Harper's "Well, all right..." as she passed through the front door.

Sandra Berkow, who had helped the group of children trace the route back to town the night before, should've been outside that night, Natalie decided. She was a math whiz at school, which was bad enough for forming friendships. She also had a deathly fear of the class cloakrooms, among other problems, having been locked in a closet for several hours by a burglar who had found her alone in the house one night. Sandra felt safe only when she was apart from her body, and sought escape each night from the need to lie awake in her darkened room until she fell asleep from exhaustion.

Natalie walked outside to the Berkows' backyard; perhaps Sandra was swinging from the big sycamore they had in the back. She was startled by a huge German shepherd—she'd forgotten they had a dog. For a moment she ran back around the side of the house, then caught herself and remembered the beast couldn't hurt her.

She returned to the backyard, and again the dog lunged. It stopped a few feet away, however, and resumed its loud barking. A few nearby windows lit up, one of which was on the second floor of the Berkows'. Natalie took another step toward the dog. It was strange to feel no fear of a dog that had once nearly bit her. The dog was still barking, but as she advanced the bark became more like a whimper. Backing off now, the dog didn't bark at all. It was...afraid of her. Deathly afraid.

"There," Natalie said. She followed the hound to the opening in its doghouse, one Sandra's father had built too small, years ago, having misjudged how large the dog would grow. She chuckled at the panicked whining coming from within. *"So you do still fit,"* she commented.

"Rogue, you stop that noise now! Stop it, boy." The voice was Sandra's, and the girl slammed the window shut. Natalie wouldn't walk upstairs—she was too curious. She floated up to her friend's window and peered within.

Sandra was sitting, in the dark, on her bed, her back against the wall. She curled her arms around her crouched legs and stared, trembling, out the window. Toward the moon. She was crying.

Natalie had had several stops she'd wanted to make, but it was too difficult for her to piece together what she'd already seen. She had to see Gerald next. His house was a few blocks away, in the direction of school, but what was distance, especially now? She had to find a way of reaching him, and he of all people would be out tonight.

While the little girl had felt safe on her nights of floating high above the neighborhood, walking outside late at night—or what she called walking—frightened her as it had in life. Large hedges could still hide bad men who took away kids, and vans driving slowly down the street still seemed like cruising "preverts," as the boys in school called them.

It would take a long time before she realized that she was not only denied the simple pleasures of life, such as sucking a cold chocolate shake through a straw. She also was invulnerable to life's hazards.

A car passed by, and Natalie stuck out her hand as it passed by; as she expected, the car passed cleanly through it. Natalie thought of the stories she'd been told about why you shouldn't stick your hand out a moving car. Next was the ultimate test: when another car approached, Natalie stood in the center of the street. Her every instinct was to run, jump, anything, but she managed to hold her ground and keep her eyes open as this car, too, passed through and continued down the street. Natalie watched the taillights until a curve in the road took the car around a bend. Maybe, she supposed, the driver felt a brief chill at this point in the road.

Gerald's fence was ahead, and she passed through and into the yard. Jasper, in his doghouse, emitted a low growl. She passed around him, watching his eyes upon her as she circled. The cellar door was closest to her, a good place to start looking.

She slipped inside, saw the bare concrete floor upon which an exercise mat and a weightlifting bench were arranged. A workbench leaned against one corner—Natalie didn't want to look at it—and the car, in the adjoining garage, was empty.

Passing up to the next floor, she spotted what had to be Gerald's parents sitting in opposite chairs, not speaking a word to each other. It looked like they'd had a fight, and Natalie left that room, too.

Upstairs Gerald's older brother, Mark, sat on the upper bunk, one leg hanging over the side, as he talked on his cell to someone who sounded like a girl.

"He don't mean nothing by it, Chloe, he just was saying, like, guys, well, they just say things sometimes, and—you know I didn't say, like 'You're right, Jimmy,' or nothing like that. It was just, like, *talk!* You know? No, I didn't *agree* with him. What do you mean, I nodded when he said it. You had a freakin' video man there or somethin'? Chloe...Chloe...I'm sorry, I didn't mean that, I just—"

Gerald lay motionless in the bottom bunk.

Natalie ran over.

"Shit, it's gotten cold in here, lemme..." Gerald's brother pulled a comforter over himself and brought the dangling leg up to warm it also. "I'm sorry I said 'shit,' Chloe.... I didn't mean it, I was just surprised...What do you mean, 'I said it again?' How are you supposed to know what I'm sorry about? Geez..."

Natalie leaned over his body, but she could not tell whether her friend was merely asleep or if he—

"Natalie," came a voice from behind her. In spirit form, there was no stuttering.

She spun around, ecstatic that Gerald—his spirit—could see her and that he had spoken her name. Without thinking, she ran to embrace him.

"Uhhhhh..." He was backing away.

"Wh-what's the matter, Gerald? What's the matter with *everyone* around here!"

"You shouldn't *be* here." Gerald's eyes were wide, and he shuffled nervously from one foot to the other, looking past her.

"What do you mean? I was outside looking for you, looking for all...of our friends...outside."

"Nobody's outside. Nobody *will* go...ever again. And I won't go outside this way. I shouldn't even be...ghosting at all tonight. I don't think I'm gonna do it anymore."

"But...why?"

"Natalie, go home. Go...somewhere."

"Geraaald, why?" She made a motion toward him, and again he backed away. "Gerald?"

He was crying. "Get out of my way!"

"Out of your w—" Natalie had positioned herself between Gerald's spirit and his body.

"No!" she said. "Not until you tell me why everybody is afraid to go outside."

"They're not afraid. They just don't wanna do it anymore...that's all. Now move!"

"No! Why *don't* they want to do it?"

"Because of *you!* Now move!" He charged at her and she instinctively jumped out of his way. He jumped back into his body but, now that he was safe, kept the upper part of his spirit outside. "You think we can still play with you? You think we can go outside with you out there waiting for us?"

Now Natalie was crying; she rubbed at her eyes though no tears rolled down her face. "W-why not?"

Gerald, half in and half out of his body, shook his spirit head in frustration. "What's the matter with you? Why can't you just leave me alone?"

"Gerald, I just—"

"Natalie, just go away! You don't get it, you're *dead,* don't you know? You're dead! You're dead—oh, shit, just..."

Gerald returned fully into his body, and Natalie was left with only his brother's monotone. "...so Saturday, what time? Aw, c'mon, I promise to be a *gentleman,* yeah, yeah..."

Natalie's last friend in the world lay on his bed, pretending to ignore the intense chill in the room. Before rolling over to face the wall, he pulled up his comforter.

15

"Damn this dishwasher!"

Jennifer heard the kick from the dining room and turned around in time to see her husband shove in the dish rack and slam the door shut.

"Phil..." In the living room the baby was crying, obviously agitated by all the banging and shouting coming from the kitchen. Grant, close by, wanted to pick her up, to hold her against his chest, to take her upstairs where it was quiet. Quieter, anyway. But he didn't trust himself to keep his grip. Tonight, it was bad. He'd taken the biggest dose he dared of his medication, and his insides were nevertheless ignoring its potency as though he'd taken Tylenol.

You need insides for the drug to act upon, son.

He resigned himself to remaining on the couch, crouched over as much as he could while keeping an eye on the kicking, shrieking baby in the infant seat they'd detached from the stroller.

And rocking her in motion with his own convulsed spasms.

"Damn thing, why won't it ever close right? So y'see these goddamn little wheels just roll right in when they sell you the fuckin' thing, and now with a few dishes it just—"

"Phil, please stop—"

"Grant! Would you pick up Carolyn or something?" Philip hollered from the doorway of the kitchen. "Try to concentrate on something, like closing the damn dishwasher, and you just can't—"

Jennifer placed, nearly dropped, the last dinner plate back onto the dining room table and stormed into the kitchen. "Philip," she gasped, her voice lowered in her anger, "just get the *hell* out of this kitchen. You are so *ripped* you don't know what you're doing." She wiped away sweat from her brow; the boiler's heat was coming up with a fury tonight! Or was it just her mounting sense of helplessness bringing on the anger at her husband? For all intents and purposes, he was useless against anything this...thing might think up tonight.

"So I'm just trying to do a little housewo—"

"Go. I don't need a drunk in my kitchen."

"*Your* kitchen? Now I need an invitation to come into the—"

That was it. "Philip, get out! Just get out of my sight. I'm scared tonight—really scared! I need you with me more than I ever did before, and what...what do you do? You go for beer after beer and get wasted!" She was crying now, but she didn't care. "W-what am I supposed to do? Are *you* going to watch over us?"

Philip took another drink from a fresh one and, without answering, carried it past her into the small office off the living room. There was a love seat there, too, which was where Jennifer was sure he'd end up before long.

On the other side of the wall, Grant's hands trembled as he tried once more to insert a pacifier into the baby's mouth. He...he kept missing, his hands were so bad off. Was it nerves over what he felt was surely approaching? Of course, he'd been wrong about the arrival of death once before. Or was it merely residue from yesterday's frustrations?

A real man can handle his tools.

There was that voice again, he realized. He thought about whose it was for a few moments with as much concentration as his pain allowed him. Then it hit him. He realized, of course, that it was his own. He was full of snide common-sense quips to direct at himself, always had been. They reminded him of who he was, kept him in line.

Keep your head on straight, too, mister.

He looked into the baby's eyes, what little he could see as Carolyn cried, and tried once more to reach over with the pacifier. Goodness knows she needed more than that with all the shouting those two had been doing in the kitchen. It hurt too much to move his arm this time, hurt in the chest area.

"H-heeere's the tucky, Carolyn. Here it is, Honey. Just take the tucky..." he said—but stared, incredulous, as it was slowly wrested from his hand. It drifted quickly over and plunged into the baby's mouth.

"Natalie," he whispered. "Natalie, no..." He couldn't see her, though she was there. But the cold! He hadn't known of her approach; even in his occupied state, he'd have felt that intense cold. It wasn't there, yet she was.

And now she was brushing her hand over the infant's brow. Gently rocking the seat, too. Grant could even hear faint cooing sounds as Carolyn's eyes closed: first only for an instant, then for an entire second. The argument died down for a minute in the kitchen—either that, or they were now wrestling on the floor. That was all it took. The baby turned her head and was out.

"Natalie," he whispered, "you shouldn't do that." But it worked! This dead...child had been the calming force necessary to quiet the baby.

Grant watched as the thin, light hair on the baby's head flattened and rose at the touch of the spirit. She shouldn't be doing this, he was thinking. Oh, God! Get away from that baby! You... "Natalie, no," he whispered, about as loud a voice as he could muster.

He felt a touch on his ear, heard the voice and froze in terror at the stark logic of the spirit's explanation.

"It's okaay, baby knowss mee..."

* * *

Was it pride? He didn't know. But Grant had waited till his daughter took the baby upstairs to her room before he attempted to rise from his position against an arm of the recliner. She knew he was in trouble, had to know by now. But he'd been keeping to himself as much as he could—mostly to avoid the doting attention.

Don't need no help to die, thanks.

Right. The way he saw it, it was his job, not Phil's, to protect the family. He'd realized that, over the weeks since they'd moved in, the ghost had gotten bolder in many ways. Her familiarity with the baby—and vice versa—made that quite clear. Shockingly clear, though he should have expected it. Every little girl loves to see babies, after all. Why should she be any different?

This, however, was no ordinary girl. She could be vengeful, he had no doubt. He had to win her over before he left for...wherever. He wasn't sure how, but there was one thing he also felt he knew.

That tonight would be his last chance.

He slumped out of the chair and was surprised at how weak his legs were. The blood, perhaps, had all traveled up to his vital organs, which were fighting for their very existence. No wonder he couldn't walk so well.

Catching hold of first the edge of the couch, then an unsteady pole lamp, Grant passed Philip's office on the way to the small half-bathroom next door. A glance, all he got of his son-in-law, saw the drunken man draped half over the edge of the secondhand sofa. Good thing you're out cold, Phil...this one's gonna be a doozy.

He barely made it into the room when it came, the flood he'd felt coming up for the past half hour—or perhaps since Natalie had whispered in his ear. He knelt over the toilet and let it come, the onrush colored brown from the steak dinner, deep red from the battle waging within him. When he finished he tried to stand, felt too weak, and leaned back against the door, his chest turning inside out. He closed his eyes, felt his own sweat mingling with his tears. Lord, take me tonight, but please...not in a bathroom.

In his fog, he slowly realized he hadn't closed the door behind him; yet he was leaning against it. And the swirling sounds he was hearing were those of the toilet flushing. A wad of toilet paper was running around the edge of the toilet.

She was cleaning up after him.

"Natalie...Natalie, you...you don't have to do that..."

The toilet stopped after another flush but more water was running. The faucet, it sounded like. Grant opened his eyes to see...what?

Water, literally floating in the air before his face. Natalie...the little girl. She was cupping an invisible hand to give him a drink of water.

His first instinct was revulsion—he couldn't drink from *those* hands. She was death! Yet...water was life. He wouldn't drink from a corpse, which was what it had to feel like. To...taste!

But of course he drank, one helping after another as the spirit went for refills, drank until he felt he might bring this up, too. He wiped his parched lips and swallowed, but not easily. "You're...you're a good girl, Natalie," he said but received no reply. He tried to get up, this time with her aid; she seemed far stronger than a nine-year-old girl. He found the doorknob and, leaning against what he sensed was her shoulder—any support would serve at this point—made his way to the recliner.

Could he talk to her now? He craned his neck to look upstairs. Jennifer hadn't come back down, it seemed. And, again, Philip had to be still out cold in the love seat.

"I-I'm dying," he whispered. "You know that."

Her hand touched his shoulder. God! To have a...lost soul at his deathbed! He longed for the presence of his daughter. Even for Philip, drunk as he was. Not...but he needed her here. Her alone. It could be no other way.

"I doon't wwant you to die..."

It hurt to shrug, but Grant managed. "The good Lord w-wants me, it seems. N-Natalie. Y-you helped an old man. I...want to help you. I don't know how."

She suddenly clenched his trembling hand, seemingly releasing her control over her surroundings. The chill returned with a fury. Grant stiffened at his proximity to the child's spirit. "N-N-Nata-Nat..." A moment later it was gone—the room again grew intensely warm.

And Natalie appeared before him, a child kneeling at his feet with longing in her eyes. He couldn't see her well in the light of the living room, but what he could see was all he needed.

A bluish, transparent tear was running down her face.

"Taake me..."

"Hmm?"

"Take mee wwith you..."

"Natalie, I—"

"Please..."

This wasn't going to be easy. "I'll try. N-Natalie," he said, "I've—I've never done this b-before...I...I don't know what to expect. All I can say is, I'll try."

He could see her nodding in acceptance, could feel the touch of her hand. True, the chill had dispersed across what must have been a very wide area. Still, however, he could feel the *wrongness* of what gripped his hand. These two hands were tightened on his with the intensity of a young child. Nevertheless, they were the hands of age, of great age. Of death. But he could not, must not, recoil from them. Like the water he took from the same hands, minutes before, to keep up his strength, now he must treat her as he would any other child. To keep up the strength of his family.

"N-Natalie, please tell me h-how you came to be...a spirit."

It took some energy on her part, the old man could tell. But after she began to speak, Natalie seemed to be able to overcome even more of the great differences between their two planes of being. Always stretched out and with letters dropped from the beginnings of words, her words began to sound more and more like those of a living girl, which was frightening in itself.

What was even more frightening to him was the concept of "ghosting."

He wondered if the haze of pain and disorientation was clouding his understanding of what she was saying. "Y-you mean some children...have the power to leave their bodies? They are alive, but for a time, they live...as spirits? Natalie...you wouldn't...play games with a dying man."

"No. Only some kiids. N-not the happy ones."

"You said...your father killed you. You were out playing late...you said. And when you came home—"

"Was out ghostiing!"

"You were out gho—then you were home all the time. Your father came in your room and shot you while you lay in your bed. I fixed the hole a couple of weeks ago."

"Ghosting, you know when theere's daanger. He shot through the wall and..."

"And?" Natalie, however, was suddenly staring straight ahead, a look of stark terror on her face.

"Noooo..." she was saying.

"N-Natalie?"

"MY MOTHER! MY MOOTHER DID IT! My mother killed mee! She had the gun! It was my mother, but she didn't meean to! She didn't meean to! She..." The spirit leaned her head against Grant's lap, and it passed through for an instant before she withdrew it, withdrew altogether for a moment.

She vanished, and all Grant knew of her presence was a faint sobbing. This wasn't working out very well, and he wondered how much longer he could hold out. His eyes were growing heavier by the minute, and his attention span was growing so weak that he even could ignore the nightmarish feel of her head the moment it passed into the same space as his leg. He otherwise might have vomited; that surely was the proper reaction. But there was nothing left anyway to bring up, no surprises left for him. He wondered: where was Jenny? Upstairs, probably cooling down from her argument and sitting as close to the baby as possible. And Phil? Easy answer. Even if Grant died in this chair, he would hear the drunk when he stumbled out of the little office.

"Natalie."

She gradually reappeared before him, still sobbing.

"Natalie, I think you're...a very brave little girl to have gone through what you have. I want you to know I admire you...very much."

"Not brave. Not me."

"Y-yes, you are. But please listen to me. I don't have much more time. Stay close to me. When I go, you will see me...my soul, I guess, come out, go somewhere—up, I pray, though I'm sure...directions really don't matter as...much as we think.

"Where I go, you follow. Stay with me, and don't let go for anything. Got it?"

Nodding, Natalie floated up onto the chair. Onto his lap. And stared into his eyes, waiting for the moment.

Again Grant felt the revulsion, the vile, sickly churning in his stomach at his closeness to this long-dead child. But he was already going through too much on the inside. He'd felt blood welling up in the back of his mouth minutes before; Natalie was hardly to blame for that. Now, he could taste its first drops as they slipped out the corner of his mouth and ran down the side of his jaw. What a sight I must be, he thought. His mind was clouding up. It was coming, he could feel it.

What if...? "Natalie." He hardly recognized his grunting voice.

The spirit kept her gaze fixed on his.

"N-Natalie, I don't know...if this...works. If it...doesn't, promise me...promise to be good to...my family.... Please...promise..."

His head dropped down to his chin, and Natalie poised for action. This was it! She would follow him to Heaven, she would see her mother and would tell her Mommy, Mommy, I know you didn't mean to do it, it was an accident, I love you Mommy and—

Movement. She stared as...as it happened! The old man's spirit, his soul he called it, was beginning to rise up high, up from his body. And he was looking at her, extending his hand, saying Come, Natalie. She reached up to grab for the hand.

"Goddamn!" came a voice.

Natalie jumped—her father was behind her! Her father had somehow—

139

But when she turned her head for a mere instant, the little girl saw only Philip, who had rolled off the love seat and lay contorted on the floor of the office.

"Natalie! Try! Try!" The old man called after her but he was rising not of his own power, going up, up, over the roof, up high into the sky. Natalie raced after him.

Past the clouds in the dark November night came an opening in the sky—a doorway of sorts, a parting in the bluish curtain that was only light. Intense light. Grant was heading right for it, and like no soul ever hurtled toward eternity, the old man spread out his limbs as though doing so would provide wind resistance to his spirit. He leaned back to beckon Natalie along. Come on! Come on! You can make it! You can make it!

She rushed onward after him and watched, helpless, as he passed into the light. "Pull me in! Pull me in!" she screamed but the gateway was closing behind him. Squinting, she rushed the gate and tried to pry apart its opening. It was too strong for her—she couldn't do it! When she began to try again, an arm rushed out from between the gates. It was Grant's! He groped for her; she grabbed his hand with one of hers and tried even to latch on with the other hand but the closing was shutting her out, squeezing even the arm that had passed through. The little girl felt her grip loosen—become loosened—by forces she could not understand, by a Heaven that did not recognize her as one who deserved entry.

When she found herself fully alone in the night sky, she began to cry and found she had no tears. There was only anger.

16

Thank God for Carolyn! thought Jennifer. Generally docile except when hungry, tired or otherwise uncomfortable, the infant squirmed against her mother's shoulder, rendering her too distracted even to think much about where she was. Where the two of them and, until moments ago, Philip had been for hours.

The stream of people had been fairly steady. Well-wishers, some of them in tears, approached her with arms open. Because of the child, they refrained from throwing their arms around their beloved friend's daughter. This was just as well, for, try as she did, Jennifer was too shaken up to know or care who most of them might be. To the relatives she did know—there were indeed many despite how far from home she'd moved—Jennifer spoke a few words about her father and, gratefully, changed the subject to her baby at the slightest question.

Am I being ungrateful, Daddy? She had wept earlier before the open casket, a tear dripping on the edge of the silken padding. She had whispered that question to his lifeless body moments before Philip laid a hand on her shoulder, strengthening her till she could finish her prayer. No, she could not think too much about her father. For to dwell on his death was to relive again and again the sight of his head cocked unnaturally against the vinyl seam of the recliner...the drying stream of blood that had slipped out between his lips in his last breaths.

And, for Jennifer, the most painful thought of all: However sick he was, had he truly died a natural death?

No, she would use her fussing child as an excuse to change subjects, to leave the viewing room, to go anywhere away from these well-meaning friends and relatives who could not but further stir her fears.

At one point in the late afternoon, shortly after Philip drove off to pick up a few groceries for dinner, she reached the point at which she had to excuse herself. By some coincidence, Carolyn was hungry as well. Jennifer, over the past day or so, had taken to nursing her baby exclusively—putting aside the occasional bottle. She did it, she'd realized, because she lately needed the intimacy as much as her daughter did. Her actions lay at the heart of her family's survival of the events that had been rocking their household. Their unity, only their unity, would help them weather the crisis.

By memory alone, she carried the baby past the sliding divider and into the hallway. Jennifer barely looked where she was going but nevertheless found the break in another divider that led to an empty viewing room she'd used earlier that day. God! How could she endure this for another full day?

She opened a few buttons of her black blouse once she reached the end of the back row. Here it was quiet. Carolyn anxiously cupped her lips over her mother's nipple and began sucking, loudly at first.

Jennifer gazed at her child's busy facial muscles, her puffed cheeks filling with mouthfuls of this nourishing fluid before swallowing. Eventually, the rhythmic sucking motions lulled her into a near-sleep. For these moments, all the world was her and this child.

The woman herself drifted. Drifted. Until a sound alerted her, something in the room she had been hearing for...how long? The muffled recording of organ music often used in the background during viewing. It had to be coming from another room. Yet it was not. It was...

The lights in the room had brightened; had someone turned them up? Her mind was still not clear, but she was making out something at the head of the room—not centered but off to the side. A closed coffin. It shook on its covered stand. Flower displays nearby tottered as if blown by a sharp wind in this windowless room. A gasp froze in her throat, and Jennifer wanted to leave. Her legs would not obey. The baby sensed her mother's terror and cried out with Jennifer when the coffin lid flew open and a woman sat up, a beautiful blonde-haired woman dressed in a pink dress. She sat up straight and held out her arms...toward nothing. No—the woman began to turn toward Jennifer, her arms beckoning, and stepped to the floor. Over and over again she said something Jennifer could not understand. When the woman faced her, Jennifer made out the words: "My baby, my baby, my baby..."

"No!" Jennifer screamed and turned to leave. Chairs flew in her path and she stumbled, clasping her daughter against her still-bared breast. More rattling behind her. Over her shoulder, she stole another glimpse at the coffin.

The woman had remained in place, still muttering the most frightening words Jennifer could ever hear. But the rattling sound was not from the woman. Rather, it came from another coffin nearby—Jennifer had not seen it—and when the coffin lid exploded into pieces, she saw only a man's face before she leapt through the maze of chair legs and into the aisle of chairs. His eyes were those of hatred—dark, malicious hatred. And he, too, had been looking at her child. "Little bitch!"

Jennifer snapped back awake. It had been...oh, too much was happening to her. To all of them. Hastily rebuttoning her blouse, she shushed her baby and returned to the crowd.

To the living.

* * *

Eggs. Formula. Diapers. Milk. Philip knew he was forgetting something. Several things, probably, that he and Jennifer knew they needed for home—what little time lately they were getting to spend there. Would this madness never end?

It wasn't enough that his supervisor had been strangely quiet toward him over the past couple of weeks. Philip's strange moods regarding his ongoing home situation had certainly contributed to that. Add to this the presentation he'd botched, and those critical occasions that the business cards he kept in his wallet were oddly not at hand when needed. When the boss was present, particularly before new or prospective clients, was not the time to be scribbling his name, title and contact information on a drink napkin.

Grant's death could perhaps be the clincher, and the notion of being jobless with a nonworking wife tending their new baby was more than he wanted to think about. He had to make it in tomorrow, despite Jennifer's wishes. Too much was riding on his performance for him to get away with being out another day.

He approached his house from down Oak, seeing it in the distance at the three-way intersection a block before he reached the driveway. What a beautiful house, he thought. Their dreams, in fact, had revolved around it: new job, quiet neighborhood in the suburbs, a home they could stay in for years and years, with two or three children who would make them proud.

He caught himself. As he stopped at the intersection of Mason and Oak, Philip realized he'd been thinking about this house in the *past* tense. Of course their situation wasn't hopeless. He'd do whatever he needed to restore peace to his household. He only hoped he could act before everything he and his wife had worked for crumbled into dust.

The house was dark, though Philip was sure he'd left a couple of lights on when they'd left that morning. A dark house, he remembered commenting to Jennifer, was not what they wanted to see after the first day of viewing at the funeral home. Was it the... He felt ashamed for feeling so sure it was an outside force lurking at every turn.

If it was, it wasn't funny. He pulled out his phone and clicked unlock on the Doorlock module. No sound—though the app reported the lock was disabled. He turned the knob. Nothing. He reached for his keys, inserted the right one, turned it and pushed.

It didn't budge.

That's strange, he thought. He must have locked their top lock, a vestige of the precautions they regularly took in the city. He turned his other key in the top lock—it hadn't been locked—then returned his attention to the bottom lock.

Still nothing.

Philip paused for a moment to think about the situation. He methodically set down the bag of groceries on the step beside him, then examined his phone app. It said the door was unlocked. He closed the app, then reopened it—no different. He restarted his phone and tried again. This was a brand-new app and lock, with weeks of beta testing before their release.

He sighed, then checked his keys. It was the right one. The key had always worked, even before Grant shot a bit of graphite in for lubrication. And it didn't look damaged. Neither did the lock appear to have been vandalized. No, the right key, undamaged, was turning perfectly in the lock. *But the door would not move.*

He shook his head. It wasn't any ghost. It was...

Already Philip's collar began to moisten as he stood on the porch of his own house and wondered what to do next. He loosened his tie. After his first walk around the house to check the windows and cellar door, he took off the tie altogether. Holding the key turned in the lock, Philip threw all his weight against it, to no avail. He thought about breaking a window, then shook his head. In this condition, the house at least was no invitation to burglars.

He circled the house once more and looked around at neighboring houses, in which the inhabitants sat, ate, relaxed, did normal things without a second thought of how they got past their front doors. Damn this...thing! His own house, and no way to... Again he tried the windows—and retried them. The door, too, held fast.

With a flash, he remembered the garage-door module on the same app. Gotcha, he thought. He switched the app to Garage Door and clicked open. The garage door began to rise. But before he could reach the door, it had changed direction—and had shut once again. Trying and retrying the app, even with another restart of his phone, made no difference. The app itself reported that the garage door was wide open.

As had the app's Doorlock module.

Philip was livid, beaten, by the point he sat down on his steps. It wasn't fair! he wanted to cry out. His eyes were already growing moist. Cut it out, now! Jennifer was right about his trouble handling crises—they had yet to discuss the possible effect his behavior and their recent argument might have had on Grant's last hours. But for the moment, he'd better think this thing out.

He dreaded the thought when it came to him, but there seemed no other choice: a neighbor could probably help him get the door open. He knew of only one such person.

"Who izzit?" the voice repeated.

"It's Phil Carter, Harold. We met when I moved into the house down the street...the former *Leffingwell* house," he added. "So you said to stop by if I needed a hand with anything. I thought I'd just..."

"It's Howard."

"*What?*"

"Howard."

Howard stalling for time, thought Philip. "How—"

"Not Harold."

"Howard, sorry. *Please.*" He sighed.

Slowly, Perkins unlocked the rest of the door but did not unbolt the chain. The door opened some four inches; the face that greeted Philip was one of suspicion. "Whatcha need?"

"So I'm sorry to bother you, Howard. But I seem to be having trouble getting into my house, even with the keys. I dunno how these old houses might swell up on a humid day, maybe, but—"

"Hang on." The door slammed shut. Philip could hear some hollering from within—either Mrs. Perkins didn't want him to go or she did and he didn't—for two minutes that seemed like an hour. Philip had already strayed to the end of the driveway, staring at his house down the block and considering trying again, alone, when the door opened. Perkins emerged wearing a coat that seemed much too heavy for the temperature. He blew into his hands and rubbed them together. "Let's go, buddy."

Philip explained the situation further on their way down the block, from his father-in-law's unfortunate demise to the extent of Philip's efforts to gain entry to his home. And that he never would have left a bag of groceries unattended were the Carters still living in the city. Anything for conversation.

Perkins, however, seemed miles away. Or, perhaps, a few houses away. In front of his TV with his feet up, his front door locked, and, safely packed away under the mattress, what had to be the pistol that now bulged from within his coat.

"Yer sure, now, that you don't keep unlocking one lock and locking another."

"Very sure."

"Easy to do, you know?"

"So Howard," Philip explained, turning his key in the bottom lock, "there are only four permutations of two locks. Both locked, both unlocked, or just one or the other locked. Watch." He demonstrated, each time throwing his weight into the hardwood door, as Perkins stood by shrugging.

After the fourth possibility had been exhausted, Howard uncrossed his arms and placed his hands on his hips as if he were in charge. "Now, what about the top one turned and the bottom unturned?"

Already believing he'd consulted the wrong neighbor, Philip shook his head. "Did it, Howard. So there's also my phone app, which can also lock and unlock the door—it's a smart doorlock.

Look." He pulled out his phone, showed his neighbor the Doorlock module and how it said the door was unlocked.

Howard sniffed. "That a smartphone app?"

Philip sighed. What had he just shown him? "Yes, that's what it is, Howard. A smartphone app. So my employer makes these."

"And the lock is smart, too?"

"Yes." Philip was tempted to raise his intonation like he'd heard tween girls at the local mall use when they answered stupid questions.

The neighbor shrugged and thrust his hands into his pockets. He looked off to the side, perhaps with a grin, before speaking. "They don't look so smart to me."

Shaking his head, Philip let out another sigh, this one deeper. "Tell you what. So let's go through each one again, and this time, could you help me push?"

"Yeah, I'll help you push," said Perkins as though he had been helping all along. Together, the two slammed their bodies into the door with each repetition. And together, the door remained in place. The door and its jamb, thought Philip, had been installed with a craftsmanship worthy of Grant O'Keefe himself.

"Try the windows, buddy?"

He was going to kill this man. Yes, I've tried the windows, idiot. I said five minutes ago that I tried the windows several times. What the hell is the matter with you? I can't get into my goddamn house, and you're treating this whole thing like I'm doing an oil change and my filter is stuck. "Yes. So I tried the windows. Maybe if we both pushed..."

They worked their way to the back, pushing unsuccessfully at the windows along one side of the house; even the basement ones were sealed tight.

"Try the back door?"

"Yes. Let's try the back door." Perkins' look of boredom began to change after this, too, wouldn't budge. A front door, well, was one thing. And city folks in the suburbs always seemed to lock their windows. But the back door, too?

"Y-you do have the right keys, don'tcha? I mean, it couldn't be something really simple like—"

"Right keys. Right way to turn them. Right fucking house. I've tried everything, Howard." Philip, too, was still having trouble believing all this. His own *house!* And he was supposed to bring his wife and child back here from the funeral parlor?

"So Howard...what would you do about something like this?"

His neighbor was already backing away, very slowly. Like he'd run out of ideas and was now wondering how he could conveniently stroll away without being called, well, a chickenshit. He stood out in the space between the Carters' house and the next one over, staring out at the places across the street as if deciding which family might next be able to help him. Philip followed aimlessly, to Perkins' chagrin, but stopped short to notice the sudden look of surprise on the man's face. Perkins had spun around and was looking up at Philip's house.

"Carter, y-you better look up there in that window. I just saw somebody *up* there!"

"Where? You saw a person?"

"I—yeah! N-no, not a person. A shadow. Yeah, that's right. A shadow of someone. Listen, buddy, your wife musta come back and didn't come down. She's putting your kid to sleep or something so couldn't come to the door. She—"

"Perkins, no way could my wife get back here so fast. And no way she'd let us stand around in the cold pushing again and again against the door. So what do you think, she—"

"I don't know. All I know is I gotta go. Get your wife and kid, spend the night in the motel or something. Me, I gotta go. Take it easy, buddy."

And he was gone, leaving Philip in the beam of the lone streetlight, staring up at the corner window. The one Perkins had been staring at.

The window of his daughter's room.

17

"So where is it?"

Lana didn't look up from the card she was putting in her hand, didn't answer till she discarded another. "Where's what?"

Cynthia burrowed into the nearby bowl and spilled a few more kernels of popcorn on their way to her mouth. "The gin," she said.

"The gi—oh." Lana giggled. "Must have geeen to play geeen rummy."

Her friend nodded. "And popcorn to watch scary movies." She wiped her hands on her jeans and took a card. "You laughed."

This time she did look up. "You really do want me to find my mother's gin? I don't even know what it tastes like."

Cynthia glanced at the screen, where *The Haunting*, the good one made in the sixties, was showing on cable. She loved the movie. They both did, even though you never did see any of the ghosts. Lana once said that was the point, that the ghosts you could dream up in your head were much scarier than anything some movie director could conjure up. Shivering, Cynthia had changed the subject. It...had sounded like a very grown-up thing to say. Lana was always coming out with things like that. So...she didn't know. Superior? It wasn't something Cynthia wanted to think much about. Lana's mom slept around; her father, Cynthia assumed, walked out rather than put up with it any longer. Her own ma was a drunk; her pa, a stone who talked to nobody at home and worked late as often as possible. Maybe he had a secret girlfriend, too.

Add to this crowd the pals from school, who regularly tormented her—excepting Lana, of course. She sat and stared till whoever was taunting her looked down, called her a crazy bitch, laughed nervously and went away. The pair were friends who felt they truly had nobody else in all the world. What perhaps worried her the most was that Lana sometimes didn't seem to really need anyone—something to do with her orphanage years. This coolness on her friend's part regularly put Cynthia on the defensive, made her the one obligated to break through the occasional conversational lapses, which still bothered her a year after they'd become close friends.

She looked down at her cards to refresh her memory. "No...I mean you're not in a very good mood tonight."

Lana shrugged. "The bottles are locked away anyway, I bet. Want some more Dr Pepper?" She got up and used the tip of a steak knife to pry open the flip-top.

"No, really, what's the matter?"

Lana tipped her head and, heading back into the relative darkness of the den's worn carpet, fastened her eyes on the scene taking place on the TV. "Here's where they hear the cane."

Cynthia nodded and awaited her next turn. Tonight, this frightening part of the movie made her want to change the channel to Nickelodeon. Disney+. Anything but this part that made her realize that—blame it on their nightly excursions—ghost stories were no longer much of a fantasy. She couldn't put her finger on it, but the very idea of this strange power they shared was gradually becoming more and more unsettling.

Take tonight, for instance. Lana apparently felt it, too, for she hadn't once suggested they go out and be *immaterial* for a while. No, something had changed, and it came out when Cynthia suddenly reached over, just as the film's Eleanor watched the engraved doorknob quietly turning from across the room, and switched the TV to *Mister Ed* on one of the oldies channels.

"Hey, what's the big idea?" Lana picked up the remote control.

"Put it back, and I'll leave. It's too creepy!"

"Wilbuuurrr..."

"So? You saw it before. Lots of times. Hey, what's the matter with you?"

"I asked you first."

Lana reached over for a card, looking over her glasses at Cynthia—knowing her friend hated when she did that—and sighed.

"I'm thinking about Jason Pleva."

"Me, too. And about Nancy." Cynthia finished her soda and opened the fresh can Lana had known she'd want. "I...I can't do it. I try all the time."

Nodding, her friend discarded and thrust her hand into the potato chips. "Me, too. I try to think about my body. I think, you're resting, like you're dead. You're not using much of that energy, just enough to—y'know, breathe and make your heart beat and stuff." Kneeling, she jutted out her chin and shut her eyes to act out her story. "I...I command you to let me hold things even though I am just *immaterial*. I command you, body, to let me—I dunno, just *move a paper clip or something!* Nothing works, Cyn." She wrapped her legs into a lotus position and crossed her arms.

"Maybe she's, I dunno, like it runs in her family or something. She said her big sister showed her how to do it."

"And you believe her."

Cynthia cocked her head, pretending to watch Mister Ed sneaking around the back of the house. "I guess maybe." She picked up a card, daring not to say—in the middle of a hand—that she wanted to play something else, or even nothing at all. Especially since she had only two pairs out of ten cards and couldn't seem to decide whether to take a helpful card each time the opportunity arose.

"So," Lana continued, "how come Nancy said she couldn't explain how she did it if her sister explained it to her, huh?"

"Oh, never mind." Cynthia got up and parted the curtains to look outside. A fog enshrouded Oak Drive, the sight of which made her hurry back around the TV and grab another handful of popcorn.

"Care to do some 'ghosting' on this vonderful night, my dear?"

Cynthia was in no mood for the Lugosi voice tonight and shook her head. And besides, it sounded like some drunken crazy was trying to break through a door down the street.

* * *

"Phil, I still don't get why we can't call the locksmith who put in the new locks instead of going to bed in the same clothes, the same everything. I don't even have enough clothes for Carolyn. If she has one more messy diaper, we'll have to—"

Her husband shut off the ignition, quietly thankful that he'd been able to park the car under one of those LED streetlights that made it seem like daytime. He peered from the car into the motel's office window, where a young man sat with his feet propped up on the lower counter, a television beaming from out of Philip's view. "So Jennifer, please. We'll work things out in the morning. Trust me, we're doing the right thing."

"You say you have to go in to work, I understand, but you don't have your briefcase, these little motels never make their wake-up calls at the right time, and...Phil, I'm scared I'm scared I'm scared I want my house back!" and she was in his arms, the baby shuffling in restless sleep behind them.

"Phil, I was really scared in the funeral home. I even had a man look in and he said he saw 'nothing amiss.' Amiss! Philip, I know it was probably just a dream, like a dream, but they were after Carolyn, oh, I want to h-hold her now, Phil..."

"It's okay, Jen. So everything'll be okay, everything'll turn out okay," he repeated, feeling her face pushed against him even as her eyes peered under the headrest at the baby. He would repeat this crap again and again, he thought, until *he* began to believe it.

Who was in his daughter's room?

No, he hadn't told Jennifer the whole story. Instead, he'd said it looked in the dark as if some kids had stuck something in the locks. Some probably did think he, or someone in his house, had had something to do with that Halloween prank-turned-bad. And they laid low for a while, waiting till the excitement died down. Yeah. That was it. He'd think about that, and tomorrow, before the viewing room opened again for a few last hours before the funeral service and the burial itself, they'd get the locksmith back to take care of everything.

So who was in his daughter's room?

"Phil," his wife whispered. She was staring at the baby, watching the gentle rise and fall of her zipped-up coat with the little pink bears on it. Several times she had glanced over to check whether the back door was locked, and twice she even pushed on the door's handle to ensure the door hadn't opened on its own. When finally Jennifer's gaze met her husband's, she appeared a different woman than Philip had ever known. Her straight hair seemed always to have a shine all its own, but tonight it looked haggard, the hair of a woman much older than twenty-nine. She swallowed dryly. Her parched lips trembled as she attempted to form words.

"No one's going to...take away my baby, Phil."

"No, no, you're right, no one will." Her husband shook his head and carefully reached behind him for the lever that opened the door. Considering the baby's crib was at home, he thought, it would be pretty hard to get at an infant who's sleeping on the bed between her parents, too.

Not, he added wryly to himself, that any self-respecting ghost would be caught...dead at a prefab motel. Philip shook off the chuckle and wondered how his mind could possibly come up with a joke at a time like that.

"Phil..."

In his heart, he knew what she was going to say. And knew she was right. "Yes?"

She paused before replying. "We need to go home."

"Jen—"

"I want to just...drive over, and let's try the locks again. Together. This..." she gestured with a wave of her hand, shaking her head, "this isn't right. You know it, I know it and..."

Philip sighed. Yeah, he thought with a glance at his daughter, who was stirring uncomfortably in her car seat. Somehow the kid knows it, too.

The three-mile trip back seemed endless. Philip and Jennifer remained too shaken to speak to one another, too worried about waking the baby as well. What awaited them at home, in the days to come? Would they ever get their lives on course again?

For his part, Philip found himself wishing to God he could talk to Grant. Problems awaited him at every turn. Once back, Jennifer would find the doors the way he had, stuck shut although the keys turned freely in the locks. The baby would start crying from the cold, and Jennifer would get hysterical once again—though that might be healthier than her current icy silence.

Tomorrow, he would be out of the office again. And this time, his boss would probably be waiting at his desk to take the call himself. It was no time to cause additional hardship for him or his family, Garrett would surely begin, but he was seeing little on Philip's part for him to believe anything other than.... Philip was ready for it. No. He wasn't actually ready at all, no matter how many times he repeated the words, over and over, to himself.

You didn't tell anyone, especially not his finger-wagging employer, that your family was feeling threatened by a...ghost. You couldn't say sorry, I'm not feeling too productive today, I had to sleep on the couch sitting with my wife and screaming child. Or, I couldn't fall asleep wondering whether I'd wake up with a pillow shoved against my face, snuffing out my last breaths or—no, he just couldn't tell anyone. He might well be fired from his job tomorrow, he and his wife and child were driving home to spend the rest of the night with this vengeful *thing,* and...

No, there wasn't anyone he could talk to about it.

Grant, for all his own problems, would have understood. To the end, he seemed to know what was going on. Even to know more about it all than he was letting on. More than anything, he was a *man*. Philip needed a man to talk to about the troubles he faced. A man, not this Howard Perkins whose house was just ahead on the road. Not this ordinary man Philip envied for his ability to simply walk away from this whole situation.

I have to see it myself, Jennifer had been telling herself from the very instant the car's back seat grew silent. If we can't get in, well, we could call a locksmith or, at the worst, go back to the motel. We'd stop at the 7-11, pick up some diapers, a few other things, and they'd sit tight—she hoped restfully—till they decided on their next move.

Jennifer knew Philip's job was on his mind. It was one thing to get diapers, quite another to get a pressed suit, the rest of the clothes he needed, and his briefcase. (She didn't have to ask Phil if he'd brought work home the other day.) If he lost the very job for which they'd left their hometown, what next? No unemployment checks would go very far toward paying the mortgage.

The mortgage. Their home was becoming a nightmare, she thought with a shake of her head, and here she was fretting about potentially losing it. The silence enveloping the drive home was overshadowing what most distressed Jennifer: the threat of this thing to her child. Let them move out, go anywhere, go cross-country to stay with Philip's pushy parents if they had to. She was going home because it was where she belonged, where her family belonged.

Until they found out otherwise.

She bit her lip when they passed the Perkins house and felt her heart rate rise at the audible stirrings from the back seat. A sudden sense of foreboding gripped her, and she spun around to see her baby merely stretching, a soft whimper escaping her lips. Jennifer reached out to tickle her daughter under her chin and barely noticed when the car stopped before Philip could swerve it into the driveway.

"Oh, my God..." he said.

Jennifer turned slowly to see their house shining like a beacon on this dark street. Every light in the house had been turned on, and they glowed with a flickering intensity no wiring system was meant to allow. An electric hum filled the chilly night air. And the garage door was wide open, and just as brightly lit.

To add to the strange effect, a chubby schoolgirl, ten or eleven years old, stood staring from across the street. At two o'clock in the morning.

"Phil..." The baby on her shoulder, Jennifer pointed toward the front of the house, where the porch light had just flickered on.

The door was ajar.

18

They gasped. Philip's first fleeting impression, that they'd entered the wrong house, quickly gave way to ripples of shock. Of recognition. He'd seen these things before. Both recognized them the same moment: the day they'd moved in. Incensed, he had grabbed armfuls of what had been left in a pile on the floor. And had unceremoniously thrown everything he'd found into the garage.

But it was all back.

Jennifer began to cry as her gaze swept the living room. The art she had hung, two of the pieces, gifts from an artist friend, were gone. In their place, crookedly hung, was a seascape. A city skyline photograph. A painting of a boat on a pond. Not necessarily...ugly things. But...

not *their* things.

Gone were their couches, a straight chair, the coffee table—but not, for some reason, their recliner. In their place were a strange assortment of boxes in three separate groups: Two medium-sized boxes were stacked; another abutted the bottom one to form an L-shape.

Chairs.

Above, the oak and brass chandelier for which they'd scoured the city was gone. In its place was a cheaply made Tiffany-style lamp she didn't recognize. The wires, in fact, were not even connected to the wiring from the ceiling—more like tied. But the lamp was nevertheless lit...very, very brightly. All around, they could smell the

157

ozone crackle of overheating wiring.

There was more, much more: on the mantel and on every shelf, the little knickknacks Jennifer realized she cherished for the memories had been replaced. By a ceramic cat. A bowl arranged with dusty dried flowers. An ashtray from Niagara Falls. A pair of Hummel-knockoff figurines that seemed to wave evilly from across the room. A...bowling trophy. She dared not approach to read its plate.

Carolyn squealed, and Jennifer realized she'd been squeezing the baby against her chest. The stereo's power button crackled as though struck with a fist. The radio switched on and filled the house with the loud cacophony of a rap station.

> *That's how it goes, yo, throw y'hands high*
> *ATF at the door, the deep shit's nigh*
> *Kilos in a stack—joy powder on your face*
> *Your ass in Club Fed, your soul in deep space*

From the kitchen, a cuckoo clock—not theirs—began to crow quickly, repeatedly. She wanted to cover her ears but couldn't while holding Carolyn.

"Phiiiil!" She pressed against him, crying profusely, and they embraced in a three-way hug. "Make it stop. Please! Make it stop!"

"So it's—it's g-gonna be okay, Jen. Let's just step in further, step in quietly, and s-see what else it did." Philip took a step, and his foot hit something that was moving. He looked down. It was their vacuum cleaner, a robotic vac from his company, another connected product from his company. The radio drowned out the vacuum's reassuring beeps.

But he hadn't fully set it up; it should never have left its base.

Jennifer closed her eyes, concentrating on her daughter's frantic cry as the only sound real to her home. She whispered to Carolyn as Philip inched them all, still locked in their embrace, over to the rack system. He reached over, slapped the power button. "So the AC outlet with those audio components," he said quietly, "had no electrical power to it. My app is supposed to control it—it's a connected outlet."

The cuckoo had stopped the same instant, and all was quiet.

Quiet but for the sound, from the kitchen, of what sounded like bones. That, at least, was Philip's first thought. With a reassuring look over his shoulder, he broke gently from his wife, stepped around the corner and immediately cried out as he slipped and fell.

Jennifer smelled it before she saw it, knew this stink and wondered why she couldn't tell it the moment they entered the house. After all, she had smelled it on her husband plenty the other night.

It was beer. The kitchen floor had a puddle of spilled IPA, and a sopped Philip, now getting up, almost tripped on the empty bottle that lay on the floor. Their garbage can, situated inside a cabinet door left ajar, was full of bottles someone had emptied. The one on the floor? The perpetrator had apparently dropped it. It was the moment they needed, a sardonic bit of slapstick relief that could only help them get a grip on this unreal predicament.

"Whatever it is," she couldn't help saying above her daughter's whimpering, "it doesn't seem to approve, either."

Philip allowed a slight grin, shook his head, and reached for...*whoever's* dish towel it was. Jennifer heard the rattling again, turned quickly and saw the

bones?

wooden chimes hitting against one another and sighed. She hated to admit it, she thought as Philip stepped through the puddle to take them down, but they made a pleasant sound. Philip reached over the counter and—

The dishwasher, apparently no longer connected, glided out from its bay and knocked the wind out of him. He fell back in surprise, slipped again on the beer and hit his head on the wall. The machine...was rolling further out from the wall. It swayed from side to side as it drew nearer, a heavy weight difficult for this...thing to maneuver; the effect was that of a giant swaggering toward its prey. He tried to get up, slipped again, and the giant was upon him. Philip cringed as the door swung open—at this speed, its upper edge could crush his windpipe if he stayed there.

At the last instant, he flattened himself on the floor. The door passed above him, dented the wall, and Philip raised himself up to force the door closed. But the machine pressed in further; it pinned him to the wall, digging its knobs into his shoulder. In pain, the man reached down, gripped the bottom of the machine, and heaved it up and onto its side. It crashed to the floor and was silent.

Jennifer spoke first. "Phil, maybe—"

"The answer is no."

"Phil, are you crazy? This thing—"

"So Jennifer, we are stronger than *this thing*. I think I've proved that. Case..." he added, wincing from the pain, "case closed."

Jennifer shook her head. Staring resignedly at the torn-away hose and power cord protruding from the rear of the fallen dishwasher, she decided she would bring the matter up again before much longer. She scanned the room and recognized little other than the major appliances. These, she thought, were common things. Many of them, she might have picked out for herself.

But she hadn't.

And where *were* their things?

The spice rack remained. But on a nearby nail when she'd hung newly purchased potholders, a "round tuit" potholder she did not recognize hung on a nail. A mug tree stood at the end of the counter. So did one of those drinking bird ornaments that periodically doused its beak into a vat of red

blood

colored water. On the refrigerator, two cookie-shaped magnets seemed to stare at her. It took a moment for the rest to hit her. "Phil...there's a list here." But it wasn't a store list. It read, in child-like bold capital letters,

HERE YOUL'L
NEED A FEW
OF THESE

Philip sighed. "Stand back, Hon."

"Phil, we don't really need to—"

"Jen, we *have* to stand up to this thing," he stated, even as he checked the bottom of the refrigerator for wheels. "Now—"

"No, we don't, not right now. Could we just—"

"Stand back, *now*. Wait outside in the living room if you want."

With a sigh of her own, she stepped back and to the side, recommending that Philip do the same. He cautiously placed one hand on the top of the appliance; with the other, he gripped the handle. The two exchanged glances. He inhaled and gave the door a sharp pull.

The two of them leapt, but not from anything within the refrigerator. Rather, the cuckoo clock behind them was repeating its rapid-fire crowing again and again. Philip reached up to lock the bird's door, but each time the latch seemed to unhook itself. "Damn it!" he shouted. "Stop this!" He reached up to drag the clock off its nail. "Stop—"

Gripping the clock's face with his hand, he shrieked in pain as he tried to release his hand from the wooden bird's face. Blood dripped down from the palm of his hand and turned pink with a splash on the floor. Another moment passed before he pulled his hand free and held it up, trembling, to stare first at his bleeding hand, then at the clock.

The cuckoo had stopped crowing. A single drop of blood fell from its splintered wooden beak.

"Aaaaahhhhhhh!" Philip reached for one of the weights hanging from the clock's underside, swung its chain over his head and slammed it squarely into the bird. The carved figure snapped off its wooden pedestal. Next he crashed the flat of his hand into the side of the clock, sending it to the floor. Jennifer stopped him after the third time he stamped it with his foot.

"Phil."

"What!"

She remained calm, though the baby had been screaming since the cuckoo had started up the second time. She handed her husband the dish towel and pressed it against his wounded hand. "Phil, the fridge."

It took him a moment to remember what she meant. He turned around to see, in the middle of the top shelf, a metal box of Band-Aid adhesive strips.

"It's joking, right?"

Jennifer said nothing, preferring to take a shot at rocking their tired daughter to sleep.

"I mean, it's *fucking* joking with us, right!"

"Phil, please let's just wrap up your hand." She opened the box with her free hand—she did most things with one hand these days—and found it had four large strips; she spilled them onto the counter. A folded piece of paper came with it. Philip grabbed it, shoved it into his pocket and went to the sink.

"Aren't we going to..."

"Yes, we are," he said, doing his best to keep calm as he held his bleeding hand under the cold water. "Yes, we are going to read what it says. And yes, maybe we'll play its little game until we know what the hell is going on. But first I am going to patch up this hand. And then we are going to do things at our own pace. Even if all we accomplish is helping Carolyn sleep for a while."

"She'll be all right. It's you I'm worried about."

In the instant they met eyes, she saw again the man she loved, the harried but caring man who was determined to get his family through their every hardship. If there was a way to make this house their own once again, she saw in his eyes what she also believed: They could not run away tonight. Only if they stayed could they win.

The bleeding had slowed down enough for Philip to see the actual puncture wounds. They weren't deep; how would a wooden bird sharpen its beak, anyway? But there were four wounds in his hands.

Four wounds.

Four Band-Aids.

Philip turned to his wife and grinned. "So I need a beer."

She shook her head. "I think you'll have to lap it up off the floor."

The note, when he retrieved it from his pocket, had the same scrawled block letters they'd seen on the last one. It read:

TRY THE
FRONT
CLOSET
MISTER

"'Mister'?" What are we dealing with here? A kid?"

Jennifer shrugged and continued to rock Carolyn to keep her dozing. "Or a child-like adult."

"Well, whatever it is, it's getting predictable. I open the door, things fall out. Right?"

He sloshed out of the room, removed his drenched sneakers and socks, and stepped back to open the door. Out fell but a mop. "Sense of humor," he said, and looked inside.

Everything was gone—their sweaters, shirts, jackets, boxes they'd stuffed onto the shelves, boots, umbrellas. All that remained was another note, this one taped to the edge of the top shelf:

AFTER YOUR DONE
IN THE KITCHEN
TIME TO TRY YOUR

OFICE

"So my briefcase is at least in the car," he said, crossing the room to veer around the dining-room table. The light of the small office was already on, but his jaw dropped open before he even entered. "Oh no..."

She was behind him in a flash. "What...?"

"Everything is gone. It's all gone!" Empty was the desk's surface, normally littered with papers and office accouterments, and empty was each drawer—he saw as he opened each and slammed it shut one by one. "Jen, I need this stuff! I've got a big project going at work that I can't—you know what's at stake now—and I..."

He slowly walked back to the doorway, where his briefcase stood conspicuously at the threshold. He seized it, opened it. "Empty! It's—damn you! God damn you! Where are my fucking thiiiiiings! I-need-them-back. Now! Now, damn you!"

The baby was awake and crying again, and Philip stared blankly as another piece of paper fluttered down from above the dining room doorway. Jennifer was crying now, right along with Carolyn. The note read:

THAT PLACE
SURE DOES FIT
ALOT OF
STUFF

"'That p-place,' Jennifer repeated. Her eyes lit up. "Phil, the garage! Our things are in the garage! Where you put—"

"So I'm going there...my papers. My papers must be there, too."

"*We're* going there, Phil. We stay together, okay?"

Philip didn't need to turn on the garage light, either, but he tried with his phone app, to stop the door's continuous opening and closing. Before crossing the threshold, Jennifer paused. She took a deep breath and patted the baby.

The two of them stared, open-mouthed, at the sight of their things. Unceremoniously dumped into boxes, atop boxes, in piles. Their few paintings lay damaged beneath a sheen of broken kitchen glasses. The clothing from the front closet, the items from the shelves and a favorite dress of Jennifer's lay bunched up beneath Philip's work boots, and the hinge of Philip's company laptop had split where it was dropped upon the concrete floor.

There was no sign of his missing papers.

Hearing a slight rustle behind them, Philip spun around and saw a new note, this one taped to the doorjamb:

COME INTO MY
PARLOR

"Jen," he wanted to say, "we can still go out the side door." But to what? No home, no job. Only one another, and sorry, he'd be damned if he had to go running with his wife and daughter to stay, penniless, with his parents in a little apartment that was barely big enough even for...though of course it wouldn't get to that. No. Because they were going to march back in and just...

He led the way. Once out of the garage, though, he smelled smoke. The light from the fireplace caught his eye first; the stack of papers burning, second. "My thiiiings!" He flew out of the dining room and charged across the living room, but he was too late. He struck the outer hearth with his fists, his eyes tearing as he saw the last of the top page crumble, his company's logo curling into blackness. "Noooo..."

Behind him, Jennifer screamed and began to sob uncontrollably. "Phil! Oh no take it away! Phil make it go away, make it go away Phiiiiil!"

He had passed right by it: in the recliner, a figure, stuffed with old newspapers. A figure wearing Grant's red-plaid casual shirt and blue gabardine pants. Leaning back, its cantaloupe head stared at Philip with white eggshell eyes.

* * *

"You're crazy. You're absolutely crazy."

Philip had stepped out to the side of the house to remove the mock-up body—his wife, all the while, remaining within view in the doorway, using her coat to cover the sleeping baby. And now that the two of them had gotten the chance to sit down, at least on the sturdier boxes, he could not believe she still wanted to stay.

His job, he knew, was lost in the flames of the fireplace. Your dog did not eat your homework in the corporate world, and Phil mulled quietly handing in his resignation rather than suffering the disgrace of actual termination. But at least if he was fired, the unemployment compensation could carry them through for a while. Then again, they'd surely lose the house either way—the mortgage was just too much.

Was that such a bad thing?

Better to walk away from it now, he thought, than to have it taken away piecemeal. And now here was his wife, right after the fright of her life—worse even than whatever she said she saw at the funeral home. Saying she wanted to stay.

To stay!

"Phil, I am not crazy. You said it yourself, we can't let it beat us." She looked over the edge of the bassinet, which they had brought down from their room. At least their beds and sheets had been left alone, if little else in the room. Surprisingly, the baby's room had been left completely intact.

Except that the music box was back on the dresser.

He shook his head. "So Jen, we...we don't really even know what this, this *thing* is. You told me about that music box you found in Carolyn's room. You found it after I know I cleaned the closet out. I mean, it seemed to *like* you. Or not *mind* you. Carolyn, either. Damn it, it seems to want me *dead* or, at the very least, hurt. Very badly. And now..."

"Phil—"

"And now, Jen, it wants to do whatever it needs to get us out. *All of us.* The—"

"I don't think—"

"So Jennifer, that effigy downstairs certainly wasn't meant for *me.*"

With that she paused, and Philip believed he hit home. He thought briefly about generations of old, in which the husband did the thinking for two. True, this was a major decision of the type many families never face, and they had equal share in the outcome. But it would be so much easier if he could simply say, "Jennifer, we are going," and see that decree become reality.

He shook his head. What a joke. Reality. In this insane course of events, he'd be so blacklisted as unreliable that he would probably be watching Carolyn while his wife went out to look for work. All was as it should be for the moment: By the end of the following day, week, or however long it took for his company to put its headhunters to work in finding a replacement, he would be out of a job. It wasn't his fault, yet...nevertheless, his wife *should* be the one making the decisions.

He looked at his wife, realized she was quietly weeping, and reached over to embrace her.

"I...I was ju-just thinking about one night when...when I was a little g-girl. I don't know, I w-was maybe ten. I was sitting on Daddy's lap, and h-he...he was telling me how proud...he was of m-me, that n-no matter what I did, he would always be proud of m-me." She paused, blew her nose, took a few breaths. "Do you know what I told him? I remember just what I s-said. I told Daddy that what I want is a nice family, a house just like the one I lived in, a nice chair to sit in like he had and—I don't know—there was lots more. But Phil!" She grabbed his hand and squeezed it so tightly he winced. "Phil, you and Carolyn are my family. *This* is the house. Everything I've ever wanted is wrapped up in this place, Phil. Don't think I don't know that if we walk away from it now, we may never have anything like it again. Never a house, and...we as a family would never be the same again."

"So Jen, believe me, the last thing I want is for us to lose what we've dreamed of. But Hon, I'm thinking about us when I say we've got to go. I'm thinking about you, about Carolyn—"

"We'll just have to keep her real close for a while. And we'll get someone over. A priest. As many as we need. A medium, too."

Shaking his head, Philip knew he was getting nowhere and stood up. "So we'll talk more about it tomorrow. Things seem to have quieted down around us, and I...have a pretty busy day planned for tomorrow. C'mon up, I'll carry her upstairs."

Jennifer nodded and began to rise. "But Phil, can I tell you something?"

"Yeah, Hon?"

She wrapped her arms around him. "I...I don't think this is the time to go. It won't be, I think, for a long, long time. But..."

"Mmm?"

"When it's time to go, Phil...I think I'll know it."

* * *

She was staring into the light of the streetlight.

A voice within, some voice of reason in a house where reason had taken leave, this voice was insisting. Their room did not face the streetlight, you must not be in your own room.

You must be dreaming.

I must be dreaming, she was telling herself..

Jennifer had quickly fallen asleep, and the LCD baby monitor, on the nightstand, showed no motion. She remembered few dreams from the dead of night before the sun rose, knew of none she could remember where she consciously knew that she was dreaming. Yet here she was, staring into the glow of the streetlight. She felt like a child, felt she could just rise up, kick up her heels and...fly. I can just take my family and—

With that thought the scene changed, and again she looked down at the damp handkerchief she clutched in her hand. But she was through with this! In the haze she stared dumbly as face after face appeared through the gloom, each distorted as though viewed through one of those fish-eye lens. In off-speed slurs they spoke, leaning closely, and asked, each in turn, what will you do now?

What will you do now?

What wiiiill you dooo now?

What will you do now?

What do you mean? she cried out in the dream. Phil, tell me what they mean. Phil, tell me, pleeease.

Phil?

And then she heard her father's voice. The air had grown thicker with the smell of flowers, and she cried because she could not see him. Daddy? Daddy, where are you? What's happening?

His voice was heavy, distant. *Jenny, Jenny, I want to be there, I'm trying to be there and I can't get through. Can't get through...*

"Daddy! Where are you? Where—"

"Jenny. Jenny, get up. Jenny, I'm talking to you. Get up and do what you have to do. Do what you have to do. Do..."

She snapped awake; she was drenched, though the room was chilly. Phil—he was there. She sighed and wanted to just kiss him in the middle of one of his lawn-mower snores. And let's check Carolyn, too.

The LCD monitor's image was completely dark.

"Phil! Phil wake up—" she punched him awake—"she's gone my baby's gone oh my God!" She turned on the light and ran into her child's room. The crib was empty. The baby cam was still on the dresser. But it now faced the wall.

Jennifer looked under the crib. Under it. Around the floor. The closet. The stairs!

Philip was still waking up. "Jen, what's—"

"Carolyn is gone, God damn you! Wake up, wake up we have to find her we—"

"So you looked all in this room, right?"

"Yes yes find her my baby oh my baby oh Phil, we have to find her!"

He ran out of the room, hurried down the hall, checked the upstairs rooms—Carolyn's room, Grant's old room, the bathroom, the hall closet—then ran down the stairs. Jennifer could hear him trip over the boxes, turn over each one, look inside. He checked the doors and windows. He slammed doors, threw things out of the way. She heard it all.

Yet she knew her daughter was somewhere close.

She shivered. It *was* chilly where she'd stood in the doorway of their bedroom. Uncommonly so, the way it had felt a few times before. Whatever had Carolyn, it was indeed close. It was...

Somehow, both she and Philip had missed her. Carolyn had to be in her room, the one room left untouched in the recent melee of rearrangement. Never mind that they'd scoured that room first.

This wasn't for Philip to do.

It was hers alone.

She walked the few steps slowly, seeing through the half-open door the light of the corner streetlight. And there was another light, a...glow. It lit up the room for a moment, and then it was gone. She reached the doorway and pushed the door open further.

Philip was still banging things, yelling now too, as Jennifer saw her daughter lie suspended, in mid-air, beside the crib. The baby was awake and looked up.

But not at her mother.

"My baby...give me my baby...give me..."

As she stepped closer, the spirit appeared. The mother's love and instinct alone kept her feet rooted as the bluish glow became the form of a young girl. A little girl with an angry face, the face of a child who had learned to hate.

"Please..." Jennifer could say nothing more as she extended her arms toward the spirit and...a most comfortable infant. A baby who somehow *knew* the one who held her.

The mother's hand flew to her mouth. *Then she...before...*

Calmly, the spirit handed the baby to Jennifer, but not before stroking the baby's forehead once more. Jennifer clutched the baby close and faced the one bathed in the bluish glow.

The spirit came only a step closer, and when she spoke, her words carried more weight than any brave, irrelevant utterings the woman could ever hear herself say, now or again.

"It's time for you to go now."

PART 2

19

The house lay still. With the Carters gone, even a few weeks of neglect were enough to revive the lively tales that spread across the small suburban community. This time, they began not in the elementary and middle schools but in the banks, the real estate agencies, the library—wherever otherwise rational adults carried on their activities. From there they went to the dinner tables, where the stories took on lives of their own in the minds of the children.

A few of whom knew more than they were telling.

Over a period of weeks, the bank sent over a crew to tidy up the grounds. The men picked up litter that had blown over to rest in the hedges lining the right-hand boundary, looking from the street, of the property. They cleaned windows from the outside and fastened two shutters they presumed the chilly December wind had blown free. They bagged up the last of the myriad leaves, some that the neighbor next door had blown over from his own lawn, and they swept the front walk and steps.

These cosmetic measures, however, did nothing to undermine the local children's own conclusions that the house was indeed haunted. First was the obvious: You did not move out—less than two months after moving in—in the middle of the night and return, a week later and during the daytime, for your possessions.

Second was one that still had them speculating during recess, lunch, and even during class: The movers took much of the family's belongings out the *garage* door rather than the front. It was to ward off curses, a few boys decided.

Lastly, the men cleaned up the grounds but did not go inside. Of course, it was a bank selling the house. But didn't everybody clean up a house, on the inside, before putting it on the market?

In the quieter moments, the house's sole occupant stood in the window, sat on the front steps or even on the roof, or occasionally followed neighbors down the street just to listen to their conversation. From those with dogs, she shied farther away; too many growls of passing dogs had revealed her presence, which further confirmed rumors.

Natalie typically stayed close to the house, becoming a part of its seasons. She unhooked the shutters that the workmen had fastened because she liked the sound they made when the wind swung them at night. The house whose backyard abutted hers had a wind chime that was metal instead of wood. She once sat on the backyard fence at sunset and watched the tinkling metal robin as the wind waved it this way and that, this way and that, to make a music she could listen to as she spied the family within—a man, woman, and teenage girl— sitting down to dinner.

She approached closer, and concentrated on suppressing her eerie chill. On the porch, she paused beneath the chimes. Through the storm windows she watched the threesome. The daughter seemed to be telling a story—Natalie heard several "likes"—and the parents broke into laughter as they dug into their chicken. The mother asked for the father to pass her something, the salt, and she grinned as he closed the hand holding the shaker over her own hand. They kept in position an instant before the daughter rolled her eyes and said something that made them all laugh again.

Natalie passed through the wall to hear their conversation, see the steam rise from their food, watch them engage in light conversation. And...to make a difference. The scenario at play was alien to her, but not for long. The spirit slipped beneath the floor of the dining room, heard the trio giggle at another joke...and reveled in an abrupt end to the mirth when she rose up to pass through the center of the mashed potatoes on the table.

All seemed to feel it, despite the lack of Natalie's ghostly chill. For several seconds, neither of them spoke. Although the family had been eating heartily, now they picked at the food, pushed it around on the plate and finally stood up. With occasional mutterings, none including discussion of the unfinished meals, they scraped the remains into the trash, filled the dishwasher and wandered off to separate rooms of the house.

The observer giggled aloud, left the premises and snapped off an icicle from her own rooftop. She perched upon a cinder block surrounding what had once been an attempt at a garden, materialized her arms and, curious, scraped the point of the icicle along her wrist to watch the redness that would, under ordinary circumstances, eventually draw blood. Back and forth she scraped, and with every failure to make even the slightest mark she laughed all the more. Her motion took on the ferocity of an animal.

It was also the laughter of a drunk, for the spirit was drunk with power. No longer the helpless schoolgirl, Natalie was now the unchallenged ruler of the house in which she had died. Someone, without a doubt, would replace the family that had left this house in terror not very long ago—indeed, for one rooted in eternity, it may as well have been seconds ago. Or years. Whoever came next would find a lesson waiting, and it would not be pleasant.

At that moment she heard a crackle and looked up to see the air a few feet above her spatter as would a frying pan of oil into which one had sprinkled water. She first felt the icicle she'd gripped fall from her hand. Her powers of materialization, for the moment, were gone. Suddenly confused, almost afraid, Natalie stared into the blueness that seemed to form a swirling vortex whose center flashed a bolt of brilliant light. In that moment she was awash in memories of her mother—her eyes, her hair, her scent...her embrace. It flipped away, like a coin spinning on its edge, and the other side was bleak darkness. Hand-like appendages reached out from the darkness, gnarled claws reaching out. For her.

The image flipped back to the blueness for but a moment before the vortex vanished altogether. Now, dead ahead, was only the streetlight, which she swore she could not see a moment ago.

She gripped the icicle again with no trouble but tossed it across the yard. What she had seen made no sense. It disturbed her for a time until, immersed in some new activity inside the house, she forgot about it.

Except for two nagging thoughts.

That even from the grave, her mother had not forgotten her

promise. And that Natalie was less in command of this strange, mysterious world than she thought.

* * *

Weeks passed. The sun was close to setting, and Natalie was walking upside down along the hallway that passed above the living room. She turned to walk toward the front of the house, which would make her feet pass through the sloping ceiling and stick out one of the two skylights. After a few more steps she was outdoors altogether, and she grinned as she walked upside down, fifteen feet up, in the twilight.

Someone was there, standing in the snowy remains of an earlier dusting.

In a start she righted herself and regarded the woman who had stopped while walking by. To look at her?

No, realized Natalie. The woman was not looking at her, merely at the house itself. She looked familiar, she thought, then dismissed the woman and went inside. Just like the other gawkers, she decided on her way to play in the basement.

The woman shivered and wondered why she needed to pass by here as often as she did. It was only every month or so these days. But shortly after the tragedy occurred, Emily Sanders had been passing by and stopping once or twice a week.

One phone call...

Of course, she recognized it was what motivated her. Her drive to more quickly earn her master's degree and seek work with disabled children at the state hospital had all begun one night here in Hollister.

One phone call...

One night. It happened when she was nurse at the elementary school. She had acted on a hunch based on a mark, and a frightened look she'd seen on the face of Kim Leffingwell at a PTA meeting. She had called the woman...and listened in shock as the monster who was her husband shouted and, she supposed, grabbed for the phone as she cried out in stark terror. When the line went dead Emily had immediately called the police, and she had been present when the paramedics had brought out the bodies of the man, his wife and...

that poor little girl.

One phone call had changed Emily's life, and tonight she

wondered about the new homecare agency position she had just accepted, as a physical therapist for disabled children. It was a good position, lots of one-on-one responsibility, and the pay was decent. These kids needed all the help they could get, she knew.

But kids like Natalie?

A tear rolling down her eye, Emily walked on with a refreshing thought: There, at least, was one child who truly had all her suffering behind her.

20

"Claaaass..."

Mrs. Genovese was having no effect. The two boys entering the room had come from the principal's office. Hands in pockets, backs to her gaze as they sat atop woodgrain laminate desks, they felt as heroes amid a circle of enthralled classmates.

"CLASS!"

The banter hushed; a few children eased back into their seats. The two ten-year-olds holding court, however, remained in place on their elevated perches.

"Brewster and Holligan, if you do not take your seats immediately, you will find yourselves back in the principal's office for a much different reason."

"Aw, Mrs. Genovese—"

"E-nough, Joseph Holligan."

The two boys returned to their desks, but the teacher's threat had little effect on others in the room.

"You had to see *something*," whispered one.

"Didn'tcha turn around to see who did it?" asked another.

"Or *what* did it!"

The classroom exploded into laughter, and Mrs. Genovese realized there was no point in continuing any discussion on set notation. The only sets anyone cared about this Monday morning were made up of those who had been at the old Leffingwell house the night before...and those who hadn't.

"All right, then. Leonard, suppose you tell the class about your experience. In *brief.*"

All the children fell silent—all but one girl, who emitted an audible sigh. The teacher scanned the room. It was...it was that Bellows girl. Cynthia Bellows, who leaned back, arms crossed. Well, the teacher thought, at least one child in the room brought her brain to class today. She sighed with some regret for her having accepted an offer to switch from the fourth grade to the fifth...which meant teaching *this* bunch two years straight.

Leonard Brewster sauntered up to the front of the room. In general, he was a fairly timid student. Played around with a few rough types, certainly, but timid nonetheless. In the presence of Henry Waggoner, the boy in the hospital, he was a sheep. So was Holligan, a short, curly-haired boy whose front teeth protruded, giving him more than a passing resemblance to SpongeBob SquarePants. But both were now celebrities—at least for today.

"Me, Joe here and Henry, we were just passin' by the ol' haunted house on Oak an' Mason. It was cold, you know? And I say—"

"Henry said it!" rang out Holligan's voice.

"Okay, okay, so Henry says let's go in! And Joe here says, 'No, I don't wanna—'"

"You didn't wanna *either,* Lennie!"

"Boys, boys, only one of you can tell the story at a time." She motioned for Brewster to continue.

"We didn't wanna go in, like, you know? And, you know, we told 'im, Henry, why don't *you* go in? He's like, you know, I asked you first, so I says—"

"Let's just go on with the story, young man."

He looked up at the teacher, bewildered. "Right. So, you know, I'm like, you know, it's gettin' cold, it's like late, and," he glanced sideways at the teacher, "you know, there's *schooool* tomorrow!"

The class groaned.

"So Henry's like, okay, but before we go, I wanna toss a rock in the window!"

Having recaptured the class's attention, he paused before resuming. "He's, like, lookin' around for a rock. Joe and I, like, we're cold. Like, we heard enough about this place, you know? Some things you just don't mess with on a cold...dark...night. You know? So Henry's, like, he can't find a rock? Joe and me, we start walking. We're like, 'Goodbyyye, Henryyyy...' And he's like, 'Okay, okay, I'm

178

coming.' He's still lookin' around. That's when we hear a funny sound from behind, and like Henry's voice, and we see him lyin' on his face. His head's bleeding like nothing I ever seen."

"Surely," said the teacher, "someone had been hiding in the bushes."

"Oh, no, Mrs. Genovese, there ain't no leaves on those bushes anymore—we'd'a saw someone. Like, we looked that way and didn't see or hear nothin'!"

The class was silent. Silent for a moment until Cynthia released the snickering she had been keeping within her. She held her hand over her mouth, but it was not enough. The class had begun to stare at her, her friend Lana included—though not without a grin of her own, a face she rarely exhibited in class. Leonard turned red with anger.

"Well, what do *you* think is so funny?"

Cynthia took a few breaths to regain her composure. "Well..." she inhaled once more, "this is the first time a haunted house ever threw a rock at the *kid!*"

Now the laugh was on Brewster. "Didn't see *you* there, shit-for-brains. Getting drunk with your mom?"

"Stop this, both of you," Mrs. Genovese said, her hands on her hips, "and sit down."

Cynthia held her anger and delivered a comeback she felt sure would make Lana laugh. "I'd rather...rather get drunk at home than pee my pants in the middle of Oak Drive! Did you forget that part?"

"Cynthia!" Mrs. Genovese shouted as laughter and hooting filled the room. But she aborted the lecture she was about to deliver when a chilly breeze passed by her, waved a few papers, and was gone. She turned around; the windows were closed.

"Ooooowwww!"

Brewster had literally bounced out of his seat. Below, a drawing compass lay on the seat, its shiny tip dripping a dark, moist red. He turned toward Cynthia, who was two rows away. There was no way she could have properly angled the implement, its point straight up, from where she was sitting.

But a last-minute glint of light off the tool's vertex told the girl all she needed to know. Apparently, no one had been holding it— yet it had been raised. At least, no one she *saw* had held it up.

Which, she realized as the bell rang, could mean only one thing.

179

* * *

Later that day, Cynthia looked up from her reverie to realize Lana had come up beside her. "Oh," she said with a start. "You scared me."

"Then we're even."

"Whatcha mean?"

Lana continued to stare straight ahead. "You said something before that just...didn't sound like you."

Cynthia giggled. "The pee in the pants?"

"I know you. You don't say something like that unless you mean it. And you weren't there."

That much was true, Cynthia had to admit. The two had been playing in the town's courtroom, taking turns playing the blubbering defendant as the other delivered the verdict of death penalty. Lana's idea once again. Her friend was never short of ideas, suspicions, plans. It made her seem, as usual, so much older.

"I just...knew," she finally replied. "So who cares how I found out, anyway?"

Clasping her books tightly against her, Lana sighed before answering. "You're gonna say it's none of my business who else is your friend, right?"

"I...didn't say that," said Cynthia. "But yeah."

"I don't trust this Nancy."

Cynthia stopped and spun toward Lana, who'd kept walking. "Lana, come back here," she yelled as she caught up. "Stop, will ya? Who said anything about Nancy?"

Lana finally stopped, confident in her control of the conversation. "I did. Nobody was looking at *me* in that classroom, you know. While you were trading insults with Leonard, I put my head on the desk and..."

"You *immaterialized* in the middle of class!"

"Nobody was looking at me, you know. I just leaned back and...stuck my head out a little. And what do you think I saw?"

Cynthia lowered her head. "She was there, right?"

"You bet. She saw me see her, too. What a look she had on her face."

It was Cynthia now who began to walk away, although hesitantly. She knew what was next.

"Uh-uh. You wait for me, kiddo."

Cynthia stopped, gritting her teeth, till Lana caught up. "Nancy told you about the pants wetting, right?"

Her friend nodded, eyes closed.

"And this thing in class...she protects you or something? She comes to talk to you at night?"

Weakly, Cynthia nodded again, close to tears.

Lana sighed again, and the two kept on walking. "Then, buddy, I'm gonna have to stick closer to you."

"What? Why?"

Lana shrugged, ready to change the subject. "'Cause she says she can materialize a little but not much 'cause it *hurts*. She didn't look so hurt in class. And did you feel that chilly breeze?"

"But..."

"She's also an awful good shot with a rock."

* * *

The older doctor shrugged. He felt a fool for having confided in an associate what he'd seen in his cancer patient moments before she died. Now, in the lounge, he was being questioned by this upstart, the one people were calling tomorrow's chief surgeon for his pragmatic, no-nonsense approach to the job.

"It's nothing much, really. A patient of mine, a deeply spiritual woman, said some intriguing things before she went. That's all."

The other doctor decided to back off, but not without a statement. "Sorry, don't mean to pry. I'm just curious. About the ways people choose to deal with strokes of fate."

"Deal? Things conjured up by the mind, in other words, to soften the horror of impending doom? Is that what you're calling it?"

"I defer to your vaster experience," replied the younger man, who appeared about forty or so. "But if visions of the Virgin Mary and my loved ones would ease my passing...then I'm sure I'd find some way of seeing those things. What are dreams, after all, but portraits of the mind?"

The oncologist rolled his eyes but agreed that in a world of pure science, the arena of all that's verifiable through the senses, his challenger's arguments were beyond reproach. "You, Dr. Stratton, may well be my equal in adherence to scientific principle." He picked up his clipboard to resume his rounds. "Just the same," he added with tight lips, "I'm going to pray for you."

Jeffrey Stratton stroked the stubble on his chin and grinned. He surely hadn't scored any points by picking a philosophical fight with Hollister Medical Center's head of oncology. But after twenty-eight hours on duty, he got a bit punchy. And became more of what they'd called him in med school, Mr. Science. Among scientists, yet.

He looked at his watch, then at the coffee that was making him pucker with every sip. It was a caffeine boost on a thirty-six-hour shift, he often reminded himself. Nothing more. But time was a-wasting; he had a call to make. He took his tray into the sleeping quarters and laid it on the small metal desk.

"Wanda? Jeff here." He eased back against the chair and bit into a vendor machine's ham and cheese. "What's up, 'Da?"

"Still with that label after all these years, I see," the woman replied with a chuckle. "But there's nothing up."

"Nothing? More and more I'm entrenched in this bum town, the last of the old gang is helping me hunt down a house, and there's nothing? It's not the city, but it's also not *that* small a town!"

The realtor was unabashed as usual. "First of all, Buddy Boy, it's winter. I'd apologize for the slim pickings except that they aren't slim: You and/or Maureen have pooh-poohed everything I've come up with so far. I also don't apologize."

"Yeah, that's us. That's you. That's why you're such a friend."

"And being a friend, I'm going to tell you another thing. I know you're doing most of the looking for...obvious reasons. I mean..."

"Right. Go on."

"But some house-hunting requires your *joint* presence, if at all possible. What I could now think of to show, you might even differ...some properties require a joint decision."

Jeffrey's phone, during the call, had been going crazy. "Break's over soon, Wanda. Whatcha been holding out on me?"

"Just one..." she paused for effect, sighed and, he knew, took a drag from her ubiquitous cigarette, "the local haunted house."

"You're kidding me."

"Gorgeous house, bit of property at a three-way intersection, three bedrooms plus an office/den, smallish kitchen and dining room, one-and-a-half baths, good construction, big basement, skylights, one-car garage...owners left in a panic about a year ago, and the bank has foreclosed. It's not as large as you'll eventually want, but it's a steal.

"Bring the wife if you're interested, Jeff. This is a storied house,

182

and a local boy has just claimed he was assaulted outside the property—by something he never saw."

"Assaulted?" Jeffrey grinned. "You don't mean the Waggoner kid? The hospital is abuzz over him and that house—they just sent him home. What an imagination! I'm off tomorrow morning. Nine o'clock?"

The realtor was typically not one to show indecision or concern, but he was hearing it from her now. "Nine, fine. But talk to your wife first, Jeff. If there's any truth whatsoever to the rumors, and there are plenty..."

"Uh-huh. See you tomorrow, 'Da." But the more he thought about the house, the closer he came to deciding not to talk to Maureen till he'd had a chance to see the place himself. *By* himself. He would actually get off from work that evening, not in the morning, and over surgery a fellow doctor had mentioned where the place was.

Of course he'd meet with his old friend in the morning. But if you were going to see a haunted house, you went first alone. At night. When you could see for yourself what bullshit the whole idea of a ghost was.

* * *

He'd decided against hitting his motel for a bite and a shower before heading over to the house. The hospital was a mere eight blocks away, and Mason Street—one end of it, anyway—was just off the highway. It was practically along his route.

Jeffrey parked along Oak Drive and, by habit, checked his phone. It was not unlike the ER to contact him even within the hour after a long shift had ended. Looking into his rearview mirror and combing his grayless blond hair, he checked his appearance and grinned. Of course he was being boyish, he knew. First, though, he was a scientist. All science began with a childlike enthusiasm and curiosity. An open mind, too, but certain things a scientist didn't consider options. It was a physical world, a godless world of senses and sensibility. He would approach this house and, at least from the outside, see its sights, smell its smells, hear its sounds. That was at least what the Waggoner boy had done.

He checked that he'd locked the car—with kids like that hoodlum around, he was taking no chances. Ahead stood the house, completely dark but for a nearby streetlight. Flashlight in hand, he crossed Mason Street and was standing before it. The Leffingwell house, he'd heard the boy call it, but the mailbox read "Carter."

At night, he thought as he shivered, it looked like a nice place. Nothing out of the ordinary. A big bay window covered much of the front of the house; off to the left he saw what looked like the kitchen. Following the driveway around on the left, he saw a garage and, at ground level, small basement windows. Have to check for leakage, he thought, although the springtime was best for that—not early February.

Jeffrey circled around the right side of the house, occasionally flashing his light up toward the bedrooms. These and what looked like a bathroom wrapped around three sides of the house, and the roof above the house's first floor angled back toward them. Now in the backyard, he noticed a basement door.

Now what?

He again considered checking for an unlocked door, but of course, breaking and entering wasn't an option. So he stood there in the cold. Other houses he'd seen, a few of which he'd discussed with Maureen, had been too cramped—the converted summer cottage. Others had been too old, too close to this or that, too far from something else. This one...this one was a perfect distance from the hospital. It was sufficiently close to the interstate without being just off the access. It was close enough to the same elementary school but on the other side of the district, close enough to the therapist he'd found through the agency and...

What was he doing? Jeffrey realized he was freezing in the backyard of a home he'd never entered, practically buying the thing on the spot. It was fatigue, he thought. And hunger. It was time he just—

A car pulled up in the driveway. Jeffrey ducked behind the house and peered around the corner, feeling more foolish than he had during anything he'd pulled in his college days. A car door opened, then shut. Someone with boots, light footsteps, was coming up the side. He pulled back—what would he do? Then he heard the voice: "Ringolevio one-two-three, one-two-three, one-two-three!"

He peered out from the darkness. "Wanda?"

Jeffrey smelled his friend's cigarette first, and then saw her. Her silvery red hair slipped out the side of her parka's hood. Her face, already beginning to wither from the steadiness of her habit, beamed in triumph. "So you think I don't know you, Jeffereee? I know you, and I know many, many people in town. A few of whom work at a certain nearby hospital. The boy spun a good story, didn't he?"

Jeffrey sighed, his face red as much from embarrassment as from the cold. "Magic Wanda strikes again. Um...got your keys?"

She jiggled them in the air and stepped over to the back door. She turned the key and fumbled with the lock. "That's funny. Nothing's...it won't budge. Let me..."

Jeffrey had turned away for a moment and hadn't heard her. "Could fit a nice swing set here," he commented.

"Oh there, that's funny. Now it opens right up," she said when the catch suddenly released.

"Hmmm?" He returned to the realtor's side. "Lead on."

She crossed her arms and stepped aside. "There's electric but only enough heat for the pipes. You first, Dr. Fancy-pants. This was *your* idea, remember?"

21

The little plaque leaning against the hutch of her dresser displayed the old, familiar saying: "Lord, nothing is going to happen today that you and I cannot face together." Maureen had found the plaque in an old suitcase, where she'd put it soon after her mother gave it as a gift for her high school graduation. These days, it was a saying to which she clung.

"Motherrr," called her daughter from the other room.

Maureen looked over her shoulder, then replied, "In here, babe."

Janice, a girl of eleven, bounced into the room. Her blonde curls covered the designer-brand tag that protruded from within the collar of her blouse. She had kicked off her shoes upon entering the house twenty minutes before. In her hands she held her favorite doll, and a blue button that had fallen off.

The little girl went straight to her mother. "Could you sew this back on for Casey?"

Her mother sighed. "Sure, Jan. Give me some time."

"Okay, Mom." She turned to leave the room.

"Janice, aren't you forgetting someone?"

Her daughter paused, then stepped over to the window, where a younger boy sat in an electric wheelchair, his head slightly craned in her direction, his right side facing the view of a teeming metropolis that spread out as far as the eye could see.

Just beneath his jaw, a chin control allowed him some painful but self-reliant mobility.

Janice touched the boy's shoulder. "Hi, Mickey," she said, remaining standing.

Maureen had asked her daughter often enough to bend to eye level as a sign of respect. Now wasn't the moment to remind her, she knew. Not before her brother.

Her brother.

"Hi, Janice," the boy replied, craning his neck to look up at her. His voice, weak with a trace of sadness, nevertheless rang with the unshakable optimism of youth. "How was school?"

Janice shrugged and managed a smile. "Okay, I guess. What are you doing?"

Her mother groaned within at what she interpreted as possibly the stupidest question she could have heard from her daughter. Nothing much, she imagined an adult would answer. Just sittin' here exercising my eyes, mouth and neck, seein' as how nothin' much else'll listen to a damned thing I tell it. Any more questions?

But of course, Mickey took the question better than that, just as Maureen knew her daughter had not asked the question to hurt. It was all most children would have thought to say. We're all children in this one, she thought. It was the only way to keep things going.

* * *

It had been the year of bad luck. Janice, then eight, had begun making playful chicken noises the day Maureen told her little daughter that Grandma would be coming to watch her for the next couple of weeks. Mommy had gotten chickenpox, perhaps from one of the children at a nearby pediatric medical group, where she had a new job as an insurance coordinator. Her daughter—whose merriment faded at this news—would surely be getting it, too.

Her illness itself wasn't the concern, Jeff and Maureen agreed. The issue was that the two of them, Maureen in particular, had been wanting a second child, and any efforts toward that goal would have to wait.

Of particular worry was that Maureen was going on thirty-nine, well in the range of what doctors called "advanced maternal age," and the risk for complications was greater.

"How can this happen!" she had shouted over and over. "How can this—Jeff, I didn't take this job for *this* to happen. You know why I—"

"It'll be all right, Maureen." Jeffrey reached out to take her in his arms. She jerked away.

"Was it so *wrong* to want to work just a few days a week, to have somebody else care for Janice sometimes? My God! Jeff, I want another child..." She wrapped her arms around him, then let go and pulled away again. "I'm a mother! I wanted to be...a person again, too. Was that so wrong? *Was that so wrong?*"

"Of course not, Mau. But it happens. We'll get through this."

They did, but the chickenpox wasn't their only challenge. When Jeff began to have trouble sleeping and developed a tremor that came out only when he was holding an object—such as a scalpel during surgery—he had his suspicions checked with a full blood test. Given professional courtesy, within a day of having the CBC results he saw an endocrinologist friend, who confirmed his diagnosis: Graves' disease.

One symptom of this autoimmune disorder, erectile dysfunction, would not go away until the meds he was prescribed had been in his system for at least a few months. The day he told Maureen about his illness, however curable it tended to be, was when he first suggested they consider adopting. He predicted her initial response, and it didn't take long.

"IT'S NOT THE SAME THING!"

"No." Maureen could see him weighing the situation by the look that came over his face. He was a practical man; that, she had always admired. But the same pragmatism had its cold edge, and she could almost read his mind: *But baby, it's the only thing.*

"No. Absolutely not."

She'd stormed out of the room of their high-rise condo and, shortly after, even went so far as to take Janice away to her mother's for a few days. "Don't try to call," she'd said to Jeffrey, who'd dropped her off at the airport on his way to work a double-shift. "I'll be all right. And when we get back, we'll talk some more. Okay?"

Maureen had looked to her husband, whose blond hair was just long enough to toss a bit in the wind that whipped around the terminal. Few words were needed.

She needed her time to absorb what she knew in her heart was perhaps the only practical solution for a woman determined to raise two children. And he was practical enough to step back and let her work things out.

She gripped his windbreaker and almost picked up his tie, then remembered he disliked the way she absent-mindedly played with it. Inevitably, it would wrinkle.

"It's okay," he said. He picked up the half of his tie that wasn't clipped down. "Here," he said sheepishly and extended it toward her.

"Oh, Jeff..." She leaned close to kiss him and wrinkled his tie.

"Mommy, the plane is gonna leave!"

"What? Oh okay, Jan, we'll go get on the plane now." She turned back to Jeffrey. "You take care, my man. I'll ring when I hit terra firma again."

"Leave a message," he said by habit.

"Righto."

Maureen knew that by the time she returned, she'd have come to her decision, bad luck be damned. Let it be a healthy child, she'd decide. A happy, healthy child, boy or girl, whose only need was a loving family. Could they find one like that?

* * *

A snap decision, she later called it. It had taken her more than a week and the trip away to think about it. But in the context, it was a snap decision. As it turned out, after the seemingly endless forms, interviews and background checks, another year passed. It was a year of follow-up calls, classes and impromptu trips to foster homes. Disappointing visit after visit—both online and in person—to see children of crack addicts, battered and unresponsive toddlers, and other tragic wards of the state.

In the meantime, Janice had grown into a skinny ten-year-old who took ballet and piano lessons. Maureen had remained with her job at the clinic and was now going for a master's degree. Jeffrey had insisted they stay in the condo till he saw what happened at the hospital. He was awaiting a superior's retirement; Jeffrey was next in line, he was convinced.

Eventually, the social worker assigned to their case did her best to hammer home the realities they faced. First, it was nearly impossible to get a baby other than one plagued by a host of drug-related or other developmental problems. Of course they also needed love, she stressed, but not all prospective parents were up to the challenge. If they were interested, the adoption process could be over within a month or two. From there, the choice narrowed to kids as old as five or more, most of whom had already been through the system long enough to grow a thick shell. "Here are some wonderful children who need lots of TLC," she said. "Of course, we can't guarantee that a loving home would make all the difference, but..."

As the woman went on, Maureen realized she'd gone back on her original idea. The two of them had gone on with their busy lives, addressing the subject now and then but never stopping to check their course and ask themselves exactly what they were looking for in a child. Was it the perfect infant left on the doorstep by a loving but poor young woman who wanted more than the streets for her child? That sort of thing didn't seem to happen anymore—if it ever did.

Without catching themselves, they had fallen into the trap of expecting, day by day, that special phone call on her cell that would alert them to a baby who, at that very moment, was being placed on the list. "Arrive within the hour," the voice would promise, "and the child is yours."

For years, she had waited for that call. As she understood better and better the bureaucracy inherent in the child welfare system, she came to the conclusion that if such a child did materialize and the call came...why, her phone would be out of range.

* * *

The boy had a bright smile despite a missing tooth. Straight, reddish-brown hair seemed permanently matted despite the regular care he received. He typically walked slowly with his arms folded and head down, a defensive posture formed over five years of care from an aunt who swung her open palm in his direction often enough to forge a habit that could last for years.

His guardian, the adoption officer explained, had been arrested two years ago for manslaughter when her car had struck and killed a girl on a bicycle. The aunt had been drunk, which was not unusual. But Mickey still had frequent nightmares about seeing the girl. Shrieking to his aunt, who'd been nodding off. And watching as the empty bicycle flew into the air, then landed, its wheels spinning for seconds more. "He says these things in the night, so we've pieced together what we know of the story," she said. "He won't discuss them by day. Not to us, anyway."

By and large, however, the eight-year-old was healthy so far as they could see. The officer went through the boy's medical files, his immunization reports—missing a few doctor receipts though the aunt had completed the immunization record—and evaluation reports from the various counselors and other mental health professionals who'd seen Mickey over the past year. Oh, and there was the boy's passport. The aunt had apparently taken the boy, less than a year old, with her for a few months to Central America on an English-teaching position. From which she was soon fired. "If you like," said the officer, "you can take him out for an afternoon, then a full day, then an overnight. After each meeting we talk, and ultimately you all make the decision."

Maureen noticed she was biting her lip. She peeked through the door, which was ajar, to catch another glimpse at the boy swinging his feet in the molded plastic chair outside the office. Oh, he was the one, wasn't he? She turned to Jeffrey and saw the hopeful look in his eyes, too. They would make this work. They would give this boy a family.

One hurdle, of course, would be Janice. An only child for ten years wouldn't just welcome a new brother, two years her junior, with open arms. Not sincerely, anyway. If they did end up adopting Mickey, they'd have to spend plenty more time with their daughter, too. Especially because of the support the boy would need in dealing with the tragedy that had landed him in foster care.

* * *

Maureen and Jeffrey's first problem didn't follow the usual path of conflicts over commodities like toys, desserts and TV time. Initially, the two were heartened by how the boy seemed to sense that Janice was determined to keep her possessions to herself and thus kept his distance. But no. They later realized, as they got him his own toys, that they'd entirely missed the point.

The boy got along fine with Janice because he didn't feel entitled to *anything*.

If served ice cream, Mickey would swish it around a bit on his plate till it melted, occasionally looking up like a boy who'd been served spinach or liver. Could I please be excused? his eyes pleaded—though of course he didn't feel he deserved that, either.

"Mickey." Jeffrey would never have believed he'd be someday lecturing a kid to eat his dessert. It was one of those evenings, four months after the adoption process had completed. Janice had finished long ago and scurried away, but not before asking in vain if she could help Mickey finish his dessert. "We don't give you ice cream, cookies or cake because it's good for you," Jeffrey began. "It's not going to make you grow up to be a big boy, and it doesn't build strong bones. We give it to you because it's *fun.*"

"Fun?" he whispered. Maureen, across the room, wanted to cry.

"Yes, fun. You get it because we love you and want to put a smile on your little face. We want to see the ice cream drip down your chin and run all over your shirt so much that we have to scrub out the stains. You're a good kid, and dessert is your chance to be a kid."

The boy betrayed traces of a grin. "But...I *am* a kid!" he said meekly.

"Right. Now, I'm going to leave the room, and you're going to sit here a while and dwell on that. When you're ready, I want you to put a little, just a little, on your spoon and taste it. I want you to think about something nice when you do. You can stop there if you want or finish it. After that," he leaned closer, "come to me quietly and ask for some more—this time."

With that Jeffrey left the room, rolling his eyes. He sat before the television, staring at but not comprehending the sitcom Janice and Maureen were watching together. Finally, he could stand it no longer and signaled Maureen to check on him. Your turn, his eyes told her.

Loud laughter rang from the kitchen, and Jeffrey sprang from his armchair to see Mickey grinning guiltily at the table. Ice cream covered most of his face, his chest and his hair. He had smeared it around on the linen tablecloth, and his spoon was balanced on one ear.

"Well, I'll be damned..." was all Jeffrey could think of to say.

Grinning, the boy replied, "More?"

Toys took longer. Maureen had been braiding her daughter's hair while the little girl fondled a stuffed raccoon her mother didn't notice at first. When she spotted it, Maureen paused in her braiding and realized that both children had a raccoon doll; Mickey's was missing its nose, and that was the one Janice held. The other one was on Janice's pillow. "That one is Mickey's, right, Honey?"

"Oh," said Janice, "Mickey let me play with it."

Her mother nodded, but then she spotted another of Mickey's toys: a dump truck with a little horn that automatically sounded when the vehicle was pushed backwards. "And what about this one?"

"Mickey brought it in and left it."

"But—"

Yesterday!" the girl added with pride.

"Ohhh." She tied off the braid and looked around some more. Mickey's Tonka dump truck. Mickey's G.I. Joe. Protruding from beneath the bed, Mickey's Operation game. "Honey, excuse me for a minute." She wrapped an elastic band around where she'd stopped.

"Where are you going?"

"I'll be right back."

Of course, Janice knew where her mother was going. "Mickey," Maureen said to the boy who lay on his bed, his legs and feet facing up the wall. He was stretching a rubber band and singing a little song to himself. His lamp, with a grinning clown's arms wrapped around the post, was in place on the dresser. Above, in slight motion, was his mobile of fighter planes. The window curtains, printed with assorted race cars, further brightened up the room.

The usual array of scattered toys, however, was not to be seen; alone sat a blue ball in the corner. She looked into his toy box: empty but for a headless plastic robot and a few pieces of other toys. "Where are your toys?" she asked.

The boy rolled over and scanned the room as if he himself had just noticed they were missing. Then he shrugged, returned to his supine position and walked his feet back up the wall. His sweat socks curled around his ankles, and his pillow lay bunched against the headboard the way it looked when Mickey awoke from the nightmares he still had now and then. "They're around."

"Do you like your toys, Mickey?"

"Yeah. Sure, I do." His reply was unconvincing.

"Mickey..." She sat on the bed; this was a tricky one. "Mickey, do you know what it means when something is 'yours'?"

His head, upside-down to Maureen's view, cocked in reply as he considered her question. She was about to repeat her question, or simply leave, when he said, "Means I play with it."

"Y-yes, Mickey, it means you play with it. Or it means you can play with it if you want. Anytime, we mean. If you want to play with your G.I. Joe or your dump truck—"

"Not my G.I. Joe anymore. Not my truck."

"Of course they're yours. I bought you the truck, and Daddy must have gotten you the G.I. Joe."

"Jan says they're hers. But I can play with them if I ask."

So that's what's going on, she thought. It took many more days of such conversations—with Mickey and with Janice—before Jeffrey took things in his own hands.

"Daddy! What are you doing!" Scooping up Mickey's toys was what he was doing, he told her. And throwing them out.

"But they're Mickey's!"

"I don't see Mickey asking me to keep them around," he calmly replied.

The girl ran past him and literally dragged the boy out of his room. "Look! Want him to throw out all your toys?"

The boy stared at his father and said nothing. He'd never been allowed to have any toys *before* he came here. Why should now be any different?

"Okay, then." Jeffrey took the little red plastic racing car, the last he could spot, and put it into the opaque trash bag.

"You can't!" shouted Janice as her father disappeared from sight. "They're Mickey's!"

He stopped. "Oh?"

"DON'T YOU TAKE MY BROTHER'S THINGS!"

"Well, where shall I put them, then?"

The little girl paused a long time before speaking, her head down. "They go in *his* room," she quietly said.

Jeffrey shrugged, then slowly turned around to head toward Mickey's room. His daughter stopped him; she reached for the bag. "I...I'll do it."

* * *

Months later came the blow. Things had been going well for the Strattons. Jeffrey's long hours and patience were rewarded with a promotion to the position he'd sought. Maureen was up to her final thesis before receiving her M.A. Best of all, the children were getting along fine. Mickey clearly needed to improve when it came to standing up for himself at school, where he was in the third grade. In the meantime, his big sister protected him every step of the way. Three grades ahead, she possessed a knack for showing up in the right place in the schoolyard, in the cafeteria, the hallway. She egged him along when he needed it, and if she felt her brother needed her to shove another boy over, she did that, too.

One day, however, Mickey arrived home complaining of a

headache. Maureen, her day a busy one of errands and library research, noticed he also was walking peculiarly. She held him close, instantly realized the boy felt unusually warm, and carried him into his room. "You, little man, have a fever," she told him.

In her and Jeffrey's bedroom she unplugged the little TV, as per the special treatment they gave either child when one was hit with a bug—and took it to Mickey's. This had happened often enough in their first months at Hollister Elementary. Then, all comic books belonging to either child went on loan to the sick one. Later, once the illness seemed to subside, the child received the special dessert of his or her choice. First things first, though.

The night passed, and the fever seemed to be going nowhere. It didn't go up, didn't go down, and Mickey wasn't showing any cold symptoms except for the headache. His back and limbs felt stiff and achy, he mentioned when he complained at all. His throat felt sore, and his stomach bothered him.

As soon as Jeffrey came home from his shift—he still did an occasional back-to-back—he gave the boy a thorough going-over and came to the conclusion it was influenza. It was spreading in various forms around Broward County, along with the rest of the state, he said, and it was only a matter of time before Mickey began sniffing and sneezing like the rest of the cases he'd been hearing about.

A few more days passed with no change in symptoms. After checking on his son one evening, Jeffrey took Maureen aside. "I'm taking him in, Mau. We're doing everything right, and he's just lying there—aside from going to the bathroom. This may be something more than flu."

"What?" Maureen replied, reacting mostly from the concern on his face. "What do you think?"

"I don't really know what to thi—"

"MaaaaAAAAAAA!" came Mickey's cry accompanied by a loud thud. Blood trickled from the boy's nose as Jeffrey lifted him up to return him to the bed.

"Daddy, I can't walk! I can't walk! I can't..."

And his parents saw it, too, that Mickey could not even lift his arms to wrap them around his father. Janice watched, a shaking hand gripping the belt loop of her mother's terry cloth robe, as Jeffrey scooped the sobbing boy into his arms to take him to the hospital.

The crushing news came after a month-long barrage of tests that included a lumbar puncture to examine Mickey's spinal fluid. However rare a case this was, particularly in the U.S., a close associate of Jeffrey delivered the verdict: undeniably, it was paralysis due to poliomyelitis. Paralysis below the neck. His question echoed what had already occurred to Jeffrey. "Hadn't the boy been immunized?"

Maureen gasped for air. "W-we...got him a booster shot...just before he started school."

"Which should supplement the shots he received as a child," said the doctor, bewildered. "While it is remotely possible for a child to contract the virus from a vaccine, the odds—"

"Yes, the shots he recei—" Jeffrey's mouth dropped open. "Oh, shit."

He grabbed his wife's hand.

"Oh, no. This didn't happen. Ohhh...shit!"

A moment later she figured it out, too. Mickey's aunt, who languished in the women's state prison miles away, had actually had two victims. The first had died quickly on a leaf-strewn residential street and lay buried in a nearby cemetery.

The second lay paralyzed in a hospital bed, his records falsified, the money for his immunization visits perhaps laid on the counter of the local liquor store. He'd been exposed, most likely, during their brief stint abroad.

And by the point he received the booster shot, the infection had already reached the boy's nervous system.

* * *

He sounded less rushed than usual over the phone. "Maureen?"

"Hi, Jeff."

He paused. "You've been crying," he said.

Maureen wiped her nose. "It's all right, Jeff. I'll be all right. How're you doing?"

"Things're okay. Strange being in this little motel when it's only thirty minutes' drive home."

"Yeah. Well, you've got enough to do, setting up Mickey's therapy, looking for a house—"

"I think I found one."

She wasn't into this conversation at all. Mickey had been unusually testy tonight as she fed him, ran him through the range-of-motion and stretching exercises that were hers to attempt in between clinic visits, bathed him, brushed his teeth, dressed him for bed and read him a story to ease the thoughts that ran through his head at night. Not to mention help him fall asleep. Janice, usually grateful for the minutes her mother spent with her alone—Maureen made sure to go right in—tonight was distant and replied to questions with "Yes, Mother" and "No, Mother." The only full sentence she uttered, in fact, was to ask whether her mother had sewn the button back on Casey.

Maureen nevertheless remained with her daughter till Janice went to bed, earlier than the girl had to. And then she walked down the hall, past the kitchen with the piled-up pots, into her room and cried into her pillow for the next half-hour.

Until her cellphone rang. "Okay, tell me about it."

"It's two floors plus a full basement. Three bedrooms on top plus a little room downstairs where we can put the exercise gear. Construction looks solid enough to mount a chair lift. Got a garage, a full back door to the basement, kitchen and dining room, level front and backyard. Six blocks from the school on the other side from where we are, a mile to the hospital, half-mile to shopping. What else do you need?"

"It sounds...sounds good, I guess. When can I see it?"

"I'm free tomorrow afternoon. Why don't I swing on over and pick all of you up about two-ish?"

Swing. "Fine. See you then." She hung up.

22

Defending the indefensible. These weren't the words Lana, at ten years old, would use to describe her desire to help Cynthia. But in so many words, this was exactly what she thought as she lay against the corner of her bedroom, her feet curled warmly under a pillow that leaned against the warm baseboard. And now, alone in the house, she thought about someone else: her father.

And the last time she had tried to help her mother—or anyone.

Oh, it wasn't as though the young girl didn't clear the table after meals, tidy her room on occasion or put her dirty clothes into the appropriate bins in the basement. "You're not helping *us* so much as doing your part," her father used to say with a gentle smile she could still see in her mind. From early on, Lana had learned to be an active member of her adoptive family. And, like many daughters, she was clearly Daddy's girl.

Lana blew bubbles through a straw into her chocolate milk and remembered early one morning—she must have been six or seven— when he woke her up. She had smelled coffee before she opened her eyes. He was dressed in red plaid and old jeans, had shaved too quickly, and gazed at her with his deep blue eyes. She could see her father wake up a bit more when he returned her smile. "You're going fishing!" she'd said.

He'd shaken his head and run his fingers through his flaxen blond hair. "No," he replied. *"We're* going fishing. That is, unless you want more sleep."

Lana had never, ever gone fishing. It was one of those things he had promised her, that they'd get to do when she was "ready." She'd never known quite what that meant. She knew what it meant to be "patient" but once confessed she didn't know what doctors and patients had to do with it at all.

The closest times she had shared with her Daddy had been while they watched many of the old movies he'd watch whenever they came on. Mother never seemed to be around those nights. She was seeing a girlfriend, it always seemed, when Lana asked.

But fishing! That day was one of Lana's fondest memories. They'd sat for hours in a rowboat he'd borrowed from a friend, and it didn't even matter that the sky was overcast and they'd caught nothing. She and her father had talked and talked...about everything, it seemed, and best of all, he made her feel like a grown-up.

They'd left early when storm clouds approached. On the way back from the lake they talked some more—about her friends, classmates, teachers—but as they pulled into the driveway, she noticed he had stopped listening to her. She, too, had noticed the living room curtain pulled, then released. And although she didn't know what it meant, she also heard the back door slam closed.

He was a different person after that, and it seemed he and her mother were always fighting about something. A short while after each argument, Lana would hear her door open. Daddy would step quietly in and tell her a story to help her relax, and he would often explain that married people sometimes had problems they needed to solve, and that it took time.

After this kept on for a few months, Lana began to act asleep when he came in. The words took on less and less meaning. Words in general meant less. The only reality was the fighting, which inevitably began after her mother returned from "seeing friends."

Lana had figured out what kind of friends they were by the time her parents divorced. From the first week after her father moved out, *the men* began to come. One of about two or three at a time would visit on a regular basis, and her mother's orders were explicit. At the sight of headlights in the driveway, Lana was to go up to her room, close the door and the light, and make no sound whatsoever until her mother's guest left—sometimes in the morning. It was an arrangement that frequently led to harsh punishment. What young girl could keep out of the bathroom for hours, or at least could resist sneaking downstairs for a cold chicken wing?

Breakfast and dinnertime at home were hardly out of the ordinary, at least for a divorced mother and her daughter. The two talked little; mostly, they stayed out of one another's way once past a few cursory questions about school and the importance of keeping up studies. But where most other children wrestled with siblings or sat riveted to the Xbox, Lana followed a different ritual four or five nights a week.

Her father had tried several times to persuade his wife to let Lana stay with him across the state, but it was no use. Despite the woman's nocturnal activities, she had apparently been discreet enough during the court proceedings that custody of Lana fell to her for lack of evidence of continued infidelity. Also weighing into the court's decision was the man's work position: a salesman who frequently traveled to meet clients and attend conferences.

Once won, Lana had become a prize to be withheld from the person who could most provide a loving home. And her mother wasn't going to relinquish her one way to hurt her now-former husband for the embarrassment he had put her through with the divorce.

After a time, regular visits became even more difficult. Lana's father was transferred to a nearby state, and when he occasionally needed to swap her scheduled weekends with him, his wife inevitably came up with reason after reason that no other time would fit her plans. The result: spans of several weeks the girl spent weekends at home. When she did see her father, he'd promise things would work out. He asked, too, that she remember her mother was a good woman, however hard that could be for him to say.

Perhaps because of the old movies she now watched alone, Lana did believe that her mother was basically good, the lovers basically bad. Why else would Lana have to stay so quietly in the dark of her room as she listened to the giggling, the laughter and...? She knew the men by their voices, and she remained convinced that someday she'd need to describe one to the police—by voice rather than face. "That's the one," she'd tell the officer. "Sure, I'm sure, that's him." And then her mother, in the hospital with a minor injury, would apologize for everything and promise to be the mother Lana had always prayed for...

The night Lana now thought about, for the thousandth time in the corner of her room, was the night, about two years ago, that she heard a new voice. It wasn't unusual. Mother's boyfriends lasted from a couple of nights to a few weeks, and it didn't take Lana long to learn a new voice. (She even imitated their voices to herself, imagining their being gunned down by police after an elusive chase.)

What was unusual was that this man, his first night over, had gotten into a loud shouting match with her mother. She didn't know quite what they were talking about—words like "bitch" and worse kept coming up—but Lana began to get worried. Three times the girl almost ran into the hallway, big flashlight wielded high, to chase the bad man away and restore peace to their house. Each time, however, she talked herself out of it.

When the front door slammed, Lana collapsed on the bed, both from hunger and from sheer exhaustion. She awoke two hours later from a sound down in the yard. Someone was there, she realized. He was looking up at their windows from the shadows, and he wore a hoodie that obscured his face. No matter: She hadn't seen the man's face in her house, anyway. He came closer—to the latticework up against the house! It looked like he was going to try climbing up among the vines, and the first place he could get in...was her room.

She'd fix him. This was her chance, and she could almost see the gaze, rich with love and relief, on her mother's face as eight-year-old Lana sneaked down the stairs, dragged the big cast-iron saucepan up the stairs and heaved it onto the windowsill. Looking down before opening the window, she couldn't see the man. That meant, no doubt, he was on his way up.

Lana understood the element of surprise. She kept her bedroom light off, gathered strength for a moment, and flung open the window. "Take *that,* suckeerrrr!" she shrieked, and thrust the heavy kettle.

Too late did she recognize her father's face. The kettle struck him squarely and knocked him to the concrete patio. He was dead before the ambulance arrived, and a part of Lana—the part that loved, perhaps—died also with the vehicle's fading taillights.

* * *

The moonlight pierced through the shadows of the belfry, where Cynthia clung—hovered beside, rather—the massive hook from which the church bell swung. This was one of many places forbidden to children and even most adults of the local Episcopalian congregation. Climb too far up the spiral staircase leading from the vestibule while the bell is ringing, came the warning, and your hearing would never be the same. Stand beside the bell while it rang, and your dizziness would send you right over the rail.

Just like little Jesse Colter, a five-year-old who, some forty years before, had fallen one bright Sunday morning. His ghost, Natalie had told Cynthia, was said to haunt the belfry still—but they needn't be worried. How could a ghost threaten the living, especially when these particular living were present in spirit only?

"Don't go down to ring it yet, Nancy," Cynthia said to her mysterious friend. "I need to know something."

Natalie saw it coming, knew from earlier that day when she wafted, unbeknownst, beside Cynthia and Lana on their way home from school. "Sure! What's up?"

There was no good way to ask. "H-how can you ring the bell? Or hold up that pencil? I like that you, um, st-stuck up for me—oh, God!—but..." She was as embarrassed by the pun as by what she was intimating, and she remained on the bell, head down, as it gently rocked in the breeze.

Natalie matched her friend's ashamed tone. "I...I wasn't lying. N-not really, you know?"

"No. Please tell me."

"Well, it's like throwing a ball or jumping rope. Some kids can...um, do it better than other kids. You and Lana didn't learn to *immaterialize* from someone. You had bad nights and...just did it. I said my big sister showed me, just before she...I dunno, got a little older and forgot the whole thing. That's what happens. You start being a teenager and...it goes. Everything. I guess I...just had a head start or something.

"Look, if I showed you at your school how easy it was, you wouldn't be my friend. You woulda been..."

"Scared?"

Natalie paused; she was getting good at this. "Yeah, scared. It happened one time before. In the city."

"Well, why do you come around here all the time? You live over there, you told us, don't you? And how..."

"What?"

"How can you *immaterialize* during the day? A school day, too, and in the...same clothes. Where...*where's your body when you're here?*"

So, Natalie realized. Cynthia had been thinking hard about what

Lana had said. "I told you...I don't like where I live. Lots of kids in the city do what we do. But some of them are real bad. Some can materialize a little the way I do. And they break things and hurt people. I just—" It came to her.

"Look, I have no parents, all right? I live in an orphanage and—and nobody but my sister cares about me and if I go to class or not or just stay in my little room and...oh, forget it, all right? I'll just go back!" She turned to leave.

"Nancy, n-no! Please don't go. I'm sorry. I didn't m-mean to make you cry." She dropped down from the bell and sat beside Natalie, now crouched against the inner wall of the tower, head between her knees.

Smiling.

Cynthia was angry now. Angry at herself for being so cruel when she should have known Nancy had something she couldn't say. Angry, too, at Lana. Why wouldn't she stay out of this? She, who acted so damn...grown up all the time, why didn't she just—

"Did you ever..." Natalie's voice trailed off.

"What?"

"...ever wish you could leave your...body behind forever, just stay...*immaterial* and fly around in the clouds and see what you want, learn what you want, and...not have to listen to parents or anybody else? Did you ever?"

Cynthia sighed and slumped further against the wall, almost passing through it. "Oh, brother." She thought of her mother, hung over and nasty when she wasn't drunk and nasty. Her father, who hid behind his newspaper and stayed late at work whenever he could. And friends? She had just two. "A lot," she said.

"What would you do to be that way? I think I know what I'd do." Natalie's head had lifted; the girl was staring into Cynthia's eyes. As if she had the power to grant her own wish?

Cynthia pondered the question. "Um, I-I don't know what I'd do. Um..."

"Sometimes," offered Natalie, staring intensely, "I think I would die for it." She looked back to Cynthia.

The reply came quickly. "Yeah...I think sometimes I would, too."

* * *

Nobody but Lana's mother, the police and her school administrators knew what had transpired that night long ago. Her classmates knew only that Lana, while the same age, was no child. Her thin, bony face and tight-lipped smile, her jet-black hair firmly bound behind her head, the long-sleeved turtlenecks she wore virtually all year, despite style or season, gave more the impression of a spinster schoolmarm than an intelligent, curious ten-year-old.

Her nightly activities—at least till the girl chanced upon "ghosting"—were in fact what had given Lana her best defense: a mature adult's knack for holding her tongue in the face of danger. But in a child, such an ability was in fact harmful. It made her silent or at least monosyllabic when called on in class, where peer pressure was the greatest danger of all.

Her test scores, at least, were flawless; she had plenty of time, if not always the concentration, to study. But if a teacher sent her to the front of the room—most, like Mrs. Genovese, did so only once—she would read her report with icily calculated delivery. It was not that she was merely able to shrug off the guffaws of the many classmates who openly referred to her as "Dragon Lady Junior" once they'd tired of "class corpse." Rather, she seemed convinced of the existence of only one other person in the room.

That person was the teacher, who typically sat toward the back of the classroom during presentations. Lana never glanced at the page she held in her hand, though she read it word for word with near perfection. The gaze of her startlingly blue eyes, instead, fastened hard to those of the teacher from start to finish. And said, over and over: You will not repeat this mistake.

It mattered little where image extended beyond reality. Lana had learned early how to blur, even obliterate, the distinction in the eyes of those around her. The result was that classmates with any sophistication whatsoever knew enough to stay far away from her— to taunt her only in open areas, when among a crowd of friends, if at all.

Others, like Cynthia, were the innocents.

Lana watched glumly from the far row as someone nearly every day prodded or humiliated Cynthia. These rituals were inevitable, Lana was convinced, until her friend took her advice and put up the proper defenses. But while Cynthia was on her own before her peers, there was another who seemed to pose a far greater danger.

Was it worth it to think she could, or should, try to help anyone ever again?

Lana's every instinct said no. But just as she truly had believed her mother sought an end to the dark side of her life, so Lana believed Cynthia did not want whatever it was that Nancy wanted of her.

She would be sure of her facts this time. There was no undoing the horror she had brought upon her own life...but Lana would do whatever she needed to help the only friend she'd managed to keep.

23

"Oh, Jeff, it's beautiful!"

Priding himself on his own taste as well as his understanding of his wife's wishes, Jeffrey fully expected to hear these words as he ushered his wife into the former Leffingwell house.

Instead, he heard: "Oh. It's...nice, Jeff."

Wanda, with no need of psychic ability, had deliberately fallen well behind the couple on their way up the snowy walk. For one thing, few wives on earth, at least in America, let their husbands pick out their houses.

She also didn't need to have heard the rumors to feel a certain...something about the house. It was trouble, her bones told her, though she would never, could never, admit such stirrings to anyone.

"Nice? I think it's a great place, Maureen. Just wait'll you see—"

"Jeff, give-me-a-chance. I know all too well that you saw the house and fell in love with it. Please keep in mind that you have had quite some time to spend looking at the place, and it's not till now that I've even been able to arrange time to join you. Did you ever think I might want—"

"Yes, I thought about that. But let me show you through it. It's got—"

Maureen shook her head. "Je-eff," she said, her voice taking on a musical condescension that did not fail to get her what she wanted, when it was important enough, "would you *please* wait outside for a few minutes? I want the pleasure of seeing the place without—a sales pitch. *Without seeing the movers carry my furniture in ahead of me.* Even Wanda is letting me use my own eyes."

Jeffrey was seething, but Wanda had known him too many years to let that upset her. "Coffee at the Thruway Diner is real hot stuff, Jeff."

He stormed out.

Maureen sighed when the door slammed.

Wanda shrugged. "Solid door, huh?" The two giggled, and Maureen felt free and suddenly relaxed enough to see the house with some objectivity. Part of her anxiety, she realized, was that today was the first morning she had ever left Mickey alone with Emily Sanders, the therapist they'd been fortunate enough to have found from among this very community. The woman had readily agreed to be reimbursed for travel to and from the old neighborhood until the family moved closer to Hollister.

Janice was staying for a few hours with neighbors, which left Mickey and Emily alone for the first time. Was she wrong to feel so nervous? Their agency itself, in stressing Emily's impeccable references—including five years as nurse for Hollister Elementary—had noted the two would eventually have to build their own relationship. Maureen knew that.

Just the same, she could not stop thinking like a mother. And, after all, why should she?

Maureen let Wanda lead the way around the house. She fought the urge to find fault with the house at every turn (really, her husband could be so damn *right* sometimes), but after thirty minutes she had to admit she liked it, too. The modest skylights above the living room made the place cheerful, even if they did need a good washing. The stairway banister and the railing of the upstairs hallway had obviously been reinforced by a good carpenter. The rooms were spacious, though a surprising amount of clutter remained from the previous owners. (She'd have to learn more about these people.) And, she conceded to Jeffrey, she did have her eye on that dining room. A nearby extra room even had ample space for Mickey's particular needs—all they'd need for his therapy.

By the time Jeffrey returned from the diner, ready for a fight from heavy doses of caffeine and donut sugar, the fight was over. The two had long before researched the neighborhood, learned that the community was right for them. And with Jeffrey's nodding assurance that they would make further decisions of major significance together, she agreed the house seemed perfect after all.

* * *

How far she'd come. Natalie was thinking about another prior episode, from the last days of her past life, and what she learned about her body's understanding of its surroundings. She needed to be absolutely sure for her plan to work.

That night, she had used too much toilet paper. At least, that was the apparent reason her father had swung at her the moment she'd opened the bathroom door. One look at his deep blue eyes, and she'd tightened her every muscle. She almost knew by then which hand would come at her.

Almost crawling into her bedroom, her head spinning, she whimpered to the carpet an excuse no one would hear. That, in fact, she had used very little toilet paper. What she'd been doing was twirling the roll backwards on its holder; the paper's cardboard tube was more oval than round, resulting in a rhythmic rattle when rolled. She had giggled at the sound it made. Like a rattlesnake, she thought, from the scene of a western movie she'd recently viewed. Hey thar Joshua watch out fer thet thar rat'ler...*ghugaghugaghugaghu...*

Was it the few extra minutes she spent that night in the bathroom that had set him off? Was it truly the rattling of the paper roll that had gotten him yelling outside the bathroom door?

Or was it the muted sound of a child having fun?

Frozen in age at nine years, Natalie was spared such tormented musings. Now in the backyard of Cynthia's house, she instead thought about what had followed that night. She had climbed onto her bed, still reeling with pain, and it had taken very little concentration for her spirit to escape her body that time. There was no place in particular she really wanted to go this time. She floated around anyhow. Soon, she found herself in the local movie house. Playing was Disney's *Fantasia,* which had already started.

The theater was an old one, the only one in the vicinity that hadn't been converted to six or more smaller theaters. Natalie grinned at the prospect of seeing a movie...for free, yet! She'd perched on the railing of the balcony, wished for popcorn, heard the opening notes of Dukas' *The Sorcerer's Apprentice,* watched Mickey Mouse stare, transfixed, at his master's work—

Trouble. In a flash Natalie merged into her body before her bedroom door had opened halfway. "Get up off the goddamn bed and help your mother fold the laundry," he said. She was up a moment later, her head still stinging, the lesson learned. She didn't understand how or why, but no matter how far she was from her body, it seemed she could recognize a threat back home and could return swiftly when she had to. It was all about how her body, on the bed, continued to listen for danger. Her closed eyes were of no use, and she wouldn't smell anything unless there was, say, smoke from a fire. It was all about hearing.

That warning of danger, of course, would later fail her—since the very first shot fired was the one that had killed her. How could she have foreseen death would steal her, however incompletely, from another room? That the shouting, nothing unusual those days, was in fact a prelude to the death of her entire family?

In her present quest to have a friend, one who was all hers, Natalie couldn't think about that. She knew Cynthia was with Lana. Natalie had seen them floating high up above the neighborhood and even into the clouds. It was time, then, to test out her theory.

Cynthia's body sat slumped into two big pillows that leaned against the headboard. Natalie first put just her face into the room, then the rest of her. She spotted the chubby girl, looked around a bit, and stepped in the rest of the way. Natalie was intruding. She knew that, and, if Cynthia returned, that would be the end of their friendship.

Along with Natalie's plan.

Concentrating deeply, Natalie ignored the pinup posters and curios that any young visitor would want to regard one by one. Instead, she passed into Cynthia's closet all but her face and her left arm. On that hand she materialized a single pinkie—something she could not have done a year ago.

And she waited—ready to vanish in an instant should her friend return, having sensed a threat. While she was away and *immaterial,* Cynthia wouldn't notice Natalie was in the room. And once the girl re-entered her body, she'd never know what had transpired.

Nothing happened. Cynthia did not return.

From everything she understood, it was sound alone, such as footsteps in the hall or a door creaking open, that alerted the spirit about impending danger to the body. So as long as she remained up with Lana in the sky, Cynthia would not respond, plain and simple, because she *perceived no threat.* Despite Lana's efforts.

That busybody.

Natalie solidified the rest of her hand, waited almost a full minute, then passed halfway out of the closet and did the entire arm. Still nothing. Wherever Cynthia's spirit currently roamed, she felt no sense of danger to her body from Natalie's presence. If this worked all the way, only one part of Natalie's plan remained before her—one object that must make its way, nonthreateningly, into this room. And Cynthia's own sense of curiosity would shortly take care of that.

Within minutes, the girl could fully materialize—as much as she was able—and remain in this state, by Cynthia's side, for about fifteen or twenty seconds. It got difficult then. She could feel herself fading back, but before she did Natalie caught sight of herself in Cynthia's mirror. The look she saw in her own face was resolute, determined...yet still hinting of a sadness, the emptiness of a young girl denied the

God-given?

right to grow up. It wasn't fair, she reminded herself even as she scowled to shake off the thought.

No, it wasn't fair what had happened to her. What she was contemplating, here in Cynthia's room, perhaps wasn't a fair thing to do, either.

But, she reminded herself as well, her ethereal world, like the physical, was not a fair place.

* * *

"When danger calls, I am not slow..."

"It's hip hip hip—"

"And awaaay we goooo!"

Cynthia sighed as she and Lana drifted out of the clouds, above a vast comforter of cotton over the Earth. Neither had ever flown on a plane before, but Cynthia had heard they traveled this high. "I thought I'd *die* if we never got online videos," she said.

"It's nice getting to see those old shows," Lana replied. "I bet Underdog never flew *this* high."

The two paused along their skyward path and looked down. "It's weird not being scared, huh?"

Cynthia grunted in reply, but her mind was suddenly dwelling on Nancy. Stop it, she told herself. No sense in feeling guilty about hurting her friend's feelings. Nancy seemed to understand that there were just these...things about her. About her story, anyway. And how she was around during school hours, and she always wore the same clothes, and—

But no! They'd cleared up these things. Cynthia needed now to put all that out of her mind. She didn't know how, five miles up from Hollister, she had thought about Nancy in the first place. As if her friend were very close.

No matter. Snap out of it! Get moody now, Cynthia told herself, and Lana would know. She always did. Then she'd get moody, too. And that would start a big fight.

That's what "ghosting" was supposed to get you away from, wasn't it?

"Penny for your thoughts," said Lana.

Cynthia grinned. "Inflation. Costs a buck—fifty cents for you. Hey..."

"What?"

"Wanna...naahh—yeah. Wanna go to the *moon?*"

In a rare off-guard moment, Lana didn't know what to say. "Um...I guess—I dunno..."

Cynthia was bewildered, too. After all, Lana was the idea girl. She was game for everything! And in their spiritual form... "Well, why not?"

Lana couldn't say why not, so she shrugged and, smiling, passed her fist through Cynthia's jaw. "Bang, zoom!" she cried.

"To the moon!" countered her friend.

Some time passed, perhaps five or ten minutes. But the two had stopped talking. Cynthia had just gotten another nagging feeling about Nancy, and the feeling subsided. Not without its effect, though. Add to that the creeping notion that she and Lana were somehow breaking a law, and...

Asteroids. Why, thought Lana, am I thinking about asteroids? Then she believed she figured it out. "I saw a movie once about an asteroid that hit Earth and killed practically everybody."

Blankly Cynthia answered, "It was a meteor, I think."

"Meteor, asteroid, whatever. But we're not that far up. I think one is going to come right over anyway, pass right through me, and make my body, back home, piss my pants."

Cynthia chuckled. "I *thought* you wet the bed."

Lana thought briefly of Leonard Brewster at school, then put that scene out of her mind. "Hey, I call it"—she donned an exaggerated French accent—"'Eau de Toilette.' That's what they call some perfume, y'know. Toilet water."

Innocently, Cynthia said, "Only the best for the guys!"

Lana halted in her flight. Cynthia, realizing that even in the air her friend retained her penchant for stopping without warning, returned to her side.

The two were hovering at the very edge of the Earth's atmosphere. The Earth was sprawled out beneath them. And the moon, full that night, loomed even larger than it seemed when it rose in the evening. It was big! Cynthia was enthralled. Lana was, well, in...

shock?

Lana had begun to shake her head. How could she have agreed to come up here?

The guys...the best for the guys...

And she became Monica in the book *Papa, Please Get the Moon for Me.* Her father, when she was four or five, used to read it to her almost every night. It was the one she most asked for.

"Papa, please get the moon for me."

And in her mind, her father joined her in the book and took a very long ladder to the top of a high mountain. She beamed with anticipation as he mounted the first steps on his determined quest. He can do anything, she thought. He's my daddy.

The only one I love in all the world.

...the best...for the guys...

Following the story, he would reach the top but with the moon still looming too large for his grasp. *"My daughter Monica would like to play with you,"* he said to the moon, *"but you are much too big."*

The gentle moon

Only the best for the guys...

would explain that every night, it got a little bit smaller and soon would be small enough to be plucked from the sky. Lana would be thrilled, dancing and jumping with her friend, till the moon got so small it disappeared completely.

Only the best...for the guys!

But the sky is shaken by a window rumbling open. Lana finds herself leaning out the window to see the dark form on the ladder below. "Take *that,* suckerrrr..." as an asteroid crashes into her father—the ladder smashes to pieces floating, floating through eternity and taking her papa with it. Lana found herself screaming, reaching out toward what she realized took place nowhere but in her own mind.

"Lana...?"

"G-gotta go back." She sped back to Earth.

"Lana, what happened? Tell me! Please, you were screaming and I..." Her friend had already passed into the cloud cover. "I just wanted to help," she muttered to the nothingness.

Somehow, Lana expected it. Once in her home, her room, she passed quickly into her body. And reached up to her face.

To find still-moist tears.

24

This house?

Emily Sanders held her handbag before her like the shield of a knight, realizing she should have recognized the address. She shivered in the early March chill before it occurred to her what a sight she must have looked that morning along Mason Street. She knew what people said about the house. Everyone who had lived in Hollister for any length of time knew the stories—or some variation.

Few people in town, however, knew or recalled that Emily Sanders was herself a part of the stories, at least what of the story was known to be true. Of the rest, she'd have to put those out of her mind. This was her first day she'd visit the six patients she'd been assigned at the home-care agency, after all. She had to keep her focus on each, one at a time.

Mickey Stratton was going to walk again.

She felt it in her bones, though at age forty-five the woman believed she was barely old enough to think in such terms. She knew it as surely as she knew she saw streaks of gray throughout the hair she had only recently, and for the first time, cut to above shoulder length. She saw it as only the truly faithful could believe they were not alone even before the most difficult of challenges.

Mickey Stratton, this boy whose arms and legs seemed like a mannequin's the day she had met him, would walk again. Swing a bat and hear the crack as the ball sailed toward the heavens. Run in the sunshine and feel the wind as it tried to slow him down.

Embarrassed, she brought the bag back to her side, strode up the few wooden steps and rang the bell. *Just so I don't look like the usual gawkers*, she thought with a grin. *They didn't ring the bell. In fact, from what she'd seen, they usually didn't even leave their cars.*

Maureen opened the door and flashed a quick smile that told Emily she'd been spotted dawdling on the walk.

"Mrs. Stratton, hello. I hope I'm not late!"

"Oh, no, uh, Emily. We're just getting a slow start here."

Janice came bounding out of the kitchen, took one look at Emily and did an about-face.

"Janice, that is no way to behave," said Maureen, then, to Emily: "She hasn't been sleeping well, you'll have to forgive her. I thought it best to let her stay home from school."

The little girl wore a sweatsuit she seemed to have slept in, and when she lifted her gaze to that of the therapist, the older woman could read the greeting: *You are not here for me, you are here for my brother. I don't have to like you.* "Hi," she exhaled.

"I'm happy to meet you again," said Emily.

"Yeah." The girl's dark-eyed stare fastened to her mother for approval a moment before she turned to leave.

It mustn't be like this, Emily thought, then, before she realized what she was saying, added, "and I'm sure you'll make friends with the house before you know it."

Wrong, wrong, wrong thing to say, she told herself the instant the words left her mouth.

"What do you mean?" spat Janice, the little girl spinning around to face the woman. "Who *are* you?"

"I..."

"Janice, that's enough!" said the girl's mother. "She didn't mean anything by it." Shaking her head, she reached for Emily's coat. Janice backed away, her head shaking, and disappeared up the stairs.

Emily's apology was waved away. "I know what you meant," said Maureen, who herself looked like she could use a good, long nap. "C'mon, let's get Mickey."

The therapist was pleased to see Maureen knock before entering the boy's room at the end of the hall. It was important, when dealing with the paralyzed, to remember always their need to feel some sense of control. Mickey would know who had arrived, would have heard the doorbell and recognized the voice of the woman he had met not long before. Yet the family needed to remain consistent in the little things, such as knocking and waiting for an answer from within. Those little things, to this boy, must be considered very big things indeed if they were to make the progress she expected.

"Come in," the boy said.

"Hello, Mickey," said Emily.

The boy sat back in a deep-bucketed chair, watching an episode of *Paw Patrol* on TV. His legs dangled over one arm of the chair like those of a teenager, and the way his head tipped back in the other direction, one would think he was like any other video game junkie in the typical pose of the suburban bored. The difference, of course, was that he had been *put* there. It was but one of many frequently shifted positions intended to keep the boy's limbs from growing deformedly while the therapy regimen was getting off the ground.

"Hi," he said. His eyes snapped her way, then back to the TV.

His mother stepped into the room long enough to point her thumb toward the TV, her eyebrows lifted in unspoken question, her smile tired but pleasant. "Sure," he said, and she turned off the set.

Once Maureen left the room, Emily took a deep breath. "Well, Mickey, I thought we'd chat a bit more before we go downstairs. Tell me what you're feeling today: anxious? Ready to fight? Or...a bit scared, maybe? We do have a lot of work, but between the two of us, we'll show everyone a thing or two."

"Yeah," came the response.

She smiled to suppress the frown determined to sweep her face. His quick eye movements, unmotivated though the boy was, were swift and observant. "You'll see," she replied. "Sometimes we all need a little proof before we start to believe. We have the time, we have the road before us. And...and you've already started down the road, you know."

Mickey's eyes rose. "What d'you mean?"

"Sure," she quipped. "You got *me.*"

For the first time the boy grinned. It was a smile of hope that erupted through a wall of sadness. I don't yet believe you, Emily interpreted his expression. But I'm grateful you can believe for both of us.

"Now...it's time you took a ride downstairs. I'll work the controls this time, young man," she said, gently patting his shoulder, "but in time we'll expect you to do these things yourself."

"Aaaall by myself!"

Oh, that was the spirit, thought Emily. "Onward!"

Polio was a bad, bad thing, Janice said to herself as brother and therapist passed by her closed door. She flipped herself onto her stomach and curled up tighter beneath her covers.

So why was she feeling so jealous?

She had gotten to like her new brother. Really *like* him. He'd never made like he was special when he first showed up. And the new little brother never ratted on her, even when, in his first few weeks with the family, she'd taken delight in slipping cookies off his plate and into the deep pockets of the overalls she'd have on. He was a good kid, she'd eventually come to realize. One who made her...feel like a big sister. These things made her glad.

So why was she so *pissed* at him?

Janice was too young to know there was not one but many reasons for her newfound resentment. Contributing were the recent move into the new house. (She hated it.) Her school, where she now tried to ignore the doorway whispers of her "paralyzed brother, who can't even *wipe* himself anymore." (She was ready to start swinging the next time she heard that one.) And, in general, the boredom of feeling alone at home. Dad with his crazy hours—didn't he *care* about anything else? Mom with this *regimen* she and that Mrs. Sanders were always talking about. Like, you take him downstairs and you *exercise* him, right?

Creeping around the edge of her conscious mind was the other reason. Now and then, more frequently as the sleepiness grew heavier, it returned with the cataclysmic intensity of its logic.

That the dollhouse in her room, at which she stared from her recumbent, legs-up position on the bed, had set itself up without anyone's help.

Dad hadn't. He'd been on his thirty-six-hour that day, including the whole time she was at school. Mom had begun to holler by the fourth time Janice had asked her; anyway, she'd been at that agency with Mickey for most of the day, doing some kind of tests.

That left...who?

Over Dad's protests, Mom had allowed Janice to keep the Victorian-style dollhouse assembled—it measured more than two feet high—during the move. His one condition was that every one of dozens of accessories be wrapped and packed separately for fear they'd be lost.

The movers had brought the house right into Janice's room. Its very bareness had struck her at once, and if only she weren't getting so much homework, she knew she'd have refurnished it by now.

Yet it wasn't her hands that had hung the little curtains, arranged the chairs around the kitchen table, laid the antimacassars so neatly over each armchair in the living room. The layout she'd perfected in their old condo was different from what she noticed here. Not bad per se, but not hers. Also strange was that the three figures—mother, father and daughter—sat huddled closely together on the sofa as if...watching television. The house, however, had no TV.

Who did this?

For the fourth time that day, Janice felt the urge to leap off the bed and onto the house. To smash it to pieces. It wasn't hers! Someone had taken it over and was making it *hers*. Or his. Someone in this house. Their new house!

Janice kept her tears to herself and closed her eyes. If she was lucky, she would get a few hours of sleep before...before that chill came back again.

* * *

Cynthia rubbed her bottom and tried to find a comfortable position on the bed. No, that wasn't it. She didn't want to sit on her bed, to sit anywhere in her house. She wanted *out*—she didn't care where— maybe even to see Lana, who'd been acting pretty weird since the last time they'd ghosted together. Anywhere but to be in this house. Here, where her mom had just whupped her for getting a 60 on her latest math test.

Could her parents' rare screaming match, complete with crashing dishes, have contributed during her last night of studying before the exam?

She'd been grounded, too, but that meant nothing in this house. Her mother would be out in her chair before nine p.m., and her dad—at the height of his authority amid her snores—typically let her go provided she tiptoed back in through the basement.

She'd see if she could leave now, would try Lana since Nancy hadn't come around that day. And besides, she saw Nancy only when she was *immaterial.* She needed a conventional exit to bring in what she'd found that day.

Downstairs, Cynthia found her mother out for the evening— almost. The woman remained awake long enough to take another sip of the warm beer resting on the chair's stained arm. Cynthia caught her father's gaze as he read his newspaper at the table. With her most pathetic, apologetic smile, holding her parka by the collar, she motioned toward the door. The man shot a look toward his wife, then shook his head impatiently before returning to his paper.

She sighed. She tiptoed into the living room and nearly jumped as her mother belched and rolled her head from one side to the other. Next to the can of Miller was the remote. Cynthia reached over, shut off the TV, observed the sleeping form for a reaction and turned it on again.

Again, the two met eyes; again, she gestured toward the door. This time he waved her away with a shush.

On the way out from the backyard, Cynthia snatched the small bundle she'd hurriedly wrapped in a pair of unwashed sweat socks. The chilly night air stung her face. At least it isn't windy, she thought. Smells...spring was coming. It hadn't yet arrived, but she could swear she smelled growth.

Her hand closed around the cold metal she'd wrapped in the socks. So weird to find a *hunting knife* in the yard, right in the middle of this little neighborhood in Hollister. She imagined someone had cut through their property on the way to a nearby trout stream. No one hunted within miles of the neighborhood, after all. But no...there were much better shortcuts.

She'd continued to ponder. Maybe a dog had found it elsewhere, thought it was a bone from its carved bone handle and dropped it after carrying it beneath the shade of the big maple in their backyard. Yeah, that was it. Cynthia flushed with satisfaction for a moment at the way she'd worked it all out. She couldn't wait to tell Lana.

Climbing the steps to Lana's front porch, Cynthia wished she had a sheath in which she could carry the long-bladed knife. That would be Lana's dramatic way of showing it around, she thought.

But when her friend opened the door, Cynthia lost interest in even unwrapping her find. Lana opened the front door, then the storm door, and stepped out onto the porch wearing nothing but a T-shirt and overalls. The door slammed as Lana sat on the top step; it occurred to Cynthia she had never seen Lana's long, straight hair loose. She felt embarrassed to think it: Her friend was a really pretty girl. Someday, she'd be—

"Well?"

Cynthia started at the sound, then noticed how little Lana was wearing for a winter day.

"Lana, you'll freeze!"

She responded with a shrug.

"What's the matter?"

Lana shook her head. Finally, she shivered.

"Let's go inside, okay?" Cynthia jumped up and opened the storm door.

"No!"

"Well, why n—"

"My mom's not alone."

Cynthia backed away. "O-oh." She gently guided the storm door closed and sat back down.

Lana realized if she was going to stay on the porch dressed for summer, she'd better keep moving. Which was just as well, for she needed to pace to get out what she wanted to say...to *someone*. "They're *usually* gone by morning!" she spat, remaining careful to keep her voice low...out of fear. "This one is still here," she continued without even looking at Cynthia. "He came last night—he's still here. And he's got something. S-some kind of...I dunno. Some weird white powder. They're both acting real strange."

Cynthia thought for a moment. Her dad was a wimp, she knew. Her mother was...a drunk and could be pretty mean and unfair. But at least the two of them were pretty predictable. "Lana..."

"What." She shivered. "Hey, what's that?"

She had forgotten what she was carrying. "Oh. Just, oh, something I found..."

"Wow! Where'd you find it?"

"Um, in the yard."

"Here?"

"No, by my house." So much for presentations, thought Cynthia. "Oh, what I was gonna ask...Lana, why don't you get some things and stay at my house tonight? We could—"

Loud laughter erupted from within the house. A man's laughter.

Lana turned to go back inside.

"Wait! What do you thi—"

"No. Can't leave my mother."

"But Lana, you could get—"

"Cynthia, no! Just leave me alone! Just go away, you don't understand, just—just get out of here. Forget it, will ya?"

On the earth as in the air, Cynthia was left alone shaking her head. Well, maybe this time she would take the hint.

Clutching her little weapon, its sharpened point breaking through a sweat sock's toe, she left for home.

* * *

I'm dreaming, thought Mickey. Once upstairs, he had used his chin control to wheel himself beside his bedroom window after dinner. It was one place he felt alone with his thoughts, alone but for a single streetlight, its light reflected off his ceiling. The glow already seemed a friend.

A friend.

There was nobody he could talk to about his miserable failure in the little room downstairs, where he'd wet his pants during massage on the downstairs bed. The first exercises were what Mrs. Sanders called "a bit of limbering up," and it took a while before she noticed the smell. When she did, well, that was it for the day—other than some talking she did after he got cleaned up. Whatever she was saying, he didn't think he'd heard a word. Something about God, he thought he remembered.

Mickey had only wanted to be left alone—for her to go home, for Janice to come out of her room and just to say "hi." For this stupid, *stupid* body to just...just...

He didn't know *what* he wanted it to do.

To stop hurting as it frequently did, in various parts of his arms, legs, back.

To move. To rise up, to walk, to jump. To stretch.

For starters.

And while his thoughts drifted, when his eyes closed a bit so that he viewed the light outside through a squint, that was when he thought he heard

a voice.

It was a whispering voice, and it was right beside his ear. Like someone was standing behind his wheelchair, standing where...

the dresser was.

Play with me, the voice had said.

He'd heard it first like in a dream, hadn't thought it was real and still wasn't sure when it came a second time:

Miiickey, come play with me.

"'S somebody here?" he whispered.

Think real real hard. You can do it, Miiickey.

"Can do...can do what?"

He heard someone coming down the hall. No. Not now! I don't want to talk to anyone, he thought. The door creaked open; it was his father.

"Mickey, can I come in?"

The boy sighed. "Sure."

"I...I think it's time you went to bed, Mickey. Here, mind if I...?" His father pulled Mickey away from the window. He drew back the covers and gently lifted the boy up and onto the bed.

"Son, I heard good things about you today," he began. The man waved away the mortified look on Mickey's face and nodded. "Yeah, yeah, the pants, sure I heard about that. It's Mrs. Sanders' job to keep us informed. If she didn't, well, she wouldn't be doing her job. But you know, Mickey, the fact that this happened—I didn't understand it at first, either—it means that *you* want, as badly as we do, to beat this thing. Tomorrow Mrs. Sanders is going to come again, and you'll get a little further. You'll be in the room again. You'll come in contact with what I'm calling the tools of your trade. And, buddy, maybe you'll repeat what you did today. But I'll betcha you'll be in the room *longer* next time before you do. And then not at all. Each day you get more geared up for the fight, and soon—"

"Dad?"

"Yes, Mickey?"

"Dad, do you believe in God?"

His father sighed. "Sure I do, Mickey. Sure."

"Dad..." The boy was groping for words, his head craned awkwardly back against the pillow. "Dad, I mean...I mean, do you *really* believe in God?"

How crafty are the young, Jeffrey thought, so ever ready to hear the lies that slip out between our words. "Mickey, I believe—believe that there's some God in each of us. Something that means...the best we can hope to be. And that's the most—"

"That's not what I mean. I mean God"—his eyes shot toward the ceiling—"up *there*. And saints, and angels being our friends and—"

"Mickey, I think you have to find the strength within you. You can't think too much about what's outside of yourself. I love you, your mother does, Janice too, and you know you will always have us. But you yourself have what it takes to..."

The boy had shut his eyes. Jeffrey leaned over to look a little closer in the dim light of a lamp on the dresser; he looked asleep, anyway. The man kissed Mickey's forehead and stood up.

On his way to the door, his son started right where he'd left off. "I mean do you believe an angel, a little angel, can come down to earth to play with me?"

Oh, boy, thought Jeffrey. He'd be warned this could happen. Did it really start happening so soon?

"Mickey," his father said once back at the boy's bedside, "I cannot see an angel. Or hear or touch one. I know what I can know with the senses I was born with, and with a mind that tells me what those things mean. Anything else, I can't believe.

"For the life of me, I'll never know why this...terrible thing has happened to you, Mickey. But what I do know...is what we need to bring your body back to strength. You need to *focus* on that goal. If believing in saints and angels helps you to focus on that goal...well, fine. But remember what is up to you alone."

Right answer? Jeffrey could not but believe he was doing the right thing. He knew the odds—infinitesimally high odds against Mickey's having caught poliomyelitis in the first place. Better odds of the boy someday leading some degree of a normal life, provided his spirit remained strong enough to ride through the long, arduous process before him.

Behind him, Mickey began to drift off to sleep. The boy welcomed it, greeted it as he did the voice he had heard by the window. It was a girl angel, a girl who sounded like his own age. Mickey didn't really like girls. But before his eyes closed for the night, he whispered aloud to this girl who promised him something nobody else was talking about. Who told him he could rise up, take her hand and leave behind this sick body of his...

Anytime he was ready.

25

Fairness. Compassion. Mercy. What were these but words, after all, to a child who, both alive and dead, had learned nothing of them? In her life she had watched, helpless, as all the caring in the world fell short before power, raw power. And now, in this post-life netherworld, power was the only thing she understood.

It was what she knew, and day by day her power to control her material surroundings grew stronger.

Natalie sat cross-legged upon Mickey's bed; it was positioned exactly where her own bed had been. She leaned against Mickey's headboard

no, my headboard

and, alone, made no effort to contain the cold death aura of her presence. On the windowsill, a coleus drooped and withered, as she watched, in the afternoon sun. It did not escape her notice. Little these days did.

She smiled.

Natalie triumphed in having done to a friendship what she had just done to a potted plant. Oh, it had taken months, and some lying: This Nancy who lived at an orphanage and had a big sister in the city. This girl, who had learned the advanced arts of ghosting and therefore could do things of which...Cynthia and Lana could only dream.

She had certainly gone out of her way to spoil that friendship. For with Lana at her side, Cynthia could always work out her problems. But alone? She would remain the sad girl Natalie sat beside in the bell tower, the one who would throw away life as she knew it. She would better accept

and be happy forever and ever

the plans Natalie had made to have an always friend of her own.

Yes, a friend was what she needed. She knew that from her earlier disappointment with Gerald, the night she'd believed that he, if nobody else, would be no different to her. Having learned otherwise, Natalie learned also of her sense of vengeance. She had enjoyed, even delighted in, the way she had frightened him from her window mere weeks after he'd cast her out of his life.

The girl grew excited at what was to come that night. Natalie anticipated it the way she would have looked forward to the circus, and she shrugged off her past failures as things that just didn't matter anymore.

There was one, however, that did matter. And, come to think of it, Natalie was surprised she had never before thought to take the side trip she also wanted to do that day, in late afternoon, on her way to meet Cynthia. It just seemed so right, after all this time, to stop by the local cemetery. To visit her parents' graves. For the first time, to stand upon her own.

And then?

It was time to get some real company.

* * *

The phone rang again. God, why wouldn't they answer it! Lana usually hung up after four or five rings to house phones. It often took that many rings before Cynthia's mother even realized it was ringing and began pondering whether answering it was worth the trouble. Cynthia's father never bothered at all; the land line was never for him. But when Cynthia was home, she usually bounded over to answer it within two rings. Sometime soon, she thought often, she'd have her *own* phone.

This time, Lana waited seven rings before it was picked up. "H-hello?" came the voice of her friend.

"Cynthia, I'm sorry I'm a jerk," Lana blurted.

"Lana? Lana...it's okay."

"No, it's not," Lana said. "I'm not nice sometimes, and I get all weird with these men my mom brings home. And— "

"Lana, where *are* you?"

"I'm at school. Listen, there's—"

"We got out two hours ago."

"Cynthia, will you *listen to me?*"

A pause. "Sorry."

"Cynthia, you know my father died a couple of years ago. Well...I killed him. B-but it was an accident."

"I know."

Lana gasped. *"You know?"*

"Um...Nancy told me."

Nancy! Lana stepped away from the pay phone, her fury rising within, her chest heaving. "Cyn-Cynthia...how d-did she find that out?"

"I-I don't know...maybe your school file. But Lana...I know you loved him."

"Yeah." Like hell you do. "H-hey, listen, are you doing anything? I can't stay away from home all day, and we need to talk about—"

"Lana, I can't. Nancy asked me to meet her. In the city. She's going to show me where she lives."

Suppressing a groan, Lana could only say, "Okay."

"See you tomorrow?" asked Cynthia.

"Sure. Tomorrow...is another day," she replied. But she wasn't into imitating Scarlett O'Hara, let alone a reasonably happy ten-year-old. She was losing her friend for good, and there was only one thing that would get her back.

It was proof, once and for all, that Nancy was not what she claimed to be.

Her first move, of course, was getting out of school. The substitute teacher lifted her head when Lana returned to study hall, then returned her attention to her romance novel. It was unusual, though not unheard of, for a student to remain behind voluntarily while others (usually boys) served detention. So when Lana gathered her books and left, the remaining children donned their most angelic masks in the hope they would shortly follow.

She hurried home but stopped short before she opened her door. That car was still in the driveway; the man who had so frightened Lana the night before was still inside. She cringed at what she heard him say to her mother, things he would...do to her.

In many ways, Lana was no child. She knew why these men came, if not why her mother needed them so badly. But the men, despite what she thought of them, seemed to step lightly in her father's house. Lana took it as a sign of respect that they kept their voices a bit low—particularly if they knew she was in the house. Her mother these days seemed to spill the news of her daughter's existence during their drive over.

Once in her mother's room with the door closed, they considerably lifted their moods. At that point, Lana didn't...mind as much. She relished that hush in the way they entered, something she could hear from her room, that told her each man knew it: He did not truly belong there.

Not this one, however. What Lana had seen from her window was a medium-height, stocky guy with trimmed, graying hair and a very nice suit. She imagined him the big boss of a company or some other kind of big shot. From the look, she thought him a gentleman—at least to the degree she ever expected one. Instead, she saw a man who swung her mom into him right in the front yard and pushed his big fat lips against hers. Lana turned away when her mother, squirming out of his grasp with a nervous giggle, led him by the hand to the side door.

That demonstration had occurred a half-hour before Cynthia showed up. A few minutes before the two of them started doing cocaine in the living room. And today, her mother had called in sick at her realty job. Was it the drugs? Or...the fact that the man didn't go away in the morning?

Then, when Lana was going into the bathroom for her shower, he stepped in her way to introduce himself. "Hi, Missy," he said, crouching so low she could see his baggy eyes, smell the foul cologne, hear a belch he suppressed with a deep chuckle. "What's your name, Princess?" He'd leaned closer. Clasping her arms, Lana caught a quick glimpse of a dripping razor cut on his jaw before she turned away and stared into the doorjamb.

His face moved inches from hers. She could feel his hot breath on her neck. She closed her eyes.

"I asked—"

"Wilson, you stay away from that girl," came a voice from the other room.

The man turned away, cocked his head, then stood up. "You run along, Honey," he whispered, and patted her behind as she fled into the bathroom.

She could kill this one.

228

Now, however, Lana needed to get back into the house, to leave her body (could she concentrate enough?), to stalk this girl, Nancy. She gingerly tried the basement doors—success! It wasn't difficult to lift the wooden door quietly up, then lower it closed behind her. She could hide in the basement. Behind the boiler, if she had to.

So great was her determination, she needed only seconds to will herself from her body. Within moments she was back outside, her body crouched behind a box of old clothes. And before long, she was headed down Oak Drive toward where it crossed Mason.

She couldn't believe it. There, from the Leffingwell house, she could see Nancy! Floating up from inside the house and heading...where?

Lana took off in pursuit. Cynthia and Nancy were due to meet soon, she knew. But two kids didn't need much brains between them to plan their rendezvous somewhere along the way between Cynthia's house and the city.

Natalie was traveling in the opposite direction.

This was like one of those old war movies, Lana thought, as she did her best to keep out of sight by flying low through trees. Gotta avoid the radar, in this case being spotted by her target. First they caught you on the radar, she recalled. Then came the "ack-ack"—funny that they used baby words for big guns that could blow you out of the sky.

Lana knew this part of Hollister. With Nancy drifting in and out of sight, the pursuer noticed a little shopping center, a spacious field where the town had its annual carnival, and a big building for the garbage trucks with a dirt road that led off to the local dump. Then—Nancy seemed to be lowering—a big, two-way road, a florist or two and...the local cemetery.

She wasn't ready for this. Nancy vanished into a stone office building, leaving Lana uncertain as to why they were there. And about how she could stay hidden across these rolling fields.

For a moment, Lana thought of the first time she herself had become *immaterial*. It was only a short time after her father had moved out of their house, and, at eight, she had not yet learned the expected behavior for when her mother arrived with a boyfriend. Perhaps she hadn't thought about it. Perhaps she had, and decided in her youthful way that if she were nice to the man and said hello, the three of them might spend the evening laughing together around the TV. Regardless, when the door opened, there sat Lana at the coffee table, eating a hot dog and building a card house.

"Lana!" The door slammed. The card house collapsed; a joker stared maniacally up at Lana. "Up in your room now! Do you hear me? Now!"

"B-but I'm n-not finished ea—"

"Now!"

The blond man, in a sport coat and dungarees, was beet red. "Hey, Clarissa, maybe I should just go..."

Lana's mother touched his lips to silence, then kissed him. "Come," she said when Lana had trudged to the top step.

Minutes later, the girl was ecstatic. She had wished for it, oh how she'd wished for it, and this time, before she knew what was happening she had risen out of her very body. What joy she felt at this newfound ability...no one could chase her from *here*.

Over the two years she had used this power for escape and for play, she had avoided—well, except for once or twice—entry to places where what she learned could hurt her. Her mother's busy bedroom, for instance. Chalk it up to a certain respect she felt, Cynthia too, for this forbidden part of the world to which only children in great pain, emotional or physical, were permitted access. For the most part, Lana had been able to keep that world pure.

Until this Nancy came along.

Now Lana found herself stalking a girl in the darkening cemetery where her own father lay buried. This was no place for play. In an instant, Lana would turn around and go home. What could she gain from a place of death?

Before Lana could leave, however, her target left the little stone building and proceeded farther into the grounds. With a destination apparently in mind.

In following Natalie, Lana felt coolly impressed with the feeling of hiding within a solid object. A few times on the way over she had sensed Natalie was looking over her shoulder and had ducked down into, say, the concrete foundation of a building. Now within the more open spaces of the cemetery, twice the thin girl had stepped entirely into the trunk of a wide tree. She hadn't much alternative, she shuddered to think.

But now Natalie veered to the right, into a field that was virtually devoid of elms and maples. Here she floated gently to the earth and, as Lana scrambled from behind one headstone after another, began to step along the row. She passed several stones, a few with flowers,

American flags. Before long she stopped at two stones that bore no sign that, indeed, anyone had ever paid a visit.

Lana felt a creeping terror that she would be discovered. Here, in this open field, a level acre among a hilly graveyard, the sun nearly down, she lay flat on her belly hidden—she hoped completely—behind the stone of one Giancarlo Bueti. *Grazie,* Giancarlo, she might have said aloud in cheerier times; she'd learned that word from a Fellini movie. Despite her fear, she peered around the stone and watched...watched Natalie on her knees, her arms crossed, staring at two graves that, Lana realized, had to be those of her parents. Had she been fully present, Lana would have felt a lump in her throat, so wrong she suddenly felt to be spying.

She kept watching, then, as Natalie stepped hesitantly to the side. To stand before a third stone. To remain standing, her hands hanging limp at her sides for many breathless seconds...until, Lana realized, they curled tightly into fists. A crow landed in a nearby tree; another joined it.

When Natalie spun around, Lana in a flash dropped to the ground. *Through* the ground. She raised herself up in disgust at the soil she had just entered. Of course it could not touch her. The smell of the dank, damp soil could not penetrate her nostrils, could not

claim her

hurt her in the least. Neither could Nancy, when you came right down to it. Still, she regarded herself as if unclean and peered across to see that Natalie had picked up (*how* did she *do* that?) some flowers from a nearby grave and placed half on the one of the first two she'd looked at; the other half, she placed before the third stone. She remained there a few more seconds, then turned around once more.

This time Lana intentionally dropped beneath the surface. For in the many emotions that were crossing Natalie's face—sadness, desolation, anger—Lana was sure she had also seen one of surprise. Of discovery.

Back to Giancarlo. Rose. Hermione. With the rest of the teeming dead, a few names of whom Lana had spotted. She lay only a few feet beneath the surface, and wondered which was worse. To be found out aboveground, or to

solidify

keep still, to

welcome

lurk within the soil, hiding, waiting for

231

dinner

someone far more frightening to give up her search. The hunter had become the hunted, and there was no one to help her but—

her father.

She knew he was buried here, and the thought sent a ripple of peace through her spirit. Lana's father was gone, she knew, and he could not help her. But knowing he was here did make a difference. She could, would navigate this hallowed earth as she could the sky. And, instincts setting in, she circled around the spot where Natalie had stood and came up behind it to see her pursuer standing by Giancarlo's stone. Natalie's head turned quickly from side to side; on her face, Lana saw only anger. An anger that seemed too real, far too intense for a child. It was more than vengeful: It looked evil.

Lana dove once more, beneath the headstones to which Natalie had given so much attention moments ago. And, from the ground—strangely, she did not fear it now—she looked up at the first two. The first stone with the flowers, which had been fresh only seconds before, read Kimberly Leffingwell; the other, George Leffingwell.

Leffingwell.

The Leffingwell house. The haunted house.

Lana let go a cry when she read the third stone, whose flowers also lay wilted against the granite:

NATALIE LEFFINGWELL
CALLED TO HEAVEN AT AGE NINE

"You can't stop me, Lana!" Natalie shouted behind her.

"Wha—"

Lana was alone. Off in the distance, she could see Natalie—a ghost, she was a *real* ghost, an honest-to-God *real ghost!*—speeding back toward town. Lana would follow. She had to follow. For whatever this *Natalie* was up to, Lana was sure it somehow involved Cynthia.

And I *will* do something about it, said Lana to the crowded field.

Every child who could go ghosting soon learned that, given danger, reunion of spirit with body was nearly instantaneous no matter where the spirit had floated. It was as if you were correcting a wrong; nature wanted to be restored. But traveling spirits, dead or alive, moved at about the same speed.

Natalie, with Lana close behind, thus reached Cynthia's house at about the same time. The two met in the bedroom, where Cynthia's body lay flat on the bed, facing the ceiling.

"Cynthia! Come back!"

"She doesn't hear you," the dead girl said calmly. "She's far away."

"Where did you—"

"She's in the city. She's meeting me there."

"Cyyyynthiaaaa!"

"Stop yelling."

"You can't make me, Nan—*Natalie*. I'm not afraid of you—you leave Cynthia alone, I'm going to get her." Lana turned to pass through the wall.

"You don't have time, *Svet-lana!*"

At Natalie's giggle, Lana saw the gaze of the ghost drift toward the knife sitting on Cynthia's dresser, still wrapped in sweat socks.

"You won't do—"

Natalie stamped her foot. "She's *my* friend! Not yours! You just boss her around. She's *my* friend, and she's *always* going to be my friend! Always!"

"We'll see about that," Lana spat and returned home to her body.

She wanted to stretch after lying in the cramped position but had to get up, had to get over to Cynthia's house to wake her up before...

A big hand grabbed her arm at the top of the stairs. "Where ya goin', Princess?"

Lana looked aghast into the face of her mother's boyfriend. He seemed drunk—drugged, more likely—and though he loosened his grip on her arm, he blocked her path to the door.

"Leave me alone! Motherrrr!"

The stocky man chuckled. "Don't quite think she's awake enough to hear ya, Princess."

"Where—" Lana saw past him, at her mother.

Out cold on the couch.

"Moootherrrr!"

The woman stirred, uttering a sound, and when the man craned his neck to see, Lana slipped free and darted between the knee and elbow he'd leaned against the wall.

He grabbed hold of her shirttail. It ripped before she broke free and—with him close behind—dodged him again to run through the kitchen, around through its other doorway, into the living room. Plants, tables, chairs flew as the man lunged at her.

She stood before her mother.

"Mooootherrr...!" she gasped, reaching back to tap the apparently unconscious woman twice on the head.

He leaped at her—she dodged again. He landed across her mother and tipped the couch backward. In his rush to get up, her mother flailing as she came to, Lana got her idea. She rushed to the kitchen, opened the door to the basement and stamped her foot twice on the top step. Lana switched on the basement light and left the door open. Then she leapt into the kitchen and quietly lifted the saucepot off its rack beside the stove. Taking a big step sideways to the right, out of sight, she waited.

The man yelled "Shut up!" from the living room and lumbered, dazed, to the basement door. He opened it and stopped after taking two steps down. "Oh, Princess! Come baaaa—"

Still woozy in the living room, her mother whipped up her head just in time to see the cast-iron kettle crash down upon the man's head. Hear the resonant gong and the howl of a man with an open, gaping skull. Watch the hulking form totter, tumble down the basement steps.

Lana opened the basement door wider and paused only long enough to say it: "Take *that*, suckerrrr."

* * *

Big words. Against a crafty enemy like Lana, Natalie had needed them. The girl now knew her secret, after all. And her plans. Natalie had to act quickly, certain that Lana would soon return.

The thought of a friend, trapped as was she herself in this other world, was too exciting for her to think about at this juncture. Natalie would show Cynthia, oh, how she would show her, all the fun things she had learned over the past year and more. They could play day and night, never get tired, never have to listen to *anybody*.

First...first, however, Natalie had to bring her over. And when her spirit materialized her hands to grab the knife and peel away the socks, it occurred to her that—well, Cynthia might be mad at her. *Real* mad, so much so that the two could only fight. While no one living ever yelled at her for long, Cynthia might...

No. Natalie had learned she could control Cynthia, could pull her away even from her best friend. The girl already trusted her; of that, Natalie became convinced the night she materialized in Cynthia's room. It would take time. Lots of time. But, she reminded herself, there'd be lots of that.

It was a simple matter, she knew. Just fly right over to the unsuspecting Cynthia and take the knife, the one she had left in three different places until Cynthia found it. And plunge it into her heart.

Time was running out—within a minute Lana would be back and would somehow shatter the calm state a child required in order to remain outside the body. She had to do it. Do it now.

Come on!

Natalie floated over to Cynthia's bed and stood above her. She held the knife, fondled its razor-sharp point, wondered whether the sporting goods store had noticed it missing. But no—her mind had strayed again. It just...

The spirit lowered the knife, suddenly unsure of precisely where on Cynthia's body she needed to strike. It had to be perfect; if she missed the heart, and hurt the girl without instantly killing her, from miles away in the city Cynthia's spirit would re-enter her body...just in time for it to depart in a natural way. The way the old man, Mr. O'Keefe, had left her.

It had to be just so. Natalie remembered what she had heard, that the heart was a bit off to the left—she focused on a spot and thought, no, Cynthia's left. She lifted the knife an instant before she could accidentally touch the point to Cynthia's breast. Any physical contact before the actual stab, even so slight, and it would be all over.

Now. It had to be now.

Natalie stared straight ahead at the window, raised the knife high above her head—and froze at the return of those bright-blue flashing lights. They appeared and disappeared. They blinded her in their intensity—she held an arm, to no avail, instinctively over her eyes and saw through it the same whirling hole in the air she had seen that night in her yard. The brilliant lights alternating with a blackness, again like a huge coin spun on its edge, a pure blue of goodness alternating with a darker, malignant shadow from which erupted groans. Natalie had stepped back and, to her surprise, realized she had dropped the knife to the floor. Like the icicle of the previous occurrence, the weapon had fallen because Natalie's power to materialize had dissolved.

No! The spirit remembered, as the bright-blue vortex faded, that her powers last time had come back right away. Whatever the nature of this intrusion, it had delayed her for only a few moments. Now the knife was in her hands again; Natalie raised it high into the air. Now was her moment.

A shard of patio slate smashed its way through the opposite window. Glass fragments sprayed across the room.

Lana, apparently, was a good shot herself.

Cynthia opened her eyes. From her body she could have seen only the knife floating in the air, held tightly by two disembodied hands, and felt a disturbing chill. But an instant earlier, upon its return, her spirit had seen all she needed to see.

"Nancy...wha-what are you doing?"

26

Two weeks later, Jeffrey Stratton awoke to realize he was freezing—had been for the past half-hour. The first rays of dawn were creeping in through the blinds. At this time of night, from what he remembered setting his last time before the thermostat, the temperature should have been at its lowest: seventy degrees, he and Maureen had decided. But this?

Jeffrey looked at the sheet, bedspread and comforter covering them. They hadn't slipped off. Two days before, he'd carefully checked the room's windows. Once again, he climbed out of bed and touched the baseboard—there, they had heat. Plenty of it. He sat back against the headboard, shook his head and turned his head to see Maureen also sitting up. Awake—for hours, the redness around her eyes told him.

"Don't you feel it?" she whispered.

Jeffrey squeezed his wife's hand. "Sure. Time for a home energy audit."

"I think it's more than that, Jeff."

Furling his brow, Jeffrey shook his head. "Heat's escaping, that's all. We need a utility guy. He needs to—"

"Jeff," she interrupted. Sheer exhaustion alone kept her from shouting. "It's not just the *cold*. Can't you feel it? It's more than cold...it's *gloom*. There's—I c-can't explain how I feel any other way—there's a gloom over this whole house. Day and night. Except for—"

"Honey, don't you think you're overreacting?"

Maureen crossed her arms. "Don't treat me like a child, Jeffrey Stratton."

"I just meant—"

"I know what you meant, Mr. Science. Do now what I've done about three times tonight. Go check Janice's room. Then go into Mickey's room."

She pointed toward the floor beneath them. "Then come back and tell me what you think."

Jeffrey sighed, shrugged, stepped onto the cold floor once again and out to the hallway. He made a right, not a left; if Janice's room was warmer than theirs, he'd have less to compare with the chill he now felt down to his bones.

He stepped past Mickey's door, which by night they left open. Amazing, he thought.

The room was toasty warm.

Leaning over the comforter and holding the gleaming metal rail of the electric bed, Jeffrey touched the wall that was adjacent to his and Maureen's bedroom. Warm also. Wherever the cold was leaking in, he decided, he saw no problem with the insulation *there*.

He looked down at Mickey—silently exhaling in the position Maureen had left him—and walked back into the frigid hallway. His foot kicked something: a miniature basket of bananas from his daughter's dollhouse. He scooped up the wooden accessory and started at the frost he blew in the entrance to his daughter's room.

Here it was coldest of all.

Janice's eyes followed his, and Jeffrey stepped around the bed and sat on the edge of the pastel-striped outer cover. She lay curled up, three layers of comforters around her body as her teeth chattered in the dim light.

"D-daddy," she whispered as Jeffrey bent over to ascertain that, indeed, this room also had plenty of heat coming out of the baseboard—and then stopping dead.

"Hi, Sugar. Been like this all night?"

Janice nodded. "I slept a little, maybe."

He rubbed her back through the blankets.

"Maybe...tomorrow we can set up the cot in Mickey's room. Just for a night or two. I'm going to see why the place can't hold the heat—get somebody to look the place over, someone...why are you shaking your head?"

His daughter sat up and curled the blankets tightly around her small frame. "I did that, Daddy."

"You went..."

"I went to the bathroom and went into Mickey's room, you know? It was *so warm!* So I took my blankets and...like, I laid down on the floor." She sniffled and wiped her eyes with the edge of the quilt.

"Well, what—"

"Daddy, it followed me!"

"Keep your voice down. What's this 'it'? *What* followed you?"

"The...the cold. Like, it came right in with me, you know? Daddy..." She lowered her voice to a whisper. "I had all these blankets on. And then I stood by Mickey's bed. It was *warm!* So I thought, like, he's not gonna roll out of bed, you know? So I got down on the floor, right next to the bed and..."

"The same. You came back here."

Janice looked into her father's eyes. "Daddy, c-can we move?"

Jeffrey released a quiet snort. "No, Janice, that's not the way to solve this. We can't just...move out whenever there's a problem in the ventilation."

"But what if you can't fix it?"

He leaned forward to hug his daughter. "I'll figure it out really soon, Honey. Oh." He reached into his pajama pants pocket and handed the wooden fruit basket to Janice. "I believe this is yours."

Wide-eyed, Janice took it, turned it in her hand and pressed it back into his. "N-no, it's not."

"Well, it certainly isn't *mine.*"

Janice sighed. "Daddy...could we take my dollhouse...like, away? Down, I dunno, like, to the basement or something?"

"Janice," her father began, "I don't quite get what I'm hearing here. You wanted that dollhouse. You *begged* for it. And now—"

"Daddy, stop!" Janice leaped from the bed and swung around to the dollhouse; it sat on the big hope chest, its open side in plain view from where Jeffrey sat on the bed.

"Janice, I said keep—"

"Daddy," she rasped in a hoarse whisper. "This—" she pulled a little breakfront from the main hall of the house—"is not *mine.* This," a bicycle in an upstairs bedroom, "is not mine. And..." she tossed to the floor a tiny vase, a colonial-design throw rug two inches across, and a grandfather clock, *"these* aren't. I don't know where they came from, Daddy. Mother doesn't buy anything for the house without me with her, okay? And if she did, she would tell me if I asked. There's nobody else who would or, like, could. I'm scared of it, all right? Okay, I said it. Are you happy? Daddy, please take it out."

This last had too much an element of pleading for Jeffrey to do other than nod in agreement. This house of theirs, this house...he felt he alone liked living here, and remained convinced the place was as good as they could get—for now, at least.

It was the cold weather, he decided. They'd moved into the place in the middle of winter, when it was easy for everyone to get a little stir-crazy. But soon the warm weather would show. The house would seem much brighter; there was nothing like a house in the springtime.

"A-downstairs it will go," said Jeffrey as he gently lifted the house off Janice's dresser.

His daughter called him after he stepped through the door.

"What?" he said with some impatience.

A thin smile formed across her lips. "The cold...it's not cold anymore."

She was right. She was absolutely right. Jeffrey smiled and nodded. Maureen had come out of the room, relief across her face, and she grabbed an end of the dollhouse. Janice heard her mother mumble the question, on the stairs, of where they were supposed to be going.

The little girl closed her bedroom door, sat on her bed and looked up toward the ceiling. "Now leave us alone," she whispered. Janice lay down and fell immediately to sleep.

* * *

Mickey, in his room, had an active night for a different reason. It had begun with the heat—cranked up for reasons he didn't understand—and the sweat that trickled down the side of his cheek.

The boy didn't like sweat. He dreaded all the things that, by virtue of working our arms and legs, typically represent but annoyances. Sweat: he could feel it moistening his skin all over his body but could do nothing about it without help. Mosquitoes. Bees. And, in the city, even the occasional cockroach. When he wasn't dreaming of his drunk aunt and the bicycle flying, the August sun glinting off the polished chrome of the slowly spinning spokes, he dreamed of insects. One spider, two spiders, tickling their way up his bare thigh, one stepping across his gym shorts and onto his belly—joined by six, seven, *ten* others as they approached his neck, his chin...his eyes.

It was during just such a dream that he felt himself pulled out of danger. Yet he believed he was still asleep. A hand, in his dream, was rubbing something across his forehead. He could hear humming, that nursery song about the pretty little horses. It...was a girl's voice. But not his sister's.

Mickey opened his eyes. From his limited perspective, he could see nothing strange. On his dresser, a clown bank smiled amiably toward the doorway; from a knob hung a Sheriff Woody doll with his cowboy hat. But what he could ascertain was that he had been sweating. And, no dream, someone had rubbed his sweat away with a moist washcloth.

"Who...who's there?" he whispered.

The silence frightened him, however possible it was that his mother or sister had stepped in to check on him. Then came a voice. *"Just me. Come play with me, Mickey."*

The voice seemed far away, yet somehow close. As good as he was getting at judging the nature and source of sounds, Mickey could not tell where this came from. One thing he knew: Whoever did say it didn't really understand his problem.

"I-I can't. Who-who are you?"

"Yes, you can," replied the voice—the same he had heard in his dream. Was it a dream at all? *"You lie there and close your eyes. Think real hard...and pick yourself up. It's easy."*

"Up?" he whispered incredulously. "But I can't even—"

"You leave your body where it is. Your body rests, you play. You can dance, and run and fly!"

"But I ca—"

"Try. Play with me, Mickey."

"A-are you...a-an angel?"

"I...guess I'm like one. You can be, too. Just try."

Mickey was smart enough to keep his voice low—there were no angels, his father had said—but his exasperation was making it difficult. "I-I'm not dead. If I go with the angels, th-that means..."

"Mickey, we won't go anywhere you don't want to go. Do you want to move by yourself? Do you want to walk?"

The voice paused, then changed tone. *"I...have to go now."*

"No...wait." He almost shouted after her, after the voice. Instead, Mickey closed his eyes and released a tear that, once he fell asleep, Natalie wiped from his face.

* * *

Emily Sanders found the Stratton household in a consistent state of irritability. It seemed they all were in pajamas and mumbled when they spoke at all. She removed the cardigan sweater she'd been toting for her past several visits, thankful for the warmer temperatures. Not that it should be *too* warm, she subjectively felt; too much heat would render Mickey less willing to progress—rather, make the boy feel too sluggish to try.

But what she had felt throughout the house lately was, well, like the stone chill of a mausoleum.

"So, Mickey, what shall we try today, hmmm?" Hands and wrists, she knew from the boy's muscle tests, including the electromyograph he'd received during a total of three months Mickey had spent in the hospital. Hands to grip. To hold a fork and knife, to press the TV remote or the buttons of the stair lift. The telephone. Anything to give the boy confidence. Arms, for holding himself up against his wheelchair in pursuit of the next, far-off goal: mobility. Legs. Feet.

She was getting way ahead of herself, Emily knew. A few children, despite the best therapist's efforts, the best course of therapy, simply did not progress well. Mickey had shown little in these early weeks to account for the time they'd spent—but then, triumphs were not guaranteed in this profession. Nor were they immediate. The aim, she reminded herself now, was to maintain her patient's spirits till he reached that first plateau.

Whenever that would be.

It was just a few minutes into their session that the boy broke out from his reverie. Emily had been talking about Mickey's favorite cartoons, which she tried not to miss. It was another thing for them to discuss, after all.

"Mrs. Sanders, are there angels?"

"Yes, Mickey, there certainly are."

The child considered her answer. "You didn't have to think about it," he said.

Emily paused in her up-and-down maneuvering of his right wrist, then regained her stride. "Well, I have learned that what comes from the heart has a short stop in the head." Or something like that, she thought.

"My dad says no." The boy winced from a flash of pain.

Keeping up the rhythm, Emily replied, "Maybe he doesn't look for them." It occurred to her: Such things were not for her to say.

Mickey, however, was taking this in another direction. "I dream about an angel," he said.

"What is his name?" asked Emily. "Here, let's turn back and forth in this direction now...like so..."

"*Her* name. I don't know."

"Oh," Emily said. "A woman angel. You know—"

"No, Mrs. Sanders. She's a girl. She wants me to play with her."

Emily shrugged off the slow chill that tickled her spine. "Well, what do you tell her?"

"I...I tell her no, I'm...I'm a cripple."

She frowned and tapped Mickey's temple. "Know what's up here, Mickey Mouse?"

The boy grinned. "My brain!"

"Righto. Up there is the word 'cripple.' And down here..." She waved her arm to indicate all below the neck. "Here is the baseball player waiting to get out."

The boy lowered his eyes. "I was only kidding."

"Let's instead call this spring training, shall we? And you...you are the batter on deck."

"I...asked her how could I play with her. She said to leave my body, and I could do whatever I wanted."

Now she stopped. Stopped cold.

"Mickey, did you dream only once about this angel?"

"Well, she said she's only *like* an angel."

"Only once, Mickey?"

"Um...once a night, maybe."

Religious, yes. Superstitious? No. True, Emily knew well the tragedy that had taken place in the Leffingwell house—no, the *Stratton* home. What worried her far more than any visitor from beyond, however, was clear evidence that the boy was forming a new reality in his mind. She had been warned of dissociation in her training. And it was something to watch very closely. To bring to his parents' attention if it progressed anywhere beyond imaginary-friend status.

* * *

Any living person in the basement would have heard gentle sounds of shuffling wood. Figures in the dim light of the high windows comically weaved left and right as they were walked throughout the dollhouse. Occasionally two would stop and exchange words—muttered softly by the new owner of the dollhouse—that, inevitably, led to the wife or one of the children jumping up and down over the father's trembling figure. Any living person, left undetected, would also have heard a young girl's giggle: after the father, back on his feet, fled shrieking from the little wooden collie.

Natalie had always wanted a dollhouse. Now that she had one, she had been delighted to loot a nearby toy store for additional furnishings. Scale didn't yet make sense to her; a few things, like the little silver and red iron, were apparently too big in proportion to the rest of the house. She would learn more about such things later. For now, at least, what mattered was that it was hers. It would provide her, in quiet moments, a break from pursuit of a greater goal.

One she would achieve soon. Soon, indeed.

27

"Mother. Pleeease?"

With a sigh, Maureen found herself breaking into a smile. She couldn't help but nod—it was all Janice needed to pounce upon the ringing landline phone before its third ring—as she hazily recalled her own pre-teenage years. How quickly they pass, she found herself thinking. Though soon, she realized as well, her daughter would have her own cellphone.

Maureen reminded herself she was only forty-one: not so old. But with virtually all of her free time spent worrying about Mickey, Janice, the house and even her own marriage, she could swear she'd spotted a gray hair cropping up in her auburn hair.

"What's so funny, Mom?" asked Mickey, his head propped up on the headrest of his chair as he awaited the next bite of breakfast.

His adoptive mother knocked over the bottle of pancake syrup but caught it before the thick, brown goo could spill out onto the cluttered table. "Oh, my—what? Oh...I was just remembering how much I used to talk over the phone when I was, I'm thinking, right about your sister's age. Until I was eighteen or so."

"Who's she talking to?"

Maureen shrugged. "Regina, I think. From the sound of it. She's..." Her voice trailed off. Not right to go on about how proud she was of Janice's having friends, even considering the trouble she'd had until a few days ago. Mickey, after all, didn't have *any* friends. He'd lost so much time of the third grade that she and Jeffrey had decided to let him get a head start on his therapy, get into a routine there and, she hoped, with some sort of counseling, too, and restart him at the same level in September. Had it been a poor decision?

"Janice doesn't like me," he flatly stated.

Her face changed as if she'd been slapped. "Oh, Mickey. Why do you say that?"

He flashed a false grin, the closest the boy could come to a shrug. "She never talks to me. She walks by and doesn't say hi."

Only Janice's knees were visible from where the girl sat on a chair she'd grabbed from the dining area. And her mother suddenly felt the urge—unfair, she knew—to storm into the kitchen, wrest the receiver from Janice's hands and slam it down on the cradle. How dare she chatter in such a happy tone while her brother...her brother...

"Mickey," she said, "all of us have many, many things to think about right now, many new things. For you, of course, you have the biggest job and you're being very brave about it. For Janice, it's a new house and neighborhood. We all need a little time to settle, that's all." She mussed his hair; he smiled.

Of course she couldn't blame the little eleven-year-old. That was the trouble around here—no matter what went on, Maureen considered, she couldn't blame a soul for it.

She recalled with a shiver the look she saw in her daughter's eyes whenever, those few nights, she'd checked on Janice in the hope that exhaustion had overtaken her for a few hours. Constant chill gets you fever, flu, pneumonia, Maureen kept in mind as she watched and waited for symptoms. None came. Two days after the mysterious return of the heat, in fact, Janice had seemed completely herself in the way she slammed doors. Left them open. And left clothes scattered throughout the house.

Sure, Maureen thought. Kids are resilient. But if this little girl had any of her mother's blood, the anxiety of the previous week had just dipped below the surface for a while. She couldn't nudge her daughter to make more of an effort at being a sister—not yet. Unless Janice brought it up first, it seemed the girl first needed a few more days...at just being Janice again.

When Maureen cleared the table and began to load the dishwasher, Janice swung the chair out of the kitchen and, with a passing glance at Mickey, sat back down and resumed her conversation, picking up where they'd left off.

Mickey, on the couch in the living room, routinely watched what he could in the few minutes it took his mother in the kitchen. This morning was no exception. What was different this time was his sister, equally within earshot, chatting away in competition with the Saturday morning cartoons. He tried to tune her out, listen only to *A Pup Named Scooby-Doo*. What little he heard was enough to do the job:

"What? You're taking *ballet?* No...maybe gymnastics. Last year I was watching the Olym—what? ...yeah, the *summer* ones. You know, that's where those girls—and they're, like, fourteen..." She paused to listen. "...so he comes running up behind me and, you know, he stamps his *foot!* I thought, like, did you *reeeally* have to do that. He says..." Another pause, this one longer. "...well, I don't care if he *is* on the football team. Even if my father did let me out on dates, I'm not gonna go out with a boy I'm taller than...yeah. And he better stop waving at me, everybody's gonna laugh at him...yeah, right? And..."

Tears spilled down Mickey's face. "It's not fair!" he shouted. "It's not fair!"

"I'll call you back," Janice said flatly and hung up the phone. "Mickey..."

"Why do I have to *be* like this? Why do I have..." His mother was hugging him, then, and her shoulder barely muffled his sobs. "Mommy, why? Why, Mommy? Why Mommy why Mommy why Mommy why Mooooommmmmmyyyaaahhaaahaahhhhaa..."

"I don't know, Honey. Oh, I...don't know why things happen." She closed her eyes; she was crying as hard as he was. At a loss for words, she opened her eyes. In the reflection of her glasses lying on the table, she saw Janice, standing frozen behind her. Staring for a few more moments before she turned away and went upstairs.

* * *

You can do it, Mickey. Think real hard...all you have to do is try.

How?

Mickey lay motionless in the bathtub upstairs, his hairless body dry barely a minute since his mother had pulled the plug. She had been hurrying to give him his bath before Mrs. Sanders showed up for his brief Saturday session but, as the doorbell demonstrated, she had begun too late. To keep him safe, she had waited a moment to let enough water drain—most mothers could let this fear go after a child's toddler period—but was now, he supposed, downstairs greeting the therapist.

Where was she?

The boy longed to cover himself. He knew by now that the voices he regularly heard, no longer only by night, were no dream. And it was no trick to piece together that she who could hear him could also see him. It was embarrassing enough for Mickey to get a bath from his mother, but to be seen by a girl? He didn't like that idea at all.

Out of utter, frustrating helplessness, he put that thought out of his mind. It was like hiding from God. Or from an angel. But although he could dismiss his embarrassment, Mickey could not get her words out of his mind. They remained on the edges of his every thought after his mother returned to his side. He muttered in response to her apologies at being behind schedule, barely spoke as she got him dressed for his session.

Emily was all smiles despite the way he gazed ahead at some nonexistent object at her approach. He grunted in approval at her reference to his stair lift as the "royal chariot" and lowered his gaze when, at the sight of his therapy room, she referred to it as the "Olympic gym." It occurred to him that his mother had told her he'd been crying; it was why she'd taken so long downstairs. From there, he further shut her out.

He had an appointment that night.

Not that he didn't listen to her and, in his way, respond to her encouragement. There was something, he sensed, in the way she was speaking to him this day, something she seemed to be looking forward to—did she know something he didn't? The fact that his thoughts were elsewhere left his body free from the second-guessing Emily knew could block progress.

That was when it happened.

Emily had been repeatedly raising and lowering the fingers of his right hand when, after a dip, she noticed two of his fingers tremble and—barely noticeably—lift. "Mickey! Again! Do it again!"

He gritted his teeth and did it again, though with a little less power.

"Wonderful!" She hugged him. "Mickey, Honey...you...are getting better! We have to build on this, get this hand back in commission all the way. But first...let's tell your family, huh?"

Mickey's face fell. "Yeah. Fine."

His mother, just out of the shower, ran down the stairs in her bathrobe. Janice trailed, less out of interest than from obligation to see whatever was going on before she got into more trouble for not being present.

"Ready, Mickey?"

"Alright," came his reply. Impassively, Mickey repeated his movement and glanced up at his whooping mother and his nervously giggling sister.

"There's gold in them thar knuckles, I tell you!" said Emily.

It was a breakthrough, he guessed. But for all the excitement he could muster up, it was as nothing compared to the promises he heard by night.

You can dance, and run and fly!

Without such words, his triumph surely would have charged him up—given him the boost he needed to carry him onward to each new success.

Through the remainder of the session, he instead repeated the thought: It wasn't even a whole finger, just the tip. Just a little part.

And

Play with me, Mickey. You can do it. You can do it...now

By bedtime, he was ready to meet her. In nights past, she had come to him, standing *somewhere* near him

an angel

and coaxing him ever onward.

like an angel

This time he would not wait. "Are you there?" he whispered. "I...I think I'm ready."

* * *

Oh, but for a cookie.

Maureen didn't know which feeling she was enjoying more, however much with guilt: the idea of having a cookie, just one, or the freedom of spirit that left even a little room for so minute a luxury. After relishing the breakthrough in Mickey's therapy, she had been too excited to sleep.

So here she was, after midnight, staring at an inane talk show and thinking about...just one.

She almost didn't hear the shuffling of stocking feet to her left. "Hi," came her daughter's voice. "Whatcha doin' up?"

The parent in Maureen nearly commented, I should be asking *you* that question, young lady. She merely shrugged, however, and patted the empty end of the couch in an invitation. "How about you?" she asked Janice.

Her daughter shook her head in reply, the girl's lips tightened in dismay, as she flung herself into the couch.

"What is it, Honey?"

Janice rolled her eyes and again shook her head. "Nothing, Mom. You'd just think I—" She cut herself off and glanced at the stairway before locking her gaze on a car commercial.

Maureen brought a knee up and faced her daughter. "Janice..."

The girl looked quickly and returned her eyes, if not her attention, to the TV.

"...do you know that I love you?"

Slowly came the nod; Janice's lips were trembling as she fought back the tears. She crossed her arms. She leaned over to rest against her mother, and that was when the tears came.

Maureen said little, held her close, wondered with shame whose shoulder she *herself* could cry on. First must come the tears, she thought. Then they'd talk.

The two of them watched the pendulum of their mantel clock swirl one direction, then the next, in its endless rhythm. "Mom, h-he scares me," the girl said without warning.

Her mother drew back, still holding on but feeling a need to see Janice's face. "Scares you? But *why*, dear?"

Janice shrugged. "I dunno. He just..."

It was wrong to say it. She knew what she felt was not something people talked about. But—"I get scared the way he sits, all bent...funny with his head tipping back and his eyes...*looking* at me, always *looking* at me from, like, sideways. I...feel like he's saying *look* at me, feel *sorry* for me, and I feel...oh God, Mommy...I feel like if I look at him too much or touch him I'm gonna go to bed some night and...I'm gonna wake up all twisted, too, and he'll look at me and he'll smile and say, 'See, it's not so bad.' Oh, Mommy! I'm sorry, I'm sorry I feel that, I'm sorry I said..."

"It's okay, Honey, it's okay," her mother intoned. "You know, you didn't have very much time getting to know Mickey before this...horrible disease came along. Because of that...well, you think he's a different person. Or you forget who you knew. But inside, he's still the same Mickey, and you are still his sister."

"I know—I know that."

"It's...not easy. I know that. But I remember, too, how proud I was the day he said you pushed a boy against the lockers in P.S. 169 after he knocked down Mickey's books. He was a grade above *you*, I think I remember him saying."

Janice straightened up and wiped her eyes. "Oh, Mom, all the sixth-grade boys are dorks."

"Well, this little boy upstairs said the nicest thing about you that day. He said..."

"What? What?"

Maureen grinned. "First, go get us some cookies."

"Mom!"

"The chewy chocolate-chip ones, thank you."

With a grunt of exasperation, Janice sprang from the couch and returned, a minute later, with the cookie bag, two glasses of milk and a full mouth. "Ess oh oo 'on ass or il eh."

Chuckling, Maureen replied, "Beg pardon?"

Her daughter swallowed. "I saaaid, 'Just so you don't ask for milk next,'" she translated. She handed over a glass and sat back. "Now *tell me.*"

"Well," she said, staring at the chocolate chips but daring not speak while chewing for fear of spoiling the effect, "he said he thought you were his best friend in the whole world."

"Oh, Mom, I feel..."

"And he couldn't wait till he got older and bigger so he could protect *you.*"

The tears came again, Maureen content to remain in silence. After a while, Janice lifted her face up from her mother's shoulder. "Mom...?"

"Mmmmm?"

"Now...now I'm scared he doesn't like me anymore." Her lips tightened into a hint of a smile.

"My little sweetie, I think he'll surprise you. But Janice...think about things a little different now. At school, you protected him from the bad kids. Now..." She trailed off.

"N-now what, Mom?"

"Now you have to protect him from the sad kid inside. The one who sometimes wants to hang it all up and quit."

251

* * *

"Tell me how to do it. Now. Please?"

The voice that responded was steady, confident. This time he was ready for her instructions. *"Mickey, the hardest part the first time is to lie still. You don't have to worry about that. Just...think about floating. Think really really hard with your eyes closed...relax your face...think...about floating...you don't—you don't feel anything against the pillow. You're floating up...that's it...don't...don't talk...you're doing it! I can see two of you! You're..."*

The boy gasped in the realization that he *was* doing it. He was joining that vast world of play, where paralysis was nothing but what he was leaving behind on the bed, more with each passing moment. He saw the sinking outline of his covers as he rose slowly, then more swiftly with the revelation that he had *done it*. This was the triumph he needed to egg him on—not some little finger-twitching in a therapy room that made him so anxious. Here were no sessions, no baths, no waiting for someone to feed him or move him or... He flipped wildly about in the small confines of his room, somersaulting through the air and raising his arms, legs kicking, toward the heavens.

Mickey crouched, then sprang up to the ceiling. He clenched and opened his fists, turned his wrists one way and the other, bent and twirled his arms, finally flapping them like a puppy shaking free the raindrops. It took several seconds before Mickey could even begin to calm down. And once he did, he turned, a bit shamefacedly, to greet...

his savior.

"Just like I said?" she asked him.

The boy studied his friend. Pretty though he would never admit it, the girl stood before him with her arms crossed over everyday clothes. She had long hair he supposed was blonde when the girl was in her body—her spirit as well as his appeared a wispy gray—and a thin face that seemed...bothered by something. But, to him, as friendly a face as he had ever seen. She looked younger than his sister; Mickey wondered who would win in a fight. His sister, though, was sometimes friendly, sometimes, well, weird. Like she didn't like him anymore since he got sick. This girl was different, he could tell with the complete assurance of a child. "What's your name?"

The girl paused. "Um, Natalie. I live here."

Mickey chuckled and began to jump up and down. "What do you mean, you *live* here! You do not! You're funny, Natalie."

"Well," she replied, shrugging. She rose to meet Mickey at the ceiling and, upside down, continued. "I do, kind of. Um...can you keep a secret? And not be, like, scared or anything?"

"Yup, I can keep a secret, all right."

"Okay. I, um, left my body and...never went back. My daddy was—is—a very...mean man who h-hit me all the time. Hit my mom, too. One night I was hurt real bad—it's easier to leave your body when you're real sick or hurt—and I left...my body and never went back. I came here; the house was empty then. This is your room, but...it's mine, too. Is that okay?"

The boy nodded. "But...that means you're...dead, right?"

Natalie shrugged again and said, with a grin, "Well, nobody told me! I don't think so. I'da went to Heaven, right?"

Smiling, Mickey floated to the window and passed his head through to gaze at the docile corner of Mason and Oak, and his streetlight. It was true. If you died, you had to go to Heaven or hell. Otherwise, this neighborhood would be packed with millions of ghosts so close together they wouldn't know whose arms were whose. He looked back at Natalie. "I can go back whenever I want, right?"

"Sure. Want to try now?"

"Um, no. Let's explore the house!" He needed not tell Natalie that while he knew he'd have to return to his body come morning, it wasn't hard to imagine the notion, the sweet notion, of staying outside his body and never going back.

Which was, of course, the point.

28

Mickey was sleeping soundly.

Too soundly.

His mother had given the boy's door its usual light knock before entering. Funny, she thought on her way in, this morning the door was closed. Neither Jeffrey nor Janice would have done that, so much had she stressed that Mickey should feel a part of the household routine—even if it meant he heard each and every sound they made near his room.

Maureen noticed something else: a loud creak in the door's hinges. While nothing unusual in itself—March humidity needed no help—she realized it had also failed to awaken her son, a light sleeper. She knelt beside his bed and stroked his cheek, watching the faint rise and fall of his chest beneath the tucked-in covers.

"Oh, Miiickeeey..."

Considering the disturbed sleep Mickey had been having even until recently, she should have been glad to see him so lost to the world. Nevertheless, Maureen wanted him awake now. She couldn't put her finger on the reason; she just wanted him up.

"Mickey, wake up," she said.

In an instant, his eyes opened wide. "Hi, Mommy," he greeted her without hesitation.

"Good morning, young man. Were you...already awake? Pretending to be asleep, I mean, to play a joke on Mommy?"

He furled his eyebrows in confusion at the remark, then grinned.

"Um, yeah. Practicing for April Fools!"

"How long have you been awake?"

Again he hesitated, which, Maureen observed, wasn't like him. "A long time," he announced.

Maureen felt his forehead. "And how did you sleep?"

He shrugged with his eyebrows. "I dunno. Okay, I guess."

"Hi," Janice said from the doorway. Her mother and Mickey stared as she came and propped an elbow up on the dresser as if she came in this way to greet her brother every morning.

"Hi, Jan," her mother finally said.

Mickey was still staring; a hopeful smile was forming in the corners of his mouth.

Janice swallowed and sat on the edge of her brother's bed. "Can your dumb ol' sister make you some breakfast?"

"Um...sure!" A frown crossed his face, and he turned toward his mother. "Can she cook?"

Funny you should ask, thought Maureen with dread despite her pride at what she was observing in her daughter. "Janice, Honey, I think you're a dear to offer. Since it's a school day, though, why don't you just start things up while I get your brother dressed. I'll pick up in a minute." And give you two a chance to talk, she thought, even if it means you miss the bus and I have to spring for an Uber.

"Okay, Mom!" She leapt for the door but caught the jamb and sprang herself back in. "Oh...what do I make?"

"I like scrambled eggs eeeeevery morning!" cried Mickey as his mother leaned his back against the headboard. "Um...applesauce, too."

"Got it. Anything else?"

While the three were engaged upstairs, Jeffrey dragged his slippered feet across the kitchen floor and poured his coffee from the drip coffeemaker. He sneezed—it occurred to him he was the only one who ever thought the house was still drafty—and pulled the sugar bowl down from the open shelf above the counter.

Let's see, he thought: a touch of milk for the java, one of those frozen bagels and...yep, a banana would do it for this morning. He was doing rounds with the interns first thing that day, and he had a presentation on abdominal aneurysms right after. Oh, and he'd have to remember to take along some notes he'd brought home the night before.

First, he went to the refrigerator, opened it and took the milk.

The refrigerator, however, didn't close right away. Janice had hurried into the room. "Hi, Dad," she said and reached for the closing door. She caught the handle—and the egg tray flew off its holder, overturned and smashed its contents onto the floor.

"Janice! How could you do such a stupid thing?"

"No! Dad...I didn't...I couldn't—"

"Now you can clean it up." He stirred milk into his coffee. "Damn," he muttered with a shake of his head.

Janice began to cry. She bent over with a dishcloth to wipe up the gooey mess, staring up at the egg compartment. It wasn't something she could put into words, but...the refrigerator door hadn't been closing quickly enough for anything to have slid out when she grabbed the handle. She began to wipe the ledge of the open refrigerator.

"For Pete's sake, Janice! Use the dustpan to get up the shells and yolks *first*. Then wipe the rest. With a moist *paper towel,* not our good dish towels!"

"O-Okay, Daddy," the girl replied. She was thinking not of the mess on the floor but rather her brother upstairs.

With whom she had just struck out.

When she returned to Mickey's room, she found him all dressed, in his wheelchair and headed out the door. Mickey's smile, brighter that she had seen in a long time, faded when he saw the look on Janice's face.

"Janice! her mother said. "What's wrong?"

Her eyes lowered. "I...the eggs fell."

Maureen had heard some shouting, so she kept her voice low even as she felt her frustration level rising. "All of them, Janice?"

She nodded. "I'm sorry, Mickey. I don't know how I did it. I just..."

"It's...it's okay. I think I'm in the mood for something else today," he said.

You're blaming me again, she wanted him to say. She was ready to cry again—seeing that cocked head, his wide-eyed stare—and run from the room. "C-could I m-make—"

"Janice, you're sweet for wanting to help, but you'll hear it from Mrs. Thurmond if you're late for school."

"Oh...yeah." She crouched to look across at her brother. "You have a good day, okay, Mickey? I'll see you later."

"Yeah. Thanks." His faint smile reminded Janice of how much

making up, in general, she still faced ahead.

* * *

No wonder he'd been sneezing in the house, Jeffrey thought as he pulled the storm door closed behind him; it looked like a cloud had made its home on Mason Street. That's all fog was, after all, he mused, just a low cloud. Good for him he had a short drive these days. Otherwise he'd be late for—

He stopped in his tracks. His notes! He'd been so upset at Janice that he'd nearly forgotten them. With a sigh, he swung open the storm door and stuck his key in the lock. The door opened without his help, and Janice rushed past him, crying. She gripped her books tightly to her chest, and Jeffrey watched her blonde curls bounce as the girl stepped down the walk.

"Hey, Ja..." Have a nice day, he was going to say. Maybe he did overreact, however unlikely the chance that he would apologize. But wishing her well wasn't going to erase what had begun as merely one of those awful mornings. He sighed again and went into the house.

Upstairs, he realized he hadn't said goodbye to anyone. Maureen was washing Mickey up in the bathroom; he could stop in on his way out, though he'd have to hurry at this point. His notes: he'd left them on top of the small desk in their bedroom. Jeffrey found them where he'd left them—he skimmed them to be sure—but noticed something else. A drawer, where he kept a few personal files, was ajar.

He didn't have time to ponder what this meant. Instead, he opened it, retrieved one particular manila folder and shoved it into his briefcase with his notes.

"Gotta run," he snapped as he barged in on Maureen and Mickey. "Bye, Mau," he said and pecked his wife on the cheek. He patted his son's head. "Knock 'em dead, slugger."

"Bye, Daddy."

* * *

"I...I didn't hear the question." And, come to think of it, Janice wasn't quite sure at all what topic Mr. Ruben had been discussing.

The burly science teacher had a long neck, and students joked among themselves that he could turn it all the way around, in brontosaurus fashion, to stare at a wayward student before the rest of his body completed the rotation. No one dared cross him; the penalty, after all, was close proximity with the dark sweat spots beneath the arms of the long-sleeved shirts he wore buttoned to the neck each day.

"The question, for the benefit of Miss Stratton and anyone else lost..."—he faced Janice but craned his neck to survey the rest of the class—"in *Wonderland*, was, what gives a green plant its color. Could you return from your...*fugue* long enough to answer the question?"

Janice stammered amidst a low tittering. "It...it's—"

"Will the Muses kindly aid Miss Stratton in her efforts to—"

"Chlorophyll."

Mr. Ruben's slow movements would not allow a double-take; instead, he raised his eyebrows and straightened in the aisle. "I beg your pardon?" he said in almost a whisper.

"Chlorophyll. It makes plants green and, like, also catches light that the plant needs. To make food."

"Uh, yes. Please, next time, do not make me repeat the question."

A half-hour later, Janice looked up from her tray in the cafeteria at her friend Regina, who had sat down, across from her, at the end of one of the three long tables. "You really made a dummy out of Ruben," said Regina in place of a hello. "How'd you know that answer?"

Janice shrugged. Between slurps of her iced tea, she explained how the time her mother spent with Mickey made it easier for her to get into the habit of studying. "Also," she added as the idea occurred to her, "I...want to know answers to things when my brother starts school again."

Regina, a slim brunette who prided herself in having had her first period before starting sixth grade, nodded in admiration. "You sound like a good sister," she said. "I don't know how I'd do if...um..."

"If your brother was paralyzed? Regina, it's okay to say it. Really." Janice realized it was a subject the two hadn't touched on during the month since they met in social studies class.

"I'm sorry," Regina said, pushing her hair back.

"It's all right. Please." Janice did not like the silence that followed, nor the way her friend avoided her gaze as the two ate their lunches. There was more that bothered her. It didn't only involve Regina. It was the way most of her classmates generally *looked* at her. Studied her face, analyzed whatever she said, the way she acted, throughout the school day. Janice had moved in mid-year from one end of the school district to the other, which meant spending more time catching up on schoolwork—and less time with friends. But that couldn't be it. Janice could swear she heard occasional whispering in the halls as she walked by one clique or another.

Were they talking about Mickey?

"Um, Regina, I was thinking."

Her friend had just been wiping her mouth after downing one last noodle. In fact, she had been rising to leave. "About what?" she asked.

"Do you want to come to my house tonight to study for the science test tomorrow? I'd have to ask my Mom, but I think she—"

"Tonight?"

Janice sat back in her seat. "Well, yeah, the test is tomorrow..." She paused as the tone of Regina's reply sank in. "Regina, please don't say you never want to come over. We're friends, aren't we?"

"Yeah! Sure we are. But..."

Janice sighed. "But what?"

She couldn't comprehend the way her friend's eyes darted from side to side before she came up with an answer. "How about, like, right after school?" Regina countered.

Puzzled, Janice nodded in confirmation. Right after school was when she wanted to sit down with Mickey. It was also not when she could best sit down and concentrate. Whatever her friend's strange reasoning, however, Janice wasn't about to argue. If that was what it took to keep a friend, well, that was when she'd study.

And after what happened that morning, Janice wasn't sure her mother would let her in the kitchen to help with dinner, anyway.

* * *

Hadn't she just done this room?

Maureen hardly considered herself a heavy-duty house cleaner. She grinned whenever she remembered the day she told Jeffrey— yes, before their wedding day—that she'd be the proverbial white tornado only when assured she was but one of a pair of such storm systems.

Jeffrey, to his credit, generally picked up after himself. His schedule made it difficult for her to tell whether he would help with the household chores if he could. But what he was able to do, he did.

Which was what made the mess in the bedroom so unusual. Jeffrey's dresser looked as if he had been frantically searching for something—drawers askew, articles of clothing spilled out. Even his pajamas lay on the floor beneath the foot of the bed. He always hung them up.

Maureen shook her head and sighed. When she awoke each morning, she left her own disorder behind in her haste to get the kids—Mickey in particular—ready for their day. Emily had settled into enough of a routine that Maureen felt free to do what she wanted for a few hours. She typically began by making the bed, showering and having a nice cup of tea while she checked in online. Then she straightened up the upstairs rooms.

In short, it was a time for letting her thoughts wander.

Now, however, she was wondering whether they could have wandered so far. She stared in silence at the dresser, the floor. She shook her head. She looked down; in her reverie, she had spilled some of her tea on her bathrobe. The heat of the drink had kept her from realizing, even with her wet hair, that somewhere a window had opened.

She turned. There was only one wind—

A frantic flash of black and her tea went flying as she raised her hands in defense. The black bird flapped, screeched, panicked, fanned past her face and flew in crazed circles around the room. She kept an arm across her face and searched with half-closed eyes for...something. Anything, a—a weapon. Her robe was wide open, and she held it closed for a moment. Her own turning with the encircling bird made her release her grip.

Maureen waved away feathers and lunged for the corner of the comforter. It was hers. She spun again, and the robe fell to the floor. It was not vulnerability she felt but confidence. There it was, perched atop the overhead light's translucent dish. The crow, panting, awaited her next move.

"Get...*out of here!*" She screamed and swung a half of the blanket. The crow took off, resumed its circling and

No!

headed for the open doorway. Maureen swung. The blanket grazed the bird, and it touched off the doorjamb and landed on the bed. Maureen slammed the door shut.

"I said...GET OUT OF MY HOUSE!" With a screech, the crow

took off—directly at her face. It careened off her forehead as she dropped to the floor, and then spotted the open window. It took off and was gone. Maureen hid her face in the blanket for several seconds before...

Before she realized it was quiet. Quiet but for the sound of Emily's running feet on the stairs. "Mrs. Stratton! Mrs.—"

The door opened, and the therapist gaped at the sight of her employer, clad only in her nightgown and panties, hair disheveled and with a red scratch on her forehead that seemed to grow redder as she stared. "Oh, dear," she said, resuming her control. "Here." She helped Maureen on with her robe, guided her to the bed.

"No!" Maureen screamed. "Not there! It—"

"What? Mrs. Stratton, this is definitely the best place for you right now. You just—"

"Death!"

Emily shook her head. "Excuse m—"

"Death was on this bed. My grandmother always said, a black bird in the house is...a message of death." Maureen shivered, shook her head to ward off the shock of her experience.

"That's what I thought you...why, Mrs. Stra—"

"A...bird. A big, black bird." She stared absently through her disheveled hair and extended her hands to indicate its size. "It flew at...it flew at me and...I swung at it. It landed..." She gestured toward the bed and backed away. "I can't..."

"Mrs. Stratton, you cannot *fear* your bed. All right, don't *lie* down if you feel that way, just sit for now. Although I can't guarantee anything if you start showing signs of shock."

Maureen did as she was told. Emily propped up her pillow, then turned to get a cold, wet cloth. "Oh," the therapist said. She stepped to the windows, firmly lowered and locked them. On her way out, she picked up the mug from the floor.

When she returned, Maureen was shaking her head, still taking deep breaths. "I'd *locked* them," she was saying.

"Pardon?"

Maureen began to brush her hair. "I know they were locked," she said. "They're always closed and—we, we're practically city folks. I lock them when they're closed."

Emily shrugged and dabbed Maureen's forehead with the cloth. She had already left Mickey for too long; by now, he'd be worried sick and might even be in tears. "You don't suppose your husband could have had it open and forgot to lock it afterwards?"

Maureen leaned her head back against the headboard. "I guess you never know," she said.

"Do you think you'll be all right now?"

"Um...yeah. I...no," she said. Maureen was staring at the open door of the closet, across the room. A door she remembered having closed before she took her shower.

She leaned over for the comforter, waving away the therapist in an effort to summon the concentration she might soon need. Maureen wrapped part of the blanket around her arm and slowly, quietly, approached the closet with her quilted shield before her.

Easy now, she thought, it's gone. Still, she heard the bird's mad cawing and saw the black flash in circles through the peripheral vision of her mind's eye.

Without another thought she sidestepped the wooden louvered doors and thrust the protected arm into the closet. She shoved coats, sweaters, dresses to one side then back, all the while with her eyes squinted, her teeth clenched. Maureen tasted blood, realized she had bitten her tongue.

When she finished waving her arm across the lower part of the closet, she closed the door, sighed and smiled. *"Now* I'm okay," she said. "But I think I'll take another stab at some tea. Downstairs, where I can reach the broom next time I have company."

"I'm with you."

The two descended the stairs, and Maureen followed Emily into Mickey's exercise room. The therapist had left the boy in his wheelchair, assuming he'd use the chin control to wheel over to the TV and switch it on for a few minutes. And now it appeared to both that he had fallen asleep without leaving the room.

Emily crouched beside the wheelchair. "Hey, champ," she said closely into his ear.

A second passed, then another. His eyes flashed open with no indication of sleepiness. "Hi, Mrs. Sanders. Hi, Mom."

"Um..." Emily began. "Mickey, were you asleep?"

"I was visiting...um..." He lowered his head, frowned, and bent it awkwardly upward to meet his mother's gaze. "Mom, is the black bird gone?"

Maureen and Emily could only look at each other.

* * *

Call her the new Natalie.

The girl smiled softly to herself, for no one else was there to see her. There, atop the chimney for a fireplace that had never been used for as long as she could remember. It occurred to her: The Strattons did talk about firing it up, "to flush out the spooks," Jeffrey had joked. His wife hadn't laughed. But what these people didn't know about houses was that you didn't just build a fire without having some man in a top hat come and brush it out first.

Occasionally, she ran a materialized finger along the corners of the chimney cap. She nodded at the potential of a neglected chimney, then shrugged. She had better ideas than this.

Her new plan could work. Would work.

It would work because it was simple.

No ruses to lure this person here or there, no knives or rocks, no trickery. That hadn't worked with Cynthia, that former friend, because leaving her body for good was never her intention—no matter what she'd said.

Mickey would become her playmate forever if he could come to feel he had no other choice. There was unlimited mobility, a carefree life devoid of wheelchairs, stairlifts, therapy. And then, she thought with a slight clenching of her fist, there was this family of people who...

should stay out of her way!

...were finding everyday life more difficult by the day.

Call her the new Natalie.

True, her living years were cut off at age nine. But experience, she was learning, went on and on. Although Natalie had made her presence—and, eventually, her demands—known to the Carters from the very day they'd moved in, she now knew that a different approach was necessary this time around. If these Strattons quit and left as the Carters had, Mickey would go, too. They had to feel comfortable enough in the house to stay.

But be too weak and confused to get in her way.

She pretended to stand, upside down, on her hands as she gripped the cap of the chimney. Swinging her legs back and forth, she pondered her next moves. Each had to frighten its target, yet it couldn't be traceable to anything other than...bad luck. No more dollhouse extortion, if she could help herself.

Now it was temperatures. Eggs. Birds. Whatever else she could think of, plus...

The letter she'd found.

And once Mickey was hers, the rest of them could just find another place to live.

Barely at first, Natalie heard voices from the street. She righted herself and, gazing over the ridgeline of the roof, spotted Janice and another girl crossing Mason Street.

She stared coldly at the pair. Whenever she saw Janice, watched those blonde curls bounce around on her shoulders with every light step, Natalie wanted to rush at her. Hear the intruder shriek as she tore loose a few handfuls of that primped hair. Take those purple sneakers, tied together and hanging from the ring of a magenta knapsack, and shove the toe of one into her crying mouth. Then—

Natalie cut herself off. No, this wouldn't do. The spirit knew she could snuff the life from this girl as easily as she had nearly done with her aunt, Sarah Leffingwell, and that—she snickered—smartass egg thrower. In fact, Natalie would enjoy taking care of this one. What she had to remember from her triumph over the Carter family was how the threat to a child invariably sent a family packing. If they couldn't do anything more for Janice, that still left Mickey.

And he was *hers*.

Which left a problem. Janice's true threat, Natalie reminded herself, was her ability to make Mickey feel a part of the family even when his parents, for whatever reason, did not. Natalie had never had brothers or sisters. But she always felt that, however much they might fight, they sided with one another when parents seemed unfair. She couldn't think about her feelings toward Janice.

What she needed to rein in were Mickey's feelings toward his sister, whose friend had fallen back a few steps. She was now staring up at the house.

"Come on in, willya?" Janice called from the doorway.

With a glance at the lowering sun, the dark-haired girl quickened her pace and followed Janice into the house.

Natalie floated facedown, spread-eagle, through the roof. Past the rafters of the half-cathedral ceiling, through the rail of the upstairs hallway and to the center of the living room. Janice's friend looked frightened—she'd gotten a good dose of those stories at school, Natalie surmised with a schoolgirl's grin.

Maybe...

Maybe she could keep those stories going strong. The new Natalie?

She shrugged at the thought, then grinned.

"Oh, hello," Maureen said, drying her hands on a faded dishcloth. "You must be Regina."

"Um, yeah. Hi, Mrs. Stratton!" Regina extended her hand and, in stepping past the edge of the family-room sofa, would have missed Mickey but for the sound of the TV. "Oh..." the girl trailed off, limply shaking the hand before her but with her face now toward the boy.

Here it comes, said the look on Janice's face.

"You're Mickey!" Regina suddenly said. All three watched as Janice's friend spun on a foot and sat down beside Mickey on the couch. The girl took his hand, clasped it and set it back on his lap without a hint of discomfort. "I remember you from those first few weeks of school," she said. "You were always forgetting your jacket, someone told me. And once when my class was in the yard and yours came out, I saw you come out and look right away at a bluebird in the trees, like you were listening to it sing."

The boy beamed. "I...I remember that!"

Regina's face brightened, too. "So, Mickey, you remember what happens next, riiight?"

"Uh-huuuh!"

"What?" Maureen asked.

"Ms. Salamanka comes out—we call her Ms. Salamander." She stood up, curled down the corners of her mouth, jutted her jaw till the veins of her neck protruded, and lowered her head to look out the tops of her eyes. "See?" she rasped to approving laughter. Even as Natalie wondered how to get this girl out of the house, she too let loose a quiet chuckle.

"So, anyway, Ms. Salamander is holding a green jacket, Mickey's. She holds it up high..." Regina made the face again and pretended to raise a jacket with fingers she had curled claw-like for effect. "...and says, 'Young man, I believe *this* belongs to *you!*'"

The boy glowed in admiration for Regina. "That was funny, even though everybody was laughing at me."

"Oh, they weren't laughing at *you!* Even better, you didn't even go right back for the jacket," the girl added. "You listened to that bird just a few more seconds before it flew away. *That* was the best part. You let her stand there till you were ready!"

Mickey grinned, staring toward the ceiling as though he could still hear the song.

"Anyway, it's good to see you again." She reached over and patted his hand again. "We want to see you back at school soon, okay?"

"Okay!" Mickey replied.

"Mom, can Mickey have some cookies with us while we study?"

Maureen paused before answering. "That's a good idea, Honey, but don't you girls have your work to do?"

The pair looked at each other, then nodded. "I guess we do," said Janice.

"Mickey," Maureen turned and said, "we can sit together for a while and have our *own* cookies."

Regina surveyed the living room as Janice motioned toward their books on the dining-room table. "You have a pretty house, Mrs. Stratton," she said.

Maureen was about to reply when Regina stiffened and crossed her arms.

"Why...what's wrong?"

"Oh...nothing...I—I caught—" The girl looked at Mickey, a few feet away, who seemed to have noticed nothing extraordinary. "I caught a chill, that's all." She walked briskly to the table and circled it before sitting down. "We'd better start, okay?"

The two sat down and opened identical textbooks. Maureen quietly put a few shortbread cookies onto a plate, poured some milk for everyone and left the rest of the cookie bag on the dining-room table. Janice and Regina snickered as their hands collided at the opening of the bag. Janice pulled back, and then they each loaded a few onto a napkin and went back to their schoolwork. The TV played softly in the living room.

Fifteen minutes later, the two sat back in silent agreement that it was time for a break. Regina stood up, walked to look out the kitchen window, and returned to her seat with a trace of worry tingeing her smile.

"So...what do you think he's going to ask?" Janice asked.

"Um...who?" Regina said, sitting back down.

"Mr. Ruben, silly. On the science test."

Regina closed and opened her eyes; she shook her head and smiled. "Sorry! I don't know. Maybe he'll try..." She didn't finish. She was glancing toward the living room, up toward the rafters and...

beginning to shiver again.

Her head turned, in fact, as the cold spot shifted. The bone-chill...it seemed now to have a physical form, a beginning and an end. It was not all around as it had been. It was at her side, and nobody except her seemed to have noticed anything at all.

She stiffened up in the seat, pulled her arm close and tried to concentrate on her books.

"Maybe he'll what?" Janice said, then, "Hey, are you all right?"

In the living room, Mickey coughed once and kept his gaze on the TV. His mother had returned to the kitchen and was starting dinner.

"Regina, what's the matter?" Janice asked again.

The cold spot was now behind Regina. There was nothing tangible, nothing actually touching her, yet it came closer to her back, a breath away from actually...touching it. Regina's eyes widened. A muted cry struggled to arise from her open mouth. "G-get away! Uh...uh..."

"Regina...? Mom!"

And the coldness passed through the girl's back. She began to shake in terrorized spasms. A small stream of milk leaked out a corner of her mouth and dripped onto her violet jeans.

Something, solid now, was within her. Regina cried out and began to tremble, oblivious to both Maureen's and Janice's circling, questioning.

Within her body, a hand grabbed hold of something. And *squeezed*.

Everything came up and out. It shot out to spray their books and splash the window beyond, several feet away. Regina rocked back in the chair, which fell backwards to the floor. The girl spun to avoid striking her head on the laminate floor. Then the feeling, the coldness, were gone. All that remained was a queasiness inside, the sense that something inside her had been...bruised.

"Regina, what happened?" Maureen asked the tearful girl. "Should I call—"

"I h-have to go," Regina said. She scooped up her books, shutting them over the spattered vomit and haphazardly shoving them into her bag. "I—I'm...sorry about the mess. But—"

"It's all right," replied Maureen. "We'll take care of it."

"I'm sorry, I'm really sorry, Mrs. Stratton, Janice. I just..." She grabbed her coat, shaking her head. She doubled over for a moment in lingering pain, then straightened up and shot an apologetic glance toward Mickey.

"Are you sure...?"

Regina nodded impatiently, opened the door and left.

Maureen and her daughter didn't talk about it then. In the gaze they exchanged, they didn't have to.

They both knew what they had seen in Regina, undoubtedly in her actions, her words...her eyes.

It was terror.

29

From the looks he received upon his return home that evening, Jeffrey was certain one of them had found the letter. Damn...why had he ever saved it? Did he really need to keep the issue alive, in his mind, by not destroying it at his office when he first laid eyes on it? Was it so important that—

Wait. In the moment he met the gazes of his wife and daughter, it occurred to him he could well be mistaken. It...it was not anger in their faces but relief. Something was wrong, that much was clear. But what he most dreaded, on top of what had already occurred today, had not taken place.

"Hi," he said in a voice devoid of emotion.

His wife smiled by lifting her frown and dropping it back down. She went to her husband, gave him a quick kiss on the lips and an obligatory hug. "Jeff, uh..." She glanced at her daughter as if for approval. Janice flashed the same unconvincing grin and cocked her head in a shrug. "Janice's friend Regina was here this afternoon to study, and she had some sort of...an experience we...can't make a lot of sense of."

Sighing, Jeffrey slumped onto the couch and threw back his head. He felt a grin, a stupid, sappy grin, beginning to form on his face, and he gave it a shake to keep it away.

"There's nothing funny about this, Jeff," Maureen remarked.

"No, of course, I know. It's just been...a strange kind of day." He noticed the two of them look to each other before continuing. "So are you going to tell me what's going on?"

Maureen relayed the events. Janice frequently broke in, appropriate since she alone had been present when her friend first exhibited that faraway, pained look. Jeffrey listened to both as he removed his wool overcoat. He looked from one to the other before beginning his questions, as he had earlier while doing rounds with the interns.

He undid his tie, which he'd loosened in the car on the way home. "Janice, how did your friend seem on her way over from school? Any anxiety? Complaints about her stomach? Chills, maybe?"

His daughter shook her head. "We were mostly talking about Dougals."

"Dougals?"

"Yeah. His name's really Douglas, but the teacher once misspelled his name on a list she put up on the bulletin board. He's a real—"

"Janice, save it for another time. No strange behavior till you got in the house, I take it. What did she have for lunch—do you know?"

"Um...tuna sandwich. But I had one, too. It was good, I thought. For school, anyway. But..."

"What?"

"She was looking up funny at the house. We were in front and I got to the door, opened it and she was way back at the curb. Staring up, you know? But then she came in."

Jeffrey sighed and leaned back into the couch. "And nothing strange until after she was here a while," he said flatly. He was processing their answers, fitting what he took as incomplete information into a picture he would need to complete on his own once they told him what they could. Tuna salad. Janice ate it, too; she's fine. Maybe Regina already felt ill before she came in the house but forgot it when she talked to Mickey. Okay, no discomfort on her part whatsoever; funny, people seemed to feel one way or the other about the handicapped. No, he'd been hearing it called "physically challenged" these days, wasn't he? He would suppose it was harder when you saw a problem with a kid; older people, you more or less expected problems at a certain point. Not that he knew. His sister halfway across the country took care of his folks, and she'd stopped writing.

He shook his head at his own mental tangent—where was his brain?

The cookies. He knew how he used to down cookies. And the subject of their test: biology. That had to be it. It wasn't an easy subject to stomach—he forgave himself the pun—and with a belly full of cookies on top of a mayonnaise-laden lunch and probably a soda or two...

"What was Regina reading before she lost it?"

Maureen groaned. "Jeffrey, is that the best you can suggest?" she said. "In school they dissect frogs and fish...nothing. She comes over, *reads* about a frog's guts and throws up *here*?"

He countered, "Have you got a better explanation? Her biology class, if I remember right, is before lunch. It wouldn't have come up before."

"Janice," Maureen said, "have you or Regina ever skipped lunch over a dissected frog?"

"Maureen, this is ridiculous," said Jeffrey.

"Janice?"

The girl shrugged. "Well, I don't. Regina, I...don't always see at lunchtime."

"Anyone else from your class?"

"I...can't see them from my table."

Jeffrey was ready to reply—Maureen, for some reason, seemed determined to make him look foolish—but he happened to look up toward the second-floor landing.

Past the landing, toward the door to Janice's room. The door was halfway open, its hinges on the left side of the doorway.

And through the balusters, he could distinctly see the maroon seraph type of a logo, on a letter taped to the doorjamb.

The letter he had been shocked to find missing from the file he'd rushed into his bag that morning.

He had just finished his rounds—or rather, had begged off early in his growing anxiety. The senior resident could handle things fine, he knew. Or, at least, he could this morning. Jeffrey had been slowed down behind one school bus after another on his way to work, and he'd had to rush to his rounds without pausing to check his briefcase for what he was sure was inside.

After his presentation, he had a mere fifteen minutes before prepping for surgery, a peripheral artery bypass he'd done enough of to let him take just a minute...to check the file in his briefcase. He opened the file; the letter wasn't there. He rummaged through the briefcase. Nothing. Several minutes later—he'd run through each drawer, much of a file cabinet and now his briefcase once again, its contents spilled out onto his desk—a nurse came in to see why he hadn't joined the rest of the team downstairs.

Frantic. Unprepared. Foolish. That was the way he'd felt, his office in upheaval as he stared at the nurse a moment before he brusquely sent her back with affirmation that he'd be right there. And now he...no, he couldn't think any more about Janice's bratty friend. How? Who would've taped the letter, that damned letter, onto Janice's door? He shot his daughter a look; she drew back, uncomfortable. He looked back up and started for the stairs.

"Jeff? What are you doing?"

He ignored her and clambered up, and in two strides from the stairs he reached the door to find...nothing.

"Shit!"

"Jeff, what's the matter with you?"

He looked down at them. What, were they playing a *game* with him? If they, if one of them found the goddamn letter, why didn't they just...

Jeffrey knew the answer: They hadn't found it.

But he had seen it. Someone was playing a cruel trick on him. It had to be nearby.

He swung open Janice's door and peered behind it. He stepped into the room, hearing footsteps coming up behind him. He saw nothing. It was gone.

Jeffrey took a deep breath and emerged from the room, to answer that he thought he saw "something" but was surely mistaken, looking as calm as he could.

Under the circumstances.

* * *

"Where did you go?" Mickey asked his friend. The two had been exploring the school, Natalie impressing him with her ability to turn lights on and off, when she said, "Be right back" and, so to speak, vanished. She'd been gone for ten minutes and Mickey, despite his incorporeal state, had begun to grow afraid of the remaining shadows in the hallway. He was just about to head home when she returned.

"Sorry," Natalie replied without remorse. "I just...thought your father might be home and wanted to hear what they were saying."

"That's not polite," the boy said automatically. "It's called...it's called 'ears-dropping.'"

"*Eavesdropping,*" she corrected him. "They talk about you sometimes when you're asleep, or like now, when they think you're asleep."

Mickey shrugged and floated through a row of lockers before swinging around. "Saying what?" he eventually asked.

Natalie clicked open a padlock, swung open a locker and dumped out a small plastic bag of marijuana to the locker floor and the waxed hallway. Girls learned to materialize bits of fingers faster than boys, she'd been able to explain the first time he'd asked. And besides, she was older. "Oh..." she replied casually, "it's not nice to gossip."

"Come oooooon."

"No," she said. "People say nice things, and sometimes they say not-so-nice things. You oughta listen yourself if you want to—"

"Tell me. Please."

Natalie rolled her eyes and, for a few seconds, turned her back on him. "It was Janice. She...she..."

"What? *What?*"

"She asked why you still have to live there."

Mickey's jaw dropped. "No. N-no, n-no no no noooo!" He stepped backwards, almost through the wall, and grew into a rage that got worse with the realization that he could hit nothing with his clenched fists. Instead he whirled around and around in the doorway of the cafeteria, passed through the double-glass doors, out of the building across the hall, down from the ceiling above. Eventually he lay facedown on the floor, motionless until the moment he came up on his knees and, as if anticipating a blow to his midsection, asked, "W-what did someone say back?"

"Well, your mother...gave her a hug, and your father said something..."

"WHAT DID HE SAY!"

Natalie put up her hands in defense. "I'm sorry, Mickey. I didn't want to tell you, but...he said something like...'We all have to live with our mistakes.'"

* * *

She was losing her husband.

It wasn't merely the impatient *"What?"* that formed his reply when, the moment after they'd shut the bedroom lights, Maureen remembered she hadn't told him about the crow. He couldn't have known she had never before been so frightened in her own home. And in the flurry of what had happened to Regina—whatever that was—it had slipped her mind until then.

Now, Maureen was replaying the scene in her mind, the image of that black bird flitting about the room. Despite Jeffrey's talent for observation, which clearly grew excruciating at times, he hadn't noticed that every piece of furniture in the room had been moved away from its place, then moved back. She'd changed the sheets on the bed, too, in her post-lunch quest to find and remove each and every black feather. She had come very close to throwing out the comforter.

No, what ached at her was both the irrational and the rational. It was her husband's increasing coldness toward her, toward Janice—and, yes, even toward Mickey, who needed the encouragement of his adoptive father perhaps more than anyone else's. She saw it in the interrogative manner he'd taken on when they told him about Regina. And, in general, she saw it whenever she spoke to him, made a little joke or merely tried to snuggle up close on a cold night—and in this house, there were enough of those.

She was losing him.

To another woman? She doubted it.

To his job? A distinct possibility. Dr. Stratton could, without a doubt, get obsessive about his work.

A black bird in the house meant death. Maureen didn't need to know the source of what Jeffrey would dispel as an old wives' tale. She knew it in her heart in a way a woman could never explain to a man.

The death of...

She shook her head, in the darkness, despite the sense it made.

The death of a marriage.

Sitting up in bed, Maureen felt chilled at the thought. But it wasn't in her head—the room had grown chilly in spots. At her feet; she drew in her knees and clasped her arms defensively around her legs. By her right side; she shivered, and it was gone.

In her desolation, she suddenly wished she were with her children. She wanted to hold them both close to her heart or, at the very least, to see them sleeping. To know they were safely tucked in. And then, with her thought came another feeling.

Mickey was in the room.

She knew, of course, that the very idea was preposterous. It must be that she was lonely, wanted her children, and had spent the past half-hour beside a man who, day by day, was becoming more and more the stranger. That sort of thing, after all, happened often.

But Maureen felt lonely for her children. She was familiar with the emotional, even psychic, bond a mother could share with her children. She had no doubt but that Janice, her true flesh and blood, was right in bed where she was supposed to be. It wasn't just because she missed her son that she could feel *his* presence so strongly. It was...

She got out of bed and felt the itchy fibers of a woven mat beneath her toes. For a moment she began reaching for her robe; she changed her mind. It was uneasiness, not cold, that made her think of covering the cotton nightgown she wore. This *was* her son, wasn't it? He was here...somewhere in this very room.

Maureen shook her head. No! Her son was in his own room, fast asleep in the same position as she'd left him. She should get back into bed now and...forget whatever it was she felt. Whatever it was she felt, it was ridiculous. She would just check the kids and—

A slight sound behind her made her turn around. The faint light of the moon slipped between the slats of the venetian blinds, and what fell on the exposed sheet of her side of the bed showed...

The indentation, as of two feet, being made, slowly, repeatedly as if...

It couldn't be.

...someone was jumping on the bed.

In slow motion, as if gravity were no consideration.

It wasn't her imagination. The bed vibrated slightly with each iteration. Maureen stared, her mouth hung open, as she watched a disheveled lock on the side of her husband's head jiggle with every slow, agonizingly slow rise and descent of...what?

She backed away, too scared to do anything but watch the repetitive depression on a single part of the sheet. More than ever she felt the presence of her son. And of...something else. Once her husband stirred, Maureen seized the chance and lunged at the bed.

To feel nothing. A faint trace of intense cold on the mattress— gone in an instant. Then nothing.

Jeffrey had awakened and, in the darkness, stared at her without speaking.

"H-hi," she whispered without expecting an answer.

"Trouble sleeping?" he asked.

Maureen lay back down and, wrapping an arm around him, was elated when he returned the hug. "Not anymore," she said, wiping away a tear. "Not anymore."

But hours after her husband rolled back to sleep and she was left with the cold, cold question of what she had in fact witnessed, Maureen admitted she would get little sleep after all. She had gotten up, some time ago, to check first on Janice and then on Mickey. As she had gone past her own doorway, she had tripped over a pair of slippers.

Not hers. Not her husband's.

They were Mickey's.

30

"Mom, I'm leaving now, okay? I made my breakfast and cleaned up, too." She was already in her hooded jacket, with her shoes on.

Struggling to open her eyelids, Maureen wasn't sure she had dreamed the words. "Janice? But it's—"

"I know the school bus doesn't come till seven-thirty. I just...feel like walking today."

Her mother sat up in bed and rubbed her eyelids—two, three hours of sleep, maybe. From the corner of her eye she could see Jeffrey, already shaven and showered, tying a careful knot in his tie. "Um...all right. Have a nice day, Sweetheart." In an instant, she ran through her head any reasons her eleven-year-old daughter should not be walking to school alone. But she'd been outside that time of day; Janice would be one of many people out at that time, walking their dogs if not heading to school or work.

"Okay, bye. Bye, Daddy!" She took off down the stairs; a moment later, the heavy oak door slammed, followed by the gentle sweep and click of the storm door.

Without taking his eyes off the tie clip he was fastening, Jeffrey asked, "Does the school bus driver molest little girls?"

Maureen began making the bed. "I'm sure she doesn't," she said, then stopped straightening the sheet. "Jeff, did you find Janice's answer strange last night? I mean, about sitting in the cafeteria. She doesn't usually sit with Regina, she doesn't sit with anyone in her biology class. I wonder: Is she sitting with anyone?"

Jeffrey shrugged. "Well, it *is* a new neighborhood for her, Maureen. She'll make more friends, or better friends, when she's ready. And besides," he added, tying his shoes, "there's nothing wrong with eating lunch alone sometimes."

"Easy for you to say," Maureen retorted. "You ate your lunch alone in the gym bleachers, buried in your science books." She pulled the bedspread up over the pillows and ran her open hand over the wrinkles.

"Well, I couldn't eat in the library," she heard her husband defend himself behind her as she left the room to see Mickey.

The boy's eyes were closed, which was unusual since Mickey usually woke up while his parents shuffled about in the next room. "Oh, Miiiickeeey," she sang and touched his cheek.

No response.

"Mickey, Honey." She shook his shoulder, lifted his head in her hands. "Mickey? Mickey!" She darted from the room. "Jeff! Mickey won't wake up. Oh my God, Jeff, where are you? Jeeeeeff!"

She barely heard the coffee carafe hit the counter below. Her husband ran up the stairs and flew past her.

"Mickey," he said. "Mickey, can you hear me?" He waited a few seconds, gripping the boy's wrist. "Pulse is normal." He forced open Mickey's lips and leaned close. "He's breathing—normal breathing, I can't..." He opened one of his son's eyes, then the other, and ignored Maureen's questions as he ran for the leather case he kept in the bedroom. Out came the stethoscope, otoscope, even his sphygmomanometer, the blood-pressure cuff. Barely a minute later, he tore off the cuff and sighed. "Get his coat."

"I have it right here. Sweater, too. Jeff, what is it? You're not telling me, I have a right to know. I'm his—"

Her husband cut her off with a shake of his head. "I'm not telling anything because there isn't anything to tell." He sat the boy up and pulled the sweater over his flannel pajama shirt with the fire engine on it. "Let's get him a change of clothes, too," he said. Then, "As far as I can see, everything's normal."

Maureen gulped. "Could it be a...a coma?"

"I don't think so. There's a lot of slowdown of body functions in a coma—breathing, BP, pulse—they'd do as little as they needed to in order to keep the system going."

Maureen wanted to swing at him. He's a boy, not a *system!* She knew, however, that it was her anger, her sense of utter helplessness, that would be talking for her. And from within came the reminder of how fortunate she was that Jeffrey had been home that morning.

Her husband had gotten the boy's coat on and was now trying to stuff a foot into a sneaker—no easy task in general due to the paralysis. Maureen clicked back into gear and finished the other foot. Then she threw on some clothes of her own, quickly brushed her hair and grabbed their keys and coats.

The ride to Hollister Medical Center was brief, with Maureen clutching Mickey in the back seat and Jeffrey on the phone. Once there, they met with a swift reception. Two of Jeffrey's former coworkers immediately began to look over Mickey, while Jeffrey reshuffled his schedule of meetings and surgery with a few calls from the ER desk.

Hollister's emergency room was top-notch, Jeffrey had told Maureen. Then why, she asked herself again and again as she sat alone in the waiting room, did her husband have to remain behind with the other doctors? Ten minutes grew to twenty. By forty-five minutes she was pacing and trying to keep her gaze away from the wall clock.

Maureen pulled out her phone but got no reception...too close to the MRI suite. She reached for a magazine but couldn't read it—yet more revelations about a millionaire celebrity suspected of child trafficking. She found another and, absently flipping pages, looked up after a few minutes to see her husband closing the door marked "AUTHORIZED PERSONNEL ONLY." A second doctor accompanied him.

"Jeff!" She sprang from the seat and met the pair halfway. "What's going on? How *is* he?"

Her husband held up his hands and said, "There's no difference from what we saw before, Maureen. It's no coma, and his vital signs are nothing out of the ordinary for what we'd expect to see."

She turned away and began to grate her fists against one another. "Then what...?"

"Uh, Mrs. Stratton, I'm Harold Joy. I'm a psychiatrist, and your husband asked me to look at Michael."

He extended his hand; Maureen studied his intense gaze, but his faint trace of a smile warmed her, at least for the moment. Hesitantly, she nodded and shook his hand.

"Let's find a room where we can talk, hmmmm?"

She followed the two of them a short way down the hall to a

small room with only a few chairs and a coffee table.

"Mrs. Stratton, I've spent a little time with your boy and have conferred with both Dr. Stratton and the two residents who saw Michael in the ER. But I need to ask you a few questions before I can start to feel comfortable with my diagnosis. Let me start, if I may, by asking you how you, as his mother, feel Michael is adjusting to his paralysis. Of course, at his age—at any age—he could handle it acceptingly or...well, handle it poorly. And I know you've been planning to get the boy some counseling, but decided to wait till the boy was in a routine with his rehab. Does...does he seem happy? Is he optimistic about his therapy?"

"Happy? But what does this have to do—"

"Please."

Maureen shrugged. "I don't know. Sometimes he's happy, sometimes...he knows what he's missing out on, I guess, and...yeah, I guess he's had more than his share of off days about the therapy."

"He has a sister, Jeff has told me."

"Yes, Janice."

"Is she generally supportive?"

"She tries her best."

"Any odd behavior in your son over the past week or so?"

Maureen paused to think. "Only..." She watched Joy's eyebrows rise with her words and knew she'd have to complete her sentence. "A couple of times in...that period, he seemed to..."

"Yes?"

"I don't know what you'd call it. Tuning out? Like, he seems awake but just...somewhere else. The first time I saw it, I...thought he was asleep and said his name again, louder. But he wasn't quite asleep. His eyes opened right away—not like he was asleep at all— and he started talking to me. Kind of like he was reading, the way you read or...listen to music. Your attention is elsewhere and you realize you're being talked to and snap back? I don't know..."

Maureen watched as Joy met glances with her husband, who shrugged.

"What?" she said. "You know what this is? Is this the same—my God! This is the same thing, isn't it? I can't belie—I'm so stupid not to see it. Only..." She looked up questioningly at Joy. "...he's not coming out." She picked up her handkerchief again.

Joy sighed. "Mrs. Stratton, what I believe may be happening here is a phenomenon that is not entirely accepted by the medical community. In cases where children meet with extreme trauma of any sort, some are better able than others at dealing with the intense feelings of frustration, isolation, that are bound to come up. Now, I'm still not ruling out more common, medical explanations, but if your son has been keeping all that inside, then what can arise is something we call *dissociation*. It's a fancy word for just what you said: tuning out, so to speak."

Maureen swallowed. "But where *is* he when he's...not here?" A chill ran up her spine as she thought of the previous night.

The doctor hesitated before answering. "We don't really know. In the cases I've studied, the patient is awake but nonresponsive. In extreme cases, we see behavior exhibited that doesn't seem to match that of the patient." His lips tightened in dissatisfaction at his own answer.

"What he's saying, Maureen, is that if we don't work on this, the next step may be multiple personalities," said Jeffrey.

This was too much. "*Multiple* personalities? What are you, nuts? Sorry, but...at this moment, my son has got *no* personality, all right? You're...you're saying all this stuff and...Dr. Joy, you haven't even *talked* to Mickey."

"Mrs. Stratton, we're still running our tests," said Joy, keeping his voice low to hide his annoyance at Jeffrey's interruption. Apparently he'd heard right that the man could be a coldhearted prick. "And you're absolutely right: I haven't yet had the opportunity to speak with Michael.

"But as far as our tests show, Mrs. Stratton, your boy is wide awake."

She had one more thing to say. "The cases you've heard about— not treated, right? The ones you've *heard* about...you said the patient is awake, and I assume you mean eyes open, sitting somewhere, say. Awake in the normal sense but just not responsive."

Joy nodded. "Yes. But—"

"In my son's particular case, can you honestly say you know what you're talking about?"

* * *

Jeffrey was a vascular surgeon, not a psychiatrist. And if further tests showed the boy needed some other form of specialized treatment, well, he'd ensure they found the best specialist they could get.

With that resolved, he drove home, "to do a few things," having promised a disappointed Maureen that he'd remain reachable until he returned. He shook his head, in the car, when he realized he'd forgotten his cellphone charger—and the phone battery was low. "Should've gotten it," he muttered as he braked for a red light coming off the highway's exit ramp. But there was always the house phone.

When he passed near the school, he felt glad once again that he and Maureen had decided not to pull Janice out of class over Mickey. Between her biology test and the simple fact that she could do nothing to help, it made more sense to let her know later.

School, Jeffrey thought with a sigh.

Those certainly were the days.

* * *

Thank God, Janice was thinking, she hadn't noticed before the biology test. She felt sure she'd aced it, but somehow the victory quickly withered to irrelevance when she noticed the looks she was getting in the hall.

Regina. She *had* told. She'd said something to somebody, and—whatever else kids were thinking that made them stare and whisper even before today—now her family served poisoned cookies, too. No, Janice realized, she probably left out the part about getting sick. But she'd said something that had quickly spread throughout the classrooms.

There was talk about something else, too. Oh, how the halls were hopping with news today; apparently some boy with some drugs in his locker had been taken away to see the principal and probably the police. Do you go to jail at eleven years old? Put me there, too, she thought, so I can get away from this crowd.

What little she could hear of conversation that stopped at her approach, nobody was talking about the young pusher. It was all about her. Things about the house: "that place," she'd heard someone call it. Once, even, she'd inched close to a group of fourth-graders—they hadn't yet learned to form a circle from which they could see the subject of their conversation approach—and had heard the word "haunted" before they spotted her.

Haunted?

The thought unsettled her. It had been school alone that had helped her leave behind, even suppress, the memories of those first few weeks her family spent in the house. The bone-chill that seemed to...follow her from room to room. Even into Mickey's room, although...God, she'd almost forgotten about that. But it was such a short time ago.

And then there was the dollhouse. The figures, the furniture that no one had ever admitted buying for her. She'd been through this already: It wasn't like her mother. Her father would say he did it right away, had he done it at all, so she could thank him, and Mrs. Sanders was too new. Besides, it would look weird, the hired help or whatever she was, buying her things. Strangest thing about it, all the weird stuff ended, at least for a while, once her parents put the dollhouse in the basement.

Haunted.

It was a coincidence. She could go down to the basement today, ask her mom to help her carry the house back upstairs—though her textbooks now cluttered the top of the hope chest—and notice nothing different except that she'd have back what was *hers*, right? She'd do that. She'd do it that very afternoon.

It occurred to her that she had not gone down into the basement in nearly a month.

She realized as well that the hallway was practically empty. Well, why was *she* standing around during lunchtime?

Janice went to her locker, tossed in her backpack and snapped shut the combination lock. She gave it a few extra turns by habit and went to the cafeteria. The food today was Salisbury steak, regarding which she nodded absently to the food-service people. She nodded at everything she heard, and when the last person handed her the plate, she took it without even looking at what she'd asked for. The whispering. It was a buzzing that was becoming a roar. The whole cafeteria seemed to sizzle over it, and her worst fears were confirmed when, having paid for her meal, she swung out into the eating area.

The entire roomful of students stopped talking at once.

She dropped the tray to the floor and ran out. Stopping only at her locker for her coat and books, Janice sobbed as she ran past the security guard, ignoring his protests and swinging the iron gate closed with a dull clang.

It wasn't fair. She didn't do anything wrong, and everybody was talking about her. All she was, was unlucky enough to be in this town, go to this school, live in this house, have—

Someone was walking closely behind her. Closely behind. Janice glanced over her shoulder to see a girl, one of the fifth-graders, trying to catch up.

"Wait up," the girl said.

Janice was a sixth-grader; fifth-graders were scum. Nevertheless, she slowed her step to let the chubby girl with the tousled hair come astride. "Well, what do *you* want?"

"You...have a problem at home," said the girl, gasping for breath. "And everyone at school thinks they know what it is."

"Yeah, right," she snapped. "Everybody knows what my problem is. Why don't you just leave me alone, all right?"

"Janice, my name is Cynthia Bellows, and I'm one of only two kids in school who know, *really* know, what the problem is."

There was a certainty in the girl's voice, a strange kind of sincerity and not a little maturity, that stopped Janice in her tracks and made her look closely into Cynthia's eyes.

She remembered something she'd heard the first week of the school year. "You...you and your friend, Lana. You're the ones they call the weirdos of the school."

The girl snickered in reply. "Correction," she said. "I'm the weirdo, she's the psycho. But from what I heard today and what else I've heard, to the class there's only one crazy now. It's you."

"But I'm not—"

"Me neither, but if nobody tells you what the school already knows, and more...they just might be right someday." Cynthia grabbed Janice's arm to pull her through one of many backyard shortcuts. "My house—it should be quiet for the next hour or so."

"I—I have to call my mother to—"

"No! Um...I mean, please don't call. If a certain person knows I'm involved..."

"Who? If you're playing a trick on my family or something—"

"Janice, this is a *house* thing, okay? It's not...not a...a *Stratton* thing. I'm trying to help you. And if you even say my name over the phone to your mother, well..."

"Well, what?"

Cynthia shivered and turned sideways to pass through an opening in a neighbor's hedges. "Let's just say you might not see me at school anymore."

* * *

286

The white-haired nurse took one more sip of her cooled machine coffee and noticed the clock. Michael Stratton's mother had finally gone downstairs for a bite, and now that the phones had died down for a few minutes, she decided it was time she checked on the boy herself.

A few steps from the station she paused, convinced the phone was going to ring. It did not. Had the patients' relatives and friends all gone to lunch? she thought. The ones, at least, who were not already here, visiting their children in the pediatric ward. On her way down the long hallway she thought of her little charges, then of the poor Stratton boy. All those problems, and now this.

Whatever it was.

It was that normalcy of his vital signs that in fact had prompted her to suggest she and her nurses check on Mickey no less often than every half hour. A few of them, of course, had initially chuckled about doctors' kids getting preferential treatment. But that was before they learned more about the boy than that he needed to be frequently looked in on. Every time any of them checked, the bedside instruments indicated nothing out of the ordinary. She expected the same this time.

The woman was a slow walker these days. Atypically mindful of the rest patients needed under the hospital's care, she slowly swung open the door, ready to speak to the boy until she stopped, speechless, at the sight of a young girl sitting beside Mickey...who was awake! The girl froze and stared unwelcomingly at the head nurse.

"Mickey! Your mother will be right back, and you cannot know how happy she will be to see you awake." She turned her head toward the girl. The light in the room was strange, the woman thought, and her eyes were playing tricks on her. The girl, this...smirking girl was crouched before the room's cartoon-character curtains, and the nurse could swear she could see right through... "Little girl, I'm sorry, but you are not allowed in this room."

This was wrong, the woman thought. She knew every child on the floor. And the way this child was *looking* at her! Of all the things—"Where is your mother? Come with me." The nurse extended her hand.

The girl smiled again, a taunting smile that reflected no fear whatsoever, no respect for the woman's authority in the ward she had run for twenty years. She opened her mouth as if to speak—no, to laugh, a tittering laugh that sent the old woman's heart dangerously racing. And then she was gone. The curtains fluttered as a cold breeze wafted momentarily through the room.

Shaking her head, the nurse stepped to the spot, even went to her knees to peer under the bed. "Uh...uh...I..."

Uncontrollably, Mickey began to giggle.

31

Yes, his adopted son lay motionless in the pediatric ward. Yes, he should have been checking on Mickey's tests—he'd used his influence to rush their processing, after all. And yes, barring that, he at least had volumes of paperwork he could have tackled while still remaining within the hospital building.

Instead, Jeffrey Stratton had gone home to find the letter.

There was nothing to be alarmed about, he told himself. Just the night before, he had thought, he had been close enough to the letter that he could read the logo of his lawyer's firm. Of course, he had since decided, the document simply could not have appeared on his daughter's door, then disappeared before he could climb the stairs. Any of the senses could be fooled, particularly after a long, exasperating day.

One fact, however, remained apparent: Since the letter was not at his office or in his briefcase, it had to be at home.

Yes, he would be sticking by the phone. While he did so, he would search the place from top to bottom.

One lousy letter. He had written to his lawyer shortly after Mickey had become paralyzed. Just looking out for his family, he had explained away his reasons to himself.

And the reply, which he had nearly memorized, came addressed to his office at the hospital at the time Jeffrey was working longer hours, prior to his promotion. Beneath the letterhead and the date, it had read:

Dr. Stratton:

First, let me apologize for not passing along this information by phone. Apparently, you have not had the time to return my calls.

I have reviewed your inquiry about revoking the adoption of your son, Michael, and reviewed the photocopied documentation you forwarded to this office. Based on this information, and pending your approval to my contacting the Dept. of Social Services' Office of Adoption and Foster Care, it is my belief that such a process could not, using your own word, be transacted 'cleanly.'

The agency, to its defense, would be sure to claim it has no legal recourse against falsification of records when said falsification was not carried out, or known about in advance, by a representative of the Department of Social Services.

Above all, I urge you to reconsider the effect of these proceedings upon the child in question. As your attorney, I await your instructions on how next to proceed. But as a father of three, I hope you will think long and hard about what you are considering, and confer with your spouse before taking another step.

Sincerely,

Malcolm E. Coleridge, JD
Attorney at Law

Where to begin? He supposed the best place to be his daughter's room, however certain he felt that she had not taken the letter from his file cabinet. After all, that was where he thought he'd last seen it.

But no, he thought. Jeffrey repeated in his mind the decision he had made about that room. Being that the letter was not there when he'd ascended the stairs, it could not have been there moments earlier. Therefore, that room was *not* the best place to begin a search that, at any time, could be cut short by a ringing phone. Where he had last *held* the letter was in his own room.

He was getting anxious again, and it bothered him. Let's lighten things up, he thought, and turned on the oldies radio station on the stereo. In the kitchen he began to set up the coffeemaker, then shut it off and poured himself a shot of scotch. He took a sip, felt the warmth course through his body, and went upstairs to his bedroom.

The window was open. Shaking his head, he reached up, opened the blinds and closed the window. He fastened the lock snugly into place. Now for one last look in the file drawer; this time he would look inside each hanging folder, beneath them all and even under the drawers themselves. Jeffrey set down his drink on a memo pad and knelt before the cabinet.

He had already gone through half the top drawer when it occurred to him that the room had not warmed up at all. A glance over his shoulder told him why: Now, both windows were open.

Wide open.

"What the hell..." Jeffrey scanned the room. Sure, he was the only one in the room. The window handles, from layers of paint slapped on over several years, were difficult to lock and unlock even from within. So if someone were somehow outside the house—in the yard, on a ladder or even on the roof—he or she would have no leverage whatsoever. The breath went out of him at his next realization.

The locked windows, of course, could only be opened from the inside alone.

He stepped to the first window, started to close it but then raised it back up. He bent over to peer out into the crisp March air; he craned his neck to look up.

Nothing. Again, he closed and locked one, then the other. He lowered the blinds but adjusted the slats to let in more light.

Jeffrey backed away from the window and relaxed his legs to perch on the edge of the bed. This wasn't happening, he thought. It was not possible. He looked toward the file cabinet and noticed the shot glass, one sip left, sitting atop. Bad liquor? You never knew, he thought. He stood up to get the glass; he would pour it out. Lifting it to his nose, however, he sniffed the drink and detected nothing wrong. He set it back down. He turned toward the closed windows and froze.

Outside, pressed against the left window, was the attorney's letter—in plain view—through the venetian blinds. The page was worn though perfectly readable, and a corner of the sheet fluttered unsettlingly in the breeze. Something...

This couldn't be happening.

...was holding it there.

He reached behind him and put down the glass—on the edge, where it tipped over to splash its remaining contents into the open file drawer. This time, he could see it without a doubt. This time, he'd get it.

Jeffrey lunged. The blinds impeded his thrust. He cursed, passed his hand through the slats and fumbled madly for the cord. He found it and hauled up the blinds...to see nothing.

Nothing.

What...in God's name was happening? he caught himself thinking, and wondered why he would think of such a being at a time like this.

He heard giggling, a child's giggle, yet unlike any laughter he had heard before. It came from...behind, outside, all around him. Again, he saw nothing when he thrust his head out in the chill.

Jeffrey began to pace the small open area of the bedroom. No, he thought. He had to leave this room. Get out. Yes, he'd seen the letter here. If he looked elsewhere, there was no reason why it would be...he left the room. To go...where?

He ended up back in the kitchen, pulled up a chair and, before he sat down, filled another jigger and emptied it in a second. This wasn't right, he realized. Home...home was supposed to be the safe place, the familiar. And suddenly, with nothing seeming out of place, the house seemed of another world. A hostile one where...the rules he knew and clung to were of no use. On the door. At the window. Windows opening by themselves. Blinds dropping. Laughter—he knew he'd heard it. How was this possible?

Get a grip, he told himself. He wasn't chief of surgery at forty-two for nothing; he had a brilliant, analytical mind, and it was time he put it to work. He first had to concentrate on what was normal. Yes. It was still his home. He would deal with all of this in a logical way, and eventually the seemingly illogical would make sense, too. Relax, he told himself. Turn on some music.

With a start, he realized he *had* turned on some music. Minutes ago. He let go of the empty glass he'd been fondling and went to the stereo. It was indeed off. He pressed the Power button.

The barrage of hard rock at full blast sent Jeffrey reeling and made him yelp in pain. With the flat of his hand he smacked off the power and, getting up onto his knees, turned the volume controls back down from their highest setting. He turned the unit on again and, shaking his head, changed the station to where he had left it. There...that was better.

Jeffrey reached up to his face and found something unfamiliar. His eyes had been tearing. No, it was more. He had been outright crying.

He knelt there a minute, letting the words of "Unchained Melody" slowly lift him from this maddening reverie, one that yielded no answers. More tears came and stoically he wiped them, gently so as to leave less embarrassing redness around his eyes.

Embarrassing.

Who was around?

And why hadn't Maureen called, if only to tell him there was no change?

He went back to the kitchen and, without thinking, drank down the glass. He was having too much, he thought. It wasn't like him. He picked up the glass to rinse it and realized the madness was not over: The glass he had just emptied, he had not filled.

"No!" He broke the glass on the Corian counter and decided to get out now. To the hospital—he should never have left. He'd been home for...how long? He looked up at the clock.

Jeffrey had left the hospital at eleven a.m.

The clock read ten o'clock.

Great, he thought, now the clock was broken. Jeffrey looked at his watch, remembered he'd removed it in the bedroom. The living room: a mantel clock sat above their fireplace.

Eight-thirty.

"Shit!" He charged up the stairs. In the bedroom the clock radio read nine-thirty. His Rolex watch was gone from the nightstand.

"Stoooop iiiiit!" he shouted.

He would reset the clocks, he decided, panting as he left the room. His face going blanker with every step, he slowly descended the stairs and guided himself to the kitchen. He would find his cellphone and fix them all, he repeated to himself. Starting with the kitchen.

Jeffrey ran an arm across his brow; he was drenched in sweat. On the counter stood his bottle of Dewar's. Beside it was a tall glass.

A full glass.

He closed his eyes, gritted his teeth and reached for the cellphone, where he'd left it charging.

It was unplugged, its battery dead. He could not see the charger.

Seconds passed before he understood the grim implications. The phone wasn't charged at all.

He reached for the landline phone's receiver and held it to his ear—no dial tone.

Maureen could well have been trying to call both lines and—

No. There *was* an explanation: The extension upstairs was off the hook. After a period of loud beeping, it went dead; that was all. He rushed up the stairs to return that phone's handset to its cradle.

The handset was in its place.

Wearily, he returned to the kitchen, his head hung low. Without looking, he reached up to the wall phone; it was off the hook. Jeffrey fell against the wall and began to pant.

Beside the kitchen doorway, the single door to the metal pantry began to swing gently open. A soft creak accompanied its arc to a nearly open position, and the door vibrated on its return toward the magnet that typically held it fast. The process repeated, again and again, its slow and deliberate path. Each singsong creak was a scalpel's slash to his cold, unyielding logic.

Tasting blood—he'd bitten his lip—he trembled in horror, dared himself to break somehow free. He wanted to rush at the door—hold it closed. He wanted to...to flee the house, to careen out the driveway. To the hospital, to other people. To his family.

Instead he began to scream.

Again. And again.

* * *

Janice heard the sound before she turned the key. It was...it sounded like her father, but...

The call had come from the kitchen, and the girl rushed past the closed pantry to see him crouched against the far corner. Her father was sobbing and, with his head buried between his shaking knees, seemed oblivious to her entrance. "Daddy!" Gingerly, she stepped around the fragments of broken glass.

A long second passed before he lifted his head. Janice drew back at the sight of his reddened, crazed eyes, which stared into her own, at first without recognition. When he spoke, she smelled liquor and frowned. Why did he go and do a thing like this?

"Is...is it really you, Jan?" He was squinting at her, and Janice wondered what else went on each day when she didn't cut out early.

"Yeah, Daddy, sure it is. Daddy..." She pushed back a lock of his blond hair. "...are you drunk?"

He shook his head with a decisiveness that reassured her. "Please...help me up. Please..." She took an arm, and he grabbed hold of the windowsill. At the sink he splashed some cold water onto his face; she handed him a dishcloth to dry himself and went for the broom.

Seeing the bottle and the full glass of scotch on the breakfast table, Janice could not help but broach the subject again. "Daddy, are you lying to me?" Something else was wrong, she could tell. No one else was home. Her father walked to the pantry, opened the door wide and snapped it shut. He sighed and, motioning her to a chair, sat down himself. The bottle stood within easy reach; the amber liquid in the glass shimmered in the afternoon light of the kitchen window. "Janice, I-I am not drunk. Yes, I had a drink. Two or three, even, to...help me deal with something very, very strange...and wrong...with this house."

His eyes widened in astonishment when his daughter merely nodded. "We have a ghost, Daddy. A girl who died here but...didn't leave, I don't know...don't know why. Her name was—is—Natalie Leffingwell."

Now the look he gave was one of disbelief, though the downcast look that followed told her he knew, in his heart, it was true. "How...how could you know a thing like that? Are you making—"

"Daddy, I don't know what happened to you, but I think you better believe me. I can't say how I learned it. It's true. And," she added, taking a breath, "I think Mickey is in danger."

"Mickey? But why...?"

"Daddy, why isn't he here? And where's Mommy? And Mrs. Sanders?"

Jeffrey swallowed. "M-Mickey is in the hospital, Janice. He was still getting examined when I...when I stopped in here, but it seemed that, physically, nothing's wrong. What—"

"Then why is he there?" She rose to her feet. "I have to go see him."

Nodding, Jeffrey rose also, though he walked as if it hurt to do so. "Yeah, let's go," he said without conviction. "Um...Mickey wouldn't wake up this morning. As I said, nothing seemed wrong physically. It was like his mind was elsewhere."

Janice didn't get a chance to answer, for the door opened and Maureen entered. "Mom! How's Mickey?"

She glared at her husband and sat on the couch with her coat on. "Mickey," she said between breaths, "is fine. Whatever it was, he's better."

"Oh, Mom, that's great!"

"Real good news," Jeffrey said.

Now it was time for him. "I tried to call you. The least you could do was call in *once*—I ended up taking an *Uber!*" She got up from the chair and hung up her coat. "Did you leave the phone off the hook?" she said and headed for the stairs.

Jeffrey was not surprised, yet he could barely stammer out a defense. "Maureen, I...I..."

From upstairs the two below could hear a phone receiver crash down to its cradle. "You son of a bitch!" she yelled. "It *was* off the hook!"

Janice ran upstairs to talk to her. "Mom, it's not his fault," she said. "Mom...Mom..." Her mother stormed past her to the railing. "Mom, you have to listen to m—"

"In your room. *Now.*"

"But Mom—"

"Now!"

She turned and obeyed, but before she closed the door she peered out once again to catch her mother halfway down the stairs. "Momma, the house is haunted and Daddy didn't do anything wrong. It's Mickey she wants, Momma. It's Mickey. She won't stop until she gets him." The door slammed shut.

Instead of resuming her yelling, Maureen sat at the other end of the couch from her husband. She fought back the tears she knew were meant to come after her hours-long, lonely vigil. Instead, she spoke: "So talk."

With no small difficulty, Jeffrey detailed everything that had happened to him in his stop at home "for some files"—except, of course, for the particular search that was underway at the time. In themselves, after all, most of the inexplicable events could easily have happened regardless of his reason for coming home in the first place. So he did not feel he was lying.

Maureen nodded through this, then commented, "The bedroom and your breath smell like a distillery. How does that fit into the picture?"

"I got anxious and poured myself a drink," he replied. "At one point I ran at the window and dropped the drink off the top of the cabinet." Jeffrey sighed. "Just try...going through what I did without pouring another. Oh...and after I went to the stereo, I went back to the kitchen. This...thing...whatever it is, had filled the glass."

"Janice seems convinced *it* is a *she*," Maureen said. "Where did she get that?"

He shook his head. "She came home with it, heard it from somebody, I guess. Hey...what time do you have?"

"Umm...almost two-fifteen," she said. "Why don't you just look at the...oh." Maureen turned back to him. "What happened to the mantel clock?"

"The same thing that happened to all the other clocks, whatever that was." He shook his head. "And my watch and cell charger are missing altogether. My cell is dead."

"Janice!" Maureen called. "Come down here, please."

"She had nothing to do with it."

Upstairs the door opened, and Janice stone-facedly came out. Halfway down the stairs, she gritted her teeth when her slippered foot came down with a delicate crunch. She lifted her foot and gaped at the silver glint of the missing Rolex.

Jeffrey and Maureen, frowning, met each other's gaze. "Another mystery solved," he said with a grimace. "C'mon, let's head back to the hospital." On his way to get his coat, he tripped over the hassock and stopped short of hitting the bay window. "You drive," he said.

* * *

Mickey lay in bed, facing up at the TV talk show but not watching. When the boy had returned to consciousness an hour before, the nurse had put on some cartoons, but those had ended. Now all he could do was wait till she returned for another channel check.

Under ordinary circumstances.

Mickey, in fact, had again gone ghosting and was watching TV in an adjoining room. Restless, he stayed there only a few minutes before he went wandering throughout the hospital. He passed through the geriatric ward, past an elderly man moaning for a nurse;

through radiology—he quickly withdrew from the odd pull of the magnetic field surrounding a huge can with a person inside. He passed through one of the operating rooms and posed invisibly for the team of med students viewing a procedure from the big windows above. Gross, he thought, and left the room. He lay on the red tile floor of the cafeteria's kitchen and stared closely at a mop as it swished back and forth through the form of his head. And, finally, he passed from the facility to its parking lot by way of the loading dock and listened to the workers' banter.

It took some time before he faced up to what really bothered him: a loneliness that even his friend Natalie could do nothing to alleviate. Maybe it was just the way she seemed to come and go— Natalie had left, for instance, just after she'd scared the daylights out of that old lady nurse. Or else, maybe it was that she had been the one to tell him those bad things about his family. It was enough...it was enough sometimes to make him want to be *all* by himself.

Nobody to make him feel sad...nobody to keep his spirit from soaring high, high into the sky.

* * *

No more sadness. No more loneliness.

Natalie hummed softly to herself as she maneuvered figures in the dollhouse. The tiny, wooden family lived amicably together these days, a measure of the child's overall contentment with how her plans were going.

There was much she did not understand; that, she knew. She knew as well that things would get more difficult now that Janice knew about her. How had she found out? Unless...

The girl paused while pushing the baby carriage into the tiny living room. Lana or Cynthia must have told her after the day Regina came over, then went back to school and blabbed.

Natalie sighed. Sure, she had made mistakes. But there was plenty she had on her side. First, there were her powers, which had keenly evolved over the years since she first became trapped in the spirit world. Powers for making herself seen and heard by the living. Materialization developed to fullness—as full as her ethereal form could allow—for longer and longer periods. The power to suppress, through her will alone, the chilly block of stagnant air that the living felt in her presence.

This last power, matured to this point, allowed the nine-year-old to spread her death chill wherever she wanted within the house and a short distance beyond. Changing temperatures, in either direction, required power over the air; inevitably, solids came next.

What did all this mean for her plans? She wasn't following a straight line toward fulfilling her single goal. But she knew her powers, in the meantime, would win her control over the rest of the Stratton family: their moods, their alertness...their resistance.

* * *

It was only natural that Mickey receive another visitor: namely, Emily Sanders. But the woman, standing frozen just inside the doors of Hollister Medical Center, felt only unnatural about her presence. Emily's apprehension didn't surprise her at all; wasn't it only a couple of months ago, she asked herself, that the same statue—as she was calling herself—stood before the former Leffingwell home?

Having gotten the brief phone call that morning, she knew she needed to visit Mickey. His achievement of only a few days earlier had since turned to disappointment, when the boy became uninterested, even uncooperative. One step short of disrespectful. It was as if Mickey didn't care whether he progressed in his rehabilitation.

Emily shook her head and approached the front desk. Not for me to presume what thoughts whirl about in the little boy's head, she told herself. Given the one triumph, it occurred to her, perhaps he had believed the rest of the body would get the hint, shudder violently and shake off the paralysis once and for all. It didn't work that way, of course. Polio was indeed rare in the world these days, but where it did show up, it hit hard.

A nurse entered Mickey's room ahead of her, and Emily heard an "Oh!" before spotting the boy, eyes open but motionless, on the bed! The nurse spun around. "Please...you must leave the room," she said.

Emily did as ordered, being a registered nurse herself who still maintained her license. But when the woman in scrubs left for the floor's main desk, Emily couldn't help herself. She remembered more than a few occasions when Mickey was...well, not quite there at quiet moments of their time together. She shot a glance back at the nurses' station—the woman's back faced Emily—and stepped inside to the boy's side.

She sat down and took his cool hand in hers. "Mickey," she said sternly. "It's me. Come here."

In a flash, the boy's eyes livened. He swallowed and turned his head to grin at his visitor. "Hi," he said.

Aside from the fact he just hadn't *been* there a moment ago, there was something in the swiftness of his response that perplexed her. Rather than dwell on it, though, Emily thought it best this time to move along. "I brought you something," she said and produced a portable radio/CD player shaped like a catcher's mitt. The tuning knob was baseball-shaped; the antenna protruded from a dangling lace.

Mickey's expression lit up, and from deep within came a growing "Woooooowwww!" He raised his eyes. "Thanks, Mrs. Sanders."

Emily leaned over from the edge of the bed to give him a hug. "Oh, it has batteries, too. And a plug. Want to hear it?"

The boy nodded, and she found an outlet, plugged in the unit and turned it on. Slowly she moved the tuner from station to station, watching Mickey shake his head through the talk, classical and country stations plus a foreign one that seemed louder than all the others. When she hit a dance station, he said, "There!"

"So, Mickey," the woman said, settling back into the chair, "you never told me why you're here. And when you're coming back to the gym."

At this his eyes clouded, and he appeared to search for words as he listened to the frantic lyrics of the song. "I don't know. I was kind of...well, asleep. Yeah, asleep, and I didn't wake up."

"Oh," Emily replied as nonchalantly as she could. "You mean, the way you were sleeping when I came in."

"Um, yeah. Like that."

"Mmmm." From her bag she retrieved a Hershey chocolate bar and unwrapped half. "Want some?"

Mickey grinned. "I won't get into trouble?"

"I checked outside before I came in," she told him. He clamped ravenously down on the end as she held the bar in its wrapping. "A few bites never hurt anyone," she said. "So who do you visit when you sleep?" She took a single section for herself.

Mickey swallowed and gazed with longing at the part that remained in her hand. "A girl. Sometimes she visits me. She's my friend."

"That's nice. What's her name?" She broke off another section, extended it toward his eager mouth and avoided his gaze, even as she felt her heart quicken.

"Natalie."

Emily stopped chewing. But she would not stop her questions just yet. For even if this girl were merely a coincidentally named but imaginary friend, this Natalie was someone whose importance might well figure into Mickey's attitude toward recovery. "Where did you meet her?"

"At home. She's there a lot," he said matter-of-factly.

"That's very nice that you have a friend to talk to."

"We don't just *talk,*" he replied with some defensiveness.

"What do you mean?"

"We go places. I went to the zoo and looked *right* into a tiger's face. But it ran away. I rode the ferry in town, to that island. And once...once we went to the *airport*. We raced a plane that was landing! I saw in the window the pilots with their uniforms and headphones and...and..." His voice trailed off as he read the look of concern on his therapist's face. He turned away for a moment, then back. "I don't have to be in my body ever again if I don't want to, you know." He stared defiantly into her eyes.

"N-no," she said. "I guess you don't if...you believe hard enough."

Something had gone seriously wrong, Emily was telling herself. She had believed, as had Mickey's family, that while a full recovery from his paralysis could be attainable over the long term, the boy at least was positive in how he was handling the road ahead. But this...this was a complete withdrawal that had taken place virtually under her eyes.

If she could not help turn around this boy's sense of reality, he would stay paralyzed for the rest of his life.

Mickey smiled as if he could read her thoughts. "I like your cat," he said.

32

"Mickey!" Janice, ahead of her parents, ran past Emily Sanders and wrapped her arms around her brother. "How do you feel?"

"Emily," said Maureen, "I'm so happy you came by."

The therapist, for her part, had been wishing she were miles away from this hospital room. Moments before, she had backed away from this boy, this eight-year-old whose cruel expression seemed that of another person, not this shy, unassuming child she had needed to win over with her own enthusiasm. She had fallen back into the gray vinyl chair, closed her eyes in an attempt to block out Mickey's giggles.

And was she wrong? The laughter filling her ears seemed not of one but two voices. One of them a girl's.

"M-Mickey...I d-don't understand h-how you could have known anything about my cat," she said. Emily had even stood up again, as if doing so would restore some vestige of her authority.

Mickey chuckled in reply. "Your gray 'n' orange cat. It lies on the couch when you're not home and sometimes pulls on the blanket with its claws."

"Why...how did...how could—"

"Mickey!" had then come her rescue.

Emily had never been so glad to see Janice, or anyone else for that matter. "He...seems fine, Mrs. Stratton," she managed. "Do you know how...how long till he can go back home?"

Jeffrey sat down on the bed and was mussing his son's hair. "I think...think we can probably take him back home now," he said, "and wait for the other test results when they come." He put a hand under Mickey's chin and smiled back at the boy with relief. "We don't check...anybody out at this time of the day, but then..." he looked toward Janice, who sat in the vinyl chair on the other side of the bed. "We also don't let eleven-year-olds in to visit patients."

"I'm almost twelve," his daughter said.

"Or twelve-year-olds."

"Do I really have to go home now?" Mickey asked.

Maureen and Jeffrey looked at one another. "Well, sure," his mother said.

"I don't want to."

"But Mickey..." Maureen turned toward the others. "Could we please...be alone for a minute?"

Emily stepped toward the bed. "Mrs. Stratton, I must be leaving anyway. Mickey," she said, laying a still-trembling hand upon the boy's head, "I hope to see you tomorrow."

Jeffrey squeezed his daughter's shoulder and guided her toward the wide doorway. He glanced at Mickey on his way out—*dissociation, my ass,* he was thinking—and happened to glance toward the screen of the nearby patient monitor. It was his imagination, he told himself. It hadn't just blipped on.

Maureen watched with dread as they left the room. She watched her husband close the door and thought the sound of the bolt clicking home the most frightening sound she had ever heard. She was alone with her son and, for the first time, was...afraid of him.

The sound of whispering made her turn around. "What did you...?"

Her son was grinning as if a private joke ran through his head. To the left of his bed, a curtain gently rustled; an air vent, Maureen decided. The machine beside the bed quietly displayed a steady sine wave.

Maureen thought the silence alone would kill her.

Why was her son staring at her so?

She swallowed and sat at the foot of his bed. "Mickey, we...we know about your friend."

Mickey continued to stare but said nothing.

"And I want you to know we...th-think she's wrong to try—" She broke off at his smile. His giggling. This wasn't working, she told herself. Why did she think she heard whispering? And what was that flashing light? She thought to turn to see—

"You're afraid of her," the boy stated.

"No! I mean...yes, I am afraid. Yes, Mickey, I am afraid of this...*dead girl* who is somehow able to worm her...*its*, I say *its*. Worm its way into—"

"Natalie's not an *it!*" The boy shouted. "And she's not dead!"

His mother nodded. "Yes, she really is. Tomorrow we can go see where she's bur—"

"She's not dead she's not dead she's not dead!"

He had to see it. She just had to convince him, particularly since everything Janice had said in the car, all that had at first seemed but madness, rang truer with every word of Mickey's reaction. "You'll see tomorrow. And..." What was that light?

To the left of her head, the monitor was displaying madly fluctuating patterns. Its trace leapt high, literally scratched its way up and down across the screen.

It took a moment for Maureen to realize what this meant. "Mickey!" She dove for the head of the bed. Where was the—where was that nurse's button? She hurled the extra pillows aside. Where the hell was it?

Mickey, viewing the display from the side, began to chuckle.

Empty-handed, Maureen suddenly felt stupid. Here she was, frantically seeking to respond to her son's apparent...arrhythmia of some sort, and here...

Here he was, giggling.

She looked at his chest, his arms, and saw why: no leads connected boy to machine. The machine continued its quiet light show, the trace dancing erratically up and down as if possessed. She looked for the leads, from where they came out of the machine. To where they went: toward the window. Ending high in the air, suspended, their gleaming electrodes swinging rhythmically in the corner as if dancing. They *were* dancing.

Behind, the curtain rustled. Maureen backed away, slowly, toward the door.

"What's the matter, Mom?"

* * *

"Oh, it's just something I remember from when I was little. I think Mom said it with me till I was...I don't know. Five or six."

305

Mickey's proud, smug veneer had faded, perhaps out of curiosity over why his sister had come in just before his bedtime. She went to bed at ten, two hours later, and on an ordinary evening she was on the phone when he went up to his room.

Perhaps, she hoped, his reaction was out of some feelings he still had toward his big sister.

Janice felt she was the only person left who could win Mickey back over to the family. Win him back over...to life, she supposed as Cynthia's words echoed through her mind.

Words...otherwise unbelievable words, about how the very, very sad, the very hurt, while they're young, could leave their own bodies in spirit form. About Cynthia and...that other one, Lana. About that friendship, which had very nearly ended in death—and, she supposed, entrapment in that...horrible world. How had it even happened to Natalie, she wondered. And why did she now want—

Janice knew why.

Mickey looked intensely at her. "Say it again," he said.

Janice grinned and gazed at the ceiling a moment till the rhyme came back:

"Now I lay me down to sleep,
I pray the Lord my soul to keep.
If I should die before I wake,
I pray the Lord my soul to take."

Her brother seemed to ponder anew. "What does it mean, 'keep'?"

The girl picked up the glass of water she'd carried in and motioned toward him. Mickey nodded. "I think..." she said, holding the cup to his lips, being careful not to spill any. (He hated that, Mother had warned.) "I think it means to keep you safe."

"From what?" he asked, pulling his face away from the cup. "I'm asleep then, right?"

"Mmm...I think from anything that might hurt you when you sleep. I dunno, I didn't write the prayer."

"And what's 'take'? Is that like going to Heaven?"

Janice shrugged. "That must be what it means."

"Oh," said Mickey. "But..." he continued, furling his brow, "if God...if God *keeps* my soul, if he keeps it right, then why...why does he need to take it?"

"You ask some hard questions, mister!"

The two of them laughed, but a few seconds later they stopped short at almost the same time. It did feel strange, Janice realized with a shudder, for the two of them to share a joke. But it was endearing, too.

Janice and Mickey locked gazes again, and once more began to giggle. They continued for a short time, and when it again subsided Janice was still smiling.

"What?"

His sister shook her head. How could she tell him she'd just realized she no longer felt the slightest discomfort in his presence? It had taken one little talk, one good talk, and she beamed with elation that they were finally having it.

"*What?*" Mickey repeated with a child's anxiety.

"Oh. Just thinking about how I like...having you for a brother. We're gonna be brother and sister our whole lives."

"Go onnn," said the boy. But Janice could see a twinge of sadness behind his smile. "You don't like me."

"Sure I do," she replied, swallowing. "I think...but I think I'm not a very good sister sometimes. I'm still learning, and...I'm sorry. But I promise I'll try harder."

Mickey was silent for a few moments, and when he spoke his voice was low. "I think you *are* a good sister, Janice."

The girl shrugged again, this time with a smile, and she took his hand. "Mom...and Dad and me...the four of us all just want to be happy together. All of us, you know? And when we both get bigger, we can—"

"No."

"Um, what do you mean, 'no'?"

Mickey looked down at his chest; if he could have, he would have retrieved his hand. "I'm not going to get any bigger."

"Mickey, what do you me—"

"I won't grow up, and Mom and Dad don't want me around anymore. Not since I got sick."

"No, Mickey," she said, groping for words. "You *are* going to get bigger—and better, too. And Mom and Dad...how could you say that? They love you, I know they do." Don't listen to her, Janice wanted to say. But she had seen only too well the look on her mother's face in the hospital. Mom had brought up the subject of Natalie in the hospital; Janice knew only that much from the silent ride home. Mom had even had *Dad* drive, and what a vegetable he was to have behind the wheel today. And maybe...maybe Natalie had been there in the hospital, too.

Was she here now?

"They want me to go away. Back to...that place with all the kids."

Janice drew close to her brother and managed to maintain her smile. "Mickey," she said, "you don't just *bring* someone *back* to an orphanage. Do you remember when you first came to us, and for a while you just came for a morning, or for a day? Then, a weekend or something? They do that to make everybody is sure it's what they want. 'Cause you can't just change your mind."

The boy smiled meekly. "Even if...but now I can't walk or do anything."

"But you will...you will when you're ready."

The two remained silent as the words sank in. Janice stood up, went to the window and stared out.

"You're lucky," she suddenly said.

"Huh? Why?"

"Because *you* have your own streetlight outside your window. It's like..."

"What?" He was beginning to look sleepy.

"It's like the light is watching over you or something. Like a friend, you know?"

Mickey nodded. His eyes began to flutter closed. "Good night, Janice."

Janice went over and kissed his cheek. "Good night, little brother. I love you."

* * *

The streetlight shone brightly into the corner room's window as if it watched all that went on in the Stratton household.

Before that, the Carter household—but not for very long at all.

And before that, the Leffingwell home. Natalie knew how far back that had been, knew from what her friend Mickey had told her that it indeed had been more than two years she had spent in this strange, mysterious world.

When she'd stood across the window from Janice not ten minutes before, Natalie had also gazed at the streetlight and remembered she was a child. How many nights she had spent, wincing in pain yet alive in all ways, staring from her bed at the light piercing through the night sky. Beckoning her to the window though she knew she'd be punished if she were caught out of bed. Reminding her, with every sublime shaft of light, that the world indeed had its constants.

Natalie remembered these things and began to think of her mother—and her father. She must be in Heaven now, she thought with sadness. And he...Natalie shrugged and wondered if either of them could see her now. She grinned at the notion of being alone in the house with her father, had he alone lived: he in the flesh, she *immaterial* but at her current strength. Why, she thought, she would tear the very flesh off his body.

Now, to business. She floated over to Mickey and whispered his name.

The boy's head turned from one side to the other, then back. "Wh-who..."

"Mickey, it's me."

His eyes opened. "Hi. Where *were* you?"

Natalie smiled sweetly. *"Oh...around. I heard what Janice said to you."*

"Oh." Mickey looked downcast, perhaps sensing that she was about to provide another side to it all. *"You were listening?"*

She nodded. *"Mickey, I don't think you know what she's doing,"* she said.

Mickey slammed his eyes shut, shook his head, and opened them again. It was as close as he ever got to a good eye rub. He then lifted his face from his body to continue their conversation in silence. "What do you mean, 'what she's doing'?" he asked with the same suspicious air he had exhibited in Janice's presence not long before.

"Her parents sent her in to try to talk you out of leaving," said Natalie. "I even heard her mother say 'Good luck' when Janice was coming in."

He replied, shaking his head, "No. She said they don't want me to go away."

"And you believe her? Mickey, her parents will say what they want you to think till you wake up some morning from the phone and you'll hear them say, 'Oh, we can take him back now?' Who knows," she added, "maybe after today they'll take you back next week."

309

"No, no no no," he rasped. "I don't want to go back, I don't want—why are you saying that? Why do you say *her* parents! My sister says you're wrong. I..." At her beckoning, he left his body completely and continued his tirade above the bed. "...I think you're telling me lies. Why are—"

"Come," said the girl.

Still muttering, he followed Natalie down to his therapy room, "the gym," where she retrieved a sheet of paper from beneath an end table.

"I didn't want to show you what I found, Mickey, but the way you keep saying those things to me..." She unfolded the letter to reveal the logo of the firm Feldman, Coleridge & Rohm.

The house remained still without a hint of the agonized scream that erupted from the room. Outside, three starlings took off from the bushes.

33

The face Emily Sanders saw at the door was white. What she recognized was a woman starved for sleep and close to tears—probably not for the first time that day. The therapist knew the feeling, was initially even relieved that she was not the only one who'd spent the previous night awake. But this...the look on Maureen's face said more. Much, much more.

"Mrs. Stra—"

"I...forgot to call you to say not—not to come, Emily. It's...it's ha-happened again. Mickey..."

"Mickey's...gone, again, Mrs. Stratton? Oh, my...oh, how can I help? Have you called the doctor—oh, your husband. Is he...?"

"He's not here. Please...you're standing out there in the chill." Maureen's head seemed to jiggle as she dug for a decision. "C-come in, um, just come. We..."

Emily came in, set her coat on the edge of the couch and immediately sat down when Maureen did. Maureen sprang up again at once, sat down again, then rose again to ask Emily if she wanted coffee.

"N-no, Mrs. Stratton. Please. I won't add to your troubles by expecting to be served, of all things. I...I have to tell you something. Something Mickey said in the hospital yesterday that utterly...frightened me out of my wits. About a...a friend he claims to have. A girl named Natalie. I'd felt it was just a story. Children often do take on imaginary friends, but this one seemed..."

"Real." Maureen gave a nod. "Yep, Emily, we have a ghost. A badass one. And not just Natalie...no, not our ghost. This one has a last name, too: Leffingwell. Seems the whole school knows about her, too. Janice brought this wacky story home, crazy thing a girl told her." She sat back and shut her eyes to keep from crying again. "It's true, all true." She looked up at the mantel clock. "Oh, for Pete's sa—Emily, what time do you have? Every clock in this house has gone bonkers. Oh, *where is Jeffrey!* Emily, what—"

Her mouth dropped open, and Emily snapped from her moment of shock to realize how pale her own face must have been at that moment. "I...I know her," she stated.

Maureen furled her brow. "Well, of course we *all* feel we know her, Emily, but..." The skepticism slowly drained from her face. "You...you mean in a different way, don't you."

Emily nodded. "And I think...I know how I can...at least try to help you, Mrs. Stratton."

Standing up, Maureen shook her head. "You...you're going to *talk* to her, aren't you? Is that what you're thinking of, since you...*know* her? This—this thing that wants to take away my baby? Are you *crazy?* How could you think—"

The therapist stood up, too. "Mrs. Stratton, this 'thing' is a nine-year-old girl who died in this very house at the hands of an abusive, murderous father. "I—I don't have the first idea of why she's still here or what she wants—"

"That one's easy. She wants Mickey."

"I...I see." Emily sighed; of course she didn't see. Not at all. "Five minutes, Mrs. Stratton? You go on up...upstairs to your son. Close the door. I want to...try to speak with her."

"Janice is up there now," Maureen said.

"Fine. the three of you...please stay there. I don't know what I can do. But until your husband comes home, it's worth a try, no?"

"All right. I presume...Jeff is on the way home. He'd stopped in at the hospital so should...I guess, be here any minute."

"Fine."

And then she was alone, this middle-aged, frightened woman who, just the night before, had lain in bed with a nightlight on for the first time in perhaps forty years.

Emily remained standing, unsure of where she should stand, and eventually settled on the opening to the living room. I want the girl to show herself, she thought. I want...I want to see the face of this terrible...of the poor, frightened girl I once knew.

She waited till she heard the solid click of the corner bedroom door. "Natalie Leffingwell, I must speak with you," she said with as much courage as she could summon up for herself.

Nothing happened. Well of course, she thought. Why should the spirit pay any attention to her? Who was she, after all, but the meddlesome old witch who wanted her patient to revel in his power to overcome adversity?

"I...I know you can hear me, or at least believe you can. You don't have to answer me. I'll just talk a little." She began to pace around the living room, slowly meandering around the furniture and looking up and around her as she spoke. "Five—no, six—years ago, I started a job as the nurse of a little school nearby, the one called Hollister Elementary. You know it. You were the pretty little girl with the blonde hair and deep blue eyes, and held a little green book bag that you clutched ever so close to your chest as you came up the...slate walk to the entrance. I know. My office was the one on the left after you went in the main door.

"I liked to watch the children in the morning as they came in. Don't know why, really. Maybe I looked at each and every one of you as the child who could have been the one I never got to see...the one I lost in the womb, two weeks before she was due. I was married only...a half year or so longer after that, and...I saw in the kids, especially the girls' faces, the laughter and ever...everlasting hope in those rosy faces that...I know now I'll never see till I leave this earth and...go up to meet my daughter."

Was she having an effect? Emily couldn't know; what she did know was that she herself was crying and that her five minutes were about up. But Maureen remained upstairs. "I loved to see the faces of the kids, rain or shine, and got in extra early so I could sit at the window with my coffee before the first sniffly noses showed up in my office. I doted over all the children and loved them. Even the troublemakers, and Lord knows there were enough of *them*. But there was one child in particular who really worried me, and that was you. Natalie Leffingwell, who late in the third-grade semester seemed sometimes to walk with a slight limp, or hold her head down with her hair draped over a cheek. That was you, Natalie, and I was the first person in school to realize what was happening in your home.

"I approached your mother—fine woman with blonde hair and

high cheekbones, could've been a model easy—at the first PTA meeting of the year, before the first semester began. I took her aside and, not easy to do these things, asked if everything was all right at home. Poor woman, I could see where she'd tried with powder to cover a...mark next to her eye, and she turned that side of her face away when she said, 'No, everything is fine. Thank you.' She took a step away, looked back and again said, 'Thank you.' That moment I felt I was right, and I—God, I *knew* I was right! And I started looking into how I could help you."

The light of the living room's Tiffany lamp dimmed, and the room turned cold. Deathly cold. Emily's nostrils also widened at...a smell that seemed to come from the direction of the stairs and...was growing stronger by the moment. It was the putrid smell of death, of once-living things rotting. And it was drawing closer.

Emily's knees were buckling. It...she...was here. In this room, in Emily's presence. And the woman wanted to run for her life, to open that door and fill her lungs with fresh, clean March air. Air separated by only a door.

She couldn't leave if she wanted—she was frozen to the spot.

Think, woman. The little girl. The shy kid with the blonde hair and the pink sneakers. C'mon. The living, stupid. The living!

"If...if you remember, I p-pulled you out of class one m-morning and looked at your face. Such sparkling blue eyes you had. Your mother must l-love you very much, I remember thinking. And, if you remember—I g-guess you didn't recognize me—I asked you how you got the red mark on your cheek. It looked like...like knuckle marks to me, but I didn't want to say anything. You said—"

"I said I slipped in the bathtub," came an unearthly voice from the middle of the room.

The woman gasped for breath, stepped back till she felt the front of the couch, caught her balance and took a small step forward. "S-see you. I want...I want to see you, please, N-Natalie."

She waited several seconds, and suddenly the curtains and shades around the living room and the adjoining kitchen began to close, one by one. Emily watched them close in line—the spirit was swift! And how could she touch physical objects? She—

Was she doing it through will alone?

The room was barely lit now but for what little sunlight spilled under the front door and around the periphery of the bay windows' drapes. Emily faced the kitchen, where the last curtains closed. The cold and...that stink remained intense. She jumped when a voice came from behind her: *"I could tell you knew. I was afraid to tell you."*

Emily whirled around to face an image of the very girl who sat in her office that breezy day. "Oh..." was all she could say at the sight of this small-framed child in street clothes, white knee socks. It was her! And she looked...she looked not a day older than the day...the day...

But she looked closer at the spirit and saw more—a hardness in her face that told Emily that this talk of hers would only go so far. She needed to keep talking, though, till she could gain more of the girl's trust.

Emily realized she had heard, minutes before, the click of the upstairs bedroom as it gently swung open a crack. We have an audience, she thought, but she dared not acknowledge the fact aloud. "The night...you died, Natalie...I had hoped to see your mother again at the PTA meeting. To confront her with what I knew and tell her I wanted to help the two of you. I...waited and waited and, when it was over, I went to my office and called her. She...God, I never felt so helpless! She said hello and then I heard yelling—your father— and then she screamed for h-help just before the phone went dead. I called into the phone, 'Mrs. Leffingwell! Mrs. Leffingwell!' And then...then I called the police."

"You were too late," the spirit said flatly.

Emily sighed. "Yes," she said in a hushed voice. "I was..."

"You were too late then," Natalie continued, *"and you're too late now."*

"N-Natalie...what do you want? I don't know...why you are here, why you are *still* here...why you are not where...where you belong, where all children must go when they die. But—"

"They don't want me in that place. They think I'm bad, and they won't let me in." Natalie began to turn away. *"You better go away now,"* she said. *"You can't help me."* She motioned her head toward the upper landing. "And you can't help *them.*"

"Natalie...don't leave yet. Please. I think you owe me that much."

The spirit paused, then turned back to face her. *"What?"* she said as she crossed her arms.

"Natalie, where is Mickey?"

The smirk Emily got in return sent a stiffening chill up her body.

"He's in his room," Natalie said with a horrifying sweetness that

sent a wave of nausea through Emily's belly.

"You know what I mean. He's somewhere in this house, with you, isn't he?"

Natalie crossed her arms. *"Maybe,"* she said with defiance.

"Please. Where—"

"He's here with me." The spirit swooped at Emily and, before the woman could react, solidified her hand, her arm—to grip Emily's throat and lift her inches above the floor. Everything was spinning around the seething expression on the face of a girl she'd once known. She could feel her feet kicking out, flailing against empty air, and she was moments from losing consciousness when the voice broke through the haze.

"Now-get-out."

Emily felt the floor and crumbled.

* * *

Maureen rushed out of the room at the sound of Emily's struggling up the steps. "I...heard the whole thing," she said, her hands high. "The important part, anyway. My God! To think you...we have to get out of here, we have to go—but you. You heard her. You'd better leave now. I have to wait for—*where is he?"*

"I'm sorry," the therapist said. "I have to go—"

"Yes, you'd better. My Lord! I don't know how you carried on a conversation with that...that...anyway, we know what she's doing. Everything is falling into place, the way it looks. But go, please go now, Emily. I'll call...I'll call when I can."

The women embraced, and Emily left the house. Maureen wiped away tears as she stood at the railing, and crossed her arms at a chill that seemed to be coming and going that day. "Go...awaaaaaay!" she shouted.

"Mom!" Janice called from the bedroom. "It's Mickey! He's awake again—" But before her mother could reach the room, she said with disbelief, "He's gone again."

"Nooooooo! My baby, Mickey, come back!" Maureen sank to her knees and hugged the boy's motionless body with no response. She turned to Janice, who was crying, too.

"I...I saw his eyes open, and he looked at me. I said his name, and he gave me this...mad, mad face, and then he closed his eyes again."

"Miiiickeyyyyyy!"

Janice wrapped an arm around her mother as the woman lay her head on Mickey's chest. "Mom...Mom..." She kept her arm there for a short while but then, receiving no response, gradually drew away. The girl paced the tiny room and then said, "Mom, I'll be back in a minute."

After some time, Maureen's back began to hurt from the bending beside her son. She stood up, stretched, sat down again.

And noticed the sheet of paper laid across her son's nightstand.

She picked it up—had Janice left this here? First, she noticed the letterhead, remembered the firm to be the one that handled all legal matters, including both real estate transactions and Mickey's adoption.

Her eyes widened with a rage that only grew by the time, minutes later, she heard the key turn in the lock below.

* * *

Janice wanted to do something—anything. She hadn't the faintest idea how she could protect Mickey. Or, rather, she'd thought of only one thing that, if anything, would distract Natalie from her brother and maybe, just maybe, bring him back. Then they'd leave, move far, far away where this thing would never find them.

Once she left her mother, she gingerly descended the stairs, turned right in the living room and slowly, hesitantly, went down to the basement, leaving the door wide open. Her target, the dollhouse, had been moved from where her parents had told her they'd taken it weeks before. They'd first put it on the workbench, near the steps to the cellar doors. Now, it awaited her from the floor in front of the bench, its right side near the vise bolted to the bench's work space.

The girl remembered well what kind of punishment she and her mom, at least, had gone through before it had occurred to her to make what had seemed a peace offering to...the house, she'd then supposed. But now that she knew well just what had been tormenting her, she also understood that taking the dollhouse back upstairs, somehow, would get her enemy's attention. Doing so might have dire results. Still, it might be the distraction they needed.

Whatever happened, she might help Mickey. She *had* to.

Wishing the basement were brighter still, Janice stepped slowly toward the bench. She frowned over the slippers she wore. Sneakers were lots faster for running, though she realized she hadn't thought through how she alone could even carry the dollhouse two flights up, no matter what was on her feet. The air had ceased all movement. It was getting cold, cold like the upstairs during those unforgettable nights. And then...then the cold dissipated—as if she hadn't felt it at all. She stood before the dollhouse, which looked less like hers than ever. Newer figures she knew she hadn't gotten. Furniture of all colors and sizes—that kid had no eye for dimension, she thought— and too much of it all, too. Clutter she never would have allowed, and wouldn't once she had the dollhouse back upstairs.

While Janice scanned the contents of the dollhouse, something rolled out to the basement floor. It was the red iron that was too big for the ironing board it had been placed upon, almost the size of a quarter. No wonder it fell, she thought.

Stupid thing, thought Janice as she bent over to return the accessory and—

From upstairs she heard shouting. At first she thought Mickey had woken up again—Natalie was up there, and something was happening. She turned toward the stairs but, halfway up, realized she had no place in this discussion. Mickey...something about Mickey and the orphanage. Huuuhhh? Why would they be fighting about...? She listened. They were talking about a letter. What letter? Daddy had written something and...did Mommy sound pissed! This...this was a big one, and if Janice went upstairs—she wanted to shake them both and say, Hey! What about Mickey? He's upstairs and you two are—

Whatever it was, it was big. If she went upstairs, she'd surely be sent to her room. Better to stay here, where she was safe, and...

* * *

"Stop...stop it!" Jeffrey shouted. He had barely made it to the stairs before his wife swept down and lunged at him, swinging. "What are you—"

"You son of a bitch! You heartless monster! How could you..." The two struggled, and Jeffrey hit his head against the newel post before he caught his wits and grabbed Maureen's arms.

"Maureen, what...?" But, in the back of his mind, he knew what. And had been expecting this moment.

"I can't—just can't believe you wanted to send Mickey back to the orphanage! You beast! I hate you, I hate you! You bastard! How could you possibly have asked about that and...and you never even thought, 'Oh, maybe I should *see* what my *family* thinks about this.' Is it the *money,* you son of a bitch! Do you feel *inconvenienced?* How could you do this?" Again she rushed at him and landed a solid punch to his nose.

Jeffrey went sprawling and, his mind spinning, slammed against the wall and fell onto the bottom stairs. He held his hand before his face, tasted blood—God, his nose was broken—and struggled to his feet.

"I was...wrong! Okay? I wasss..." He took out his handkerchief to stop the blood. "I wass wrong. I...know it. Wrong. I...I undersssstand if you...you hate me. I...I thought I wass looking out...for usss."

"It was cruel. Terribly cruel. And I think your son knows about it, too. Guess who told him, Buster. He's gone again. She even left the letter out in the open for me to see.

"We have...we have to get him back...and then, get him out of here."

34

Janice would take the dollhouse upstairs and show them she could win out over Natalie. That would remind them both of what mattered.

Tightening her lips, she headed back toward the workbench and, on the way, snapped up the little iron.

Too late she noticed the smell. The steam. The blood-red paint shimmering on the wooden toy as if it were...melting?

Janice yelped like a stricken hound, shook her hand to dislodge the iron—it adhered to her skin before peeling loose—and flung it hard to the cold concrete floor. Her palm bubbled red as if she'd gripped a burning charcoal briquet. She let out a cry...slow sniffling first, then, as the searing pain further set in, a long shriek.

"MAAAAAAMMMAAAAAA!"

It wasn't over. The girl lay curled on the concrete basement floor, holding her hand tightly, and, from the corner of her eye, noticed the first stirrings. The movements were those of the dollhouse family—the father, mother, now two children and a collie—and the figures rose and fell demonically as they left their house and ventured toward Janice. The pleasant, painted smiles seemed now malignant. Their little arms rose to extend toward Janice, who, now on her knees, screamed. The motion, the way the family moved—no, *was* moved—seemed no different than if a girlfriend were bobbing a figure up and down, to emulate walking, within the house. But all five figures moved at once. And her playmate meant no good will.

321

It seemed forever before Janice's parents made their way downstairs. Janice felt she couldn't back away quickly enough to escape, and the wooden collie had started circling around behind her. Janice could swear she heard mimicked barking sounds, though her panicked cries were drowning them out.

"Janice!" her mother shouted. The two adults rushed down the stairs and, as they watched, saw the dollhouse figures scooped up by an unseen hand. Jeffrey held up his arm as the figures flew in his direction.

"She burned my haaaand!" she cried to her mother. "And...those people—they were—oh...mama, they were walking—they were c-c-coming toward me!"

"It's okay now, Honey," Maureen said, embracing her daughter while Jeffrey took the girl's hand.

"Here," he said, still holding the dark-red handkerchief at his nose. "Let me...oh, hmm. Let's, uh..." He snatched up one of Mickey's white T-shirts from the basket beside the dryer. "This'll do. C'mere, Janice." He took her to the deep sink and turned on the lukewarm water, letting it run. After soaking the T-shirt, he wrapped it around her wound—she screamed again—and wound a small towel tightly around that. "We'll leave that for a few minutes, and I'll put something better on it upstairs."

Janice held the makeshift bandage tightly to her chest and went briskly up the stairs to her room. Her parents wearily followed but paused in the living room.

"Maureen," he said through the clean dishcloth he now held against his nose.

She turned around sharply and stared coldly at him.

"I don't...don't know if you can ever f-forgive me. But please...let's put this aside till we know Mickey's okay, all right? We have to think of him right now."

Maureen nodded, but the cold stare remained. "Oh, I'm thinking about him, all right. It's *you*"—she jabbed an index finger against his chest—"who doesn't seem to know he's ours to keep."

* * *

In the corner room, Mickey's spirit had floated over to find Natalie beside his body. He asked her what she was doing. She stared at him in return, her materialized image flickering in and out like a candle's light. "We have to move you," she said with determination.

"Move me? But why? And why now? I gotta—I gotta hear what my parents are saying. Let's—"

"Mickey. Listen to me. They can't take you back if they can't find you. Come with me—I'll carry you to someplace safe where you won't have to worry about that. Ever again. Understand?"

The boy listened at the doorway but, with his door nearly closed, could not make out what they were saying. He tightened his lips, began to cry. "B-but my m-mother—"

"Your mother can't help you. You saw the letter. You know they don't love you. *Is this what makes you happy?*"

He cried louder, shook his head and closed his eyes. "N-n-no, it's n-not." he looked up at her eyes, through her eyes, and nodded. "Okay. G-go ahead."

Her door open, Janice had been listening to her parents' argument and now hoped, prayed, that her parents would not divorce over the letter. She herself had found the now-crumpled letter upon her return to her room and knew fully well who had put it there. How could Daddy do something so...so...

Her right hand, in its bandage, continued to sting. And as she knelt in the doorway, gasping at the intense pain, she heard other voices from down the hall. It seemed one side of another argument. The voice had to be Natalie's; how mean she sounded! And while she could not hear her brother's voice, she knew he had to be there, too. She stole closer and heard most of what the spirit said. From those few words spoken, she knew with even more certainty that everything Cynthia had told her was true. Natalie wanted Mickey.

And if Janice didn't do something now, the spirit would have him.

Natalie would take him where no one would ever find him. Where, if Mickey ever did want to return to his body, there would be no way for him to leave.

A place where no one could find him.

Where no one could hear him call.

In the room, Natalie focused her energies on solidifying her upper form. Taking the boy out of town, away from all the stores and houses, would be too much for her despite her unnatural strength. Many, many times had she traveled with Mickey, his spirit beside hers, unhindered by physical form. But she had never had to carry his or anyone else's body over a distance. It would be difficult, awkward. She might even drop him, which would present problems all its own. The sun had also not sufficiently lowered in the sky for what would certainly be an odd sight.

That's why she had scouted out two closer places. One was an unoccupied house a short walk away; the other, an abandoned factory near the cemetery. The latter was several blocks away, but once they reached the building, it would serve indefinitely.

She could do it. This was the moment she'd awaited, the closest thing to solace Natalie hoped to achieve. Heaven seemed off-limits to her always. Her mother was long gone. The next best option: She wanted a friend. She deserved his company, more than *they* did.

And now she would have it.

Forever.

She bent over to curl her arms beneath Mickey's back and knees. This would not be easy, she thought. It was not through muscle that she would transport him, she knew; her power resided in her will, a sheer mental energy that had grown immensely powerful through the years.

She materialized fully and began to lift the boy.

"No!"

The door flew open, and Janice lunged at Natalie. She could do nothing against a ghost—the girl knew it as she balled up her bandaged hand into a fist. But she swung anyway, with all her might, at her materialized enemy's glaring face.

And connected.

Natalie spun away and slammed head-first into the dresser. For an instant she curled up defensively, in her shock warding off further attack through an instinct that had never truly left her. She was in her room. *He* had struck her again, she had better—

Then she remembered who she was.

And knew what she would do.

Mickey's spirit looked on as Natalie kept her form visible and rose up in an arc that descended before the now-cringing eleven-year-old. "K-keep away! Leave us alone!" Janice shouted. She backed toward the door; Natalie circled her to slam it shut.

"Mmmmmooooommmm! She's uu...uh...uh..uueeerrr..." and the spirit entered her physical space. Janice's body shook with terror and her eyes rolled with every twist of the spirit's intermittent grasping and squeezing of living tissue within her. A yellowish fluid trickled out of her nose and the corner of her mouth. Yellow, white, wisps of red. "...uhuuuh...uuuh...uh...uh...uuuaaahhh..."

Her parents opened the door, banging it into Janice, and together squeezed into the room. Jeffrey, grabbing his daughter's shoulders, began to cry out in pain as the spirit swept him, too, into the whirlwind of anguish. Together the two trembled in agony as Maureen stared helplessly, daring not to step closer. "Jan-Ja-Janice, Jeff, I..."

Natalie was reveling in this greatest unleashing of her resolve. She had drawn father and daughter into her deadly embrace and focused her energy on partially materializing first this hand, then this one, this finger and that, feeling the squishiness of their very guts as she thought then to reach upward...to grasp a beating heart in each hand.

Maureen frantically scanned the room for something, anything, she could use as a weapon. She had to—she needed to—she needed something. She looked toward the bed.

Someone.

It would not take much longer, Natalie decided, even as she divided her immense energy between her two victims. Maureen suddenly pushed into the fray—okay, the vengeful spirit decided, then she would go, too.

But no! Maureen was holding Mickey, having wrapped his limp arms over her shoulders. She forced her way in, grasped ahold of her husband's shirt and pulled him close, pulled Janice's arm until the entire family became a huddled mass of defiance.

The deadly trembling began to subside—impossible for the spirit to continue her attack without endangering Mickey as well. And in her haste, Natalie could not be sure: Was Mickey in his body or out?

She could not tell until she heard his voice behind her: "Stop it, Natalie! Leave them alone! Leave my family alone! You're mean—you're sooo mean!"

Natalie retreated, suddenly in confusion. She remained materialized, a few feet from the crumbling family members. And, her eyes tightly closed, shoulders raised, fists clenched, she began to *will* the very house to pieces. Mickey, she gambled in desperation, would stay outside his body.

A body with little time left.

The lamp on the dresser shook free the clown's wraparound arms before it tipped over and fell off the dresser. The mobile of fighter planes dropped off its hook and crashed to the carpeted floor; the race car-print curtains leapt off their brackets.

The house then began to vibrate on its foundation. The walls and floor trembled and began to splinter. Powder and fragments began to fall from above in a room quivering as if from an earthquake.

Maureen, on her knees, covered her son's body close in defense against shards of ceiling. The others lay groggy against the door, in their stupor slowly realizing what was going on.

Mickey had re-entered his body, Maureen noticed as she held him close. "Mommy, she won't stop!"

"Mickey!" she said. "Oh, please stay, Mickey, please st—"

"You want me to go away!" he shouted. Then the life left his eyes.

Natalie grinned at the turmoil she was creating and, when a piece of the ceiling dropped inches from Maureen's head, began to laugh maniacally. *"You're not holding anything!"* she shouted. She gazed past the family, smiled as she watched something—Mickey?—float by. *"He's here now—with me!"*

But something else was going on behind her. Maureen looked up. Natalie, too, turned around to face a slowly rotating opening that had formed in the air—and continued to widen till it nearly reached the ceiling. The shaking house grew still.

The oval-shaped vortex, one Natalie recognized from twice before, oscillated at a faster and faster speed until it seemed five feet across. Maureen watched the mutating portal spin not only round and round but also, like a coin slowly spinning on its edge, from front to back.

Alternately the hole emanated a bright blue from which Maureen could...make out a voice. Someone calling out.

A woman's voice.

When the shape flipped to reveal another side, Maureen saw only blackness. Even Natalie drew back when it hovered, a long moment, before flipping again to the bright blue.

Maureen thought she was dreaming. When the hole showed its black side—could it be possible?—she could swear she saw hands.

Claw-like hands.

She caught a whiff of something rotten, decomposed. And amid a brief chorus of wails—something, someone, was being hurt

(no, tortured!)

—she thought she saw more.

Eyes peering out. Red, hungry eyes.

Now she was looking into the brilliant blue of the other side. The opening did seem like a coin turning on its edge, she realized, but...

There's someone in there!

...it was not one opening but two. Inside the blue flashing lights that formed the opening, she could make out the faint outline of a blonde woman. The light hurt Maureen's eyes; it reminded her of a much-overexposed photo. What she could make out were arms, the woman's arms, reaching out. The woman calling a name that sounded more and more distinguishable with each repetition, each flip of the dual opening. *"Natalie!"*

Maureen's mouth dropped open when Natalie replied, *"Mommy!"* The spirit lunged for the opening but halted her advance when the coin turned again to expose the black, fetid cavern of cackling beings that beckoned her. She backed away, narrowly dodging a talon of one foul being.

The portal flipped again; Kim Leffingwell appeared. *"Dear Natalie, these others..."* A flip away, then back. *"They have too much claim on you!"* Another flip to the blackness, the utter desolation, the growls, then back to the light. *"You have to make things—"*

The coin flipped once more, moments of growing voices that seemed louder than before. The shriveled arms that extended out seemed more numerous, longer reaching before...

Natalie's mother, bathed in the bright blue light, returned. *"You have to make things right, my darling."*

The talon again stretched far out from the portal's dark side. It scored three parallel tracks in the hardwood floor before it withdrew upon a shift back to the bold light.

The young girl understood. Natalie stared down at her feet, her powers gone, as the wide portal continued to shift back and forth between reunion and condemnation. She turned slowly toward the Strattons, still with a cautious eye toward those cackling in the dark opening. *"I was...bad and I'm...sorry. I was mean, very mean...to all of you. Mickey...you have to get better. Never, ever leave your body—it's wrong. Outside is a sad, lonely place, all wrong for you."* She turned back to the Strattons. *"P-please...forgive me?"*

"Go," said Maureen, "w-with...our blessing."

One tear fell from the spirit of the young girl, one who had been too long between worlds. Then another.

The bright side had just flipped back, and two arms were reaching out toward her.

Her mother's face, barely visible in the intensity of the glow, was smiling.

Natalie leaped. The arms enclosed her, but still the lower half of her ethereal form extended out. Feral grunts emanated from the side of shadows as the two worlds settled their claims. The girl flailed her arms and legs—they passed through Maureen and objects scattered throughout the room. Black, scaly arms gripped the girl's legs and pulled in desperation. For seconds, the family could see two halves of both worlds, two dominions, that laid claim to her soul in a tug of war for eternity.

With a whoosh everyone present could hear, Natalie suddenly fell altogether into the bluish light. A turbulent tangle of gripping arms pulled in vain as the same two humanlike arms enveloped the girl, holding her as a mother carries a young child, and slowly drew her away from the snarling pack.

The flipping of worlds quickened until the Strattons saw only bright blue, darkness, bright blue, faster and faster until both portals shrank and went away altogether.

Maureen blinked. It was gone. It was all gone. The house was a wreck. Still, Natalie was gone...all this that had so subverted their lives...it was over. Except for...

She looked down at her son. His eyes were closed, and his head tipped unnaturally over the crook of her arm.

"Mickey? Mickey...?"

Jeffrey and Janice were just struggling to their feet, Janice remembering the searing pain in her hand. She gingerly rewrapped the T-shirt and towel around her blistered palm, her eyes never leaving her brother. "Is he...?"

Maureen shook her head and carried her son to his bed. The floor, from her first hesitant footsteps, seemed strong enough to carry them; the shaking, then, had perhaps stopped before Natalie did permanent damage. "Mickey, please come back. We love you, you can't leave us like this. Did you see...is that what you want?"

Her husband and daughter made it also to the bed, their eyes red, their mouths bloodied. The three watched for what seemed like minutes, and then the boy's eyes opened in a snap.

"Mickey!" The three said almost in unison. Sighing as they embraced him, the boy was silent for several moments, long enough that his mother wondered whether he had been irretrievably affected by what had occurred in that room.

Jeffrey found his gaze rising. "My...God. Thank you. Thank you for...your mercy."

"Daddy," the boy finally said.

Maureen stopped stroking Mickey's cheek while the boy's father took his hand. He sighed, wiped his brow. "Yes, Mickey."

"Do I have to go away?"

Tears streamed down the man's face as he shook his head. "No. Mickey. Never. I...l-love you. We all love you, very much. I'm...very, very sorry I hurt you...I pray you can forgive me."

The boy turned his head in the opposite direction for a moment. When his face again showed, it wore a faint grin.

"Daddy," he said.

"What is it, my son?"

"Um...when I turn...um, twelve..."

"Uh-huh?"

"Could I have a bicycle?"

— T H E   E N D —

ABOUT THE AUTHOR

Ed Perratore's books include two other horror novels: *The Coven Tree* and *The Knock from Nobody*. His fourth published book is the nonfiction work *One Man's Journey: A Walk on the Croton Aqueduct Trail.* Ed's career was in magazine writing and editing at *Consumer Reports, PC Magazine* and other publications, but his earliest roots in horror are from TV fare such as Chiller Theater, Creature Features and The 4:30 Movie. He lives in Mount Kisco, New York, with Elena, his wife, a  short drive from Sleepy Hollow. Contact him through edperratore.com. (Author portrait by John F.X. Walsh.)

ALSO BY ED PERRATORE

The Coven Tree, a horror novel published in the summer of 2021 and set in New York's Adirondack Region, relates a dark and torturous journey for Johanna and Daniel Keane and their teenage son, Randall, as they unwittingly allow—into their own home—the instrument of their family's destruction, in the form of an elegant, hand-crafted highboy. Can they save their family from an evil as old as creation? The book is available from Amazon and independent booksellers.

The Knock from Nobody (2025) tells of childhood friends drawn back to their hometown of Mount Kisco, New York, twenty years since they last played there. They stop by a house they often skipped around, uttering a chant learned from their parents. Circle it three times, listen for the knock. For old times' sake, they walk around it again. The door soon opens. In the coming weeks, their lives shatter. This book is sold online and can be ordered anywhere.